Pirate

Pirate

THE ROCK BAND

E.Z. PRINE

PURE BARRY PRESS

This is a work of fiction. Although its form suggests a biography of a rock band, it is not one. Names, characters, places, events, and incidents are a product of the author's imagination or are used fictitiously.

PIRATE: THE ROCK BAND – First edition

Print edition ISBN: 978-1-957598-00-0

Digital edition ISBN: 978-1-957598-03-1

Dear Reader

Hey there. Dunk MacGregor, the manager of Pirate, here.

Look, our biographer, E.Z. Prine, makes mistakes and I don't always catch them. That's what happens when you're a busy rock band and people are writing lots of stuff about you. You can't keep on top of it all.

Case in point—I'm a lot better looking than I come off in this book. You'd think I'm a big brute with wild hair, when, really, people tell me I've got the same charm as that other son of Scotland, the James Bond to end all James Bonds and one of the finest actors to come out of the United Kingdom, the legendary Sean Connery. But that's just it. The bloody English never give us our due.

Likewise, if anyone is responsible for the success of Pirate, it's yours truly, the manager who takes care of everything and cleans up everyone's bleedin' messes. You think the boys are good at making music, but I'm telling you, making messes is their biggest talent.

And yet, who gets all the kudos and looks like the hero of this book? That bawbrained, control freak of a lead singer, Jack St James, that's who. It's always the lead singer, isn't it? Aye, he might be my best friend, and aye, he might be the supreme composing and performing talent of this band, and maybe even of his generation. (My personal opinion, so shut it.) But we'd be a lot richer if it weren't for him. Read this book and the next one, and you'll see exactly what I mean.

He even gets a lot of chapters told from his point of view. Far more than from mine. It's cheating you readers, is my big concern.

So, anyway, if you find any mistakes in this book, instead of whinging and moaning like our heidbanging lead singer or one of the boys, send me an email like a man (or a proper lady) and let me know what's wrong. I can't read minds, you know. Or, better yet, if you want to advocate for equal representation of other points of view, especially those of a certain charming but downtrodden Scotsman, that would be welcome too. My contact info is in the "What Next?" section at the end.

And spoiler alert: there are raunchy and sexy parts in this book, and some swearing and scenes of a violent nature. I won out against the control freak bawbrain who wanted to remove them. He said they weren't "tasteful" and might lose us fans. I put my foot down on this one. We're a hard rock band, f'crissakes. We might not be Ozzy or Mötley Crüe, but we're nae saints neither. Hey, you're more than welcome, dear reader!

Enjoy this first part of our story, and see you when it's over.

Summer 1984

One

"IT REEKED of cigarette smoke and made me gag. All of them did. Every single one."

"I heard you the first fifty times."

"Well?"

"What do ya want me to say?"

Jack glared at Dunk. The unbelievable gall, dismissing his complaint about the microphone—a lead singer's most important tool for communicating with the audience. A swapped-in spare and the boys' mikes had been just as bad.

This wasn't one of those little suggestions for improvement Jack made after some gigs to aid in their "quest for excellence." And it most definitely wasn't something that should be happening with only ten days left in their big American tour.

The life of a rock star. If people only knew. It wasn't sunshine, lollipops, and rainbows—thank you, Lesley Gore—or even sex, drugs, and rock 'n' roll. It was incident after incident of incompetent nonsense like this.

This wasn't the sixties, for crissakes, when rock bands were still working out how to do things. This was nineteen bloody eighty-four.

And hey, was it too much to ask, after four years of almost non-stop touring and three record albums, one gold and one multi-platinum, not to mention a clutch of Billboard Hot 100 singles, that the lead singer's microphone be cleaned of all germs and smells before every gig? Was that too bloody much to ask?

Jack paced in front of Dunk as he stroked his chin and beetled his brows in confusion. "So let me see if I can get this nonsense, this tripe, this *bollocks* I'm hearing from you straight in my mind."

The tour bus hit a bump and Jack grabbed the edge of the kitchenette countertop to right himself. Was Dunk suppressing a grin? Are you kidding? Jack might've let this one slip with a quick apology and a vow to right the wrong, but not now. He wanted a full admission of guilt.

It didn't matter one whit that Dunk was exhausted and in a stroppy mood, did it? When something was wrong, you did something about it. Especially when the lead singer was upset. Especially when the lead singer had made you a bloody fortune by the ripe ol' age of twenty-four. And most especially when he had just performed in front of eleven thousand screaming fans—with a smelly, germ-covered microphone no less—and was beyond exhausted himself.

Jack resumed pacing, giving the insouciant ingrate his severest glare.

Dunk rolled his eyes and took another pull from a bottle of Lone Star Beer.

"So am I now to understand that you're not the manager of this band, and that the entire crew does not report to you, and that you're not responsible for this intolerable violation of band rules that I'm bringing to your attention, because all of a sudden you simply don't feel like it?"

"Shut yer gob," said Dunk. "I'm warning ya."

"Or what?" Jack said, not bothering to mask his growing outrage. "What are you going to do? Let everything go to pot so I have to hold it together, like you always do?"

OK, so that wasn't true, not to mention unfortunate grammar. But no way was he going to take it back. Not under these circumstances.

"Ya think the mikes are a big problem, do ya? When I'm dealing with things like George and underage girls every single night?"

Jack stopped pacing and faced Dunk. "Hold on. What?" Where did this come from? "George doesn't go younger than sixteen ... Does he?"

"Sixteen?" said Dunk. "This isn't the UK, mate. The age of consent is eighteen in some states, if ya did yer bloody homework. But yer missing my point, as usual. Which is that yer problems aren't the only things I have to deal with. They're not the bloody half of it, mate."

Jack put his hands on his hips. "Wait. Go back to this George thing. Why didn't I know about this? Have you been keeping this from me?"

"F'crissakes, it's my job," Dunk shouted. "I'm the manager of this bleedin' band, last time I checked. Not you, mate. I don't tell ya how to compose yer bloody songs, now do I? Even though I think that *Señorita* song is way too slow. Besides which—"

"It's not too slow," Jack yelled back. How dare he say that? *Señorita* had exactly the right tempo. "And that's not the same thing at all, now is it, *mate*?"

"Oh no?" Dunk gave Jack his ridiculous cop stare. As if that worked on anyone but hotel clerks and little girls. "Says who? *You?*"

Now Dunk was being downright insulting. That could mean only one thing. He realized that he'd let a cat out of the bag and wanted to divert Jack's attention before Jack noticed and queried him about it. Yeah, right. Like that was going to happen.

"Have you gone barking mad? George could get arrested, and then we'd have to hire someone to replace him at great expense, maybe even have to cancel concerts. Not to mention we'd lose the bonus."

Jack narrowed his eyes as it hit him, what might really be going on here. It couldn't be, could it?

"Are you deliberately trying to screw things up? To make sure the band has to keep going?"

"I told ya to shut it," said Dunk, his flushing face betraying him.

"That's it, isn't it? You don't want us to retire. You want us to stay in this touring and recording hell forever. All the time we've been making plans, you've just been pretending to go along. That's why you're screwing everything up, isn't it? You don't want us to retire, do you?"

Dunk turned away, his face beet red now. Guilty as charged. First he'd tried to ignore the smelly, germy microphones. Then he'd revealed that George was sleeping with underage groupies. Now he was admitting deliberate sabotage of their long-discussed retirement plans. What other chicanery was Dunk hiding from him?

"What else haven't you told me?" Jack said, his voice jumping an octave. "I can't believe you, you ... you ... you sleaze-ridden excuse for a bawhaired diddy."

Dunk slammed his half-empty bottle of beer down on the edge of the sink. The bottom shattered, and he tossed the jagged top half in the sink. He turned and glared at Jack.

"That's it. I've had it. Ya better shut it now or else."

Jack pushed past him and inspected the red granite countertop. He glared back at Dunk. "Now look what you've done. You've cracked it. How are we supposed to sell this bus for what it's worth when you've damaged it? Is this another one of your sneaky ploys to prevent us from retiring?"

Dunk lurched through the lounge to the front of the bus, yelling over his shoulder. "Yer lucky it wasn't yer bloody head, mate."

He yanked open the door to the driver's area. Gus whipped his head toward Dunk, startled by this sudden intrusion into his private domain. The sound of Willie Nelson crooning about being half a man reached Jack from Gus's cassette deck. It was great music, no question about it, but the guy had been playing that same tape over and over again ad nauseam. Jack had never once caught him playing *their* music.

"Stop the bus," ordered Dunk.

"He can't stop on a motorway, you fool," said Jack as he rushed to the front.

"I can't stop this vehicle on the highway," said Gus. "It's too big for the shoulder and will stick out in the road." Jack always got a huge kick out of the way Gus said *vee-hickle*.

Dunk put his hands on his hips and loomed over their driver. "I said, stop the bloody bus."

Gus glanced back at Jack. "Is it an emergency? That's the only reason I can stop and not get—"

"Aye, it's an emergency," said Dunk in a booming voice that hurt Jack's ears. "Cause if ya don't stop the bloody bus, there's going to be a murder. Maybe even two."

"OK," said Gus, his eyes veering back and forth between Dunk and the road. "Except I could get another conviction. Like that time in Tuscaloosa when you didn't want me to contest it. And then I'd be losing my license for sixty days, which—"

"Ya won't lose it," said Dunk. "I guarantee it."

Jack gave him a scornful look. "You can't guarantee that."

"An extra thousand dollars if ya stop this bus right now."

Gus took no time to respond. "Two might do it."

"OK, two," said Dunk.

Jack crossed his arms and glared at him. That money better be coming from Dunk's own pocket and not the band's funds. They'd been hemorrhaging money, and maybe this kind of tomfoolery—knavery even—was the reason why.

Gus grabbed the walkie-talkie and barked into it. "Come in, Stonehenge. We're pulling over on the shoulder. Do you copy?"

"Come again, Big Ben," came the immediate reply from Mick, the driver of the band bus following behind them. Shouts and high-pitched laughter boomed in the background. "Got some noise here and think I heard wrong. Did you say pulling over? Over."

"You heard right, Stonehenge. We're stopping on the shoulder. Over."

Mick's voice came back. "You got some emergency there? Don't wanna put my license on the line when we only got another two weeks with these limey—"

Gus cut him off before they could hear the next word.

Jack scowled at the walkie-talkie. Why was it always the idiots of the world like Mick who were so full of themselves, while talented guys like Gus were humble to a fault? He and Dunk had been remarkably lucky to swoop in and hire Gus after a country legend announced his sudden retirement. Mick, on the other hand, was the slim pickings left after Willie, Dolly, and other country stars scarfed up all the good tour bus drivers for their luxury "homes away from home." Mick couldn't find an arena if it smacked him in the face, and had almost cost them a fortune in concert refunds when he got the band bus lost in the wilds of North Carolina. Since then, he was required to drive directly behind

Gus at all times. No way was Jack going to let Dunk offer *that* guy two thousand dollars.

Jack extended his hand. "Give it here. I'll explain it to him."

Gus held out the walkie-talkie.

Before Jack could move, Dunk snatched it, stepped out of reach, and put it up to his mouth. "Mick, this is one of the limey bastards talking. Ya know, the one ya work for? We're stopping and I'm jumping onto yer bus. Then we're getting right back on the road. And yer going to like it or ya can shut yer scabby geggie. Do I make myself clear, ya Yankee wanker? Over."

"Yeah," said Mick, his voice deflated. "I ... I didn't mean—"

Dunk tossed the walkie-talkie on the dash and turned to Gus. "Pull over. Now."

Jack looked out at the darkness framing the long, monotonous road. All he knew was that they were on the interstate between El Paso and Albuquerque. Good thing there wasn't much traffic this time of night or they might incite a major road incident and attract the attention of the cops. A turn of events that, knowing Dunk and the band, could easily spin out of control and jeopardize everything they'd worked so hard to achieve. Not that Dunk would be upset about that, as Jack was now discovering.

Gus engaged the right turn signal and flashing hazard lights. He slowed and eased the tour bus onto the shoulder.

Willie and Merle Haggard were now on to the next song, about reasons to quit smoking and drinking. Jack glared at Dunk and pointed at the cassette player. "You hear that? What they're saying about smoking? How bad it is? Two huge country stars. But my band manager tells me I should shut up about it because he's got bigger things to worry about."

Gus brought the bus to a smooth stop and put it in idle.

"Open the bloody door," said Dunk, hurting Jack's ears again.

Gus pressed the release and the door swung open.

Jack followed Dunk as he clambered down and strode toward the other bus.

"Don't yell at Gus," he shouted at Dunk's back. "He'll quit."

Dunk abruptly stopped and turned toward him, his face a mask of rage. "Oh, *he'll* quit, will he?"

They had almost reached the end of their bus, the band bus idling only a few yards beyond and illuminating them in its headlights. Jack could see the boys congregated at the front near Mick, craning their necks to see what was going on. A girl's head came into view behind them, talking and laughing. Keith quickly stepped in front of her, blocking her from view, and said something over his shoulder.

Jack narrowed his eyes. "Are there groupies on that bus?"

Dunk mimicked him in a falsetto voice. *"Are there groupies on that bus?"*

"How dare you mock me," said Jack. "I'm the leader of this band, and—"

"I'm the leader of this band, and I'm so perfect, and if it weren't for me, blah, blah, blah." Dunk switched back to his regular voice. "Jack *Saint* James. We should all bow before you in extreme gratitude that ya even *deign* to walk among us."

"Well, excuse me for actually putting in the effort to keep this band a success. Excuse me for actually caring about this band."

"Oh, do ya?" Dunk shot back. "Do ya care about this band?"

"What's that supposed to mean?"

Jack was suddenly aware that the boys had come off the bus and were standing in a group watching them.

"Ya know exactly what I mean," said Dunk.

Jack gave him a warning look and lowered his voice. "We're not going to talk about that here."

Dunk smirked. "Ya don't want them to know your plan—"

Jack drowned him out by starting to sing at the top of his lungs. He didn't know why, but "In-A-Gadda-Da-Vida" was what came out of his mouth. He extended his arms and walked toward the band, belting out the song as Dunk tried to talk over him. Fat chance of that happening. He kept on singing, as if it were the most natural thing in the world to be resurrecting a sixties Iron Butterfly hit late at night on a dark highway in the wilds of New Mexico. Without the fourteen-minute instrumental solo in the middle, of course.

Jack was not surprised when Randy joined in singing. Rob jumped in next with his baritone, not willing to be outdone by his brother, followed in quick succession by Sam singing falsetto and George making drum sounds. Keith just looked at Jack and scratched his forehead, perplexed.

Dunk had given up trying to be heard, crossing his arms and scowling at Jack. Mick was still sitting in the driver's seat, looking put out, and the groupie Jack had seen was nowhere in evidence. Told to hide when Jack was around, no doubt.

He was wondering how long to keep the song going—it didn't have more than one verse, really—when a siren became audible in the distance and grew louder as it moved in their direction. The singing died away as everyone turned toward the sound and watched a police car appear a ways down the highway.

"I got this," said Keith as he darted back into the band bus. "Where's the air freshener, Mick?"

"Oh, great," said Jack. "Now we're going to go to prison for twenty years."

"Don't be daft," said Dunk. "We just make it worth their while to let us go."

"Yeah, and then they shoot us," said Sam, the only black guy in the group.

"Let them try and see what happens," said Rob in a menacing voice.

"Can't go to prison," George said to Dunk. "Have to have sex."

Dunk smirked. "Sorry to tell ya, Georgie, but ya go to the big hoose, you'll be a very busy boy."

"Yeah," said Sam, putting on a cowboy accent. "You so purty."

"Um, what about me?" said Randy. "Wouldn't I be busy too?"

"Not with me around," said Rob.

Keith came clattering down from the bus. "All good. Hid everything away."

"What if they have sniffer dogs, Keith?" said Jack. "What then?"

Keith grinned. "Then we peg it and hope the coppers don't catch us, yeah?"

"Dibs on Dunk if we go to prison," said Sam.

"Hold on," said Rob, "I thought you'd be with me."

Jack sighed as the boys broke into an argument about who would bunk together in prison. Of course no one mentioned him. Who ever thinks about the lonely guy at the top? Whereas their smelly, short-tempered band manager was being avidly fought over, and grinning with absolute delight at his popularity. Jack would never hear the end of this.

"Zip it," he shouted as the police car approached at high speed. The boys were so embroiled in their argument they hadn't even noticed the "coppers" almost upon them. Why would he want to bunk with any of these pillocks anyway? They wouldn't last a bloody second in prison. He'd find himself a white-collar criminal with a decent chess game and a talent for procuring favors. Although really, in all fairness, *he* should be the one getting first dibs on Dunk.

Everyone went quiet and turned to watch the oncoming police car. It looked as if they might have defied fate and it would pass them by. But why should tonight be different from any other night in this godfor-saken little band? The police car swerved off the tarmac onto the shoulder and shrieked to a halt directly behind the band bus.

Two police officers got out and slammed their doors, both hiking their trousers, the older one pulling down his hat and the younger one, the driver, adjusting his crotch. As they walked toward the band, Jack couldn't help but admire their smart uniforms—dark blue with sky blue cuffs and pockets, and stripes running down the sides of their trousers, topped off by hats with medallions on the front and shiny black visors. He would kill to have one of those uniforms.

He wondered if, as head of the band, he should step forward and greet them. But he also noticed the guns in their holsters. Dunk was the hothead who'd got them into this situation, not to mention the fool who promised Gus he wouldn't get another conviction, and the knave who said they could buy their way out of it. So let him be the one who put his neck on the line, the one who got pistol-whipped for talking back, and the one who got himself thrown in the clinker. It would serve Dunk right. Especially since he was so delighted at winning the prison popularity contest.

The police officers ambled over and stopped in front of the band. The older officer put his right hand on the butt of his Smith and Wesson and the other on his hip. "Evening, fellas."

The young officer took the same stance and gave them the regulation deadpan police stare. Dunk's version was better, in Jack's humble opinion.

"Yeah. Evening, fellas," the young officer said in a tough-guy voice.

"I'm Officer Mallory of the New Mexico State Police," said the older one. "And this here is my deputy, Officer Pratt." He surveyed the group. "You folks aren't from 'round here, are you?"

Everyone started talking at once. Officer Mallory put his fingers to his mouth and emitted a sharp whistle. Officer Pratt followed suit.

In the ensuing silence, Officer Mallory answered his own question. "Clearly not. You've got them foreign accents and you're standing on the blacktop where it's not safe." He pointed at the grass. "I want you all on this here shoulder lined up." When they didn't move, he shouted, "Now!"

"You heard him. Now!" said Officer Pratt.

Once the band members had formed a scraggly line on the grass, Officer Mallory looked from one to the other and asked, "Which one of you's in charge?"

Dunk pointed at Jack and smirked. "He's your man, Officer. Right there. Our fearless leader."

Jack glared back at Dunk. "With all due respect, did we not agree that it's your job as manager to deal with things like this? And didn't you promise—"

"Aye, right," said Dunk, his brogue getting thicker by the second. "It's my job to deal with everything, int it? While you lollygag about finding fault and—"

"OK! OK! OK!" said Officer Mallory in a commanding voice. "Here's what we're going to do. I'm going to point at you, one by one, and you're going to tell me exactly who you are and what you do. Understood?"

He pointed at wide-eyed Randy, the first in line. Jack cringed. Talk about starting with the one guy who would tell the officer everything.

"Um, yeah. My name's Randy Rickman. And, um, I play keyboards for Pirate. That's who we are. The rock band Pirate. Not that sixties band called the Pirates. Some people get us mixed up, but they're from London and we're from Manchester. That's in England, where we're from. We did covers of their tunes "Please Don't Touch" and "Shakin' All Over" when we started out, because they're brilliant, right? But now we do all our own stuff. We're hard rock and they're more R&B, aren't they? And um, I guess that's it, really."

Officer Mallory turned away, grinning, and pointed at Rob. "Jus' give me your name and position, son."

"Rob Rickman, and I play the best instrument on the planet. Bass guitar."

"You two are twins, looks like. But not identical." He pointed at George. "And you?"

Jack considered George the least likely to crack under interrogation, a man of few words even in the best of circumstances.

"George Farraday. Drums."

For some reason this made the cop break into a big smile. He pointed at Sam. "And you, young man?"

Sam looked down at the ground and mumbled, "Sam Wilson. Lead and rhythm guitar."

"Sorry, can't quite hear you there, young man."

Keith took a step toward the cop. "He plays both lead and rhythm guitar, like me. He's Sam Wilson and I'm Keith Aldcroft."

"Keith, huh?" The cop gave him an assessing look. "I never did understand it. Why would a band need three guitars?"

Keith started to speak and Jack interrupted him. This was *his* band, after all, and he led all the interviews. And this *was* an interview.

"The way we do it, Officer, Rob drives the music with his bass guitar. George provides the heartbeat with his drums. Keith and Sam take turns providing the rhythm and playing the melody or counter-melody, and sometimes work together to produce a wall of sound. And Randy is the pizzazz with his keyboards. We all tell the story with our vocals. Everyone is essential to the Pirate ship, as I like to say."

"And your name?" said the cop.

"Jack St James. Lead singer and songwriter." Jack indicated Dunk with his thumb. "And this is the band's manager *at the moment*. Duncan Iain MacGregor."

Dunk puffed out his chest and gave the cop a fierce look. "Descendant of the famous warrior Rob Roy on my father's side and the former King of Scotland Robert the Bruce on my mother's."

Jack rolled his eyes. What a twit. Who provokes a cop like that? It was like waving a red rag in front of a bull.

"Is that so?" said Officer Mallory. He pointed at the first bus. "This your bus?"

Jack rushed to reply before Dunk could make some smart remark and get them in even deeper trouble. "Yes it is, Officer."

The cop turned his head toward Officer Pratt. "Get everyone off that other bus. Then put some emergency flares and direct traffic, while I have a quick talk with these two fellas."

Officer Pratt pouted like a petulant teenager. "But—"

"Todd." Officer Mallory gave him a stern look. "What department do we belong to?"

"I know, I know. Public Safety." He turned and walked toward the band bus, kicking at a tuft of grass with his boot.

Officer Mallory pointed at Jack and Dunk. "You two, with me. The rest of you, stay on this grass and don't move off it. Y'hear?"

Two

OFFICER MALLORY SAUNTERED toward the front of their bus and stopped when he reached the open door. He turned toward Jack and Dunk coming up behind him. "Mind if I board?"

"Well, we don't normally let other people on this bus," said Jack. In point of fact, he'd banned all guests from the management bus, with quick agreement from Gus. Dunk went on the other bus when he wanted to "let his hair doon."

"Be our guest, Officer," said Dunk.

Jack looked at him in disbelief as the cop turned to board. Wasn't Dunk breaking his own damn rule—don't ever let the police on the buses?

Gus was still in the driver's seat listening to Willie and Merle. He held a ham sandwich in suspended animation, his wary eyes focused on the cop.

"*Pancho and Lefty*, isn't it?" said Officer Mallory, hovering on the first step, eye level with Gus. "Great album. Would love to see them two fellas in concert. But we don't get too many stars out this way."

"Don't think them two are touring," said Gus. "Shame, really. Would give an arm and a leg to see it."

Jack looked back and forth between them. Maybe if he mentioned meeting ZZ Top? They were kind of country, weren't they? Or should he mention the country star Gus used to work for? That might impress the cop—if he needed to keep from getting shot.

The officer strolled into the lounge of their bus, Jack and Dunk following behind. He whistled as he looked around at the wood paneling and took in the TV, VCR and stereo tape deck unit recessed into the wall. He raised his eyebrows at the built-in leather sofa and grinned at the reclining leather chair, then squatted down to check out their library of VHS and audio cassettes.

"You like *Dallas*, do ya?"

"Larry Hagman came to our concert," said Dunk. "Nicest bloke you'll ever meet in your life. Not like his character at all."

"It's called acting," said Jack, miffed at Dunk stealing his thunder. Larry came to see *him*, after all. Even invited him to watch the filming. He would have too, if he hadn't been tied up with concerts night after night after night.

Officer Mallory looked at him. "This must've set you fellas back a pretty penny."

"You'd think so, wouldn't ya?" said Dunk, grabbing away the cop's attention yet again. "But we did the maths, and it's much cheaper than flying the band all over kingdom come. Not to mention, he hates airports and flying. And we can sell the buses when the tour's over to another band. Get most of the cost back." He looked at Jack with pride. "I hate to admit it, but Billy No-Mates here was the one who designed it."

"Oh, yeah?" said the cop, glancing at Jack. "Mind if I see the rest?"

Dunk led him through the kitchenette, talking a mile a minute, waving his hand at the built-in microwave and countertop espresso machine, and opening the pantry to show him Jack's wine rack and his own collection of craft beers.

Jack could hear Dunk pointing out the marble sink bowl and self-contained shower in the loo, the extra-long bed in Dunk's bedroom to accommodate his 6-foot-4-inch frame, Jack's dressing room with his concert costumes on a rack and a proper theatre mirror for applying makeup, and Jack's bedroom at the very back, with a double bed and Dolby surround sound system.

Jack stayed in the lounge, pacing and worrying his bottom lip. For some reason, he really wanted this cop to approve of the bus. He was flooded with anxiety that he wouldn't. What was that about?

He knew everything was clean—except for the broken bottle in the sink—because he'd wiped everything down that very morning. There was still the slight aroma of Wipe-It-Fresh hanging in the air. He wouldn't eat off the floor, but he could certainly vouch for eating off anything else.

They were taking forever back there. They seemed to have gone into Dunk's room and closed the door. Was Officer Mallory interrogating him? Dunk could talk for Scotland once he got started and get the band in deep trouble without even realizing it. What if that other cop was touring the band bus? Jack had no idea what he might find on there. Pot for sure, an underage girl probably, who knew what else. How many times had he made an issue about these things, but to no avail? This was not good, not good at all.

A door clicked open and Jack stopped pacing.

"We still stay in hotels," said Dunk, leading Officer Mallory back into the lounge. "Jack doesn't sleep well on the bus. He says it's the motion, and my snoring. But he never slept well at school either."

"That so?" said the cop. "Well, thank you for the tour, Dunk. It's impressive, that's for sure. Your folks must be mighty proud of you fellas. Lot to accomplish at your age."

Jack felt a ridiculous surge of pleasure at these words. It was true; they were only twenty-five. Well, almost, in his case. It was also true that they were finishing a world tour. Some people might find that impressive.

Officer Mallory addressed Dunk. "I wonder if you might go check on my deputy, make sure he's keeping himself out of trouble, while I have a little chat with Jack here." He said it as if they were going to have a natter over a cuppa.

"Ya got it," said Dunk, winking at the cop as he turned and lumbered off the bus. What was that about?

Officer Mallory walked over to the driver's area. He leaned toward Gus. "Jus' gonna shut this door, you don't mind."

Gus waved his hand. "Gonna take a walk, stretch my legs."

Officer Mallory shut the door and turned to Jack.

Jack clenched his fists in anxiety as thoughts rushed through his head. How could they leave him alone with a state cop? Why in the world did Dunk tell him personal things like his sleeping habits? What did this cop want from him?

Officer Mallory smiled. "I have a confession to make. Mind if we sit?" He didn't wait for Jack to reply. He took a seat on the sofa and pulled his hat off his head. He placed it on his lap with one hand while wetting his fingers and smoothing down his comb over with the other.

Jack took one look at the cop rearranging his hair and all the anxiety rushed out of his body. What was he thinking? This man was no threat. And where were his manners?

"May I get you something to drink? I could put the kettle on, or make you an espresso. Or would you prefer Coke? Beer? Whisky? A glass of wine? I have a fine sauvignon."

"Looks like you got Lone Star," the officer said, pointing toward the sink. "That'd be fine."

"Coming right up."

As Jack handed him a bottle of ice cold beer, it occurred to him that the police officer was drinking on the job. Or was he off-duty? "Officer Mallory—"

"Call me Bill. Bill Mallory. Jus' like the football coach. Case you know American football."

Jack knit his eyebrows. "Oh, OK. Bill."

"Have a seat."

Jack lowered himself into the recliner, angling his body toward the cop, and sat ramrod straight, bracing himself for whatever came next.

"Now, Jack, I couldn't help noticing the crack on that countertop there and the broken bottle in the sink. Wondered if maybe you two had a little bit of a bust-up. What we call a domestic disturbance. So I asked Dunk when we were back there." The cop pointed toward the bedrooms with his beer. "Thought I'd get your side of the story too, jus' to be fair."

That knobhead Dunk. He'd fallen for the oldest cop trick in the book, the "good cop" routine, acting all nicey-nice, making you relax, and then milking you for everything you know. Well he wasn't falling for it.

"It wasn't a disturbance at all, Bill." He gave him a reassuring smile. "We simply had a minor disagreement about something and—"

"So minor he paid your driver two thousand dollars to stop the bus on the highway—a convictable offense here in New Mexico, as your driver rightly pointed out to him—jus' so's he could jump over to the other bus?"

Jack's mouth dropped open in shock. Did that blathering fool tell him everything? "You can't arrest us. We have seven more concerts, and we can't miss them or we'll breach contract and ..." He stopped talking. He didn't want to tell Bill the real reason, something only he and Dunk knew.

Officer Mallory looked at him with sympathy. "And you'll lose the performance bonus you wrangled from your record company, and then you won't be able to retire after the tour like you been hoping to do."

"He told you? That idiot! He can't keep a damn thing to himself."

"Dunk told me you got blood out of a stone. Bands don't get performance bonuses from record companies, do they? Especially from one of them big fancy ones in New York City, like your Dolos Discs there. Mighty impressive, if you ask me."

Jack sighed. "We don't have it yet, and we won't get it if he keeps messing things up." They had to get it or his life would be unbearable. When they weren't playing, most rock stars drank, drugged, and screwed to get through the day. He didn't have even that.

"Listen to me, son, I'm gonna give you some advice. OK?" He looked at Jack for confirmation.

Jack nodded. What choice did he have? He still didn't know if Bill was going to arrest him, or give them a citation, or what.

"I got a deputy too." Bill pointed at the window. "Todd out there. Been to a fancy college and got a management degree, but he messes up fairly regular. Drives me crazy, copying everything I do." He gave Jack an earnest look. "But it's our job as bosses to be the bigger men, show 'em how to behave right, build 'em up and make 'em feel appreciated. You might wanna ease up on Dunk, less you want him to be the one who cracks. You hear what I'm saying?"

Jack couldn't hold back his frustration any longer. "Yes, I hear you, but for how long? It's not just him, it's all of them. They don't listen and keep getting things wrong. After hundreds of concerts! Like my microphone tonight. It smelled like cigarette smoke and made me gag. Even though we have a no-smoking clause in everyone's contract and they all know how much I hate it. And tonight they have groupies on the band bus, when we agreed, no groupies. I've told them again and again, we can't keep paying to send groupies back home. Particularly when they go through so many of them. What if they're under age? If one of the band members gets arrested and misses a concert, then we lose the bonus and—"

Officer Mallory interrupted. "Did they agree to this, or did you tell it to 'em? Or even yell it at 'em?"

Jack stared back at him. Yes, of course he yelled it at them. He was the boss. And they were supposed to get it right.

The cop continued, "Think about it. Do you want to be told what to do? Or even worse, have someone talk to you like you're a little kid? Or worst of all, yell at you like you're dumber than a block of wood?"

"Well, no."

"Course not. Fact is, you have to bring 'em along with you, even let 'em think it was their idea from the get-go even though it was yours. It might take longer, and it might stick in the craw, but in the end it's worth it because you get the behavior you want from them. You see?"

Jack furrowed his brow. "I think so."

Bill patted his hat and grinned at Jack. "I'm glad we were able to have this little talk."

Jack grinned back. He liked this cop. Reminded him of Dunk's dad. Always taking him aside for little pep talks.

The sound of multiple police sirens in the distance breached the quiet of the lounge. Jack looked at Bill with renewed alarm.

Officer Mallory suppressed a guilty smile. "So, about that confession, Jack. After the advice I jus' gave you, I'm embarrassed to admit this. But I was given strict instructions to keep you here by hook or by crook." He looked at Jack, gauging his reaction. "By my wife. My daughter has you fellas on her wall and she's in love with that George. Tried to get tickets to one of your concerts, but they were all sold out.

Annie would never forgive her old dad if he didn't move heaven and earth to get her a photo op. And between you and me, I think my wife has a thing for that Keith. Says he reminds her of me back in the day."

Jack pretended to be outraged. "Are you *serious*, Officer Mallory?" He grinned. "I'm going to have to report this to your boss."

Bill grinned back. "Be my guest. That's probably him out there now, bringing his boys, 'long with my wife and daughter. He's the one heard the CB chatter about your buses and said ... well, never mind what he said. Don't want to lose my job telling tales on my boss, now do I?"

Jack stood up. "OK. Well I better get on my costume and makeup. Don't want Annie or the boys to see me looking like this." Or, really, anyone with a camera. He and Dunk agreed that it still wasn't safe for him to be photographed without makeup, even with the tour finishing in ten days.

Bill stood up as well. "Sure appreciate it, Jack." He looked him in the eye. "I know it's going to be something they talk about for years. 'Specially if it turns out to be your last tour."

When Jack descended from the bus ten minutes later, a bag in one hand and an acoustic guitar in the other, he couldn't believe the sight that greeted him. The side of the road was lit up by police cars and passenger vehicles queued up beyond the buses with their headlights ablaze. The state police had set up flares and were directing cars on both sides of the highway, as if it were the scene of an accident. Clearly, word had leaked out that they were here. People were clustered around the members of the band, keeping them busy posing for photos and signing autographs. A loud and boisterous Dunk—no surprise there—was holding court with a group of police officers, telling a story about his surprise encounter with "Nessie," the Loch Ness monster.

Jack spotted Bill holding hands with a pretty woman as she chatted to Keith and laughed at something he said. A teenage girl bounded over and grabbed Bill's other hand, leaning her head against his arm. Jack felt a pang of sadness as he watched. Would *he* ever have that? A normal life with a wife and kids? A life where he didn't feel so separate and lonely all the time?

Bill turned his head toward his daughter and spotted him. "Hey, Jack, come on over and meet my family."

Jack took a deep breath and centered himself. Showtime! But was this guy kidding calling him Jack in front of his daughter? Big mistake, Mister Police Officer. This was his gig and *he* was in charge now.

He put on a sneer and swaggered over to the small group. "It's Blackbeard to you, dibble devil," he hissed at Bill with contempt.

Annie shrieked and clutched her dad's arm. "Omigosh! It's him! It's Jack St James!"

Jack leered at Bill's wife and winked at his daughter as he threw the bag at Bill's feet. "Me's here to rescue these fine lasses from your evil clutches. I tender these trinkets as payment for their freedom. Some photogravures of me handsome self and me bawdy crew, with our names scratched on them in pig's blood. A fine set of threads for this comely young wench." He grinned at Bill's daughter. "A pouch bursting with pieces of eight. And a few sea shanties I propose to be singing with me crew." He pulled the guitar strap over his shoulder. "I trusts you agree, you mangy scoundrel, them's trinkets enough to pur-chase their freedom."

Annie dropped her dad's arm and grabbed her head. "He's going to sing! Omigosh, I'm going to die! He's going to sing!"

Jack gave her an indulgent smile as he strummed the guitar. He'd already tuned it up on the bus. Keith and Dunk rushed to gather the band, and Jack sang one of his solos as he waited for the boys to gather around him.

He stared at Annie as he sang. She looked as if she'd stopped breathing, and tears streaked down her cheeks. He was used to that. No one was ever prepared for the emotions unleashed by music. It was emotional kryptonite and emotional catharsis all rolled into one. Who knew that better than he did?

George rocked up with his tom-toms and sang backup. Keith and Sam rustled up two more guitars. Rob and Randy joined in without instruments, singing harmony. The band went through most of their hits and fielded some requests from the kids. Jack kept up his pirate patter between songs, taunting the police officers to the delight of the crowd, flirting with the ladies, and giving the kids tips on how to be good pirates. He wasn't sure where all the people were coming from, but the crowd appeared to be expanding by the minute. He didn't mind. With state police all over the place, they didn't have the usual worry about being assaulted by rabid fans. No one dared come near them.

A while later, after their impromptu concert had ended, fan requests for photos and autographs had been sated, and the police had dispersed the crowd and got everyone safely on their way, Jack said goodbye to Bill, Peg and a tearful Annie. Annie began sobbing as he boarded the bus, and his last view out the window was of her crying in her father's arms. Bill was a lucky man.

Jack got out of his costume and makeup for the second time that night and took a quick shower. Then he and Dunk collapsed in the lounge of their bus. They each had a plateful of food balanced on their laps courtesy of Peg, who had pressed a cooler into their hands packed with barbeque ribs, potato salad, and corn on the cob.

"I invited them to the rest of our shows," Jack said as he applied butter to his corn. "But they can only make the last one."

"No worries," said Dunk. "I'll put them on the VIP list."

Jack smiled at him. "That's great. I really appreciate it. Really."

"Cut it out."

"Cut what out?"

"*I really appreciate it. Really,*" Dunk said in that same annoying falsetto. "I mean, away and boil yer head, mate."

"So what do you want me to say?"

"Just let me do my effin' job, yeah? How 'bout that?"

Jack stared at him, trying to figure out how to bring up the issues still on his mind while letting Dunk "do his effin' job." And without telling or yelling, as he'd promised Bill.

"Right," said Dunk, rolling his eyes at him. "Problem number one: Manny talked to Zeke. He ran out of Nicorette. Snuck a fag near the equipment. Didn't swap in our own microphones till the last minute, otherwise we'd've known about it in sound check and rehearsal. And besides, if ya didn't have a nose like a bloodhound, you'd probably never've noticed. 'Twon't happen again."

"Oh, OK."

"Problem number two," said Dunk. He shoveled some potato salad into his mouth. "The groupies. They're not groupies. It's just Suze and Carly."

"Suze and Carly?"

"Suze that has the black hair, looks like she cut it with nail scissors, and Carly that has the big gap in her front teeth."

"Oh, those two," said Jack.

"They've been following the tour on their own dosh, and the boys really like 'em. Keep 'em entertained and out of trouble when they're around. And"—he held up his hand to stop Jack from speaking—"I know they're legal."

"OK."

Dunk sighed. "With George, we're on it. I got a system with the roadies after the concerts. We're not letting underage girls get near him. Trust me."

Jack searched his memory and had to admit, he couldn't remember seeing George with any underage girls.

Dunk pointed a barbeque rib at him. "And last but not least, a problem ya didn't know I was handling."

"What's that?" said Jack, pausing before he laid into his piece of corn.

"There's a car been tailing us."

"Paparazzi?"

"Nah, I think it's that pimply kid who's been sneaking around and asking questions, and scampering off when I try to grab 'im." Dunk spoke with frustration. "Greasy little bassa."

"Only a few concerts to go, so don't do anything rash."

"Nah, just a trap, with you as bait. So yer going to have to suit up early tomorrow and saunter around backstage acting important." He grinned. "Yer favorite thing."

"That's an excellent solution. I would be happy to help."

"I told ya to cut it out," said Dunk. "Yer making me sick."

"Better sick than ready to kill me."

"Ya keep it up, that might still happen. Or maybe I'll can yer arse and replace ya, just like Clifford Davis did to the original members of Fleetwood Mac. Ya wear a costume, so the punters will never know the difference."

"Good thing I co-own the band. Everyone told me managers can't be trusted. Case in point."

"They told *me* lead singers are unreliable and temperamental. Case in double point, mate."

Jack took a sip of his sauvignon blanc. "Bill has a good life, doesn't he?"

"The grass is always greener, mate," Dunk said as he gnawed on a rib.

Jack stared into space, picturing himself on an estate in the English countryside, Peg greeting him at the door with a big smile and Annie jumping up and down in excitement at his return. Their dog ran up wagging its tail. No, scratch that. No pets. They were flea and germ magnets. He followed Peg into the dining room and sighed with contentment as she put food on the table and asked him about his day. Only seven more concerts and he could retire, buy that estate, and find a Peg of his own—*if* Dunk and the boys didn't mess things up and cost them any concert revenues or that absolutely essential bonus.

"Bill's got that muppet Todd," said Dunk, interrupting his reverie. "Whereas you got me. Enough said, right?"

Jack continued staring into space, willing his fantasy to return.

"Right?" repeated Dunk.

"Right," said Jack as he returned his attention to his plate. "But he's got Peg too. She's really pretty, and she can cook."

"Look at me, mate." Dunk grinned, his mouth full of potato salad. "And I can heat up pizza. What more do we need?"

Three

A FEW HOURS LATER, across the country in one of the premier yoga and meditation centers on the east coast, Lucy Sabatini sat cross-legged on the dais at the front of the Sunrise Room, facing her usual crowd of early morning meditators.

She was singing an energetic chant with her eyes closed, feet on thighs and upturned hands on knees—a position she jokingly referred to as Cramps-R-Us. At twenty-two, she was no longer the limber sixteen-year-old who could do a series of front handsprings and not even get out of breath. Oh, those were the days! But, according to Swami Zukeeni, doing the full lotus pose while chanting was part of giving the guests an authentic experience here at Spirits Rising. So, despite Cindy's scoffing, she had no choice but to suck it up and do it, did she?

Opening her eyes a crack, she surveyed the state of the room. Rows of people sat higgledy-piggledy on the floor facing her, some swaying to the music and chanting along, others sitting motionless, trying to ascend into that elusive state of bliss. Nitiraj incense, one of her favorite smells, wafted through the air and enveloped the guests in a spicy sweet blanket of smoke. The dawn of another perfect summer day in western Massachusetts crept into the unlit room and outlined everyone in a dim yellow glow.

It was time—time to take them to nirvana, or as close as she could get them. As she began to move the chant up the musical scale, she pulled first one foot and then the other off her lap. Tugging off her headscarf, she tossed it to the side, and picked up her finger cymbals and slid them on. The energy in the room jumped with each movement, as if she were deliberately poking everyone in their third eye at the same time. For a Catholic girl who believed in stigmata and miracles, this didn't surprise her one bit, but she still found it totally cool every time it happened.

As she reached the crescendo and held her voice there, she rose to her feet in one flowing move, lifted her arms to the heavens, and began whirling like one of those dervishes with the huge skirts and tall hats. She'd read in *Encyclopedia Britannica* that they were always men, those dervishes, but she saw no good reason why women couldn't whirl too. She felt giddy with a sudden and inexplicable joy as her bare feet turned in place and her long halo of hair whipped around her upturned face.

The congregation took this as their cue and exploded into orgasmic movement. The swaying chanters leapt to their feet and danced around the room in a burst of wild frenzy, while the blissed-out sitters moved their heads in hypnotic figure eights. The chanting intensified and echoed off the walls in waves of stereophonic sound.

It was so simple in her mind: music was the ambrosia of the gods, and the means through which human beings could attain some small measure of heaven on earth. That's why people were so crazy about it.

Just as she was about to push the chanting to its limit and take the congregants into a state of rapture, the side door banged open and a pale young man with beaded dreadlocks rushed forward and bounded up onto the dais. Lucy's voice wobbled at this outrageous intrusion. For crying out loud! What was he thinking crashing her kirtan ecstatic meditation session like this?

He better have a great excuse, because he'd destroyed everyone's high in one fell swoop. The sitting meditators had become still and the dancing meditators had stopped in place, their movements becoming tentative and jerky. Expressions of bliss had turned to dismay, and smiles to frowns. It was kind of like being interrupted just when you were about to come. Not that she was some big expert on that or anything.

The young man leaned toward her with undisguised impatience. Lucy had no choice but to stop whirling and return back to the more basic chant. As she continued singing, she gave the young man her fiercest glare and raised her eyebrows in a silent *What?*.

"The swami needs to see you," he said with a ludicrous sense of self-importance. "Right now. No delay."

Lucy glanced over at Cindy and rolled her eyes. Cindy was assisting her with the session, and had already danced up to the dais as soon as the young man rushed in. She'd made her sudden leaps and spins to the front look like a burst of spiritual passion. Lucy might know a thing or two about music, but boy did that girl know how to move her body.

And, better yet, being her best friend since fourth grade, Cindy knew the exact meaning of each of Lucy's eye rolls. She rushed up the stairs to take over. As Lucy slipped off the finger cymbals and handed them off, Cindy pressed her mouth to her ear. "Don't give in, Lucy Goose."

Lucy gave her a resigned look and nodded.

The young man turned on his heel and rushed back out of the room. Lucy knew who he was, the new intern in the admin office, working for that snake in the grass Mandy. No surprise that she was involved in this.

Lucy scooped up and rewrapped her headscarf, adjusted her tunic, and willed herself down the steps of the dais and to the door. As she turned to face the congregation and bow in prayer, most of them were watching her with expressions of alarm or disappointment, a few with looks of outrage.

She wiped the scowl from her face, gave them her best professional smile, and waved her hand toward Cindy as if introducing the next act in the ashram variety show. Here you go, folks, the beautiful and talented Cindy Morgan for your morning entertainment. And if you don't like it, go complain to your ridiculous—oops, I mean revered—local swami. The one with the dumb name, who wouldn't know a zucchini from a rutabaga if his life depended on it. Or good music from bad, for that matter.

The door clicked shut as she left the room and headed toward the swami's office, gulping in air to get her anger under control. Really, who did he think he was pulling her out of her kirtan session like this? It better be about the recording contract, or she was going to be really, really mad.

The door slammed open behind her.

"Where do you think you're going?" said an aggressive male voice.

She stopped and sighed. Not again. Turning to face the latest bane of her existence, she stifled the desire to shush him or, better yet, tell him where to get off. It might make her feel good, but there'd be heck to pay with the swami if he got wind of it, not to mention having to say a load of Hail Marys after her next bout in the confession booth.

"Do you think I came here all the way from L.A. to chant with the oh-so-talented, oh-so-lovely Jakananda, only to have her leave right in the middle of morning meditation at the exactimundo moment that I'm getting my groove on? Of course, that would be no, nay, nyet, wouldn't it?"

Lucy sighed again. "OK, Mark—"

"It's Megalon, like I told you. Gifted to me by my main guru guy in Beverly Hills. Not the other guy in Topanga. His name sucked. But that's beside the *el pointo*, isn't it?"

She gave him her customer service smile. "I'm very sorry, *Megalon*, but Swami Zukeeni himself called me out of kirtan, so—"

"So what?" He moved closer to her and crowded her against the wall. "Listen, sweetheart, I'm spending a fortune here and I expect to get great service." He put his arm against the wall above her head and raised his eyebrows. "If you know what I mean."

She stared into his dilated pupils. High on coke, before seven in the morning. Even in her two years on the road with Magnus hanging around dozens of rock bands, she'd never seen anyone start this early. To be fair, musicians never got up until the afternoon anyway. But still.

As he raised his other hand to touch her face, she slipped under the arm above her head and bolted away. "Sorry, Mark," she shouted over her shoulder. "Gotta run or I'll be late."

She sprinted down the corridor to make good her escape from Megalon and to make up the lost time. She was hoping the swami was going to give her the news she'd been waiting to hear—that they would be signing the music contract with Dolos Discs and she could get started on all the preparations. The swami and his second-in-command, Ramakarshivenenda—or Ramakar, as everyone else called him—had kept her in suspense, the swami refusing to discuss it and Ramakar putting his fingers to his lips to shush her whenever she tried to bring it up. They'd had her on pins and needles for weeks now.

She finally reached the swami's office and stopped in front of it, taking in one last calming breath. Yanking down her bunched tunic with one hand, she lifted the other and rapped on the door.

"Come," called a nasal voice from within.

Lucy opened the door and stopped in the doorway. The swami was standing in Vrikshasana, the Tree Pose, wearing tight white yoga shorts and nothing else. His skinny white chest sported a clump of dark hairs and his shoulder-length, blunt-cut, dark brown hair reeked of sandal-wood oil.

She gave the standard greeting, bowing toward him with her hands in prayer mode in front of her heart. "Namaste, Swami Zukeeni."

She tried and failed to hold back a sneeze. Probably allergic to this brand of hair oil too. He seemed to have every odoriferous hair oil on Planet Earth used by skinny white men trying to pass themselves off as holy swamis.

"Namaste, Jakananda," he said, fixing her with an intense stare. "And gesundheit."

Jakananda. She hated the Sanskrit name he'd given her. It sounded like a Bollywood porn star, or an Indian call girl servicing the discerning gentlemen of Delhi or Bombay. Come to my boudoir and I will do Natarajasana, the Lord of the Dance pose, before we engage in kinky-dinky Kama Sutra-style sex.

With a start she realized that she'd been zoning out. He continued to hold the stare, willing her to stay in intimate eye contact with him. She returned his gaze, and after an uncomfortable few seconds, he relaxed out of the Tree Pose and waved at a low chair facing him.

"Shut the door. Sit." He went into Downward-facing Dog and peered at her through the gap between his legs. *Oh, no.*

Lucy shut the door and lowered herself into the oddly angled chair. She hunched down, wiggling to find a position where his crotch was not in the direct sightline of his face. She didn't remember this chair being here before. He settled his crotch even lower, making it impossible to ignore the fact that, first, she could see his pubic hair poking through the tight white yoga shorts, and second, his main man bits were bulging in multiple directions. So he was well-endowed? Hadn't he heard of a little thing called a jockstrap?

She sat up straight and looked sideways toward his disheveled desk, anywhere but *there*. She had promised Cindy she would not be a goose. Why did this always happen to her and not to Cindy? The swami always seemed to have a "thing" for her. Her attention was grabbed by a large maroon hardcover book peeking out from under some official-looking papers. Without thinking she read the title out loud. "*Music Industry Directory 1983*." Huh.

Swami Zukeeni abruptly walked his hands backwards and stood up. As he sauntered behind his desk, he seized the book and the papers on top of it and tried to shove them into a jam-packed drawer, then gave up and threw them on the floor. He sat down in his carved teak wood chair, picked up some prayer beads and began to massage them, pursing his lips and giving Lucy another version of his power stare.

"Jakananda, look at me. Be fully present with me, here, in this glorious and pregnant moment."

He couldn't be serious after pulling her out of kirtan, the ultimate in being fully present and in the moment. And pregnant? To give herself time to compose her face, Lucy got up and turned her chair toward his desk. She tried to commit his words to memory, never one of her strong suits. She couldn't wait to share them with Cindy. They would die laughing. She sat back down and folded her hands in her lap.

"Yes, I'm fully present now, Swami Zukeeni."

He looked upwards and scanned his eyes along the ceiling, as if reading the wisdom of the universe. "Love is life and life is love. The two are interchangeable. Yes?"

She struggled to keep a straight face. "Um, yes?"

He turned his intense gaze on her. "I've called you here to talk about your future. I have a special position in mind for you, a promotion. I've been talking to Ramakarshivenenda, and we agree your talents are wasted running the music program and dealing with music concerns now that we're close to a deal on the recording contract."

"What?" The blood rushed to her face and her breath caught in her chest. "But it's music I composed and I—"

"I, I, I. We must not let our egos run away with us. We must do all things for the common good of the ashram."

He got up, threw down the beads, and came around the desk. Taking a wide stance in front of her, he rested his hands on her shoulders and stared unblinking into her eyes. "You could do so much more good working with me on special projects, here in the power center of the ashram. I get excited thinking about what we could do together, the music we could make." He quickly added, "On those projects."

She looked off beyond him, unable to meet his eyes. C'mon, Luce, remember what Cindy said. Stand your ground and insist on what you deserve. She took a shaky breath. "I am so honored by your faith in me, Swami Zukeeni, I really am. But we still need to choose the music and orchestrate it, rehearse the musicians and—"

"Enough! It is decided. You have laid the seeds and Ramakarshivenenda will water them and ensure a good harvest. Is this not the way of the world, the ideal balance of masculine and feminine energies?"

"But ... but ..." Lucy was at a complete loss for words. The blood pounded through her brain and her face burned red. She struggled to hold back tears. Three years' work, down the drain in a matter of seconds.

The swami cupped her face in his hands. "Aaaah, my special one. You must continue your journey of evolution and take the next step on the path. I have decided to act as your spiritual guide on this path, your shaman, your personal guru. I give this honor to only a chosen few. You are most fortunate." He slid his hands from her cheeks back to her shoulders and began massaging them.

Lucy sat frozen, unable to move. What to do, what to do, what to do? His hair tonic was overpowering her senses and his hands alarming her and distracting her from figuring out what to say. Cindy's voice had disappeared from her mind, replaced by a jumble of thoughts she couldn't seem to put in the right order. She felt like a kitten held down in someone's lap, forced to succumb to undesired and overzealous petting, without the claws or teeth to defend itself. That was it exactly. She felt powerless, defenseless, at someone else's mercy.

She sent out a prayer for divine intervention—if you could, now please! I'm a good Catholic girl, and I serve for peanuts in an ashram, and I—

At that very moment the door slammed open and Ramakar burst into the room. "That little ass—" He stopped short. "Um, that little ... aspect I was talking to you about, Swami Zukeeni, has, um, arisen and I need your wise counsel." He bowed to Lucy. "Namaste, Jakakanda. My apologies for interrupting."

The swami rubbed Lucy's arms again and gazed deep into her eyes. "I look forward to becoming your personal guide into the Age of Aquarius. We'll begin our work tomorrow. Come to my house at eight. We will be undisturbed there and I can give you my full personal attention." He stepped back, put his hands in prayer position, and bowed. "Namaste, Jakananda."

As Ramakar moved further into the room, Lucy stood up and stumbled backwards to the door. She bowed back, her eyes down. "Namaste, Swami Zukeeni. Namaste, Ramakarshivenenda." She almost collided with the doorjamb in her rush to escape. She turned and walked as fast as she could down the corridor, away from the two men she wanted to murder. She refused to say any Hail Marys for thinking that. They deserved it.

Keeping her face composed and a smile pinned on it, she willed the tears to wait until she made it back to the room she shared with Cindy. Why did they have to live in one of the furthest wings of the building? Oh, yeah, because they wanted a bit of privacy in this community of dumber than dumb, utterly ridiculous, doofier than doofus holy people. It took her dozens of *Namaste* greetings to get there, and when she finally banged into the room, she didn't know whether to cry or scream or break something. Or all three.

She slammed the door as hard as she could and threw herself on her bed face down, screaming into the pillow and kicking her feet like a toddler having a meltdown. That didn't help. She jumped up and began pacing in the floor space between their two beds. Well, actually, in the space on Cindy's side of the room. Her own half was covered by piles of dirty clothes—tunics, sweaty yoga tops and bottoms, scarves, underwear, socks. Everything she'd worn that week. She stopped and kicked at her dirty clothes a few times, then grabbed them up and flung them into her closet on top of the covered clothes hamper.

She picked up a pack of Juicy Fruit gum lying on her bedspread and stuffed three pieces into her mouth. Chewing like a madwoman, she stripped the bed and threw the sheets and bedspread in a pile in the middle of the floor, panting from the exertion. She emptied ashes from an overflowing incense burner into the bin and stacked dirty glasses from her dresser and desk, glasses she had in her room in direct violation of the rules. Go ahead, sue me if you don't like it, you stupid ashram.

Putting her hands on her hips, she surveyed the room for something else to attack. Cindy's side was the picture of perfection, as usual—all structure and neatness, with everything in its designated place and arranged in precise lines and angles. It was almost as if someone had erected an invisible barrier down the middle of the room, dividing it into opposite halves: neat and messy, order and chaos, yang and yin. In fact, there *was* a dividing line; Cindy wouldn't let Lucy get her mess even an inch onto Cindy's side. Lucy had tested the boundary early on and Cindy was having none of it. But Lucy didn't mind because she found Cindy's side oddly restful and calming. Everything was in shades of blue and green, like an underwater oasis—in direct contrast to the cacophony of colors on her own side of the room.

She turned around and contemplated her side again. It was neater now, but hadn't been dusted or vacuumed since Cindy's last cleaning frenzy. Lucy had a lifelong policy, and Cindy knew Lucy wouldn't break it even for her: never clean unless threatened with immediate expulsion from home, school or church—by your mother, the school principal, or that scary Sister Margherita. Otherwise, why do it? Sure, you needed to keep yourself clean, but what was a little dust or dirt? Look at her, she never got sick. The immune system of a sewer rat. Whereas Cindy picked up every germ known to man.

Lucy turned back toward Cindy's side and caught sight of the latest ashram newsletter sitting in the "In" tray on her desk. Prominent at the top was a head-and-shoulders shot of Swami Zukeeni and Ramakar in their formal swami outfits looking imperious and commanding. She stomped over to the desk and snatched up the newsletter. Still chomping on the gum, she rifled through the pages to see if there was anything on the music contract. No, thank goodness. But there was Mandy the Snake's name as editor. Lucy was ripping the newsletter into tiny pieces when Cindy rushed into the room.

"I came as soon as I could," Cindy said, gasping for breath. "There was, I kid you not, a lynch mob complaining about you leaving in the middle of chanting. So I had to make something up about an emergency, yada yada yada, and try not to get mad and lose my cool. I mean, what am I, chopped liver?" Cindy's gaze dropped to the torn-up newsletter all over the carpet. "Uh-oh. It must have been serious."

She grabbed Lucy's arm and pulled her onto her own perfectly made bed. "Sit. Speak. Tell all." Glancing over at Lucy's side of the room, she gasped. "You cleaned up? What did that smarmy swami do to you? He didn't touch you, did he?"

Lucy thrust out her lower lip, eager for sympathy. "Yes, he touched me here." She crossed her arms across her body and grabbed her opposite shoulders with her hands. "And massaged me like this." She ran her fingertips in slow circles on her upper arms. "It was horrible."

"That animal!" Cindy rubbed Lucy's knee to comfort her. "Did he call you out of kirtan just to put the moves on you again?"

"No." Lucy finally let the tears she'd been holding back stream down her face. "He wants to be my personal guru and steal my music and give it to that two-faced Ramakar, because that's how it should be between men and women. And I shouldn't be so self-centered, and should think only about the good of the ashram, and do special projects at his house with him because he's the power center and I need to evolve spiritually and he's the one who can make that happen. And Cin, he did Downward Dog right in my face, in those see-through white yoga shorts."

Cindy looked outraged. "Let me see if I've got this straight. He's taking the recording contract away from you and giving it to Ramakar?"

"Yes! Something about seeds and water and harvests, but I was too upset to understand what he was saying. Cin, he's going to take my music away from me forever and I don't know how to stop him."

Cindy pulled some tissues from her pocket and wiped Lucy's eyes. "Luce, listen to me. He's a swami, not the frickin' God Almighty.

There's a way to stop him, and we're going to figure out what that is. Promise."

Lucy sniffed. "Well, we better be quick. Because he had some papers on his desk he didn't want me to see, and I'm pretty sure it was the contract with Dolos Discs. And Cin, what if they're about to sign it? I would completely and totally die."

Four

﹏﹏﹏

JACK SIGHED as he wandered past the same crewmember for the thousandth time. The guy lifted his head, half-grinned, and resumed his task. What the crew actually did on a day-to-day basis—beyond putting up and taking down the set and equipment—was a mystery to Jack; Dunk and Manny handled all that. Some of the guys were on the band payroll, some of them union guys working for the promoter or the arena. He should know which was which, but he didn't. There were too many of them, and they all had odd names, like Jock and Tank and Rimsy. He didn't want to know what *that one* meant. Being among the crew reminded him of school, not a milieu he was especially keen to revisit.

He was only here, backstage, sauntering around in his costume and makeup in the middle of the day, because Dunk had asked him to do it —so they could trap the "bassa" who'd been lurking about and spying on the band. Really, Jack thought bassa was rather extreme to describe what was actually a short, hairy kid about twenty years old with a bad case of acne. But the kid had really got under Dunk's skin with his ability to evade capture and worm his way into off-limits areas. And Jack had to agree—not only because he wanted to be more supportive of Dunk, as he and Bill had discussed the night before, but also because

Dunk was right—that they needed to find out what the kid was up to and what harm he might be doing to the band. With only seven concerts to go and the bonus at stake, they couldn't afford to take any chances. That didn't negate the fact that sauntering about like this for what felt like hours was dreadfully boring, even if he was playing jazz tunes in his head.

Just as he was about to duck into the loo to check out how his makeup was holding up, he heard scuffling and a squeal, followed by Dunk's angry voice and a higher, squeakier voice responding. The words were drowned out by a loud clanging sound from the set and a crewmember letting out a stream of expletives.

Jack hurried in the direction of the scuffle.

"I'm asking again, ya little twerp," Dunk shouted. "Who sent ya?"

The kid stumbled over his words. "I'm from ... um ... *Rolling Stone.*"

"Naw, yer not. They already did a big story on us. Ya shoulda done yer bloody homework, ya dobber. So for the last time. Who sent ya?"

Jack came around a corner and there he was, the short, hairy, pimply kid, trapped by Dunk against the wall. His legs were shaking, but he had crossed his arms and clenched his jaw in defiance. Jack had to give him credit: most men gibbered or collapsed in fright when Dunk accosted them like this.

"Right," said Dunk. "Ya give me no choice." He grabbed the kid by his *Purple Rain* t-shirt, lifted him several inches off the floor, and pinned him to the wall. The kid kicked his arms and legs and shrieked.

"Dunk, that's enough," said Jack.

Dunk glanced in his direction. "Finally caught the greasy little bugger, dint I? Playin' tough with me, but now look at 'im. Wailing like a wee girl. Another minute and—"

"Let him down. Let *me* talk to him."

Dunk rolled his eyes. "OK, Kemosabe, ya think ya can do better, give 'er a shot." He abruptly released the kid and let him crumple to the floor.

The kid fell on his arse and scrabbled against the wall. He adjusted his t-shirt and checked it for damage in between quick glances up at Dunk. Not easily cowed, this kid.

Jack walked closer and stopped a few yards away. Time to play "good cop" like Bill, establish some rapport and get the kid to open up. Show Dunk there was a better way to get people to cooperate than scaring the bejesus out of them.

"*Purple Rain*. You like Prince?"

"Yeah." The kid squinted up at Jack. "The movie was cool, b-b-but the album is rad."

Jack couldn't believe how long it took him to get that one sentence out. Not only was the kid short and hairy with a serious case of acne, but he had a bad stutter with the letter "b." Not to mention early onset male pattern baldness. A very tough combination for a kid his age. Any age, really. Jack felt sorry for him, but business was business, and they still had to find out what he was doing there.

He kept his voice soft and encouraging. "You've been following us for a while now, so am I right in thinking you like our music too?"

The kid cleared his throat and looked serious. "Pirate is tight, man, b-but the b-ballads are too b-bubblegum for my taste. I know you have to appeal to the chicks, b-but you're losing some of the hard rock edge that defines you as a b-band. My only other note would be to speed up on *Señorita*, which is a b-bit too slow."

Jack stared at him like he had two heads. Who did this kid think he was? Not only did he make them listen to him stutter one "b" word after another, which was quite unnecessary. There were plenty of synonyms in the English language. Like "song" for "ballad," or "pop" for "bubblegum," or "group" for "band." Granted, the word "but" was harder to avoid, being as common as it was. But, on top of that, the kid had the audacity to criticize his music.

"*Señorita* is not too slow. It's exactly right."

Of course Dunk was smirking at him. He'd said the same thing. Jack was dealing with two musical cretins.

"But that's completely beside the point," he added before the kid could respond and take them further off track. "The point is that you've been following us around and spying on us, and we need to know why."

The kid pushed his glasses up his sweaty pink nose. "You might be a genius, man, b-but you know nothing about what's going down in your own b-band."

Dunk scowled and put his hands on his hips. Jack gave him a warning look.

"OK, tell me. What's going down?"

The kid pulled himself up as if preparing for battle. "Drugs and alcohol. I mean lots and lots of b-beer and pot. And sex everywhere, man. Not only in hotel rooms. In the elevators and pools. And orgies b-backstage."

"What do ya expect, ya weirdo?" said Dunk. "We're a rock band."

Jack gave the kid an earnest look. "So you're worried something could go wrong and derail our big American tour. And, naturally, we're worried about that too. About a security breach ... sabotage—"

"No!" said the kid.

"Or even, god forbid, a stampede like Altamont, Cincinnati, or Buffalo. Which is why we have to know exactly who you are and what you're doing here."

"And who you're working for," said Dunk.

"I'm just, um, following the b-band," said the kid. He rushed to add, "B-but I would never do anything to hurt Pirate. You've got to b-believe me, Jack."

"Why should we, twerp?" Dunk cracked his knuckles and moved closer to the kid. "Here ya are inside the arena where ya got no right to be. And even worse, in the staging area."

"Keep him away from me, Jack. Please!"

"That depends on you," said Jack, still using his gentle, encouraging voice. "Are you going to tell us?"

The kid shrank away from Dunk but crossed his arms and clenched his jaw again. Clearly, he wasn't. Well, that was it for Jack. He'd done his best as "good cop." Over to "bad cop" now.

He sighed dramatically. "Time for Plan B. Why don't you take him and show him some of our ... what do you call it, Dunk? Our finest hospitality?"

Dunk grabbed the kid's arm and the kid shrieked in terror. "No! Not your finest hospitality. He's going to kill me. Help—"

Dunk heaved him over his shoulder like a sack of dirty laundry. He grinned at Jack as the kid kept shrieking. "See ya once it's over."

Jack watched as Dunk strode toward the exit past some guys hauling cables. They moved to the side to let him pass. Not their business why their boss had a hairy, pimply kid with early onset male pattern baldness slung over his shoulder. Even if the kid was shrieking his lungs out.

Jack wasn't sure what Dunk was going to do with the kid. Probably better not to know.

Five

JACK PEERED AT HIS WATCH, calculating. It was lunchtime and he was feeling rather hungry. There was still time before sound check and rehearsal, but, unfortunately, it appeared not enough to return to the hotel and order room service. He normally ate in his suite before coming to the arena, but this situation with the kid had put everything out of whack. He headed for the hospitality room, where, hope beyond hope, he might be able to get an acceptable meal and do some reading in a modicum of peace and quiet.

Members of the crew greeted him as he passed and he gave them a smile and a thumbs up. Now that he'd talked to Bill, he would try to be more inspirational in that American kind of way, since most of the crew were American. Not give lectures or fly into rages when he didn't get what he wanted. "Inspire and excel—not tell or yell." That would be his new mantra. He grinned to himself. It had a certain ring to it, didn't it?

When he reached the hospitality room, he peeked in and breathed a sigh of relief. The band members weren't there yet. They usually rushed in en masse and grabbed something right before sound check and rehearsal, but every once in a while they managed to get to the arena early enough to sit down to a proper lunch. This looked to be his lucky day, both in terms of catching the "bassa" and "catching" a quiet, leisurely lunch on his own.

He strolled into the room and smiled at the lone occupant—a very pretty young woman standing at attention behind a table laden with food and drink. It was typical that she was pretty, as if that were an essential qualification in the job description for serving food to rock bands, but not that she was dressed in chef's whites and sanitary gloves. Dunk had rolled his eyes, but Jack had insisted that they put this in the backstage rider of their contract with the arena. Her chef's whites and gloves were undeniable proof that if you expected excellence, you were more likely to get it, and also proof that the arena here in Albuquerque had actually read their rider. It was shocking how many arenas didn't. That's why Van Halen was renowned for requiring a supply of M&Ms but banning all the brown ones. Some unfortunate employee had to fish out every brown M&M from the serving bowl, but it was a foolproof way for the band to find out if the arena had taken their rider seriously. So Jack's insistence on chef's whites and sanitary gloves was his own "M&M clause"—and also, he liked to think, an *homage* to the indisputable brilliance of the Van Halen guys.

"What can I get you, um, Mister St James?" said the pretty young woman as he approached. She blushed, her cheeks becoming the flame-like color of her hair.

"Hello, Alison," he said, reading her nametag. "It's just Jack. And may I please have ..." He pursed his lips as he inspected the food options in the chafing dishes. "The lobster tail, with asparagus and roasted potatoes. Salad on the side. No dressing. And an unopened bottle of Evian. If you don't mind." He loved lobster and asparagus, but who put them in the rider? Rather profligate given that every expense was double or triple charged back to them by those thieves at Dolos.

"Oh, of course." She reddened further. "I mean, no, of course I don't mind. Please have a seat and I'll serve you. Do you want some dessert too?"

"No pudding for me, thank you."

"We don't have pudding, actually. Just what was in the rider. Chocolate chip cookies and cherry pie a la mode."

He'd forgot. Pudding here only referred to that creamy stuff. "No, thank you, Alison." He put on his performance voice. "Need to keep me pirate figure or me crew will have me walking the plank."

He flashed her a grin as he turned and ambled over to a table where magazines and newspapers had been laid out for the band, another requirement in their rider. There were the usual American music magazines—*Rolling Stone, Circus, Creem, Faces*—but the majority were the trashy gossip rags the boys loved to read.

The cover of one of the teen music magazines advertised their "Must-Have Pirate Guide" above the title. Here we go again, coverage as if they were a boy band. He flipped to the centerfold pages and skimmed the article.

THE DEFINITIVE GUIDE TO PIRATE

If you haven't heard of this band from Manchester England, where have you been for the past three years? Sailing the high seas? In that time they've managed to climb the charts like a right ol' rigging monkey and steal a cache of gold and platinum discs from the more well-established bands. These bad boys have also stolen the hearts of many a lass in ports far and wide, just like the real pirate characters they portray. Want to know more? Here's our quick guide to the members of rock band Pirate.

Jack St James – aka "Blackbeard" – Lead singer (almost 25)

The undisputed leader of this group of scalawags, a guy who dominates the ship with his powerful singing and playing, and a man who has yet to find an instrument, a lyric, or a note he can't bend to his iron will, but also the most mysterious member of this secretive band. Even his crew members don't know: Is there a lovely senorita hidden away in some faraway port?

Keith Aldcroft – aka "Calico Jack" – Lead and rhythm guitarist (24)

Don't let the vibrant clothes of this corsair fool you. An equal opportunity pirate, he not only loves the ladies but argues to have them on ship. A man who caresses his Gibson SG doubleneck guitar on the stage and sleeps with it off, to guard it from his fellow scalawags, so he says! Deny him his share of the treasure and have no doubt you will be crossing swords. Aaaarrrrgggghhhh!

George Farraday – aka "Captain Jennings" – Drummer (24)

Want to march to the beat of a different drummer? Not on this guy's watch. He's the muscle man of the group who goes through three sets of drumsticks in one night on his Tama Imperial Star drum kit, with an appetite for the ladies to match. Playing *sans* shirt, you can't – and you shouldn't – take your eyes off this dangerous buccaneer.

Sam Wilson – aka "Black Caesar" – Lead and rhythm guitarist (23)

An African chieftain boasting a massive harem, this charismatic rogue knows how to seduce you with a smile and the sweet wails of his Fender Stratocaster. Before you can gather your wits, he's seized your treasure and slipped off into the night. Keep your eyes peeled for those infamous moves when he kisses the floor and makes love to the wall. Not to be missed.

Randy Rickman – aka "Stede Bonnet" – Keyboardist (21)

This Englishman escaped the boring life of a gentleman to become a Pirate, swearing fealty to the older and more experienced Blackbeard. Twin to Lieutenant Richards (below), he's the gentler more sensitive one, with hands that know their way around a Roland Jupiter-8 keyboard like nobody's business and a voice that sings in sweet harmony.

Rob Rickman – aka "Lieutenant Richards" – Bass guitarist (21)

The opposite of his brother (above), this privateer will make you walk the plank and swim with sharks if it brings him more doubloons. A he-man who tortures his Rickenbacker 4003 bass guitar within an inch of its life. Needless to say the ladies positively swoon at this one's feet.

Unable to see these lovable picaroons in person? Catch their sea songs on Doloo Discs and order their pirate merchandise from Pirate Booty Inc. Ahoy, me hearties!

Jack was thrilled to see the free advertising, but the article also made him a bit uneasy. It was eerily accurate, as if someone had infiltrated the band and eavesdropped on the boys. Someone with less than stellar punctuation skills but a bull's eye take on their personalities. Maybe this was what that pimply kid had been up to. But how would he know about Keith's ongoing harangue about bringing girls on the band bus, or

Randy being more sensitive? Maybe it was the work of an enterprising member of the crew. He stowed the magazine under his arm so he could show it to Dunk. Perhaps he'd have a clue.

He also grabbed *Billboard Magazine* so he and Dunk could check the rankings of the band's singles and make sure the MTV slots were paying off—they paid very good money for those rankings and slots—and snagged the latest editions of *Forbes* and the *Wall Street Journal*, which were special ordered for him. Not that anyone else in the band would bother to follow the stock market or make investments.

Moseying over to the furthest table from the door, Jack took his usual Mafioso-style position against the wall. He sat down, started to lay out his reading material, and jumped back up. Oh, f'crissakes. Would nothing ever go right?

He looked over at Alison, who was busy preparing his meal. "I'm sorry to interrupt, Alison, but there are crumbs on this table. Could you possibly—"

"Oh, I'm so sorry." Alison rushed over and brushed the crumbs off the tablecloth onto the floor. "There you go, good as new."

"With all due respect, I don't mean to make a fuss or anything, but there were germs on those crumbs and now they're on the tablecloth. Would you mind terribly replacing it with a new one?"

Alison stared at him with a startled expression. He could tell, she'd heard the rumors about him and was now realizing that they were indeed true. Well, truth be told, if she had cleaned the table after someone else in the band sat here—and only the band was supposed to use this room—then this situation wouldn't have happened. She was derelict in her duties. Not striving for excellence. He didn't want to complain to the arena management and jeopardize her job, but he should probably mention it to Dunk since they had another two nights at this arena and he didn't want it to happen again.

"No, of course not," she said after what seemed an eternity. "I'll be right back." She grabbed the soiled tablecloth from the table and hurried out of the room.

Jack stood next to the table holding the magazines and hummed one of his favorite pieces of classical music, Liszt's piano arrangement for Beethoven's *Symphony No. 5 in C Minor*. That should last until she got back. He'd learned to soothe himself with music from an early age. His mother told him she always found him in his crib singing to himself. Besides which he'd been playing the piano most of his life, and had learned a number of other instruments while at school and in the band. He was still in the *allegro con brio* when Alison reappeared.

"Here we are," she said, shaking out the tablecloth. "Fresh from the laundry." He watched with baited breath as it almost touched the floor. He didn't want to cause a scene, but really this girl was quite careless. She laid it on the table, straightened the edges, and smoothed out the creases. "Is that OK?"

"That's fine," he said. "Thank you, Alison."

"I'll bring your food in a few minutes."

As she turned away, he adjusted the tablecloth so it was perfectly centered. He placed his magazines and newspaper on the table just so, then walked as nonchalantly as he could over to the serving table where she was reheating his food in a microwave.

"So, are you a professional chef, Alison?"

He didn't hear her answer as he watched her every move. It was alarming how careless people were with their lives. Dropping cutlery and then using it anyway. Touching their shoes, shoes that had been on pavements where dogs did their business. Going to get a tablecloth and not removing their sanitary gloves, then touching door handles covered with germs—the Germans had proved door handles were teeming with germs—and going back to serving food with those now tainted gloves. You could never relax your guard around people. Never.

Alison laid his place setting, still talking, and brought over a bottle of Evian and the heated plate from the microwave.

"That's very hot, so maybe give it a minute to cool down." She looked at him with a polite but definitely cooler look. "Will there be anything else?"

"No, that'll be fine." He gave her a weak smile. "Thank you, Alison. And ... would you like a free pass to our concert? VIP section?" It was the least he could do after being his usual freakish self—and not listening to a word she'd said.

She broke into a smile. "You're kidding. Really?"

"Really." He'd arrange it with Dunk. Hopefully there was an available seat, or a cancellation. Or, if worse came to worse, she could watch from the wings. The boys would like that. Alison was a very attractive girl.

Returning to her station behind the food table, she leaned against the wall and beamed as she pretended not to watch him.

He was used to being watched like a hawk, had been his whole life— by nannies, headmasters, paparazzi, and fans. So let her observe. Naturally, he'd been raised to be a proper English gentleman. One must have a leisurely meal to digest one's food and dine properly. Many Americans ate like Philistines, using their fork like a spear and their knife like a saw, and even eating off their knife, horror of all horrors. Feel free to observe how it should be done, Alison.

He was in the middle of a surprisingly tasty meal, albeit a less than relaxing one with Alison watching, and had got through most of *Forbes*, when loud thumps and shouting came from the corridor. Drat! It sounded like the boys were arriving early today.

Alison stood to attention and smoothed out her uniform.

Jack pretended to be reading. He didn't have Dunk here to run interference, and he was in no mood for the boys' queries after the stress of this ill-planned and overly observed meal, not to mention the skulker situation earlier and all the hoopla the night before. He would finish up and make a quick escape before they cornered him.

Where the hell was Dunk anyway? Only half an hour to sound check and rehearsal. Why was it taking him so long to get a little information out of that kid? Could Jack trust him not to do something that got them in even more hot water? After last night's shenanigans with the bus, he wondered if Dunk was actually on the same page with him in securing the bonus and retiring. Was he unconsciously, or even consciously, sabotaging those plans?

Six

THE "BASSA," as Dunk kept calling him, lay on the bed zonked out. He got high so fast. It was just peach schnapps and orange juice, for heaven's sake, along with a few tokes of real good pot. The guy was a total lightweight.

Carly sat cross-legged at the end of the bed inspecting her nails. She had put her panties and bangles back on but still had her top off. She had really nice boobs, Suze said so, and she didn't mind showing them off. He sure had liked them. She'd never had a guy stare at them as much as he did, or touch them like he'd won a prize at the county fair or something.

She looked up as Suze rounded the bed and opened the door. Suze stood in the doorway and wedged the door open with her foot so Carly could hear. She was so considerate that way, always including her in everything.

"So?" Dunk said from the hallway. Carly could hear him but not see him.

"Name's Howie," said Suze. "Sent by his uncle to get dirt on the band and report back."

"Who's the uncle?"

"Guy named Barry. Seems scared of him, said he couldn't say no.

But said he really wanted to come, being such a big fan of you guys and all."

"Barry the Bastard, just as we thought. What'd the twerp tell him?"

"Nada, really. Saw some guys smoking doobies, spied on Carly getting it on with two members of the crew. More stuff like that. Doesn't even have tickets to the concerts. Seems ol' Barry was too cheap to cough up for that. Has the kid staying in HoJo's and eating at Mickey D's."

Dunk sighed. "You guys done good, Suze. Yer names are on tonight's list. But you and Carly keep yer hands off the crew until they're finished. Ya hear me?"

"Got it," said Suze. "We done here?"

There was a moment of silence before Dunk spoke. "No, one more thing. VIP seats and backstage passes for the rest of the tour, if ya pull this off." He told her what he wanted them to do.

Suze turned to Carly. "You up for it?"

Carly grinned and nodded.

Suze jerked her thumb at Howie. "But will he be up for it?"

Carly giggled. "Oh, he'll be up for it. Promise."

Suze turned away as she spoke to Dunk. "Eight minutes tops."

Dunk appeared in the doorway. He wrote a phone number on Suze's hand. "OK, do yer magic. I gotta get back, but I want to hear all the juicy details later. And bring the twerp with ya. He's ours now."

"Will do," said Suze. She came into the room and shut the door, then moved around the bed to the end table. She cracked her knuckles, then looked over at Carly. "We are about to take off, ladies and gentleman. Get into position."

Carly slithered up the bed and lay alongside the sleeping Howie, one arm under her head to be more comfortable. She looked back at Suze and nodded. She and Suze were such a great team.

"Madam," Suze said in an officious voice, "your tray must be locked in an upright position. Please do that now." Carly burst out laughing and clapped her hand over her mouth. After she got her giggles under control, she took hold of Howie's flaccid penis and began to give him a vigorous hand job.

Howie immediately started mewling and clawing the sheets, still zonked out. Their little "love monkey" thinking he was having a wet dream. She'd never seen a guy get hard so fast and come so quickly, but then she hadn't been with a guy this young since, maybe, junior high school. The older guys always took longer, thought that was a good thing because then maybe she'd come too, but never actually lifted—or moved—a finger to make it happen. Suze had already shown Howie how to make her come, and it had been the most intense orgasm Carly had ever had. Howie was a fast learner, although Suze had a hand, or a finger, to be more exact, in it too.

Carly watched as Suze picked up the handset on the phone and punched in the number on her hand. Suze winked at Carly while she listened to it ringing on the other end. After a moment, Suze said, "This is the operator. I have a collect call for Barry Bartholomew from Howard Bartholomew. Will you accept the charges?"

Suze held the handset away from her head so Carly could hear. A woman said, "Yes, thank you, operator. We will accept the charges ... Howie, where have you been? Your uncle's going crazy."

Faking a male voice, Suze spoke into the receiver. "B-b-b-b—" Carly covered her mouth and giggled, drowning out the woman's response.

"She told me never mind," said Suze, smirking. "Put me on hold while she gets him. So get ready for immediate take-off, ladies and gentlemen."

Carly grinned and redoubled her efforts. Howie was fully erect and moaning.

Suze kneeled on the edge of the bed and held the receiver so she and Carly could both hear.

A male voice exploded from the handset. "Howie, you son of a bitch! Where the hell have you been? You don't ever keep me waiting. I'll have your tiny little balls in a wringer faster than you can cry Uncle Barry. And this time your mother won't be able to save you. Where the hell have you been, and what the hell is going on there?"

Suze held the handset near Howie's mouth. He was writhing on the bed and moaning loud enough to be heard in the next county.

"Howie! Howie! Can you hear me? What are they doing to you? God help me, if those motherfuckers are hurting you, I'll have their motherfucking little brains for breakfast. You hear me?"

Howie let out a loud squeal as he ejaculated in an arc over the bed. A big goofy smile filled his face.

"Howie! Omigod, Howie!"

Suze put the handset to her mouth. "This is ... Belinda from the Howie Liberation Front. Hear this: We have liberated Howard Bartholomew from his virginity. He will no longer be reporting back to you, boring old man capitalist pig. He's ours now."

"What—"

She slammed down the phone.

"You are too much ... Belinda."

"No, you're too much," said Suze. "Your timing was perfect."

"I do take great pride in my work."

"I know you do. Ready for some backstage fun?"

"Always ready," said Carly as she pushed herself into a sitting position.

"What about our love monkey? You think he's ready?"

Howie lay on the bed, blissed out. They looked down at him and grinned.

Seven

AT THE OTHER end of the line, Howie's uncle threw his Motorola 8000X cellular phone, price tag $4000, at the wall.

"Boring old man capitalist pig! I'll show her little candy ass. I've got the best cum in the business. Calling me a boring old man capitalist pig. Who the hell does she think she is?"

He shouted at his secretary in the next room. "Rhonda, get your little candy ass in here. Now."

As Rhonda toddled into the room, with her not so little candy ass sticking out of a tight green pencil skirt, Barry said, "What's the name of that hippie broad Howie found up to that commie place? You know the one. Nice rack. Sings like an angel."

"You mean Lucy Sabatini?" said Rhonda.

"That's the one. Get her on the line. But don't let the swami's people know it's me. And get me another one of these piece of shit cellular phones."

While Barry waited for Rhonda to patch him through on his land-line, he lit one of his favorite Montecristo cigars and puffed on it to get it going. He stood in front of his wall mirror and tamped down his comb over. There was something about looking your best even if the person on the other end of the line couldn't see you. Something psychological.

"Lucy on line three," Rhonda shouted through the open doorway. He never closed the door, trusted Rhonda with his life. No, not really. He just trusted her to remember everything for him. What promises he made to which jerk-off, his heart medication, that kind of thing. You couldn't trust *anyone*, not even your fucking nephew Howie.

Barry picked up the receiver and pressed line three. He began talking with no preamble. "You want that recording contract?"

"I ... what?" said the hippie chick.

Barry took a puff from his cigar. "Listen, sweetheart, I'll give it to you instead of the swami. But you gotta do something for me."

"Really? Seriously?"

"I said it, didn't I? Now here's what I want. I gotta band called Pirate. You heard of 'em?"

There was a pause. "No."

She didn't sound all that thrilled. He didn't think he'd have to convince her, the broad panting for the contract. But hey, whatever.

"Nice English fellas. Kinda like a cross between Queen and Pink Floyd and Def Leppard, only much younger. Got a bunch of hits and now they're doing the tour thing. Like when you were with Magnus."

He took another long puff, let the idea sink in, the hippie broad quiet on the other end of the line.

"Yeah, I know all about you and Magnus. You spent what? Two, three years with him touring around. You know life on the road, what's normal, what's not. You're ... what can we call it? An expert."

She sighed. "You don't understand. I can't do that. I just ... can't."

Maybe she needs him to build up her morale or whatnot. "I know you been in that communist place for a while—"

"It's a commune, not communist. Really, it's an ashram."

"I don't give a flying—" Barry stopped himself before he said something that might put her off. He hated to admit it, but he needed her now that that nephew of his had screwed things up and the band was on high alert. The only way to get in under the radar, find out what was going on, was sending in a really pretty, sexy girl who knew how to work the situation. Couldn't send in a supermodel or actress, those broads always unreliable and temperamental. No, Lucy was the ticket—the only girl could do what he needed.

"Hold on, hold on. Let me rephrase that. It don't matter to me you been in that place and away from the scene for a while. I just need your help until Pirate finishes their tour. Just be with them for six concerts—one in Albuquerque, three in Phoenix, and two in L.A. That's it, finito. You hang out with them in the sunshine and you got yourself a recording contract." Sure, it was boiling out there this time of year, but most places had air-con and swimming pools. "Take your bikini with ya, if ya want."

"Six, that's it?"

"Yeah, that's it." He was sure he had her now.

"And what would that require? We're bound by certain rules and regulations here, so nothing … unusual, I would assume?"

So she had got religion and didn't want to break the rules of the cult. Fine by him, as long as she did what she was told. "No, course not. I'd never ask you to do nothing like that. You're just going to keep an eye on them and let me know what they're up to. Let me know they don't behave themselves. I got a lot invested in these guys. Kinda like a father to them, wanna make sure they don't piss it all away, you get my drift."

"Oh, yeah, I get it. You want a … performance."

"Well, you wanna put it like that, yeah. That's exactly what I want." She might look like an airhead, but this hippie chick was no dumbass—for a broad.

"I don't know. I have to discuss it with one of my colleagues, see what they think. I'll get back to you at my earliest convenience."

OK, now he got it. One of the swami's people was listening and she couldn't speak freely. She done good, very discreet. She'd be perfect. But nonetheless, he needed an answer pronto. "You got an hour to decide and let my secretary know, so's she can book your flight. I want you out there tomorrow. I gotta know you're in place before I tell the swami we're not signing. The bastard's breathing down my neck. Capiche?"

"Um—"

He slammed down the phone. Always keep 'em off balance. That was the only way to have the upper hand.

"Rhonda," he shouted. "Book Lucy into Pirate's hotel for the rest of the tour."

"Did she say yes?" Rhonda sounded surprised.

"Does a hooker wear a suit?" he shouted back.

Rhonda didn't have anything to say to that, did she? Of course, every hooker wore a suit, and the hippie chick would be joining Pirate. Basta.

Eight

LUCY REPLACED the handset in a daze. She had to find Cindy, fast.

"Who was that?" said Mandy the Snake. She had sat there pretending to work as she listened to the entire conversation.

"Um, that was a guy in New York who wants us to perform six songs at his son's Bar Mitzvah. But it sounds like they want a performance, like a theatre performance kind of thing, so it's probably not for us. But I said we'd discuss it and let him know."

"Make sure you run it past Ramakar."

Make sure you run your stupid snakiness past Ramakar, Lucy wanted to say as she fled the room.

She rushed down the corridor, looking into every open door and peeking behind closed doors, smiling in a reassuring way, and trying not to look like a woman possessed. She'd already checked out the dining hall, three yoga classes—Iyengar, yoga nidra, and Vinyasa—and the women's sauna. She forgot if Cindy was supposed to be teaching or on break. Where the heck was she? Lucy only had an hour!

As she popped her head into the Sun Room, two women sitting in easy chairs looked over.

"Jakananda!" one of them said, jumping up and hurrying over to her. The woman's Dolly Parton hair overwhelmed her petite body and accentuated her southern accent. "Darlin', I'm so glad to catch you alone. I've been meaning to tell you for the longest time now how your music changed my life."

Lucy blushed. "Really?" Maybe she could spare a moment to hear more.

"Really," said the woman, moving close and invading Lucy's personal space. "After my son died, I lost the will to live. Norma here said 'You're coming with me to Spirits Rising, no ifs, ands, or buts about it.'"

Her friend nodded her head.

"And I said 'Whatever' because I didn't care about anything anymore, y'know? And we flew up here for Thanksgiving, the worst time of year when you've lost someone."

Her friend nodded again.

"So we did the yoga and meditation and pranayama and aikido, and all the different therapies. But none of it made any difference. I still didn't give a damn about anything, pardon my *francais*."

The woman clasped Lucy's hands in her own. "But then I went to one of your concerts, and you sang 'Sunset,' and it touched me in some deep, deep place. The floodgates opened and I found myself sobbing for Tommy, all the pain coming out in wave after wave. And then you sang 'Saying Yes,' and it was like I could finally accept it, that he was gone, and how lucky I was to have him while he was here, and how he would be so upset if he saw me wasting the rest of my life pining away for him.

"You sang one line that touched me to the core, I'll never forget it. 'The robin comes, the robin goes, quicker every year, until our red breast breathes its last and death is at our door.' That's when I realized that life is going faster and faster, and our time here on this earth is really short, and I've been letting it go to waste, and I want to spread peace and joy the same way you're doing with your music. So me and Norma are training here in Ayurveda, and we're going to open our own practice as soon as we get our certification."

Tears streamed down Lucy's cheeks and she wiped them away with her fingers.

"Here you go, dear," said Norma, offering Lucy a Kleenex she pulled from her fanny pack.

"I can't tell you," said Lucy, dabbing her eyes. "Your saying that means so much to me."

The woman with Dolly Parton hair grabbed Lucy and gave her a fierce hug.

"We know, dear," said Norma, patting Lucy on her hip. "There, there."

People were coming and going past them, used to moments of catharsis like this. It was just that kind of place.

Lucy finally pulled away. For some reason, she instinctively trusted these two ladies and decided to confide in them. "I've got this big decision to make, about my music and a recording contract and a rock band and what to say to this guy Barry. And this has made all the difference in the world."

"Oh, I'm so glad, sweetheart," said the woman with Dolly Parton hair. "I've been wanting to tell you for the longest time."

"I would avoid the rock bands, my dear," said Norma. "Speaking from personal experience."

"She had her heart broken by one of the Cockateels," said her friend.

"Oh, really?" said Lucy.

"Sexy as sin, but they're not husband material, are they? Love 'em and leave 'em, as they say. You be careful, my dear."

"Oh, don't worry, I will," said Lucy. "I have to run, but thank you so much, and good luck with the Ayurveda."

She hugged them again and ran off down the hall. How sweet were they? Although maybe she shouldn't have confided in them. But hey ho. Too late now.

After searching up and down two more floors for Cindy, she gave up and went back to their room. She found Cindy lying on her bed, arms behind her head, staring at the ceiling.

"Where have you been? I've been looking all over for you."

"I've been right here, having a think."

"Oh, Cin, you won't believe what's happened." Lucy pushed Cindy's legs over and took up a cross-legged position facing her.

"Is it good news or bad news?" said Cindy as she pulled herself up into a sitting position.

"Um, both. Barry will give me the recording contract, but I have to go perform, quote unquote, with this rock band named Pirate."

"Wait, he wants you to sing with a rock band?" said Cindy.

"No, no, no. He wants me to go join the band on tour and pretend I'm a huge fan of their music and report back to him on what's happening and all that."

"So he wants you to be a groupie-ish spy?"

"Yeah, pretty much," said Lucy. "We called it performing because Mandy the Snake was eavesdropping and we had to talk in code."

"OK, got it. But for how long? I mean, the smarmy swami will notice if you disappear from the ashram."

"It's only for six concerts, Cin. If I get the recording contract, then who cares if he notices? And if I don't, then I come back and make some excuse. Like when Shivarandiman disappeared for a week and told them he had to rush off to take care of his sick dad. Everyone knew he'd been shacking up with that horny guest at the Starlite Motor Inn, but those idiots believed him."

Cindy furrowed her brow. "Good point, but you're not Shivarandiman. That guy gets away with everything. And besides, I'm confused. Why would Barry all of a sudden give you the recording contract for doing something as simple as that?"

"Let me see ... He said they're these nice guys from England, but really young."

"Like Menudo? That young?"

"More like early Osmonds or the Jackson Five. And how he's like a father to them. But he's worried about them getting into trouble and messing things up without meaning to. So he wants me to keep an eye on them and warn him if something looks like it might go wrong, just until they finish the tour. Because I was with Magnus on the road and I know the ins and outs of touring and rock concerts and stuff."

"Kind of like a babysitter. That makes sense," said Cindy. "So what's the bad news?"

"I don't know if I can go back into that world, Cin. I promised myself I would never ever go back ... after what happened. It terrifies me. But—"

"So don't. You'll lose the recording contract, but so what? You've got talent and you'll get another one ... someday."

"Excuse me? I can't believe you said that. Norma's friend said—"

"Who's Norma?"

"This tiny little lady with bright red hair. Her friend has big Dolly Parton hair. And Norma told her she was coming to Spirits Rising whether she liked it or not. And she came and heard my music—"

"And it changed her life forever. Like it's changed lots of people's lives. Yada yada yada. So what difference does it really make if you're not going to get the recording contract?"

Lucy glared at Cindy.

Cindy stared back, a questioning look on her face.

"You really are an annoying smartypants, you know that?" said Lucy.

"So you keep telling me. Are you going?" said Cindy.

"As that lady Susan told us last week, have that fear in your gut and go ahead and do scary stuff anyway," said Lucy. "So yeah, I'm going."

"I'll help you pack."

Nine

ROB AND RANDY burst through the doorway of the hospitality room, grappling with one another like two sumo wrestlers. They banged into the first table, spun around a couple times, and crashed to the floor.

Alison gasped and clapped her hand to her mouth.

Jack sighed. This meal was ruined. He put his knife and fork, tines up, in six-thirty position to indicate that he was finished eating. He would watch "the show" until there was a clear path to leave. The boys could be very entertaining, he had to give them that, but they could also behave like a herd of three-year-olds high on candy and let loose on innocent passersby by a bunch of bored nannies.

Randy had landed on top of Rob, but Rob handily flipped him over, straddled him, and pinned his arms to the ground. They were both gasping for breath. Rob spit on Randy's face and a big glob landed on Randy's cheek. Jack winced. Très disgusting. Blinking rapidly, Randy tried to turn his head to wipe his face on his sleeve, but Rob pinned him down even tighter.

Alison watched them with wide eyes. Jack assumed she could twig to their being twins, as Bill had the night before, what with their dirty blond mops of hair, wide open faces, and stocky bodies being such close facsimiles of one another, although Rob was noticeably bigger. Not to mention the fact that they both wore the same t-shirt and jeans ensemble all the time, except for concerts and special occasions. Jack sometimes forgot that they were the babies of the group, only twenty-one, because they were such accomplished musicians and performers. What he found impossible to ignore was the dramatic personality gulf between the two of them, exemplified perfectly in their choice of instruments—the "ballsy" bass guitar for Rob and the "cerebral" keyboards for Randy.

"I told you, runt, don't touch my stuff," said Rob.

"I didn't," said Randy.

"You took my silver pick."

"I did not. Why would *I* take your pick? Do *I* play the guitar?"

"Are you being a smartass?" Rob spat on Randy again.

The remaining band members—Keith, Sam and George—ambled into the room. Jack didn't know why, but they were always in that order, like some immutable law of the universe. Keith took his usual spot in the center of things, the other two taking up spots on either side. The three of them stood in the doorway waiting for the fight to subside.

Keith looked over and nodded at Jack, then turned his attention back to the twins. He was a head taller than the other two and wore hip hugger bellbottom jeans that accentuated his long, lean physique. Jack thought he looked like a throwback to the late 60s and early 70s with his long center-parted hair and thick mustache. No surprise there, considering that Keith worshipped at the altar of Cream, the Yardbirds, and the Zep, or more specifically Eric Clapton, Jeff Beck, and Jimmy Page.

Sam, on the other hand, standing to Keith's right with his arms crossed and a grin on his face, worshipped at the altar of "my man Jimi," and even dressed like Hendrix in extravagant peacock mode. The guy seemed to have an unlimited supply of tie-dye shirts, velvet jackets and colorful cravats, and liked to wear funky hats and scarves over his Afro in exactly the same fashion as his music idol.

George couldn't be more different from both of them, looking more like a surfer dude with his overdeveloped biceps and calf muscles bulging out of a muscle shirt and shorts, his hair messy and his beard unkempt. He had to fight off the female fans with a stick, or not, as was usually the case with George. Jack could never understand why women went crazy for George because he wasn't particularly handsome. He just seemed to have that *thing* that mesmerized Bill's daughter Annie and scores like her. That "manly man" thing.

Keith took a step toward Rob and Randy and spoke in his heavy Mancs accent. "Lay off 'im, man. *I'm* the one took your pick. Wanted to try it with me new tune. Didn't think you'd mind."

"Oh, yeah?" Rob let go of his brother's arms. "Course I don't mind." He gave Randy's face a playful smack before jumping up and sauntering over to the food table as if nothing had happened. He showed Alison his bicep and encouraged her to feel it.

"Excuse me, gents, but I see a bright red bird needs Sam the Savior," said Sam as he straightened his cravat and hotfooted it over to the food table.

George looked over with instant interest and followed on his heels, as usual a man of few—or no—words but quick action whenever a woman was concerned.

It was no surprise that Keith was the one who leaned down, grabbed Randy's hand, and yanked him to his feet. Keith pulled him into a head-lock and gave him an affectionate noogie. "Y'all right, our kid?"

Randy rubbed his head and responded in a pouty voice. "Yeah, I guess so."

Keith mock punched him in the arm and headed for the food table to join the other three.

Finally, the floor was clear. Time to make a dash for it. Jack stood up and grabbed his reading material.

"Jack!" Randy's face lit up with a big smile. He loped over and claimed the chair across from him. "Um, guess what? I finally finished that book you gave me. How not to worry so much."

"How to Stop Worrying and Start Living." If it were anyone but Randy, Jack would be making some excuse to leave. Instead, he eased himself back into his chair. "Dale Carnegie. What'd you think?"

"Yeah, it was really good. It's helping ... a lot. But um, I'm wondering ... you see, I can't help worrying ... aren't you worried about when we finish the tour? Because we don't have anything lined up yet. I mean, we don't, do we?"

Sam, Rob, and George came over with plates of hamburgers, french fries, and coleslaw. Jack removed his reading material from the table and put it in his lap where it wouldn't get soiled by the band's resident savages, Rob and George.

"She's mine, boys, I saw her first," said Rob, grabbing the end seat and launching into his burger with great relish.

"Get lost, dog breath," said Sam as he slid into the seat on the other side of Randy. "She clearly wants *me*." He tucked his cravat inside his shirt and shook out his napkin and laid it in his lap, then lined up the burger patty with the bun and took an exploratory bite.

George managed to squeeze past Jack without touching him, an unabashed miracle, pulled out the chair across from Sam with a loud scraping noise, and dropped into it with a thump. Leaning forward over his plate to bite into his burger, he spread his legs apart and bumped them against Jack's as he dribbled ketchup and hamburger juices into his beard. Jack considered it an occupational hazard sitting next to George, who exercised incredible control over his body when he was playing the drums but none whatsoever the rest of the time. As Jack had learned through contentious experience, better to channel that energy rather than manage or bridle it. Jack angled his legs under his chair to avoid being bumped again.

Keith strolled over and took the chair on Jack's right, blocking him in. He beetled his brows as he scanned Jack's costume and makeup. "What's with the togs so early, man?"

"Believe it or not," said Jack, pleased at the opportunity to tell them, "I've had to parade around for the last few hours trying to lure this kid who's been following us and sneaking into backstage areas. We finally caught him but he's refused to talk. So Dunk's taken him off to apply the screws and find out why he's spying on us."

Jack hoped the boys would now be able to see the great lengths to which he, their leader, went to protect the band. Their band. Maybe they'd take a moment to rethink their choice of prison cellmate.

"Y'mean that guy wearing all those cool t-shirts from other bands?" said Rob.

"I'd give anything for that Toto Africa one," said Sam.

"I want the vintage *Gimme Shelter*," said Keith.

"Bad Company and 38 Special," said Rob, chomping on french

fries.

Jack took a swig of water as he rolled his eyes. Cretins, focusing on the kid's t-shirts and taking his sacrifice completely for granted. That clinched it. Behind bars, he would bunk with a Wall Street banker and none of these ungrateful sods. Well, maybe Randy. He was a good kid, although with his wide-eyed innocence he would be catnip for horny cons and require some protecting. Scratch the Wall Street banker and make it a Mafia kingpin and Randy, so he could play chess, discuss books, and play music in a bubble of relative safety and comfort.

Alison hurried over and placed a plate with sirloin steak, mashed potatoes, and green beans and a can of Coke in front of Keith. She scooted behind Jack and slipped a piece of paper to George, which he thumbed underneath his plate, and scooted back to the end of the table.

"May I get you something?" she addressed Randy.

"I'll have what he's having," he said, pointing to Jack's plate.

"You don't like lobster," said Rob.

Randy looked affronted. "Yes I do."

Alison gave Randy an approving nod. "Very good."

"Oh no, love, you're mistaken," called Rob at her departing back. "I'm the very good one here."

"Too late, cock," said Keith with a smirk.

"Too late what?" said Rob.

"That's what the birds tell me," said Sam. "You're always coming too late." He grinned as he shoveled a forkful of coleslaw in his mouth.

"Better late than never, donkey dung," retorted Rob.

"You think that, Robbie me boy, probably why Georgie's already got her number and you don't," said Keith. "He don't come late, he don't come early, he comes just right, don't you, Georgie?"

George grunted as he took another big bite from his burger.

Rob looked over at George with disgust. "I don't get it, man. Why would anyone pick the drummer when they could have the bass player?"

Everyone fell silent as Alison brought Randy his plate. When she set it down, Randy casually put his arms around it.

Jack suspected he was trying to protect it from Rob, a notorious food thief who had wolfed down his meal and was now scanning the plates around him for something to nab. The guy was a bottomless pit

—and also, no doubt, too embarrassed at losing Alison to George to go over and ask her for more. Randy, on the other hand, was the perfect target for food theft—one of the slowest and most deliberate eaters Jack had ever seen, usually working away at his meal long after the others had left the room.

Jack pushed his plate toward Rob. "Want this?"

"Oh yeah?" said Rob as he pulled it toward him. He picked up the rest of the lobster tail with his fingers and dropped it into his mouth.

"Jack, you didn't get to answer about the end of the tour," said Randy. "Do we know what's going to happen yet? I mean, is there a plan?"

"Yeah, Jack," said Keith, "what *exactly* is the plan?"

The others stopped eating and looked at Jack, waiting for his answer. Jack breathed slowly in and out and kept his face blank, as he'd learned to do in school when the headmaster grilled him, or when he got caned or spanked. He didn't want to give them an honest answer and face the emotions that would be unleashed. He didn't want to tell them the truth, because he knew that the truth would likely infuriate and devastate them in equal measure. He didn't want to upset or hurt them. He liked them too much.

What in bleeding blazes was keeping Dunk so long? Why was Dunk always somewhere else when he really needed him?

"I told you," said Keith, "there is no plan. Is there, Jack?" Keith stared at Jack, daring him to disagree.

"There is a plan." Jack managed to keep his voice firm and even as he played with his water bottle. "We take some time off after the tour to recover. We all need that. And then we consider our options."

"Like another MTV video," said Rob. "Or a film."

None of the others said anything, only Rob oblivious to the tension in the air.

Keith glared at him. "What do you mean 'options,' Jack? We're a band. How many options we got?" He put his hands on the table and counted on his fingers. "Record a new album. Go on tour to promote it. Make MTV videos for the singles. What bloody else is there?"

George mindlessly drummed on the table, something he did when bored or frustrated—or stressed.

"I need some time off, yeah," said Randy. "Need to spend some time with Mum and Dad and Ronnie, see my mates, buy some—"

"Rob and me have written some ace new songs, haven't we?" said Keith, cutting him off. "No reason we can't go right into the recording studio, is there, Jack?"

Jack felt himself getting peeved. He'd already answered Keith's question, and there was absolutely no call to be rude to Randy. "Like I said, we consider our options. And you and Rob recording your songs, naturally that's an option."

"What do you mean, *we* record our songs? You mean *the band*, don't you? The band records the songs."

Jack took a swig of water so he could get his pique under control. Keith was always pushing his damn songs, and Jack had told him time and time again that they were too pop. Pirate was a hard rock band, for god's sake. There was nothing wrong with writing a crossover ballad now and again, one that appealed to a more mainstream audience. But pop audiences were notoriously fickle, and artists who didn't churn out hits became yesterday's flavor of the month.

Hard rock audiences, on the other hand, were far more likely to be fans for life. They were kind of obsessive about the music, truth be told, whereas pop audiences tended to become obsessed with the singer. Under no circumstances did Jack want to become a pop star. Nor did he want the music to take a backseat to a formulaic, earworm tune. Keith appeared to have a knack for creating earworms that grabbed you and wouldn't let you go. Jack had found that he had to play some classical or jazz piece a couple times through just to dislodge one of Keith's tunes from his head.

That was why when Jack retired, he didn't want the band to continue under the Pirate name. His legacy would be destroyed if Keith took control. But that didn't mean the band couldn't continue under a different name. Jack simply wasn't willing to have that conversation now and take the risk of upsetting everyone, derailing the tour, and losing the bonus. He couldn't retire without that damn bonus.

"Yes, I mean that the band records the songs. I'm assuming that you and Rob will lead, since you wrote them."

Keith frowned and scrutinized Jack's face. "Well, OK then."

Rob punched Randy's shoulder. "Yes!"

"Out of sight," said Sam. "I totally dig that song 'Lost Soul.'" He went back to nibbling his burger.

George jumped up, eked past Jack and Keith, and went over to the food table to chat to Alison.

Randy looked from Keith to Jack and back again. Reassured, he tucked into his lobster tail.

"So," said Keith, "me and the boys has been practicing and we're ready to perform them. How 'bout including them in the show? You know, since we don't have many gigs to go. It would be well mint for the fans. Right, boys?"

The boys froze in place and looked at Jack, waiting to see his response to this latest volley.

Jack looked at the ceiling and sighed. Why was Keith always putting his personal ambition ahead of Pirate's success? And why did he always have to take everything to the extreme? Jack turned his head to look at Keith. He wanted to yell at him, but he'd promised Bill he wouldn't. He spoke slowly and enunciated each word so there could be no more misunderstanding. "The setlist for the show is final. We've already talked about this many, many times. Help me to understand, Keith, what is it that you don't understand about the word 'final'?"

Keith reddened and glared at Jack. "I get the word 'final,' Jack. What I don't get is why you think you own this band lock, stock, and two smoking barrels, when all six of us made it famous. Why you think you get to decide every little thing, without asking me and the boys what we think and what we want. If it wasn't for Dunk MacGregor—"

"If it weren't for Duncan MacGregor, this band wouldn't exist." There was no way in a million years Jack would let Keith or anyone else take Dunk's name in vain. Or disparage his critical role in the success of the band.

"What about Duncan MacGregor?" said the man himself as he dipped his head under the doorframe and strode into the room.

Jack relaxed for the first time since the band had arrived for lunch. Everything could be put to rights again. "I think what Keith is suggesting is, if it weren't for you, they could add new songs to the setlist."

Dunk turned toward Keith. "Is that so? Did ya happen to know that Barry the Bastard's trying to sabotage us and ruin the final concerts?"

"What?" said Keith, raising his head to look at Dunk.

"So it was Barry, was it?" said Jack. "I thought so."

Keith frowned. "I don't get it. Why would he want to do that?"

"Earth to Keith," said Dunk. "Here we are getting hits and pulling huge crowds. And he wants to negotiate a new contract. But he's a greedy bastard who doesn't want to give us more clout and a bigger cut."

"So what's that got to do with the setlist?"

"Are ya off yer head, Keith? If we add songs and they don't work, we give him ammunition to use against us."

"But the songs'll work, I guarantee it."

"You guarantee it, do ya? Are ya willing to put your cut on the line? If they don't work, ya don't get paid?"

Keith thought about it for a second. "Yeah. I'm willing to do that. I know the fans will go mad for 'em. I know it."

Dunk looked at him with disbelief. Then he looked at the others in turn—George, Rob, Randy, Sam. "What about you bampots? Ya ready to give up yer pay if these new songs go wrong?"

None of them spoke. They were getting paid too much to put it on the line for a few of Keith and Rob's tunes.

"I didn't think so. Yer outvoted, Keith. The setlist stays the same. Yer songs will have to wait for the next tour."

"Yeah, that's what you always say. It's always tomorrow, tomorrow, tomorrow. And tomorrow never comes, does it?" Keith lurched up from his chair, making it slam against the wall. He pushed past Dunk and banged out of the room.

Dunk rolled his eyes at Jack as he righted Keith's vacated seat and tried to lower himself into it. He was twice the size of everyone else and too big to fit the space between the table and the wall. He decided to lean against the wall and cross his legs instead. "So the twerp's name is Howie. Sent here to spy on us and report back."

"Exactly as we thought," said Jack.

Rob perked up at this. "Is he a Russian spy?"

"Yeah," said Sam, "bugging your room and sending back reports on how sad and lonely you are."

"Well, at least there's something to record other than—" Rob faked a loud snoring sound.

"No, no, not like that, like this," said Randy, making more of a snorting sound.

"No, no, more like this." Sam put on a sexy voice. "Oh, Rita, don't stop, darling. Don't stop. Right there. That's it. Wow, you really rocked my world, Rita love." He sat back, with a satisfied smile on his face.

Rob smirked. "And what do I owe you, Rita love? Twenty quid? Here ya go, and don't think you're gonna get a tip."

"They don't use quid over here," said Randy.

"It's a metaphor, runt," said Rob. "Keep up."

Dunk rolled his eyes at Jack. "The twerp's Barry the Bastard's nephew. Didn't report much—other than Rob's sad and lonely life and Sam's cheapskate ways with the ladies."

Randy furrowed his brow. "What about me and George? Didn't he report on us?"

"Said he saw a threesome backstage. Said 'twas you and Georgie. Gonna hafta dock yer pay." Dunk stifled a smile.

"It wasn't me," Randy protested. "It could have been Georgie, but I swear it wasn't me."

"Relax, he's jerking your chain," said Rob, scowling at Dunk.

"I think it's time I have a chat with Barry," said Jack. "Let him know we appreciate his interest, but if he interferes with the band again, there will be consequences."

"Maybe I do it, scare some sense into him," said Dunk.

"No, he knows we've got Howie. That should scare him enough."

Everyone turned toward the food table, where Alison's voice and George's mumbles were getting louder.

"But he just said it," said Alison. "And I need to know. Were you or were you not in a threesome?"

"Nah," said George.

"Well, OK then," said Alison, visibly relaxing.

George smiled over at the boys and showed them the crossed fingers he was holding behind his back.

Ten

THREE HOURS LATER, sound check and rehearsal over, Jack and Dunk walked single file down the hotel corridor to Jack's suite, Jack in front and Dunk bringing up the rear. They both felt safer this way after that incident with a fan in Atlanta. The guy had jumped out from a hotel room nearby and grabbed Jack's favorite wig from his head before Dunk could stop him. After the incident in Cleveland, they made it policy to book entire floors, usually the floors at the top, and post security at all exits. Plus, even if they wanted to walk side by side, there was no way. Dunk took up the entire hallway all by himself.

Ahead, a guest room door opened and two maids came out, giggling into their hands.

"Hello, ladies," Jack said as he approached them. They were coming out of his suite. He schooled his face to look friendly, but he already knew what this meant.

The maids looked like deer caught in the headlights. It was pirate Jack, the man of their fantasies, standing right there in front of them in the flesh. One curtsied to him and the other followed suit, like he was royalty or something. Talks just like Charles and Di, he imagined they would tell one another later, since all Brits sounded the same to American ears. Except for Burt in *Mary Poppins*—Dick Van Dyke delivering a cracking performance, in Jack's book, but doing a ridiculous Cockney accent. Bad voice coaches were a hazard of the trade, as Jack well knew from a much-maligned school performance as Abanazar in "Aladdin." They said his accent was "hilarious in the wrong way." He never used Wizzy Mortimer as his voice coach again.

"We was just turning down your bed, Jack sir. And left you a little welcome gift. We hope you like it." They were shy now, not sure it had been a good idea, but too late to take it back. They curtsied again, squeezed past Dunk, and hurried down the corridor.

Jack entered the suite and walked over to the bed. Good that he still had his gloves on. The maids had left Polaroid snapshots of themselves in the nude, posing like Rita Hayworth and Betty Grable and other pinup girls from the forties. He turned the top one over and read the message: *I can make your dreems come tru, from Lori xoxo.* The 'i' had a heart instead a dot over it, and she'd given him her phone number.

"More photos for the crew?" said Dunk.

Jack picked up the Polaroids and tidied them into a neat pile. He handed them over to Dunk, who shoved them in his back pocket.

"What are ya gonna say to the bastard?"

"I don't know yet," said Jack.

"Maybe I should call him."

"No, I think I should."

Jack took Wipe-It-Fresh and paper towels out of a sports bag. He sprayed the end table next to the bed and wiped it down, then moved on to the other one.

Dunk watched him for a moment. "Right. Be back in an hour. Ya want me to send Ruth up?"

"No, not today."

The door reverberated after Dunk yanked it shut.

Jack walked over, Wipe-It-Fresh and towel in hand, and engaged the locks, then wiped down the inside of the door. He gave the locks and handle extra squirts. Germ factories, that's what they were. Next, he spent several minutes on the coffee table and the phone he would be using to call Barry. He'd have to finish cleaning after the concert. There wasn't enough time to do all the cleaning, make the phone call, eat, and touch up his makeup beforehand.

He put the Wipe-It-Fresh and paper towel roll back in the bag. The rubbish bin was already full of used towels. The room stunk from the smell, so he opened the big window overlooking the pool.

Standing in front of the full-length mirror near the bathroom, he adjusted his wig and costume, inspected his teeth, and watched himself as he took a couple of big breaths in and out.

He didn't want to get sweaty and smelly before the concert—hated that—but he needed to get his so-called brain juices flowing so he was as sharp as possible when he talked to Barry. The man was notoriously difficult, but he wasn't sure he'd call Barry a bastard. He'd known so many men like him, his own father for one, almost all of his headmasters for another. Most everyone in the music business. Barry wasn't a bastard so much as someone determined to win at any cost. Well, guess what, Barry, so am I.

He decided to take himself through the warm-up routine for Jane Fonda's workout. He had it memorized by heart, had both her book and her VHS tape, and insisted that every hotel room have a VCR player so he could watch the tape whenever he wanted. It was a damned difficult workout for a guy, Jane having legs up to her armpits and the flexibility of those bendable Gumby dolls. But he had persisted, and believed he was now good enough to qualify as one of the guys exercising behind her. That was one of his fantasies, being picked by Jane to be a member of her exercise team, then being asked to stay behind for a chat and getting it on with her.

He'd been a fan since he saw her in a double feature showing *Barefoot in the Park* and *Klute*. But everything changed forever when he saw her on the workout tape in that striped leotard with tights and leg warmers doing pelvic thrusts. What an incredible turn-on, despite her being at least twenty years older than he was. Watching the tape became one of his favorite *accoutrements* for jerking off. As well as that opening sequence in *Barbarella* where she stripped off. He had to pace himself or he came too fast, could come with her, literally, in seconds. Just thinking about her could turn him on. He couldn't watch her movies with anyone else anymore. But that was a relatively small price to pay for all the pleasure she'd given him over the past few years on the tour. Thank you, Jane.

He finished the warm-up routine, adjusted his wig and costume again, and sat down on the love seat behind the coffee table. He picked up the telephone handset and dialed the hotel operator, asked to place a call to Barry Bartholomew at Dolos Discs in New York. No, he didn't have the number. He hung up, closed his eyes, and centered himself while he waited.

The phone rang. That was fast. He opened his eyes and picked up the receiver.

"Sir, I have Barry Bartholomew's office on the line for you."

"Thank you, operator."

"Oh, no, this is Janelle at the front desk, Mister St James. If there's anything at all I can do for you, *anything* at all, you let me know, OK?"

"Indeed I will. Thank you, Janelle."

"I'll connect you now ... You are now connected. Please go ahead."

A woman's voice came through the line. "Jack? Jack, this is Rhonda. I have Barry ready to speak to you."

"Rhonda, Rhonda, Rhonda." He said her name as if it were fine wine he wanted to savor as long as possible. "How is my favorite person in the music business?"

"Oh, Jack, you charmer you. Waiting for you to come rescue me, that's what."

He smiled. Rhonda was like a mother to all the urchins of the music business. Always ready with warm words of praise when they did well or a gentle scolding when they got in any kind of trouble, and a clever quip the rest of the time.

"How is he? Anything I should know?"

Rhonda whispered into the phone. "Beside himself about his nephew Howie. Sounds like the kid got himself mixed up with some of your groupies. They had the nerve to call Barry and taunt him, said they were the Howie Liberation Front."

Jack broke into laughter. "They did? Oh dear."

"Yes, oh dear about sums it up. Be ready, Jack." A voice could be heard through the receiver yelling at her. "Putting you through now. Good luck."

There was silence for a moment, then a voice exploded on the line. "Jack, you cocksucker! What did you do to my nephew?"

Jack laughed. "Well, hello to you too, Barry. Nice to hear your dulcet tones."

Barry launched full speed ahead like an out-of-control missile. "I tell my nephew—big fan of Pirate, wants to follow the tour—you go, you don't bother the boys none. They're busy making money for your old uncle. Next thing I know I'm getting a collect call, this girl calling herself the Howie Liberation Front, telling me he's been liberated from his virginity. Thought good for the kid, about time, his mother, my sister, always breathing down his frickin' neck, never gives him the chance to get laid. But now the kid's gone missing, my sister beside herself with worry. So I says, don't worry, Mave, he's fine. My band would never let nothing happen to him. So tell me nothing's happened to him, Jack, so's I can put my sister Mave's mind to rest."

"Nothing's happened to him."

"You got him locked up, or what?"

"No, Barry, he's joined the tour as an honored guest, with backstage passes and full access to the band. I assure you he's having the time of his life, all the perks of being a member of the band. Once we learned he was your nephew, we rolled out the red carpet, naturally."

"Kids these days. What're you gonna do? They all wanna be rock 'n' roll stars."

"That they do, that they do. We did ask him to sign a non-disclosure agreement, make sure that what happens on the road stays on the road. The boys being boys and all. Nothing special, our standard practice is all."

There was silence on the other end of the line.

"Barry? Are you still there?" Jack could hear Barry puffing. Most likely lighting up one of his Cuban cigars. Or, knowing Barry, playing one of his many games. Keep you waiting, show you who's boss. Jack started humming a jazz tune in his head. He could play this game too.

Barry spent some time clearing his throat before speaking. "Listen, since you brought it up, about boys being boys and all. I did hear about that little incident in Houston."

"Oh, yes? Did you?" Jack looked up, searching his memory. What incident? He didn't know about any incident.

"Sounded like the crew got into some trouble outside that *Urban*

Cowboy place. What's it called?" Barry paused. "Oh, yeah, Gilley's. That's it."

"Yes, well. You know, the crew work extremely hard, and sometimes they let off perhaps a mite too much steam."

"Heard Dunk had to pay off some cowboys so they didn't get the law involved. Cost him a pretty penny. But that's your business. I know you guys got things completely under control."

"Yes, of course. You don't have to worry—"

"And then there was that incident in Miami with the underage girl. I know George is young, and things are different over there where you boys come from. But he could end up in jail for quite a stretch. The parents don't settle and it goes to court, you'd be looking to find yourself a new drummer. But hey, water under the bridge, yeah?"

Jack was apoplectic with rage. He knew nothing about this incident either. And this pathetic, grease monkey of a record executive knew everything, and from someone as bumbling as Howie no less. Unless there was another leak. He got up, phone in hand, and paced next to the coffee table.

"Have you been spying on us, Barry?" His voice was controlled but ice cold.

Barry cleared his throat, took an audible draw on his cigar, and exhaled. Jack knew he was getting extreme pleasure from being one-up and making him look like a fool. Payback for capturing Howie, no doubt.

"Listen, kid, we made a deal, didn't we? You get through the entire tour with no changes to the band members or the setlist, you get yourself a hefty bonus. Me, I don't get this new management world with objectives and targets and bonuses and all that jazz. I'm a straight percentages and expenses guy; my old brain can't handle anything else."

He took another draw and exhaled as he talked. "But you insisted it be in the contract. And I get it. Been in the business a long time, and I get it. Bands have fights and break up, happens all the time. Lose members to drugs and whatnot. Get in trouble with the law. So getting through the tour with everything intact, that's a big accomplishment. Or what the hell did you call it?"

"Strategic target," said Jack.

"Yeah, that's it. But listen, kid, if I'm gonna pay you this bonus, I gotta make sure you earned it. Capiche?"

"Of course capiche, of course you have to ensure we earned it. But how you do that was specified in the contract—through records and receipts and other hard evidence. Not through spying on us, Barry."

"Hey, you got your ways, kid, and I got mine. So I went too far, mea culpa, mea culpa. You caught Howie, not the best spy in the world, but you put him out of commission. So hey, there we go."

Jack could hear Barry puffing on his cigar and could picture the look of malicious triumph on his face. "We'll talk about this again, Barry. We're not finished here, but I have to go make you some more money." He needed to get off the line before he lost it. Then find out exactly what had happened and who was to blame, mete out suitable punishment, and get things back under control. Bill's management approach would have to wait. In wartime you had to act like a general, not a president or a prime minister. With his spying, Barry had made it abundantly clear: they were at war.

"Go! Go! Don't let me keep you. Do your thing," said Barry. "And tell that naughty Howie to call his mother."

"I will," said Jack through clenched teeth, hanging up the phone and placing it back in a perfectly aligned position on the coffee table.

He paced back and forth from one end of the suite to the other, his brain like a computer program executing an endless loop of outrage. Someone's head was going to roll. And that head happened to belong to one Duncan Iain MacGregor.

Eleven

AFTER WHAT SEEMED LIKE HOURS, there was a loud knuckle rap on the door. Jack strode over, checked the peephole, and released the locks. He opened the door to Dunk, not making any effort to mask his rage.

Dunk raised his eyebrows and heaved a heavy sigh. "He told ya, didn't he? About Boston and Orlando? I knew he would try to cause trouble, but believe me, they're naw a big deal. Just give me a chance to explain."

Jack's eyes widened. Boston? Orlando? He turned his back on Dunk, walked to the other end of the room, and stood looking out the open window for several long seconds, motionless. He took a few deep breaths to get himself under control. He needed to hear about these other two incidents before he let himself explode.

He heard Dunk close the door and turned back to face him. Dunk was standing with his feet planted shoulder width apart and his arms crossed, a mulish expression on his face, like a Hell's angel manning an invisible barricade and bracing for trouble.

"So, Boston," Dunk said. "The boys went to a bar called The Bottomless Keg and got into a wee rammy. Wasn't their fault, some ned called Sam a coon. Next thing ya know, there's furniture flying and some guy out cold. Claimed 'twas Rob lamped him, and yeah, maybe. Heard Rob was beside himself."

His thickening brogue betrayed Dunk's nervousness. He knew full well this was a big deal, at least to Jack. Wee rammy, my foot.

"But Manny knows a guy," Dunk continued. "Got the police to look the other way. Not that hard in Boston, ya know the right people. So I don't know what that bastard told ya, but we handled it and everything turned out fine."

"How much did it cost us?"

"Only a couple few thousand all told. Didn't know who we were."

Jack narrowed his eyes in disbelief. *Only* a couple few thousand, whatever that meant. "And what about the boys? Were they hurt?"

"A few bruises here 'n' there, couple of shiners, nothing major."

"And you hid that from me?"

"Naw that hard, is it, mate? Yer nae 'round 'em during the day and they wear makeup for the gigs."

Jack glared at him. Dunk knew very well he was around them at sound checks and rehearsals every single day, except travel days, of course. They had all conspired to keep it from him. Dunk stared back, daring Jack to contradict him.

"And Orlando?"

"So Orlando, the boys went to Pirates of the Seven Seas Theme Park on their day off. What happened ... 'twas a wee incident of public indecency. The theme park people were not amused, said, 'Give us a donation to bring a kid with some life-threatening disease and we'll let it go.' So that's what we did. Case closed."

Another wee incident, was it? "And how much was that?"

"They found out who we were. So ten thousand—"

"Ten thousand!"

"For a kid with a life-threatening disease. Charitable donation, like I said."

Jack turned and stared out the window as he processed this information—what looked to be a significant and steady drain on their finances, and a direct hit to his meticulously laid plans. Plans he'd made *with* Dunk. Good thing it was for a worthy cause and tax deductible, or there'd be a dead band manager in this room right now.

He turned back toward the traitor. "I'm assuming it was George ... or Sam?"

"I can't tell ya who. He made me give a solemn oath on my granny's grave, God rest her soul. I didn't tell him she's still alive."

"Randy? You're joking."

Dunk looked back at him without speaking.

"What did Randy ... what did this person who shall remain nameless actually do?"

"Do ya really have to know?"

Jack raised his eyebrows. You're going to tell me everything, mate.

"Right," Dunk said. "Ya remember how hot it was there. The boys had some cold brew before they went, 'cause ya can't drink in the theme park. And Ran ... I mean, he who shall remain nameless, well, ya know, he gets drunk on a wee thimble of the stuff. The others thought they could keep an eye on him. So they go to the Pirates of the Pacific and leave him alone for nae a second, and next thing ya know he's peeing in the lagoon. Bunch of parents yell at him, 'You're scaring our kids.' Makes him mad and he waves his willy and shouts, 'This is what a real pirate looks like.'"

Dunk couldn't help smiling at this.

Jack stared at him, pursing his lips. He thought this was funny? "Where was Keith in all this?"

"He stayed at the hotel. Working on his tunes, I guess."

"He should have been with them, as the oldest. Keeping an eye on them."

Dunk narrowed his eyes at Jack. "Just 'cause he's the oldest doesn't mean it's his job to take care of the boys."

"Of course it does," said Jack.

"Aye right. He's supposed to be a babysitter, is he?"

"I expect him to be responsible. I don't think that's too much to ask."

Dunk put his hands on his hips and glared at Jack. "And what about you? Where are you in all this?"

"What do you mean?" said Jack.

"Yer not going to bring up that 'I'm the leader of this band and if it weren't for me' shite again. Ya might've fooled Bill, but ya don't fool me, mate."

Jack recoiled. "How dare you talk to me like that? You know very well—"

"I know very well ya worry all the time, and ya talk about everything 'til yer blue in the face, but when it comes to lifting a finger, I'm the one who *does* everything. Aren't I?"

"Oh, yeah? Well where was that hard-working finger of yours when it came to Boston and Orlando? Or Houston and Miami? Huh? Where was it?"

Dunk's eyebrows shot up. "How—"

"Oh yes, I know all about Houston and Miami too. Did you think you could keep them from me and I'd never find out?" He wasn't about to admit that he didn't know about them until his phone call with Barry. "Tell me, what else have you been hiding from me? And how much more of my money have you wasted on these, these—"

"*Yer* money?" Dunk's face turned red.

OK, that was an unfortunate phrase to use, but too late to take it back now.

"Ya think the money the band makes is *yer* money? I s'pose the band plays hard night after night on that hot stage, and Manny and me take care of one bloody problem after another, just to make you rich. So you can retire early and have an easy life—"

"You know very well why I need to retire," Jack said, his voice far louder than it should have been with the damn window open.

"Ya want to know why I keep things from you?" Dunk shouted. "Because ya try to control every tiny little thing, and tell everyone what to bloody do all the bloody time, even when ya don't know what the hell yer bloody talking about."

"Don't you dare call me a control freak again," Jack shouted back.

"You *are* a freak," Dunk screamed at him. "Not just a control freak. A freak freak. And I musta been off my trolley when I agreed to start this band with you."

He turned, slammed the door open, and stalked out of the room.

"Control? I'll show you control," Jack shouted at his departing back as he picked up the phone, yanked the cord from the socket, and threw it at the wall. It missed and went out the open window.

The sound of the phone crashing on the pavement was followed by a woman shrieking. A man shouted, "Hey, asshole! You almost killed my girlfriend!"

Jack peeked through the gap between the curtain and the wall. The phone was in pieces near the pool, between a woman in a bikini and a man with hands on hips staring upwards. Oops.

After pacing for a while and replaying the conversation in his mind over and over again, he eventually calmed down and got the ever-so-helpful Janelle at the front desk to replace the phone for him. She delivered it personally, and as a thank you he gave her a signed photograph with a personal inscription: *Dear Janelle, thank you for making my stay a very special one, Jack St James.*

He also asked her to place a call for him to England. There wasn't much time. He was a stickler for promptness with the band and it would be hypocritical to be late himself. Call him a control freak if that made you happy. But after the fight with Dunk, he felt the unwelcome return of that old darkness. It made him face the harsh fact that, without Dunk—if he ever pushed him too far, if Dunk ever did the unimaginable and left him—who did he really have?

The phone rang and he scooped it up. Janelle was on the line and told him she had his party on the other end and to please go ahead. He heard her click off.

He cleared his throat. "Hello, Mummy. It's me. Sorry I'm calling so late."

Twelve

~~~~~

FIVE THOUSAND MILES away and seven hours ahead, Jack's mother sat in her burgundy silk nightgown on the side of an unmade bed, a glass of Johnnie Walker Black Label in hand.

"Is everything all right?" she asked.

Her classic blonde bob was crumpled on one side and the area below her eyes sported black streaks. With the migraines she had to cry, and she still hadn't found mascara and eyeliner that didn't run like the dickens.

A decorative lamp cast a weak spotlight on her and the whiskey, leaving the rest of the room in inky darkness. She imagined she must look like an actress in some pathetic amateur production of a Tennessee Williams play, and that's exactly how she felt.

"I put money in the account for you," said her beautiful son.

"Thank you, darling."

"And ... him?"

"The same."

There was a long pause.

"You shouldn't call," she said.

"I know, but I had to hear your voice."

"Oh, darling."

A man strode into the room and around the bed. She tried to hang up but he grabbed the phone from her hand and barked into the receiver. "Hello ... Hello ... Who's there?"

She could hear the click and dial tone as her son hung up.

Her husband slammed down the phone and glared at her. "Who was it?"

She took a defiant sip of whiskey. "It was my lover ... Charles."

"Like anyone would have anything to do with you." He grabbed the whiskey from her hand, sloshing it on the carpet, and strode back around the king-sized bed.

He turned at the door. "I'm going to find him. And when I do, he's coming home."

She laughed without mirth. "And then what, Winnie, and then what?"

The muscles tightened in his jaw. "And then he does what we brought him into this world to do. That's what."

He exited stage left, the longstanding villain in the drama that was her life. She pulled out another bottle and tumbler, hidden in a fancy hatbox under the bed, and poured herself a fresh glass.

Thirteen

LUCY SAT at the table in her parents' kitchen, Mittens purring in her lap and Betsy, their cocker spaniel, taking a snooze on her bare feet. Mittens made a half-hearted protest as she leaned down and kissed her head.

Lucy had absconded from Spirits Rising in a mad dash, hoofing it the half-mile down the winding driveway to the ashram's entrance to meet the taxi, where, hopefully, no one would see her leaving and raise the alarm. Namely Mandy the slithery Snake.

Cindy had wanted Lucy to tell Ramakar, her direct supervisor, that she had to rush home because her nana was ill, but Lucy had "forgot." Could she help it that she was the Pinocchio of liars, whereas Cindy made Richard Nixon look like an amateur? How many times had she been grounded while Cindy was flouncing about acting the innocent darling? Served Cindy right that she had to take on Lucy's sessions while she was gone. Although, knowing Cindy, she would have them completely reorganized and "modernized" by the time Lucy got back.

That is, if Lucy was even allowed to return. Knowing the swami and Ramakar, she could be banned from the ashram for life, as Aryakanish had been. She and Cindy called him "Aryakidding?" after that prank he pulled, which was minor compared to what Lucy was doing. She had to get that recording contract, or she was royally screwed.

She couldn't move home again, no matter how much she loved her miscreant family or how much they wanted her back. Looking around the kitchen, she sighed. It had not changed one iota in the time she'd been at the ashram. In fact, the entire house had not changed that much since she was a little girl, other than her brother moving out and her nana moving in. It was like a time capsule of an Italian American home in the early 1960s, with its formal living and dining rooms that her mother kept spotless and only allowed to be used on special occasions or for honored guests—or for visits by people with "bad energy," who should not be allowed into their living quarters. Nana was the resident expert on who had bad energy, and who had the "evil eye" and should not be allowed into the house at all.

Everyone hung out in the relaxed ambiance of the kitchen and family room. The kitchen was defined by the teal Skylark Formica countertop, her mother's pride and joy, and the family room by the La-Z-Boy recliner, her father's undisputed territory. He had fought off the move to get a La-Z-Boy reclining sofa for years, knowing it would spell the end of his rule over the color TV and *his* pride and joy, the VCR. Let the women get a foothold and, curse of all curses, dominion over the remote control would be lost forever.

Lucy looked through the double doorway at her father and brother watching a sitcom on the TV in the family room. Her brother Tony looked so much like her father, a Sabatini through and through, except for the comb over her dad used to hide his expanding bald spot. Tony always wore a New York Mets cap, a diehard fan since the "Miracle Mets" took the 1969 World Series, and even wore it at his takeout place, the Spiedi Spot. He was always getting into arguments with Yankees fans. Her brother also laughed the same as her father, a guffaw that could wake the dead, and now his toddler son, Dominick, seemed to be following suit.

Lucy, on the other hand, was claimed by both sides of the family—the Sabatinis saying she looked like Nana as a young girl, and the Santorinis saying she was the spitting image of her Great Grandmother Sirena, also a singer. Lucy didn't mind being the battleground between the Italian and Greek sides of her family because it meant they both spoiled her rotten. She could get her aunts and uncles to do almost anything. If it hadn't been for her brother and her zillions of cousins—if she had been an only child—she would have become a monster. Maybe she still was and didn't know it.

Her parents had been beside themselves with joy when she called that afternoon and told them she was coming home to visit, which quickly became outrage and concern when she said it was for only one night because she was joining a rock band named Pirate. She wouldn't have come home at all if she didn't need to get her "groupie" clothes, the ones she wore when she toured with Magnus. It was good she'd saved them, because she couldn't wear ashram clothes on a rock tour without looking ludicrous and suspicious, and she didn't have time or money to go shopping for new ones. Barry sure wouldn't pay for them. His assistant Rhonda, the poor woman, had been tasked with explaining the Dolos expense policy to her, a policy Lucy would openly flout if she weren't after the recording contract. If she wanted filet mignon and crème brûlée for dinner, Barry should darn well pay for them.

Her mother had been talking nonstop since Lucy got home an hour earlier. She was in her usual cooking frenzy, standing at the stove stirring her "family recipe" tomato sauce and shaking in more oregano. Oregano cured all ills, her mother believed, along with garlic and spinach. She looked over at Lucy and pointed her spoon at her. "Guess who's back from college? Danny. He got a degree in … what was it, Mom?"

Her nana shrugged. She sat next to Lucy clicking away with her knitting needles, making something mysterious from rainbow yarn. Knowing Nana, it was a gift she would press into Lucy's hands as she was going out the door, saying, "Something from Nana help you out."

"Con, what was it Danny studied?" her mother shouted at her father.

Her father and brother shouted back at the same time. "Accounting."

"Oh, yeah. He got that fancy accounting degree. He's a good boy, that Danny. He's joining his pop at the Chevy dealership. They had that incident with the bookkeeper, poor Dick had to file charges." She shouted at her husband again. "Hey, Con, how much did they lose?"

"Oh, for crying out loud." Her father clicked off the TV, grunted as he pulled himself out of the La-Z-Boy, and came into the kitchen, followed by Tony. "Can't a man watch a show after a hard day's work? Geez!"

"What? Your daughter's here." She turned to Lucy. "He spends more time with the Jeffersons than he does with me, his own wife."

"What? They're funny," said Lucy's father.

"Lucy's funny too ... funny-looking." Tony swatted her head and dodged her attempt to swat him back.

Betsy jumped up, ran out from under the table, and barked into the air.

"Get over yourself, Betsy," said Tony. "You're funny-looking too."

Lucy mock-glared at him. "How dare you insult Betsy?" She grinned at Betsy. "Right, sweetie girl?"

Betsy put her head on Lucy's lap. Mittens opened one eye in warning.

"I was telling Luce," said her mother, never one to be deflected from her chosen topic, "Danny came back to work for his father. Living at home, said he's saving up to buy a nice house, start a family with some lucky girl."

Her father stuck his finger in the tomato sauce and her mother hit his hand with the spoon. He grinned at her and licked his finger.

"Yeah, you better hurry up, Luce," said Tony. "You might miss your chance to marry Dreamboat Danny and have his eight kids. That is, if you got any chance at all with a dazzling dreamboat like that Danny."

"Your sister's got a chance," her mother said. "She might be too skinny." She looked over at Lucy. "I don't know what they feed you in that place. But she's got her father's eyes and her mother's you-know-whats. So he could do a lot worse."

"Yeah, but without those you-know-whats, she got no chance at all," said Tony.

"Hey, is that any way to talk about your sister?" said her dad.

Lucy smirked at Tony. "Yeah, have some respect, baby boy."

"I give you the respect you deserve." Tony swatted her head again.

She deposited a protesting Mittens on the floor, jumped up, and chased Tony into the family room, cornering him in front of the La-Z-Boy. "You take that back or I'll make you pay, *baby boy*."

Betsy took up a position in the doorway and barked in their direction.

Her brother feinted left and then right, but Lucy knew his tricks and blocked him both times. He swatted her shoulder and she punched his arm.

"Ow! Ma! Lucy's playing rough."

"When are you two going to grow up and act your age?" said her mother.

"Crybaby," Lucy taunted Tony.

Tony grabbed her, flipped her to the floor, and sat on her. "I'll show *you* who's a crybaby."

Lucy bucked and kicked to get him off her.

Betsy turned toward the kitchen and barked with more urgency.

"Say uncle," said Tony. "Say uncle and I'll let you go."

"Never!"

Their grandmother limped into the room, her walker making a distinctive clacking sound on the parquet floor, and loomed over them.

"Antonio, your nana, she want to talk to her Lucy."

Tony let go. He got up and brushed himself off, leaving Lucy lying on the floor. He kissed his nana.

"Gotta go anyway. I'm on bath duty tonight."

Their father appeared in the doorway, licking icing from a spoon and leaning down to stroke Betsy. "Bath duty? Now Em's got you doing bath duty?"

"Tone, you don't listen to his nonsense," their mother yelled from the stove.

Tony grabbed Lucy's hand and pulled her up. "It's a new world, Pop. And I wanna do it. Dom won't get much time once Nicole or Nicholas gets here." He gave Lucy a quick peck on the cheek.

"You and Em already picked out names?" said Lucy. "I love those names."

Nana turned and clacked toward the door to her room, standing open at the end of a short hallway. Nana wanted to "talk" to her, which sounded serious.

Lucy called over her shoulder to her brother as she followed, Betsy on her heels. "Tell Em and Dom I'll come see you guys when I get back. Promise."

"Dinner in ten minutes, you two," her mother yelled as they entered her nana's room.

Lucy let Betsy in and shut the door as Nana took a seat in her wicker swivel rocking chair. Nana's flowered housedress and bright orange slippers clashed with the green and blue batik-style fabric covering the chair. "Colorful" was one word you could sure use to describe her nana.

"Mind if I move these?" Lucy said as she picked up a pile of *National Enquirers* from the bed. She sometimes spent hours looking through them, finding the stories about celebrities both outrageous and hilarious. But Nana seemed to take them seriously, often brought them up to Lucy as cautionary tales of the celebrity life. Yeah right, Nana, like I'm going to be a celebrity.

"You move. You move," Nana said as she waved her hand. "Nana behind her reading."

Lucy smiled. Her nana was forever complaining about being behind on her reading and her projects. She was going to outlive them all.

Lucy got into a cross-legged position on the bed and Betsy jumped up next to her. Mittens scratched at the door.

"Too late, Muffola," shouted Nana in that direction. Nana always called their pets by Italian names. She picked up the remote control for her TV and clicked it. The TV flickered and came on.

"Um, Nana," Lucy said. This was rather unusual behavior, even for her grandmother.

Nana picked up another remote control and turned on the VCR. "You wait, mia cara. I record. For you."

"You recorded something for me? Oh, that's sweet, Nana, but—" She was drowned out as the MTV logo appeared on the TV and music blasted into the room.

Her nana motioned to the TV with great satisfaction. She had a smile on her face as some pirates appeared onscreen playing instruments and singing on a beach. A subtitle appeared:

Pirate
"Blue Lagoon"
1983
Dolos Discs

Lucy had never seen MTV, there not being any TVs in the ashram. But this was not what she expected. The video told a story of a pirate stranded on a desert island who discovers a lost tribe and falls in love with a native girl, only to be heartbroken when he is rescued and forced to leave her behind. The music was complex and haunting, transitioning from major to minor chords as the mood changed from blissful love to bittersweet loss.

Nana paused the VCR, the members of the band frozen in smoldering poses and leering looks toward the camera. "Pirate," she said, her dentures gleaming as she gave Lucy a gleeful smile. "Very popular. On MTV all time."

"Pirate," repeated Lucy. She was stunned. She'd expected a group of boys singing pop tunes. Isn't that what Barry said? But this had been a full-on rock 'n' roll band with guys well into their twenties—*men*—except for maybe the bass guitarist and the keyboard player, who looked a bit younger. And that lead singer, boy, did he look intense. Good-looking, although who could really tell with all that makeup. But definitely intense.

"Nana has gift for her Lucy. You get Nana bag in closet." She pointed to a sparkly blue gift bag with a wrapped present sticking out of it.

Lucy retrieved the bag from the closet and handed it to her grandmother, then sat back down on the bed. She looked at the gift with excitement. She loved presents, any kind of present, but especially ones from her nana, because they were always so unusual and unexpected.

"You no listen my son's wife no more. You listen Nana and be like fox." Nana tapped her temple.

Lucy grinned. "OK, Nana. Be like a fox."

Nana pulled the present from the bag and handed it to her. "Open! Open!"

Lucy took the present and tore off the paper like an overexcited child on Christmas morning. She had always been a paper ripper. Inside was a pink and silver box with a cellophane window. She looked closely at the thing displayed inside the cellophane, turned it this way and that, and furrowed her brow. "What is it? A bath toy?"

Nana put on the reading glasses dangling from a cord around her neck. She took the box from her granddaughter and read from the front of the box, tracing the words with her index finger and sounding out the words in her heavy Palermo accent. "Squirms and vibrates. Bends to your inner most curves."

She looked over her reading glasses at Lucy. "Brand new Rabbit, hot from press." She opened the box, and after some wrangling, pulled a Rabbit Pearl vibrator from the packaging inside it. She stroked the ears, letting the battery pack dangle down in her lap.

Lucy's mouth dropped open and she could feel her face get red. Was that what she thought it was? Nana!

"Much better than kangaroo or beaver or turtle. Nana know. And made in Japan. Only best for mi bella amore." She pointed at her dresser. "You get Nana batteries."

Lucy did as her nana bid and retrieved some AA and AAA batteries, not sure which ones her grandmother needed. Nana had the battery pack open and took the AA batteries and inserted them like a pro. She turned it on and the rabbit ears vibrated.

Betsy jumped on the floor and barked at the vibrator.

Lucy stared at it open-mouthed, her face feeling even hotter. Putting it on the highest setting, Nana thrust it into her hands and sat back in her rocker, a satisfied grin on her face. Lucy held it upside down at arm's length with the tips of her fingers, unable to take her eyes from the rapid movements.

"Lucky rabbit ears." Nana spoke loud enough to be heard over the noisy hum of the device. "You use, no get *incinta*—pregnant—like Nana or my son's wife. Your papa, surprise. You, surprise."

"What?" said Lucy. She and her father were born out of wedlock? "That can't be true. They said I was premature."

Nana leaned forward with a look of disdain. "Bah! My son's wife lie. Be good girl, Lucy. Say no, Lucy. *Ridiculo*." She sat back. "You use

Rabbit, no surprise. And you have, what they say ... good vibrations. Or like Nana, big vibrations."

"Nana!" said Lucy. "You're embarrassing me."

Her grandmother gave her a mischievous smile. "Bah! You listen Nana. She know."

Lucy's mother shouted from the kitchen. "Time to eat."

"Quick, quick, you hide. And don't tell my son's wife. She no need know."

"OK, Nana. I won't."

"And watch out for pirate Blackbeard." Nana gestured toward the VCR and the intense lead singer. "*Pericolo*. Danger."

"I know exactly what you mean, Nana, and believe me, I will."

Fourteen

RUTH STOOD NEAR THE ARTISTS' entrance to the arena. Damn, it was hot here in Albuquerque, but at least it was dry heat.

She took a puff on a doobie, followed by a swig from her hip flask. The flask was engraved silver, a gift from one of the boys in Lynyrd Skynyrd before that awful plane crash.

Back in the day, people often mistook her for Michelle Phillips of The Mamas and the Papas, until they saw her up close. Even now, years later, she had the same long hair parted in the middle and held in place by a tie-dyed headband, the same beaded vest and bellbottoms, and the same "look at me wrong and I'll kick your ass" look. A woman had to take care of herself, particularly with these artists. They were id, all id, that was for sure. Except for Jack. That poor guy was stuck in super-ego mode.

She was waiting for him to come. He hadn't asked for her today. Usually he wanted some part of his body adjusted. And now he was late coming to the arena, not like him at all. She was worried, had this bad feeling, and needed to see that he was holding himself together.

The guy standing near her was in a cowboy outfit, the full get-up, including roach killer boots and a Stetson. Most bands attracted a certain kind of fan base, but there was something about Pirate that appealed to people from across the spectrum. She didn't know what it was, but the band seemed to attract a lot of goofballs like this guy.

He was a really tall dude and kept sneaking looks down at her, then looking away when she looked in his direction.

She leaned over and read the words etched on his boots. "Clint Pomeroy."

"At your service, ma'am." He doffed his hat to her, revealing a slicked-back Johnny Cash pompadour.

"Wrong concert, dude. The Oak Ridge Boys are down the road." Ruth chuckled at her own joke.

"No, ma'am, I'm a big fan of Pirate, here to get an autograph from Blackbeard for my collection. You know, Jack St James. I've got all the others, but haven't been able to nab his yet."

She grimaced at him. "You're no cowboy. What the hell accent is that?"

"OK, so let me explain. You might find this crazy, but until last year I was the son of Chaim and Bartola Leibowitz, living in Brooklyn, New York City, and working as an accountant. Then I did this thing called regression therapy. Have you heard of it?"

Ruth narrowed her eyes as she took another swig from the flask. It used to have Jack Daniels in it, but these days just rooibos tea. She was addicted to the stuff. He probably thought she was high or drunk, at least enough to buy into this cockamamie story he was peddling.

"Anyway," he said when she didn't respond. "I found out that in a past life I was a genuine cowboy. I'd already been going through an identity crisis, was seeing a therapist every week but wasn't really getting anywhere with them. I was completely sick of being an accountant, dealing with a bunch of ungrateful clients who wanted me to hide their earnings from the tax man, even at the risk of me getting caught and sent to jail. So one day I just decided enough was enough. I'm going to be a cowboy, and I'm going to follow my favorite band around the country. Because why not?"

He looked at her for a reaction and she stared back at him. The guy was a bona fide loony bin.

"And you, ma'am, what brings you here, may I ask?"

She slipped the hip flask back in her pocket, took one last toke, and tossed the doobie. What the hell. He might be crazy, but he didn't look dangerous. She held out her hand to shake his. "Ruth. I'm with the band."

Instead of shaking it, he lifted her hand to his lips and kissed it. She stared up into his kind brown eyes for one long second, completely thrown, and then gathered her wits and pulled away.

She hurried over to the arena door and the security guy opened it to let her through.

Fifteen

AS RUTH SLIPPED INSIDE, Clint looked after her like a dog watching his beloved owner leave for work. Wow, that was one remarkably fine woman. He'd never met anyone like her.

Clint heard a hubbub moving toward him and the other fans gathered around the door. Clint was taller than the others and could see that it was Jack arriving at the arena with his security detail.

This was his chance to get Jack's autograph, he just knew it. He hadn't lived in New York City all his life without learning how to beat the crowd and get what he needed. And he didn't know why, but he really needed this. Civility be damned.

He advanced toward the door, lifting and placing people to the side as he did so, ignoring the loud protests and grumbles in his wake. He reached the door at the very same moment Jack's group got there. Jack looked over and made eye contact with him.

"Ruth sent me," Clint said in a commanding voice. He didn't know why he said it. It seemed the right thing to say. Jack stared at him for a long moment.

"Let him in, Manny," said Jack to the heavily tattooed guy who stood between them.

Manny nodded to the guy on the door. Jack, Manny, and the security guys went through the door and disappeared inside.

Clint stood in place, unsure what to do.

"Get in," the door guy yelled at him.

Clint rushed through the door and the door slammed shut behind him.

He was in! Now what did he do? Clearly, follow Jack and get his autograph, that's what, and then if they kicked him out, so be it. Mission accomplished.

He trailed Jack and the security guys down a hallway, and watched as Jack entered a room by himself and the security guys hurried onwards into the backstage bowels of the arena. Clint went to the doorway and looked in.

Jack was standing only a few feet away, looking across the room at a massive man with wild hair and a beard. Clint knew who it was. The band's manager, Dunk MacGregor, stuffing food in his mouth as he talked away to the members of the band.

Jack looked relieved when he saw Clint standing there and turned toward him.

"So you know Ruth?" he said.

"Yes, I'm ... I'm ... I'm in love with her." The moment the words escaped from his mouth, Clint realized that they were true. He'd never experienced that thing called falling in love at first sight. Maybe because he'd never believed in it, thought it was a bunch of malarkey made up by romance novelists and Hallmark card writers. But it *was* true. He'd looked in her eyes and realized that he never wanted to stop. That, and the fact that she was the most beautiful woman he'd ever seen. Like Michelle Phillips but even better.

Jack's eyes went wide and he turned to give Clint his full attention. "Really? Ruth didn't say anything."

"Um, she doesn't know. It's ... it's—"

"Say no more. I understand completely. How do you tell a woman like Ruth that you love her? You don't, do you? You have to show her in some dramatic way. She's not one for waffling or small gestures, is she?"

"No, sir," said Clint. He realized he still had his Stetson on and removed it, appalled he was wearing it while talking to one of his music idols.

"Don't call me sir. It's Jack. And you are ..."

"Clint Pomeroy, at your service." He didn't offer his hand, knew all the rumors and didn't want to make Jack uncomfortable, or push his luck any further than he already had.

"I've got to go warm up my voice, so let me introduce you to someone who can show you around." Jack called over to a pimply young man sitting on an orange sofa between two women who had draped themselves on him. "Howie, could you come over here?"

The young man rose from the sofa, the women trailing their fingers down his body as he got up and walked over.

"Come right back, love monkey," said the one with straggly hair. The other one giggled into her hand.

The young man strutted over, full of manly importance. "What's up, Jack?"

Jack grinned. He seemed amused by the young man. "Howie, allow me the pleasure of introducing you to Clint ..."

Clint held out his hand to Howie. "Clint Pomeroy, nice to make your acquaintance."

"Nice to meet you," said Howie, shaking Clint's hand and squeezing it a bit too hard.

"Would you mind terribly showing Clint the ropes?" said Jack. "Introduce him round, get him something to eat and drink, all that?"

"Sure, Jack," said Howie. "My pleasure."

"And ask Dunk to get him a seat with you in the VIP section." Jack looked across the room at Dunk.

Dunk looked their way and turned his back. What was that about?

Jack pursed his lips and stood thinking for a moment, then turned abruptly and left the room.

Howie ambled back to the orange sofa and turned to face Clint.

"Clint, this is Suze, and this is Carly."

"Howdy, Suze. Howdy, Carly," said Clint, bowing to each in turn.

The two young ladies were grinning from ear to ear.

"First a love monkey, now a tall cool glass of cowboy. We're gonna have us some fun tonight, aren't we, Carly?" Suze winked at her friend.

Carly put her head on Suze's shoulder as she looked up at Clint and giggled.

"I'm sorry, ma'am," said Clint, "but I'm a one-woman man, and I'm in love with Ruth."

Suze rolled her eyes. "That old sourpuss? Suit yourself, cowboy. Besides, we're actually quite happy with love monkey here."

Howie thrust out his chest. "B-be right b-back, ladies."

Clint followed as he headed toward the band members standing at the drinks table. They were all costumed and made up for the show, eating and drinking and looking up at Dunk MacGregor as he talked and gestured with great animation. Everyone except for George Farraday, the band's drummer, who was in the corner making out with a girl in a chef's outfit.

"So we pussyfooted back into the house every night for maybe two weeks," Dunk said. "Till one night, Jack got caught in a window, got his costume snagged on a nail. He was moving about like a fish on a line, trying to get free. Dropped his scepter—bam!—and woke the entire school. Headmaster came running. Whipped Jack right there in the bloody window, front of me and all the boys."

"He whipped Jack?" Randy, the band's keyboardist, looked horrified.

"Didn't even whimper. Took it like a man. And we were back sneaking out the next night. The show must go on, he said."

"C'mon, you're having us on," said Keith, creator of some of Clint's favorite guitar licks. Clint always thought he looked like one of the guys in Three Dog Night. The one who looked like Jesus.

"I would've pounded that headmaster's head in," said the bass guitarist, Rob, a bigger, rougher version of Randy.

"More like begging 'im, 'Can I have some more please, sir,'" said Sam with his hands in prayer mode. Clint considered Sam Wilson one of the best lead guitarists of his generation, although Keith and Rob were no slouches. Sam dodged a punch from Rob.

"Got caught two more times, we did," continued Dunk. "Three times yer out. But course his da fixed it, like he always did, and Jack said he wouldn't stay at that school without me. So we finished up there. 'Twas very clever, was Jack, 'cause being in that panto got us right into Footlights our first year at uni."

"What's Footlights?" said Randy.

"They're stage lights," said Rob. "Keep up, runt."

Keith sighed. "It's a drama club at Cambridge, init? We's heard this tall tale before, only a bit different." He threw back the rest of his beer.

Dunk pushed on. "We did a spoof about singing pirates in our third year at uni. Jack wrote all the music. 'Twas pure dead brilliant and went down a thundering storm. And that's when we came up with Pirate."

Clint looked at their faces. Randy was engrossed in the story, one emotion after another crossing his trusting young face. Rob and Sam kept taunting and poking one another. Keith looked grumpy and out of sorts. Dunk was in love with his own story, and wanting them to be in love with it too. And George had his tongue down that girl's throat.

"Guys," said Howie.

They all looked over at Howie, and at him.

"This is Clint. He's with Ruth."

Dunk turned toward Clint, scrutinizing him from top to bottom. "Ruth didn't mention any cowboy."

He felt Howie tense beside him. "Jack told me to show him the ropes."

"Jack did, did he?" Dunk walked up to Clint. They were about eye-to-eye, but Dunk was mammoth, about twice his size. Dunk stared into Clint's eyes, and he did his best to stare back.

After a moment, Dunk held out his hand. "Welcome, cowboy."

Clint grasped it and shook, relieved. This was kind of a loose operation, wasn't it? If you said you knew Ruth, you were in. It was clear, she was one special kind of woman.

"I'm in love with Ruth," he blurted. He couldn't stop himself. It was like he wanted to shout it to the world, or write it across the sky in airplane smoke, or put it on a billboard in Times Square.

Dunk's face softened. "Aw, really?"

"Jack said she likes big gestures," said Clint. "I'm thinking about writing it across the sky?" He wanted their advice, because after all, they knew her far better than he did. Well, truth be told, he didn't really know her at all. But he would remedy that, if she let him.

"No, no, I got it," said Rob. "You do it on the kiss cam at the Dodgers. We're going there next week."

"That's naff, init?" said Sam. "Everyone does that."

"What's your big idea then, Einstein?" said Rob.

"You put on my man Barry, pour the Dom, do the groove." Sam did a Michael Jackson moonwalk and 360-degree turn. "Have her eating out of the palm of your hand."

"Who's Barry?" said Randy.

"Omigod, do we have to explain everything to you?" said Rob.

"Barry White," said Sam. "Second god in the Sam universe."

Randy was not to be deflected. "What about the first?"

Everyone spoke at the same time.

"Earth to Randy!" said Dunk.

"Don't be daft!" said Rob.

"Wake up, our kid!" said Keith.

Sam was a little slower to respond. "My man Jimi, course."

"I know it's Jimi," Randy said. "I'm saying, why don't you put *him* on? Like 'Foxy Lady,' or 'Lover Man,' or even better, 'Bleeding Heart.' She's a rock chick, isn't she?"

"Huh," Clint said, considering. "I like it."

Keith grabbed Randy and gave him a noogie. "Not so daft after all, are ya, our kid?"

Randy squirmed out of his grasp.

"But you're still a pipsqueak." Rob gave him a good-natured punch in the arm.

Randy rubbed it and stifled a grin.

This was exactly what Clint had always loved about this band. They were world-class songwriters and instrumentalists who never failed to deliver a kickass concert, but they also appeared to take great pleasure in being together. Like a band of brothers.

A member of the crew appeared in the doorway and yelled, "Ten minutes, guys. Ten minutes to showtime."

Everyone exploded into motion, disappearing in different directions.

Howie grabbed Clint and pulled him toward the door. As they passed the couch, Howie said, "C'mon, my ladies."

"Coming, love monkey," said Carly.

Suze winked at Clint.

Sixteen

CLINT FOUND himself seated in a special VIP section with some journalists and local bigwigs. Howie sat on one side of him, flanked by what he kept referring to as "my ladies." Clint wondered who the kid was and why he was getting such deluxe treatment.

The guy on Clint's other side held out his hand. "Sid Jones. *Rock Music* magazine. And you are?"

Clint shook his hand. "Clint Pomeroy. I know *RM*. I read it whenever I visit London."

Sid looked surprised. "Oh, yeah? You in the music business?"

Clint didn't advertise his former life but saw no reason to hide it. "I was a CPA—you know, a certified public accountant—in the entertainment division. Handled a lot of Broadway productions, TV, radio, some rock bands."

"That so? What's your take on Pirate here? Professionally speaking."

Clint didn't hesitate. He knew exactly what he thought. "I would have killed for a client like Pirate. Most bands are a nightmare, but Pirate ... I mean, take a look around you." Clint gestured toward the rest of the arena.

Sid craned his neck around, scanning the multi-tiered arena. "Sold out. You expect that with the hot bands."

"No, no," said Clint. "Really look at this audience."

"OK." Sid looked around again, scrutinizing the audience. "I see a lot of weed being smoked. But that's par for the course."

"Take a look again." Clint was enjoying this, getting this journo to see things through the eyes of a money guy like himself.

Sid pulled back his head to take in the entire stadium. Suddenly he grinned. "Oh, I get it. A lot of them are dressed like pirates. It's like a huge fancy dress party."

"Yeah, that's part of it," said Clint. "The audience really identifies with the band. They want to be pirates too. But from a *money* standpoint, that's not the important thing."

Sid knit his brows. "I don't get it."

"One word," said Clint. "Merchandise."

"Say that again," said Sid as he reached into his pocket. Clint couldn't believe it. The guy was going to break the law and secretly record what he said. Well, in that case, Clint was going to give this journo exactly the story he wanted him to write.

"Everyone thinks Jack is a musical genius, but that's only part of the story. The guy is a merchandising genius too. You see those kids wandering the aisles?" Clint put a hand to his mouth and let out a shrill whistle, then raised his arm in the air. One of the kids rushed over. Clint pulled a ten-dollar note from his billfold and handed it over. "Keep the change."

The kid lit up and gave him a glossy program.

"Look at this." Clint showed Sid the cover. "It's like we're on Broadway ... or in the West End. Bands have concert programs, but I've never seen anything like this." He flipped through the program. "Here's the pirate story they tell during the concert, with the lyrics of all of the songs. They made sure they kept the rights to everything." He paged forward. "Lots of photos from the different parts of the show. And here's my favorite part: funny bios of the band members in their pirate personas, so you get history and humor rolled into one. I mean, British humor, who can beat it?"

"Oh, yeah," said Sid. "We do OK in that department."

Clint handed him the program. "Take a look. You're in the magazine business. You know the enormous markup on a thing like this. Just imagine you had a captive audience, bored and waiting for their favorite band to go on, no warm-up act, and someone came to where they were sitting and offered them the next best thing?"

"I get it, I get it," said Sid. "Genius."

"But that's not the best part. You notice all those fans wearing eye patches? Or the ones over there looking through spyglasses at the stage? Or the ones looking down at something?"

Sid looked where Clint was pointing.

"It's a treasure map," said Clint. "Have you checked out the front of house yet?"

"No, I always avoid it," said Sid. "Use the artists' entrance."

"Well, I suggest you go check it out. They have every kind of pirate merchandise and paraphernalia you can think of. Authentic replicas, from what Jack said in an interview. Even bags of sixpence. All these pirate hats and belts and costumes the fans are wearing, all front of house sales. And the markup, oy vey, the markup. It makes my eyes water."

"Huh," said Sid. "I wonder how Jack knew to do all this."

Clint was raring to tell him. "George Lucas, that's what I think."

"George Lucas? You mean *Star Wars* George Lucas?"

"Exactly. He copied the *Star Wars* merchandising strategy to a T, except for the action figures. He needs to catch up with the KISS fellas on that. But everything else, straight out of the *Star Wars* playbook. Mark my words, Sid, someday there'll be a pirate movie on the scale of *Star Wars* and they'll do exactly the same thing—and Jack the genius already beat them to it."

Sid nodded and reached toward his pocket as if he had got what he needed. Not so fast, thought Clint, I ain't done yet. He pointed toward the stage. "Take a close look at that. The guy is a design genius too. What you're looking at is another authentic replica, of an 18th century pirate ship."

Sid stared at the stage. Facing the audience was the starboard side of an enormous pirate ship. "How do you know that? You're a cowboy, not a pirate." Sid grinned at his own joke.

Clint decided to indulge him. He was used to people making fun of him, first as a Jew in a skullcap, then as an accountant, now as a cowboy. It came with those territories. You learned to let the bad jokes wash over you like water off a duck's back, smile a little smile, then move in for the kill, so to speak.

"*Art & Design Digest*," said Clint. "Interview with Jack and a full photo spread. You probably didn't see it, since it's not your beat."

"Um, no." Sid looked sheepish, like a kid who hadn't done his homework.

"He's got all the things the fans would expect," said Clint. He pointed at various parts of the ship. "There's the black flag with the skull and crossbones on it. And there's the crow's nest at the top of the main-sail, but, of course, a lot lower than a real crow's nest. See it?"

Sid nodded.

"The cannons and cannonballs on the deck ready for battle. My favorite part is the keel covered with barnacles. And the legendary gang-plank—which is usually stowed to the side on a real pirate ship, but they've kept it out for dramatic purposes."

"Cool, very cool," said Sid. He stifled a yawn.

Clint was determined that he really "get" it and do the band full justice in his article. He pointed out other features of the ship, leaning close to the journo and making sure he invaded his personal space. "There's the foresail and mainsail. There's the bow at the front with the bowsprit spanning forward from it. There's the forecastle, or upper deck, behind the bow. Guess who plays there?"

"Um, Randy?"

"No, you got the two main singers on either side. So Calico Jack, or Keith, is on the forecastle. And Blackbeard, or Jack, is on the quarter deck." He pointed to the raised deck at the rear of the ship. "That's where the captain stands and keeps an eye on the entire ship and gives orders to everyone. Although, Jack goes all over the ship. They use Nady wireless microphones—state of the art."

"So where are the others?" said Sid.

"You see the helm, or steering wheel, on the quarter deck? Randy's keyboards are there. He looks like he's steering the ship." Sid sat up and peered at that area.

"And you see that lower deck across the center of the ship. That's called the amidship. George's drum set is there, cleverly hidden right now behind piles of rope. And Sam is there doing guitar and backup vocals. Cool, huh?"

"Yeah, that is cool." Sid looked seriously impressed. "But what about Rob?"

"Rob is in the crow's nest," said Clint. "It's a platform built so he can't fall out. He does some lines in one of his solos about the loneliness of the lookout, the guy in the crow's nest. But I won't tell you any more. I don't want to spoil it for you."

"Thanks, uh ... what did you say your name was?"

"Clint Pomeroy. P-O-M-E-R-O-Y." He wanted it right if the guy quoted him. He pointed to the big screens on both sides of the stage. "By the way, you can see everything that's happening on stage on the Nocturne video projection system. You won't miss a thing."

Sid looked up at the screens and nodded his head.

"State-of-the-art sound, lighting, special effects," added Clint. "I think they use Showco over here, like the Stones and all the other top bands."

"Good to hear," said Sid. "Nothing worse than bad sound or lighting. Or special effects that go haywire."

"And can I tell you one more really cool thing?" said Clint. "Do you know what it takes to move this stage and everything?"

Sid shrugged. "No. No idea."

Clint considered this the icing on the cake for the story. "I got this from one of the roadies. It takes 42 rigs and 157 crew. Can you imagine a long line of 42 trucks crossing this country? Or crossing England? They'd tie up the M1 motorway for hours."

Sid grinned. "More like days."

The lights went down and a hush descended across the audience. Clint sat back, pleased that he'd been able to do this for the band after all the pleasure the band had given him. He saw Sid reach into his pocket to turn off the tape recorder.

He looked in the other direction and Howie was staring at him with a perturbed expression. He'd apparently been listening in on their conversation. Clint knew he sometimes talked too loud when he got excited. So was Howie perturbed by Clint's loudness, or by something he'd said? Who in tarnation was this pimply, horny young man, anyway? He'd have to find out.

Seventeen

RUTH WAS WAITING in the Band Room backstage. She'd finished a bunch of the crew; they were always needing adjustments given all the lifting and squatting they did. Now that the band had finished playing and cavorting about on that ship, they might need theirs. She had her table and ointments ready.

Jack was one of her regulars, but that's because he was always doing that Jane Fonda workout. She'd told him to cut it out, but the damn idiot wouldn't listen. So all those cricks and pulled muscles served him right. She was pretty sure she was the only one he ever allowed to touch him. Everyone told her she had the best hands in the business. Magic hands. Damn right she did.

Ruth felt bone tired, but she loved these guys, one of the best bands she'd worked with. Jack and Dunk ran a very tight ship—maybe too tight, if you asked her. Jack was all business, all the time. The boys could smoke pot on their days off, but any other drugs and that's it, they were out of the band for good. They got fined for bad language, after an incident at a concert where one of them said the f-word and some parents dragged their kids out. She had to laugh because the boys' language got pretty damn creative after that. Groupies were banned from meetings and rehearsals, but the boys could fool around as much as they wanted. And boy, did those boys fool around.

But not with her. Unlike other bands, Jack and Dunk made it clear to everyone she was not to be messed with. Sure, there was still an isolated incident here and there, men being men. She handled it herself, told them to cut it out or she would adjust them so they couldn't work, their worst nightmare. Call her a ball-breaker, she didn't care. But she'd been doing this for too long and she didn't know how much longer she could keep it up. The doctor told her to quit or else. Yeah, right. Sometimes she just wanted to cry. But what the hell good would that do?

Howie came into the room, followed by those two dumb groupies who followed the band everywhere. They huddled on the love seat, the two girls chattering about the show while Howie's head went back and forth between them like a ping pong ball. With his stutter, he had trouble getting a word in edgewise.

Groupies these days were a whole different kettle of fish. She'd known a lot of groupies in her time, and many of them had been personalities in their own right. Sure, they were damaged people in some way. Like, who wasn't? But that's what attracted them to the bands: the power to heal themselves through the music and through the men who made it. Not like now. Those girls were only looking for entertainment, for a good time, for an amusement park ride. They had not a clue what they were messing with. She had a clue. That's why she'd wasted almost twenty years on the road with different bands. But now she wondered, what the hell had she really done with her life? Had it really been worth it?

She heard voices in the hallway. Keith and Rob walked by, their latest conquests in tow, arguing about who had been off in one of the songs. Didn't even look in the room, those two going straight for the food as usual. That Rob ate like a horse.

George would already be off somewhere with a fan or two. That kid always went straight for the sex, as if he had to have as much as possible before the feast was taken away from him. He was a sexy little devil, no denying.

Sam appeared in the doorway, his arm slung across the shoulder of a woman in a bright red dress, looked to be in her thirties. That kid always went for the older ones, had made a play for her a bunch of times. He was a sweetie-pie, but she didn't do that scene anymore.

Sam looked at Howie and the two groupies, then noticed Ruth on the other side of the room.

"Hey, hot mama. Why didn't you tell ol' Sam you're off the market?" He put his free hand on his chest and grimaced like she'd broken his heart. He beamed at her and continued down the hallway with his companion.

She stared at the now-empty doorway. What the hell?

Randy came into view and bopped into the room. That kid spent too much time alone, lost in his own damn thoughts. He had his pick of groupies, but was always worried about hurting their feelings when he left them behind, said he couldn't do that to them. She told him he should found the Groupie Rescue League, take all these groupies out of their misery, starting with the ones sleeping with his brother Rob. Ruth got a good chuckle telling him that and seeing him actually think about it.

"Hey, where is everyone?" said Randy.

"Jack is doing an interview," said Howie, "and—"

"The others are chowing down next door," said Suze.

Randy's eyes went wide as he caught sight of Ruth, and he walked over to her. "Hey there, Ruth. Listen, I was wondering, well actually, I was thinking about it tonight while I was playing. If you get married, do you think you would still stay with us? I mean—"

"What? If I what?" asked Ruth.

"Oops, I don't think I was supposed to say anything. Could you forget I said that? OK, Ruth?"

He looked so earnest, she had to nod. He turned and fled the room.

She stood up and started pacing, took out her flask and took a swig. She was very sensitive to energy, and there was some crazy energy going on today. Usually she could get a sense of it, but this was really crazy shit. And off the market? Marriage? Who was spreading these crazy ass rumors about her? She wasn't even seeing anyone.

Dunk strode into the room and looked around. "Hey, Howie, ladies." They all said "hey" back to him.

He spotted Ruth, cocked his head to one side, and gave her one of those happy-sad smiles. He walked over, gathered her up in his arms, and gave her a long, tender hug.

This was so totally unexpected she didn't know how to react. She was stiff as a board, not a good advertisement for a chiropractor, but she wouldn't be able to relax until later when she had another joint. She stared at the wall, trying to make some sense of what was happening.

She heard Jack's voice as he entered the room. " ... have to introduce you to Dunk. He's the power behind the throne, so to speak."

Dunk released her and turned to face them, but kept his hand on her shoulder. It was Jack with that cowboy. What the hell was he doing here? She remembered his name. Clint Pomeroy. A nice name. A hard name to forget.

Dunk beamed at Clint, like he was proud of him for some reason. "Oh, we've met, haven't we, cowboy?"

Jack was still wearing his sweat-stained pirate costume, his makeup a bit smeared, and grinned at her in a dopey way, like a boy with a huge secret he was bursting to spill. "I think you already know Ruth."

How in the world would Jack know she'd met the cowboy? Had they been talking about her for some reason? That wasn't good.

Clint fingered the Stetson he was holding and stared at his boots, sneaking glances at her like he was shy or nervous or something. Suze was gripping Howie's shoulder and Carly had her hand across her mouth. They were all acting really weird.

Ruth shivered, not because of the air-conditioning but because everyone was giving her the damn heebie-jeebies.

Finally, when she thought she couldn't take it anymore, Clint peered at her as if he'd come to a decision and walked over to a spot directly in front of her. He was so tall he dwarfed her, and she was not a little woman. He looked down into her eyes. "Ruth, I ..."

As she looked up into those incredibly kind eyes, Ruth felt her world giving way. Everyone else faded into the background—Jack, Dunk, Howie, and the groupies—and all that seemed to matter was those eyes, looking down at her with unbounded kindness and some kind of solemn promise. Something burst in her heart, some coiled-up tension releasing and a maelstrom of conflicting and insistent emotions surging in—relief, hope, terror, joy. She started to cry. The floodgates now open, the energy pent up inside her for so many years rushed to make its way out. She sobbed uncontrollably, even hiccupping. Who was this embarrassing and out-of-control woman?

Clint lifted her into his arms and said something to the others. He carried her somewhere, deposited her on a bed, and held her in his arms, crooning to her. And she just knew: in that one moment, her life had changed forever.

Eighteen

JACK WATCHED Clint leave with Ruth cradled in his arms, a series of unexpected feelings roiling through him. Happiness for Ruth, who deserved to be taken care of by someone else for a change, given how devotedly she looked after the band and crew day in and day out. Only a smitten guy like Clint would have prevailed against that carapace she'd erected around herself. Also a bit of jealousy, Jack had to admit, because he'd always fancied Ruth but deemed it improper to come on to an employee, not to mention someone close to his mother's age. Truth be told, Ruth reminded him of Jane Fonda in some inexplicable way. But mostly it made him feel hope. If Ruth could find someone like Clint when she wasn't even looking, and when she was touring around the country with a rock band, maybe he could find someone too.

He raised his eyebrows at Dunk. "Wow."

"Yeah," said Dunk, looking dumbstruck.

Jack turned toward the others talking quietly on the loveseat. "Howie. Ladies. Would you mind leaving us alone?"

"Sure, Jack," said Howie. He trooped out with Suze and Carly.

Jack shut the door behind them and turned to face Dunk. He opened his mouth to speak, but Dunk beat him to it.

"Yer not a freak, just a flaming bawhead."

Jack smirked. "Thanks. I feel so much better."

"Ya gotta give the boys some slack or they're gonna break. Just ease up a bit."

Jack wasn't about to tell Dunk that Bill had said exactly the same thing, but about easing up on *him*. He wasn't going to give him that ammunition. Besides, they had a much more pressing problem than his less than stellar leadership. "I hear you, but listen. We've got much bigger fish to fry. Clint used to deal with Barry and said he's got a lot of dirty tricks."

"Wait. Clint the Cowboy knows Barry the Bastard?"

Jack started pacing. "He said Barry is a master at manufacturing expenses and cheating bands out of their hard-earned cash. Keeps you churning out one album after another and touring forever, and laughs all the way to the bank."

"So wait ..." Dunk looked confused.

"We've got to hire Clint. Now he's with Ruth, it shouldn't be too hard to convince him. Get him to chase the money—"

"Whoa, whoa, whoa," said Dunk, putting up his hands in a stop gesture. "Slow down, will ya? How do ya know all this?"

"I was doing the interview with Sid Jones and he said, 'That cowboy is an accounting genius. If I were you, I'd grab the guy.' So I grabbed Clint after Sid left, and it turns out that he worked for one of the Big Four accounting firms in New York and then ran his own firm handling bands like us. He knows all the record company tricks. I couldn't believe our luck."

Dunk beetled his eyebrows. "But he's a cowboy."

Jack smiled. "Yes. So he used to be Bernie Leibowitz until he converted to his true cowboy path in life this past year. Isn't that perfect? He's a freak, just like us."

Dunk did not look entirely convinced. "OK, first, speak for yourself. And second, I'll have Manny make a few calls—check him out, make sure he's legit—while I have a little talk with our Howie, see if he knows something."

Jack stopped pacing and faced him. "Do you really think Barry would send another spy, right after we discovered Howie? Would he be that stupid?"

"Howie was an amateur. I wouldn't put it past the bastard to up his game, send in a pro with the bonus at stake. So let's check out this Cowboy Clint, claiming to be former ace accountant Bernie Leibowitz, and make sure he's the real deal."

Jack scrunched up his face. "I don't know, Dunk. I think he's the real deal. You saw how he looked at Ruth, and how he carried her out of here. Let's be on our guard in case Barry does decide to send someone else. But seriously, who could he send now that we wouldn't suspect?"

"Yeah," said Dunk, grinning. "Who in their right mind would be daft enough to mess with us?"

Nineteen

THE NEXT MORNING, Lucy strolled into the lobby of the Albuquerque hotel where Pirate was staying. She didn't expect to run into any band members yet. Those young innocents Barry sent her to babysit—ha!—were likely holed up in their rooms, or someone else's, sleeping off a night of hard playing, followed by casual and extended debauchery with one or more willing partners. She knew the lifestyle of rock stars only too well from her time with Magnus.

She approached the front desk, bellboy in tow. The poor kid was struggling to lug the big black Samsonite suitcase she'd borrowed from her dad.

"May I help you, dear?" said the middle-aged woman behind the desk. Her nametag read "Janelle." She smiled at Lucy over her pink cat's eye glasses with rhinestone swirls on the edges. Lucy could tell she was eager for distraction.

"Oh, hi there, Janelle. I believe I have a suite booked ... on the top floor." She gave Janelle one of her most innocent smiles. There was no reason she couldn't get into this spy stuff and play her role to the hilt, have a little fun while she was earning her music contract. She already knew from experience that the band was likely to have the top floor. The hotel would want to keep the band as far away from the other guests as possible. And probably give them the suite, so if they damaged it, the hotel could get itself a nice little payout and replace the tired old furnishings with some brand new decor. These rock stars were such excellent guests.

"Oh no, hon. It couldn't be on the top two floors. They're completely booked out." Janelle leaned toward her like they were neighbors about to have a good gossip across the fence. She lowered her voice. "We've got that band Pirate here. Only eight of them and they've got two whole floors."

Lucy leaned toward Janelle and matched her hushed voice. "Really? That's crazy."

Janelle looked over at the bellboy. "Pete, could you go get a complimentary fruit basket for this guest, please?"

The bored teenage bellboy brightened and headed off for the kitchen.

"And don't hurry back," she called after him. She turned to Lucy. "I had to get rid of him. He's such a gossip. Now where was I?"

"Two whole floors," said Lucy. "Why would they have two whole floors? Are they having wild parties?"

"No, that's the thing of it. The lead singer—that's Jack, real sweetheart—and his personal assistant, Vic, have the entire top floor to themselves. Everyone else is on the next floor down, all bunched up together at the other end. Darnedest thing we've had since Mötley Crüe stayed here, but theirs was more sex type stuff, you know what I mean."

"Are Jack and Vic you know ... together?" Lucy said. That would make her assignment so much easier, if that intense lead singer was gay.

Janelle looked affronted. "No, they're both very manly. I don't see Jack all that much, except when he goes to perform all made up in his costume and makeup. He stays in his room most of the time. But Vic comes and goes quite a bit. And they're both quite handsome, if I don't say so myself as an old married lady. But look and don't touch, like I always say to Bob. That's my husband. Bob."

Lucy needed to get Janelle back on topic; the woman couldn't seem to tell a straight story. "So the rest of the band—"

"I've got all their pictures right here." Janelle darted her eyes around the lobby, empty except for one man reading a newspaper. "Come on around here, hon, and let me show you. Quick, quick."

After a moment's surprise, Lucy scurried behind the reception desk. This could be very helpful since she didn't have the names and faces of the band members down yet.

"Now let me assure you I'm not spying on them or anything. I might be a member of the Pirate fan club and read everything about them in the magazines. Them and Duran Duran. Love those boys. And sure, I might have died and gone to heaven when I heard Pirate was coming to stay here. But I'm a professional manager in pursuit of excellence, so their every wish is my sacred command."

Janelle held up the full-sized, autographed publicity photos like she was showing off wallet snaps of her own kids.

"So this one here is Sam. He's a happy boy, always smiling, talks kinda slow."

"He's a guitarist, isn't he?" said Lucy.

"Uh-huh," said Janelle. "And this here is Rob. He and Sam are always together. And this here is his brother, Randy. Rob told me he was born five minutes earlier and 200 IQ points smarter than his brother. That Rob, he's such a card."

"Oh, so Rob and Randy are twins?"

"Uh-huh," said Janelle. "Randy is the sweet one. Always stopping to ask me how I am. But oh lordy, does that boy need to get laid. He's wound as tight as my Playtex control top girdle."

Lucy laughed and Janelle smiled over her glasses at her. Janelle was clearly enjoying this distraction from her desk duties.

"This here is Keith. He's very serious and likes to practice his tunes in his room. That's what he calls them, his tunes. Strong accent, that one, sometimes can't understand what the heck he's saying. The opposite of this here George, hardly says a word. But it doesn't matter because mischief is written all over that boy's face. You watch out for that one, get your bra unclasped and your hooters hanging out before you have a clue what's happening."

"I will," said Lucy, grinning. "Thanks for the warning."

Lucy knew that if Cindy were here right now, she would be tutting and complaining up a storm. Why is she telling you all this? Is this any way for a hotel manager to act? How do you get people to tell you this kind of stuff? Cindy thought it was because Lucy looked like a puppy with her floppy long hair and big eyes. Lucy thought it was simply because people loved to talk given half a chance and a sympathetic ear. Her family was a major case in point. They *never* stopped talking. That's how she always knew *everything* that was going on. She just asked—and listened.

Janelle took out a key and unlocked a drawer. She pulled out another photo, encased in a plastic sleeve. "And this is my favorite, although I don't like to play favorites." She held up a photo of Jack for Lucy to see, but didn't hand it to her like she had the others. "See the inscription? I made a call for Jack ..." She leaned closer to Lucy. "To a lady in London."

"Oh, yeah? Does he have a girlfriend there?"

"I think so," said Janelle. "But that Vic, I think he's single if you're in the market. Are you ... in the market?" Janelle stared over her glasses at Lucy.

Lucy blurted the first thing that came to mind. "I'm here to check out the band ... for a record label." Damn, damn, damn. She shouldn't have said that. It was too close to the truth.

"Oh, you're the one from Dolos Discs," said Janelle. "Why didn't you say so? I got your key, *Miss Wonderly*." Janelle winked at her. "And a message from Sam Spade."

Janelle handed her the key and the message slip. It was perfect timing, just as Pete came around the corner with a little fruit basket.

Janelle looked at the bellboy with exasperation. "Pete, you take Miss Wonderly and her luggage up to her room, and then you come right back down and get her a *big* fruit basket. You tell that Leon to give her the works, you hear me?"

"Yes, ma'am," said Pete, sighing and slumping his small shoulders.

Janelle turned back to Lucy. "Anything you need, you let me know, Miss Wonderly." She winked at her, and Lucy grinned back.

Pete juggled the fruit basket in one arm while trying to pick up Lucy's oversized suitcase with the other.

"Let me carry the fruit, Pete. I can't wait to eat one of those peaches." Lucy smiled at him and looked in his eyes as she removed the basket from his arm.

He stared at her, rooted in place.

"C'mon, Pete, get a move on," said Janelle. "Remember our corporate mantra—Efficiency Plus Effectiveness Equals Excellence."

Facing away from Janelle, Lucy smirked at Pete.

He gave her a goofy smile back.

She turned and headed toward the elevator, glancing back at Pete as he resumed his struggle to drag her uncooperative suitcase. "I bet you're really strong from moving all these heavy suitcases around."

"Yes, ma'am," said Pete. "I've gained five pounds, all in my arms."

"Call me Lucy," she said as the elevator door opened.

One of the band members emerged and walked right past her.

She held the door open as Pete maneuvered the suitcase in and put it down. She got in next to him, clutching the fruit basket and trying to act nonchalant, even though she was starting to feel a bit nervous.

Pete pushed the floor button with an air of authority and self-importance.

Lucy watched as Keith turned around right when the doors were closing and looked at her, a puzzled expression on his face. That one is certainly up early, she thought.

Twenty

KEITH WALKED over to Janelle at the reception desk. "Hey, I think I know that chick."

Janelle leaned toward him and whispered, "She's with Dolos Discs, here to check out the band. But"—she gave him a meaningful look—"you didn't hear it from me."

Keith made a gesture like he was sealing his lips and gave her a conspiratorial smile. "You're a babe, Janelle."

"Oh, you go on," said Janelle with a flirty smile and a wave of her hand. "I'm an old married lady."

Keith grinned and winked at her as he turned and made his way toward the rear door of the lobby. The chicks, always putty in his hands, even the older ones. He could make a living as a gigolo if his rock career petered out. But that wasn't going to happen because he'd do whatever it took to stay in the scene and keep making music. This was his *life*.

He rushed past the pool, where people were sunning themselves and enjoying the refreshing water before it got too damn hot. He could never live here, the desert heat like a sauna that bathed you in sweat within minutes. He'd never been a sauna guy, but a Jacuzzi with a willing chick or two? Now you're talking.

He let himself out through the gate into the hotel parking lot, and zigzagged through parked cars to the far end of the lot where the band's two buses were parked. Jack always insisted that the buses stay at the hotel within easy reach in case he needed an escape. But then Jack and Dunk had a much more luxurious bus and didn't have to share it with a bunch of kids like Keith did. He should be on the management bus too. Of course Rob was taking full advantage of the situation, using the band bus for "other" activities and paying Mick to look the other way. A few Benjamin Franklins and Mick would do anything. Unlike that Gus. You'd have to pry his cold, dead fingers off the management bus before he'd let anyone but Jack or Dunk use it.

Keith knocked on the door of the band bus, waited a moment and knocked again. A bald guy in a muscle shirt and arms covered with tattoos opened the door and let him in. Must be a member of the crew, probably enjoying some rare time off.

"Ya gotta do something before this asshole cleans us all out," the guy said before Keith could say anything.

The bus reeked of pot and stale beer, more so than usual. Keith followed the bald guy back to the galley table, where a card game was in full swing. Rob and two muscled hulks were looking at the cards in their hands, a reject pile and a big pile of cash between them.

Keith had no clue what they were playing, had never had any interest in games. Where was the fun in learning and following someone else's rules? Or in playing with bits of paper with pictures and numbers on them? Once he picked up a guitar in middle school, that was it for him. Love at first sight with something that gave him unending pleasure. He didn't need anything else, except getting laid and hanging with the lads. And getting fed. A man did have some requirements of a non-musical nature.

The bald guy sat down, picked up his cards, and furrowed his brow.

"We gotta talk, man," Keith said to Rob. "Like now."

"OK, hold your horses," said Rob. "I'll finish this hand, and then we'll talk."

Keith paced and bit his fingernail as the card game continued. After a few rounds, Rob laid down his hand. "Read 'em and weep, ladies. Read 'em and weep."

"Goddam you all to hell, you cheatin' limey bastard," said the bald guy as Rob gathered up his winnings. "I know you're cheatin', I just don't know how."

"Yeah, ya cleaned me out," said one of the others. "How'm I s'pose to get through the next week?"

"You play with me, you play to win," said Rob as he put the cash in his pocket.

"We did play to win, ya cheatin' s.o.b."

"C'mon, c'mon," said Keith as he manhandled Rob toward the exit. Keith didn't think any punches were about to be thrown, but he didn't want to take any chances. He hustled Rob off the bus. When they descended onto the pavement, Keith grabbed Rob's upper arm to stop him from leaving.

Rob swung around to face Keith, still flushed and distracted from the excitement of the game.

"Listen, man," said Keith. "A chick from Dolos is here. I saw her getting into the lift."

"Dolos sent a chick?" said Rob. "Like what? A gift?"

Keith rolled his eyes. "No, ya daft ape. I mean someone checking out the talent. Checking *us* out."

"What?" Rob looked thoroughly confused. "Why?"

"So OK," said Keith. "I mighta called Barry the Bastard and had a chat. I was going to tell you, but you was otherwise occupied."

Rob smiled at the memory of something. "Oh, yeah."

"I said 'Listen, Barry, me and Rob, we're not happy and the other guys aren't neither. We know the contract's ending and you'd be looking at all your options. And me and Rob, we think might be better for all concerned if we take over the band. We got lots of tunes in the can, guaranteed number ones, but current management won't even let us play them.'"

"So what'd he say?"

Keith grabbed both of Rob's upper arms and looked him dead in the eye to make sure he had his full attention. "He said, and I quote, 'That's a very interesting proposition, Keith. A very interesting proposition. Why don't you call me every day and fill me in on things, so I get the full picture. 'Cause I gotta convince the powers-to-be here it's the right move, capiche?'"

"Capiche? What's that mean?"

"That's I-talian, like when you say 'You getting me, man?' and I say 'I got ya, man.' Capiche? Capiche."

"I like it. Capiche? Capiche."

Keith took on a very serious expression. "But listen, mum's the word. Ya don't tell Sam. Ya don't tell Randy. Ya don't tell nobody, yeah?" He made the same seal-the-lips gesture he'd made with Janelle. "This is our little secret—you, me, and Barry the Bastard—for the next six concerts. Then it's read 'em and weep, Jack. Read 'em and weep. Capiche?"

Rob smiled. "Capiche."

Keith held out his hand. "Now gimme the dosh you owe me. And lend me a couple Ben Franklins, would ya? I'm a little low."

Rob pulled out his wad of winnings, peeled off five hundred, and handed it to Keith.

Keith put it in his pocket. As nonchalant as possible he said, "You don't cheat at cards, do ya? They're just crap players, yeah?"

"Me? Cheat?" Rob smiled mischievously. When Keith continued to stare at him, he said, "Naw, course not. I count 'em. It's the only way to win."

"Yeah, thought so." Keith pretended to be looking for something in his pockets. "I think I left me comb on the bus. You go ahead, I'll catch up." As Rob headed toward the lobby, Keith boarded the bus and went back to the galley. He found the bald guy and the other two members of the crew still sitting there smoking spliffs and drinking cans of Budweiser.

"Listen, guys," said Keith, "he kinda owned up. He did use one little trick. It wasn't really cheatin', but it wasn't exactly a level playing field, ya get me drift. So he wanted ya to have this back." He threw the five hundred down on the table.

The bald guy grabbed the cash and counted it. "Thanks, man. Me and the guys, we got another problem with Rob. About the grass he's selling us. We think he's ripping us off, but he says he got costs. We can't figure it, can we, fellas? Like, what costs?"

The other two guys nodded.

"Don't seem fair," he went on, "how hard we're working and all to make him and the band look good. Guy needs a toke end of the day, what with all the aches and pains go with the job. Forget to buy it when it's there, then find you need it and hafta go to Rob. So we says to one another, not fair, is it? He should be giving us a fair price, shouldn't be ripping us off, should he?"

The other two guys, still nodding, said, "Yeah."

The bald guy stared earnest and unblinking at Keith, waiting for a response.

Keith looked back at him. OK, he hadn't expected this. But if he was going to lead the band going forward, this kind of thing came with the territory and he needed to step up and take control. "Leave it with me, yeah? I'll chat to Rob and make sure he's giving ya a fair price."

"Thanks, man," said the bald guy, saluting Keith with his can of Bud and taking a swig.

Twenty-One

LUCY STOOD in her hotel room and opened the message from "Sam Spade." It was written in barely legible writing on one of those hotel message slips.

She read it aloud. "Miss Wonderly, guard tresure Calfornia and call for reword. Sam Spade."

She looked at it, puzzled. What the heck does that mean? Maybe Pete the bellboy wrote it when Janelle had to run to the Ladies, or something.

One thing she knew for sure. She had not signed up to be that two-faced murderess Miss Wonderly. She had agreed to be a babysitter and keep the band out of trouble. That was it. Hardly Miss Wonderly. She crumpled up the paper and threw it in the direction of the trash bin. It missed and landed on the floor nearby. Oh, well.

Pete the bellboy had put her suitcase on the luggage rack. Lucy unzipped it and flung the top cover over the side, letting it clang against the rack. Hands on hips, she eyed the tangle of clothing and shoes she'd thrown willy-nilly into the suitcase the evening before. She'd never been a good packer, unlike her meticulous mother. She rummaged through the mess and growled with frustration as she couldn't find anything to wear. Pulling out each piece of clothing, she held it up to inspect it and flung it over her head toward the bed.

"What to wear? What to wear? I need to be sexy, but record executive sexy, not groupie sexy ... Oh, I know." She pawed through the rest of the clothes and pulled out her favorite outfit from her days with Magnus. She always felt great in this.

An hour later and she was ready to go. She'd gotten her outfit pressed in record time, thanks to the efficient, effective, and excellent Janelle. She'd scarfed down some food, thanks to room service. And she'd taken a shower and washed her hair to get rid of that travel smell.

She'd also concealed the massive bags under her eyes. Rhonda had reserved one of the Dolos corporate jets to get her from Binghamton to Albuquerque that morning. She'd gotten little sleep at home, her parents so excited to have her there, and no sleep on the four-hour flight because she'd been too busy talking to the flight crew and enjoying the luxurious amenities. The pilots had even let her join them in the cockpit, explained all the controls, and let her fly the plane—under their attentive guidance. She'd promised not to tell anyone. Apparently that was a no-no.

She looked at herself in the full-length mirror and was satisfied with the overall result. She hadn't worn makeup in her three years at the ashram, being a sexual renunciate and all. But to her relief, it turned out that putting on makeup was like riding a bicycle; you never forgot your old tricks. The bags under her eyes were invisible under concealer, foundation and powder, and her blood red lipstick and sparkly blue eye shadow helped draw attention away to other parts of her face. She adjusted her clothes to make them a bit sexier, checked her teeth for lipstick, and wiped away some stray mascara below her eye.

She smiled at herself in the mirror. "OK, you pirates. Ready or not, here I come."

Twenty-Two

JANELLE ARRANGED a taxi to take Lucy to the arena. She said she'd seen Dunk round up the band—except for Jack—to take them over there for something called a sound check. So that's where Lucy would find them. Bless that all-knowing, ultra-helpful Janelle.

On the ride over, Lucy avoided conversation with the driver and peered out the window at the passing scenery. She needed to come up with a believable cover story. She wasn't even sure how she was going to talk her way into the arena. She bit her lip in concentration. Who was she? Why was she here? What would they believe? What would convince them to let her stay and hang out with the band until the end of the tour? Think, Lucy, think.

How about I miss the rock 'n' roll lifestyle, and it's your lucky day, boys, because I've decided to become your devoted groupie? Well, at least, for the next six concerts. No, that was ridiculous. They'd yawn and roll their eyes, and the beautiful young girls hanging off them would sneer at her. "A groupie at your age?" they'd say. Twenty-two *was* old for a groupie.

How about I watched your video on MTV and fell in love with one of you? That might work, but which one? It would have to be that sensitive one, Randy. No, she couldn't do that. She'd violate her renunciate status in the ashram and she couldn't play around with his feelings like that.

Maybe she should tell them, straight out, she was there to babysit them. Isn't that what she'd spent most of her previous time on the road doing anyway? Soothing off-their-head and out-of-control musicians. Persuading them to sleep it off. Dispatching unwanted groupies. Healing rifts between the guys. Holding heads over toilets and, on a few occasions, dealing with overdoses. People thought it was glamorous and exciting to tour with a rock band, but, really, she'd spent most of the time being a mom and a therapist—to the band, the crew, the groupies. Even members of other bands sought her out for advice. If she'd had the good sense to charge them, she'd be sitting pretty right now. That said, she'd managed to get what she really wanted out of the bargain—to be close to the music and learn about composing and singing. All in all, it had been worth it. But these Pirate guys, they wouldn't have a clue who she was after she'd been away from the scene for three years. A babysitter, you say? Get the heck out of here.

Damn, she was too tired. Nothing even halfway believable and persuasive was coming to her. What if they didn't let her in? What if they didn't want her around? She'd lose out on the recording contract. She'd have to think of something in the moment. She'd just have to.

The taxi arrived at the arena and stopped near the artists' entrance. The driver jumped out and rushed to open the door for her. She pulled out the envelope of money she'd been handed on the plane to cover travel expenses, courtesy of that lovely Rhonda. No doubt Barry wouldn't have been so generous. She handed the taxi guy a twenty-dollar bill for a four-dollar fare, and he protested that it was too much, but she waved his protest away. Barry had a lot of money and this guy had a smelly old taxi. Maybe it was immature, but she wanted to get back at that oily old slickster who'd lied to her about the band and was probably lying about other things as well, and who had the nerve to call her Miss Wonderly.

Lucy started walking toward the artists' entrance, wobbling a bit on her platform shoes. How the heck had she worn these things for years? They were like stilts.

Two men chatted as they leaned against the wall next to the

entrance. As she approached, they glanced over at her and one of them did a double take.

"Lucy?" The guy pushed off the wall and stood to attention. "Lucy, is that you?"

The other guy stopped talking and stood to attention as well.

"Jigsy?" It couldn't be! She ran up to him and hugged him. "What are you doing here?"

"I'm running the arena." He showed her his assistant manager badge with a look of pride. "Had a kid. Lenore put her foot down. Said we're gonna do this right, settle down somewhere, and give this kid a good life. So guess what, here we are."

"You're still with Lenore? And you have a kid?" Lucy's eyes teared up. "I'm so happy for you."

Jigsy turned to the other man. "Bruce, this here's the famous Lucy L'amour."

Bruce's eyes opened wide. "Lucy L'amour? *The* Lucy L'amour?"

She smiled at him and he stared back at her. The rock world was so silly, always giving people dramatic names. Magnus said he couldn't be with plain old Lucy Sabatini, how boring. So he'd anointed her Lucy L'amour and always addressed her as Lucy Love. "Get me a drink, Lucy Love" or "You're not going out in that, Lucy Love." He'd always thought it was so clever and funny.

She smiled at Bruce. "No, what you should be saying is Jigsy, *the* Jigsy? Have you ever watched this guy handle power tools? Out comes this work of art like you never could've imagined. Remember that staircase you made for Magnus?"

"Oh, cut it out. I'm not that good," said Jigsy, looking both embarrassed and pleased. "So what the hell happened? You disappeared." He snapped his fingers. "Just like that."

She pulled a fib out of thin air. "Oh, you know, got tired of being on the road. Decided to take myself off to ... India and all. Hang out with a swami for a while." Part of that was true. She'd say some Hail Marys later for the part that wasn't.

"Lenore thought maybe it was, you know ... Buffalo."

Heat flushed her cheeks and she looked down at the ground. Three years and she still couldn't hear the word "Buffalo" without feeling overwhelmed. At least she no longer went to pieces when someone said it. "No—"

"No, no. Sorry I brought that up." Jigsy rushed to change the subject. "You coming to see Pirate?"

Lucy looked up at him and let out a breath she didn't know she was holding. "Yes, I'm here for Pirate." At least this was the truth.

Jigsy opened the door for her. "I'll put your name on the list. You come and go as you please. So great to see you, Luce."

She gave him a grateful smile. "Thanks, Jigs. You too. Congratulations to you and Lenore on having a kid. Can you tell her 'hi' for me?"

"Sure thing," said Jigsy.

She turned to Bruce. "And nice to meet you."

He just stared back at her.

Jigsy pointed down the hallway. "So the band's room is three doors down on the right, and the hospitality room right before that. The band should be in there any time now."

She smiled and touched his arm as she walked past him into the building. Jigsy smiled back and pulled the door shut behind her. Their voices started up again, but she couldn't hear what they were saying. Probably something about Buffalo. She seemed to be defined by that now, rather than the rest of the time she spent on the road with Magnus. But, of course, their entire lives had been changed and defined by Buffalo. She and Magnus.

She stood inside the entrance and gathered her wits. Miracle of miracles, she was in. Well, maybe not a miracle because arena rock was a small world and she was bound to run across people she knew. But she could come and go as she pleased today, while the band was here in Albuquerque. Hallelujah!

Now she could concentrate on the next challenge—embedding herself in the band. Not bedding them, as someone else in her place might do. But winning their trust so they let her hang out with them until the end of the tour. It hadn't seemed like such a big deal when Barry said it on the phone. "Just babysit my band for a few concerts and I'll give you the recording contract." She'd fallen right into his well-laid trap, focusing on the recording contract and neglecting to think about what she would have to do to earn it. But in her defense, he hadn't given her any time to think. She had to make the decision in an hour and get on the plane the next morning. That Barry, such a trickster. She'd have to make darn sure he didn't weasel his way out of giving her the contract.

OK, time for action, Lucy Goose. She peered down the hallway, trying to ignore the butterflies flitting about in her stomach. She fluffed her hair, smoothed her clothes, and checked that her hoop earrings were firmly attached while taking several deep breaths to calm herself.

Truth be told, she was anxious about returning to this crazy world after being in a well-ordered, quiet, predictable ashram for three years. She was nervous about being accepted by a bunch of pampered rock stars. And she was terrified of being back in an arena and getting anywhere near the stage. Maybe she should just leave and go back to the ashram. Oh, that's right, Lucy, you can't do that either, because the swami has fired you from running the music program and "promoted" you to the privileged role of serving as his personal assistant. You lucky girl, you.

As she stood there debating with herself, a man came out of the hospitality room and stood in the hallway, looking down at a folded magazine in his hand and pursing his lips. Judging from the MTV video she'd watched with Nana and the photos Janelle had shown her, she didn't think he was a member of the band, although who knew what Jack St James actually looked like under his elaborate costume and makeup. The other band members weren't so glammed up, for some reason; she'd recognized Keith the moment she laid eyes on him. This guy was in a Pirate t-shirt and jeans. He wore what looked to be a classic Patek Philippe watch on his left wrist and had a pricy rock star haircut. Magnus used to pay a fortune for that sleek devilish look.

Showtime, Lucy! She forced herself to start walking toward him, despite another part of her wanting to run back out the door. One of her platform shoes scuffed the floor and he swiveled his head to look in her direction. Too late now, she'd been spotted. The game was on.

He stared at her as she came toward him. She focused on walking with her head held high and her hips swaying back and forth. She hoped she looked regal and saucy, not totally ludicrous the way she actually felt. He might not have been a member of the band, but he was clearly *with* the band, which meant she probably needed to impress him, or at least get on his good side. You never knew who had influence with the band and who didn't. He had that look the swami had, that master-of-my-universe look. And now that she was getting closer, she could also see how good-looking he was. Lucy's cheeks burned as he stared at her. His look was so direct and intense, like he was trying to decide whether she was friend or foe. Her face flushed hotter. Darn it, not the first impression she wanted to give, blushing like a silly little schoolgirl.

Twenty-Three

JACK WATCHED her coming toward him. How did *she* get in? There was no one else around, none of the band members or crew. Dunk would have to have a word with arena management about their lax security procedures. She didn't look like a security risk, he had to admit. You couldn't hide anything in those sky blue flare trousers that hugged her slender hips, or that red and white striped tube top that left her arms and shoulders bare. No, with that outfit she looked like she could have been on the cover of some teen girl magazine in the seventies. Even ironed, it looked like it had seen better days.

But who cared? His breath hitched just looking at her. She had a sexy little navel peeking out from her tube top as she moved, and her long shiny hair swung from side to side, revealing big gold hoop earrings dangling from the cutest little ears. Her bright red lips, he couldn't take his eyes off them. As she got closer, he watched her face turn bright red as well. He shouldn't be staring at her like this—it was rude—but he couldn't tear his eyes away.

"Oof!" she said as she tripped on her platform shoe and pitched toward him.

Without thinking, he caught her in his arms and broke her fall. She turned her head and looked up at him surprised, with those green ...

wait a second, no, they were brown ... no, no, they were hazel ... those startled hazel eyes. He realized he'd been stroking her arm as he stared into them. Her arm was so soft. She felt so   comfy. A part of him didn't want to let her go.

Fortunately, another part of him quickly brought him back to his senses. He lifted her upright and helped her stand up. He could *not,* under any circumstances, allow her or anyone else to distract him right now. He had to keep the band under control and make sure they made it intact until the end of the tour. He had to keep his eyes on the ball—and ensure they got that bonus—not on a very tempting little damsel like this one.

She seemed a tad unsteady on her feet, so again, being the gentleman he'd been raised to be, he kept hold of her arm. Time to go into his Victor persona. He couldn't have her revealing his real identity to anyone, not even this late in the tour. No telling what damage it could do.

"Allo, I'm Vic," he said. He loved doing a Cockney accent. "And 'oo might you be, princess?"

"Um, I'm Lucy," she said, peering up at him through her eyelashes. She tried to push her hair back off her face.

Again, being the gentleman he was, he did it for her.

"Perfect," he said without thinking.

Jack couldn't stop staring at those lips. He was dying to kiss them. His traitor mouth moved in their direction, but he managed to regain control and divert it to her right ear. "I'm wif the band, me love. So whatevah you need, whatevah at all, don't be shy. Jus' let me know, Lucy love."

He released her arm and strode off down the corridor. After going around a corner where she wouldn't see, he stopped and hit the wall. Idiot! What was he thinking acting like that? He needed to talk to Dunk. This was not good, not good at all. He needed to get his senses back under his complete and total control and focus on his work. Not on "Lucy love," but on his work. Dunk had to get rid of that girl, whoever she was. She had to go.

Twenty-Four

LUCY WATCHED him stride away and round the corner in a state of bewilderment. What the heck just happened? She felt desired and dumped all in the space of ten seconds. And she was equally confused by the lingering scent of his cologne. It smelled like a strange combination of Wipe-It-Fresh and Paco Rabanne. She'd never smelled anything like it.

Well, now she'd met Vic, the personal assistant to Jack St James. Rather than having her removed from the arena, he'd offered to help her. That was a good start. However, Janelle had neglected to warn her about how direct and intense he was, just like the lead singer. What was it with these Pirate guys? Keith had stared at her too. They seemed alert and focused, not high or strung out like a lot of rock guys. That meant she couldn't rely on slipping into the maternal role with them, like she often had in the Magnus days. She'd have to keep her wits about her.

Jigsy had said the band members would show up soon in the hospitality room. So maybe she should wait in there and think about what happened with Vic. She wasn't going anywhere near the stage, that was for sure. She walked over to the door of the hospitality room and looked in.

A young woman in chef's whites was alone, pacing back and forth and talking to herself. "George, before we go any further, I need to know—" The young woman cut herself off as she caught sight of Lucy.

"Just looking for the band," Lucy said, making a sorry-to-disturb-you gesture.

"Oh, no, that's fine. They went to do their sound check and said they'd come back for some lunch before they do their rehearsal."

Lucy walked over to her and extended her hand. "I'm Lucy."

"Alison," the other woman said, shaking her hand. "Don't worry, you'll know when they're coming. They sound like a herd of elephants."

Lucy grinned. "I take it you're practicing a talk with one of those elephants. The hairy one. George."

Alison grinned back. "Yeah."

"You're seeing him?"

Alison got a troubled look on her face. "Well, only since yesterday, actually. But he's already ... well, he's ..."

Lucy gestured for Alison to come sit with her at a table. "Should we sit? Until they come?"

Alison nodded, a look of relief on her face. They pulled out chairs and sat down across from one another.

Lucy smiled at her. "So let me guess. He's already trying to unclasp your bra and get your hooters out, or worse. Am I right?"

"Yes! How did you know?"

"Oh, I heard about him from Janelle. She's the lady at the front desk in the hotel where I'm staying, and the band is staying there too. Well, really, I followed them there, but ..." Lucy noticed Alison looking confused. "But, also, I've got a lot of experience with guys like George."

Alison played nervously with her fingers. "He seemed really attentive at first, not like the others, who were all busy hitting on me. Or that Jack, who pretends to be listening but is watching your every move to make sure you don't do anything wrong."

"Oh, yeah?" Lucy stored away this knowledge for future reference. Jack was a perfectionist, was he? That figured.

"George really listened, y'know? I thought he was interested in me ... as a person. But then all of a sudden I find myself kissing him, right there in front of all the guys. And within seconds he has his tongue down my throat, and then he's trying to sneak his hand inside my uniform. He swore he hasn't done a threesome, but I don't believe that for a second."

Lucy laughed and Alison looked offended.

Lucy put her hand on Alison's and cocked her head. "I've spent a lot of time around rock bands. Let me give you Lucy's Guide to the Rock Stars. I think that might help."

"OK," said Alison, sounding skeptical.

Lucy looked up at the ceiling and counted on her fingers, then looked over at Alison. "There are at least six different types of rock star. Here we go. Number one. What I call Old Faithful. That's a guy like Charlie Watts in the Rolling Stones. He's been married to Shirley for twenty years and wouldn't think of cheating on her. There aren't a lot of guys like him around, at least among the younger guys. Too much temptation. Are you with me so far?"

"Yeah," said Alison.

"Then you've got the complete opposite, what I call the Sex God. That's usually your lead singer, sometimes the lead guitarist, and any guy in a band who's really hot. Those guys can have it all. The gorgeous wife, and the family, and all the sex they want with anyone else on the planet. They're the quarterback in high school who gets the head cheerleader *and* the rest of the cheerleading team in the locker room or under the bleachers, if they want them. You know the type."

Alison stared at her, horrified. "I think George might be a Sex God."

"Well, let me tell you the others, so you can know for sure. You've also got the Dad. He wants to be a good guy and makes a real stab at being a family man. But he can't resist all the goodies offered by the rock 'n' roll lifestyle. So he goes through one addiction after another, and keeps losing one wife and picking up a new one. But he always takes care of the kids. That's the thing about this type. He's a really devoted dad."

Alison grimaced. "That doesn't sound so good ... to me."

"Oh, you ain't heard nothing yet. There's also the Pollinator. That's the guy who comes, gets you pregnant, and leaves. Love 'em and leave 'em, as they say. He can't be bothered with birth control, that's your responsibility, and if you get pregnant, hey, that's your problem for not protecting yourself. If you take the kid to see him, it makes no difference whatsoever. You have to take him to court, and even when you've proven paternity, you have to fight him every step of the way."

"Who would want a guy like that?"

"Are you kidding?" said Lucy. "Lots of women. The Pollinators are usually incredibly charming and great fun to be with, until they grow tired of you. And they can be amazing in bed, from what I hear. Not like the Jackrabbit. That's the guy who can never get enough sex. You're just one in a long line of women he picks out of the crowd. In and out in ten minutes. Slam, bam, thank you, ma'am."

"Oh, no! George might be a Jackrabbit."

"And last but not least, there's what I call the Leprechaun. He's totally hard to resist with a mischievous smile and a sparkle in his eye. He likes the ladies and lets them know it. I call him the Leprechaun because he loves to party, but don't try to pin him down, he has to be free, even when he's married. He's a funner, more down-to-earth version of the Sex God."

Alison furrowed her brow and bit her thumbnail.

Lucy smiled at her. "So, sweetie, it depends on what you want ... and what you don't want."

Alison looked surprised. "But doesn't everyone want Old Faithful?"

"No," said Lucy. "Not at all. There are all kinds of women, too. Sex Goddesses. Lovers. Sirens. Divas. Bosses. Ladies. Queens. Mommies. Devoted Wives. You get the picture. And they all want different things."

Alison stared at Lucy. "What kind are you?"

Lucy laughed. "Oh, that's easy. I'm a Greek-Italian Catholic girl with a Nana who told me to act like a fox and gave me a Rabbit—"

"What?" Alison looked horrified.

"No, no, that didn't come out right. Forget about me. The question is what kind of man *you* want, and whether George is that type of man."

"I want a Charlie Watts, that's what I want," said Alison with conviction.

"Then I think your man might be sweet little Randy rather than mischievous George. If that Janelle is to be believed."

Alison looked unsure. Lucy had to admit that George was very good-looking in that he-man kind of way and would be hard to resist. She felt sorry for Alison, who clearly was not used to dealing with entitled and temperamental rock stars and could get emotionally hurt, or even knocked up. Lucy felt a responsibility to make sure that didn't happen to Alison, like other girls had done for her.

"I have an idea. Here's what I think you should do to figure this out." Lucy outlined a plan to her. It might work or it might not, but she thought it was definitely worth a try.

Alison stopped biting her nail and grinned. "Really? You think that might work?" She thought for a moment. "OK, I'll do it. But can you be here too?"

"Are you kidding? I wouldn't miss it." She leaned toward Alison. "In the meantime, I want you to tell me everything you know about this Vic guy."

Twenty-Five

"I GOTTA FINISH, doll. I got company."

Barry took another puff on his cigar and exhaled slowly.

A woman's voice with a heavy Long Island accent came from under the desk. "You're too tense. Relax already."

"I'm trying, I'm trying."

Barry needed a new chick to fantasize about. Problem was, his fantasies were all getting too stale, didn't do it for him anymore. So who could he use that he hadn't used yet?

All of a sudden it came to him—that hippie chick. He started thinking about Lucy Sabatini whirling in front of him like he'd seen her do up to that communist place, then stripping off pieces of clothing one by one while looking at him like a porn star.

"Aaaaaaaah!" he yelped as he came. Wow, that was fast. He'd have to use that fantasy again. But save it for occasions when he didn't have much time and knew he really needed to get off. Like right before board meetings when his blood pressure would be going through the roof, which was pretty much all the time these days.

He zipped up his trousers and fastened his leather belt, pushed away from the desk and stood up. A woman crawled out from the cavernous space underneath and looked up at him.

"What's with you today? I told you, get yourself some Valium already. I never seen such a tense cock."

He shrugged and took another puff on his cigar. He wasn't going to take any fuckin' Valium. That was for sissies. He watched as she pushed herself to her feet.

She went over to her oversized purse, rummaged around, and took out a lipstick. She moved in front of the mirror on the wall and redid her lips. Some kind of orange color. Like a tangerine.

Barry put his cigar in the ashtray and pulled a billfold out his back pocket. He took out some cash and threw it on the desk.

"Listen, doll, I got some people waiting—"

"I know, I know. I saw 'em when I came in." She grabbed the cash from the desk and shoved it in the purse. She walked to the door and turned to face him. "See ya Thursday. And you get yourself some Valium or I'm gonna double charge ya."

He gave her a dismissive gesture. She opened the door and walked out, leaving the door open behind her.

"Rhonda, send 'em in," he yelled.

An indistinct woman's voice could be heard outside, followed by a man's response.

Almost immediately, Swami Zukeeni appeared in the doorway. Continuing to puff on his cigar, Barry watched as the swami stopped short on the threshold and looked around. Like the guy was thinking of buying the place, and yes, this place would do.

The swami grinned and sauntered toward him, taking his sweet little time as he stopped to look at all the signed photographs on the walls, Barry with his famous clients—bands and singers that were household names. That's right, swami, you're lucky I'm giving you the time of day. The swami caressed the arm of the white leather couch with his fingertips. That's right, Swami, hand-tooled Italian leather. Big enough to hold a decent-sized orgy, and yes, to answer your unspoken question, I have been so inclined.

The Ram-a-Ding-Dong character followed closely behind the swami, almost bumping into him, all tense and nervous. That guy could do with a good B.J. right now. Barry expected the both of them might need one after this meeting.

They were wearing their ashram duds, looked to be their fancy ones. Dressed to the nines to come to the Big Apple and see him. Some sort of loose robe in that color all them spiritual types went for, reminded Barry of mustard. And them white trousers looked like they might fall down around their ankles any minute. The two of 'em smelled to high heaven, probably using all that oil shit in their hair those Asian types went for. Piece of dark blue cloth wound round their heads, made 'em look like snake charmers. Not going to be able to charm him, that was for sure. And the piece de resistance of their get-ups—leather sandals like they were still in India or something. You just couldn't make this shit up.

The swami reached Barry's desk, a big grin on his face and his head nodding in approval. He extended his hand toward Barry. "Mr. Bartholomew, let us shake on this auspicious day in the Sanskrit calendar, and on our blossoming relationship as partners in the making of beautiful and life-changing music."

Forward prick, wasn't he? Barry took a puff, staring at the swami's hand. The swami narrowed his eyes and waited. When Barry thought it was long enough, he transferred the cigar to his other hand and shook the swami's. Now that they were clear on who was boss.

"Sit." Barry gestured to the chairs in front of his desk.

The swami and Ram-a-Ding-Dong sat down, making a big show of gathering and arranging their robes like they were holy men. Holy men, my ass. If they're holy men, he was the fuckin' Dalai Lama.

Ram-a-Ding-Dong lifted his briefcase onto his lap and opened it. The swami put his hand on the lid and lowered it back down. Ram-a-Ding-Dong looked over at him and the swami flashed him a warning look. These two were like a comedy double act—Dean Martin and Jerry Lewis.

"My colleague here, Ramakarshivenenda, has been paving the way for this unprecedented advancement within the ashram," said the swami, giving Barry that ridiculous stare of his. "We are a simple organization and unused to all the glamour of your world, Mr. Bartholomew." He waved his hand toward the photos and couch. "Yet we strive to honor and worship the divine through our musical offerings. And we cannot ignore it when the universe brings us an opportunity like this to do so in a more profound and profligate way."

Profligate? Barry took a puff on his cigar to hide his smile. The swami was very entertaining, you had to give him that. And he'd make a superb marketing director, if he ever wanted to get on the corporate bandwagon.

"Ya brought the contract?" said Barry.

"Yes, our law firm has reviewed it and given their approval."

Barry stifled his smile again. Yeah, sure.

Ram-a-Ding-Dong looked at the swami. "Now?"

A spurt of irritation flitted across the swami's face. "Yes, now, Ramakarshivenenda." The swami smiled at Barry and crossed one leg over the other to appear relaxed and confident.

Ram-a-Ding-Dong took the contract out of the briefcase and stood up to hand it over, forgetting he had the briefcase in his lap. It fell to the floor—bang!—and a bunch of papers spilled out all over the carpet. The putz looked panicked, got down on his hands and knees—again, who could make this shit up?—and rushed to gather up all the papers and shove them back into the briefcase. Then, no kidding, Ding Dong sat back in the chair with the briefcase in his lap and looked back and forth between him and the swami. Until suddenly, the light goes on and he realizes that he hadn't handed him the contract, had actually stuffed it back in the briefcase with the other papers. Barry puffed on his cigar to hide his grin. Jerry Lewis, like he said.

"Um, oh, sorry. Um, just a second. It should be right here." The shlimazel furrowed his brow as he rifled through the papers in the briefcase.

The swami continued to smile at Barry and rolled his eyes as if to say "What can you do with these ridiculous mortals?".

"Oh, here it is." Ram-a-Ding-Dong pulled it out and the swami snatched it from his hand. Uncrossing his legs, the swami stood up, and walked around the desk to Barry's side.

Barry removed the cigar from his mouth and looked up at the swami, all his amusement dissipated. Was he an idiot coming behind his desk?

The swami failed to notice, too busy opening the contract to the last page.

"I wanted to bring this to your attention, Mr. Bartholomew. Our attorney advised us to sign with our real names, meaning our Western rather than Sanskrit names. We have amended and signed the contract accordingly." He handed Barry the contract with one hand and touched Barry's back with the other, as if they were old buddies.

"Uh huh. Have a seat there, swami." Barry gestured to the chair the swami had vacated. Get out of my space, you macher. And don't come in it again or I'll have you circumcised without anesthesia.

Barry leaned away from the swami and glared up at him. "Cause I got some news from *our* legal counsel, and it's not bad, but it might put a slight delay in the picture, all depending."

The swami moved back around the desk and took his seat. "A delay? What kind of delay?" He didn't ask what the news was, he went straight for the delay. This guy was chomping at the bit to finalize this contract. Well, too bad, buddy boy.

"A delay while you get another signature. I'm talking about that hippie broad wrote all the music. Can't sign without her. One, she's gotta sign away her rights as the composer, yeah? And two, I tried to argue your case, but Dolos ain't interested in a one-record deal. No real profit in it. Gotta have regular releases to make the deal worthwhile. That means we gotta have the composer involved. Capiche?"

The swami stared at Barry and Barry stared back with an innocent expression.

"No!" said Ram-a-Ding-Dong. "I mean … what I mean is, Jakananda wrote that music as a member of the ashram, so it belongs to us … I mean, the ashram. It belongs to the ashram."

"You got a job description and employment contract says that? You pay her for her labor? Cause if not, ya need her John Hancock on the dotted line." Barry made a gesture like "Hey, what can ya do?".

"I see," said the swami, pursing his lips and giving Barry an even more intense stare.

Barry would worry for the hippie broad if she was still at the ashram, wouldn't put it past this guy to use torture to get her to sign away her rights and agree to be a composer slave as long as he needed her. The swami would make a damn good gangster, or a crooked cop, or hey, let's be honest, a record producer. Lots of professions this guy would do good in.

Barry stood up, walked around the desk and to the door. "Rhonda, please show these gentlemen out." He turned to the swami and Ram-a-Ding-Dong. "Glad you decided to stop by so's we could get this little matter resolved."

As he shook their hands, he called them by their real names. "Roderick ... Elmo."

Ram-a-Ding-Dong did a quick shake, avoiding eye contact.

The swami looked backwards at Barry's office and then stared into Barry's eyes. "You've got an excellent set-up here, Mr. Bartholomew. By the way, you've got something white right here." The swami touched his own nostril to show Barry where it was.

Barry gave him a hard glare. The swami walked past him out of the office and joined Ram-a-Ding-Dong and Rhonda at the elevator. Barry shut the door to his office.

If that guru boy thought he was going to threaten him and still get a contract, he had another think coming. The swami was ridiculous, but he was also focused and determined, and Barry knew from hard experience, you should never underestimate your opposition. He did not underestimate that swami.

Twenty-Six

LUCY CAUGHT sight of Keith when he appeared in the doorway of the Hospitality Room. "Looks like sound check is over," she murmured to Alison.

Keith strode over to them and looked down at Lucy. "Could I have a word with you, in private? Like toot sweet before the band gets here?"

Lucy raised her eyebrows. "OK."

This was a surprise. What did he want with her? She got up and followed him out of the room. As they left, she called back to Alison, "Remember what we agreed."

Men's voices could be heard coming nearer. Most likely the other members of the band. Keith put his hand on her back and steered her down the hall and into the empty room next door. She knew from Jigsy that it was the Band Room. Keith locked the door after them.

She could still feel where he'd had his hand on her back. He was already acting too familiar. Time to get this onto a more business-like footing. She stuck out her hand. "I'm Lucy. It's nice to finally meet you, Keith."

She could sense his impatience as he shook her hand. "Listen, I know why you're here," he said. "I been in touch with Dolos."

"You have? I mean, with who? Was it Barry? Because Barry didn't

147

say anything about anyone knowing I would be here." Lucy cringed. She let the cat out of the bag again. Some spy she was turning out to be. And why didn't Barry tell her?

"Just me and Rob know. And our lips are sealed with superglue. Problem is, we gotta give you a disguise. Only one thing I can think of, you don't mind."

He would give her a cover story. Hallelujah! Her problem of how to infiltrate the band would be solved. Unless it involved doing things she wasn't willing to do. She saw from his look that it would.

"Let me guess, Keith. Your girlfriend?"

Keith scrunched up his face. "Well, not girlfriend, exactly. Gotta be believable. Ya know, life on the road and all that."

"Yeah, I do know. And I'm OK with that. But with conditions." If he thought she was going to play the devoted groupie and sleep with him, he was whistling Dixie.

"Yeah?" said Keith.

She planted her feet apart and folded her arms across her chest to show she meant business. "It's all show, Keith. No real hanky panky. No groping. We only kiss when we have to, to keep up appearances. You can hold me and put your arm around my shoulder all you want. I'm used to that."

A hurt look crossed Keith's face. She didn't want him to feel bad, and she didn't want to blow this opportunity. "Nothing personal, Keith, except I promised my nana I would be a good Catholic girl. And you're a good-looking guy. Not the best idea to tempt fate, as Nana would say."

Keith's face brightened and he leaned closer. "Could we have one big kiss so's we can establish, like, you know, that you're me bird and all that? So none of the other guys makes a play, y'know what I mean?"

She could give him that much. They did need to make her cover believable or she might get kicked out. "Yeah, that's fine."

Someone rattled the doorknob from the other side.

She grinned up at him. She liked him. This could be fun. "Looks like it's showtime."

"You ready?" said Keith.

"Ready when you are."

He grinned back at her. "Oh, I'm always ready, darlin'. Don't forget that, case you fall in love with me."

She smirked. "Oh, I won't, loverboy."

He unlocked the door and opened it. He put his arm around her shoulders and she put hers around his waist, and they walked down the hall to the Hospitality Room arm in arm. It wasn't the most comfortable fit in the world, Keith being a lot taller and his waist level with her you-know-whats, but she'd have to make do.

When they reached the doorway, Keith stopped right inside the room and waited for everyone to notice them. She looked around and all the band members were there except Jack St James.

Keith steered Lucy toward the food table, leaning down and making a show of whispering in her ear. "Time for our big moment. Ready or not, here I come."

Lucy looked up at him. What did that mean?

He stopped, turned to face her, and said loudly, "C'mere, you sexy wench." He leaned down, took her face in both hands, and gave her a kiss that went on and on, and on some more. It was like those kisses in the movies, a lot of dramatic lip play. Keith slipped his tongue in at the same time. Cheeky monkey, as the Brits would say.

Keith finally removed his lips from hers and let go of her face. He looked down at her in triumph.

She was a bit breathless, and flushed under his scrutiny. There was no denying, that was a darn good kiss.

He leaned in and whispered, "Remember what I told you, darlin'."

She was only able to muster a half-smile in response.

He turned to the guys. "Listen up. This here's Lucy. She's with me. You touch her and you're dog meat. You hear me, George?"

Lucy looked over at George for his reaction. He was glaring at Keith and sneaking looks at Alison. She was standing behind the food table, her arms folded across her chest and a look of disbelief on her face. Keith took no notice, completely oblivious to the trouble he might be causing between the two of them.

Rob and Sam both grinned at Keith, Rob's face full of admiration as if Keith had scored a big goal. Rob knew she was here for Dolos, and probably thought Keith was a genius for putting her in this role and kissing her like that. Randy, on the other hand, was looking at her and furrowing his brow. She might have to work to get that one on her side. She gave him a bright smile and he smiled back.

Keith steered Lucy over to the food table and let go of her shoulder. He turned away from her and gave his order to Alison. "I'll have that same steak I had yesterday. With a double order of chips. Yeah?"

Alison looked from Keith to Lucy and back again. Lucy knew she was waiting for Keith to turn to her and ask her what she wanted, but he kept staring at Alison, waiting for acknowledgement. Lucy rolled her eyes at Alison. Alison burst out laughing and Lucy joined her.

"What's so funny?" said Keith.

"You, loverboy. You're funny," said Lucy.

"You *guys* are funny," said Alison.

Keith looked at George. "*Women.*"

Twenty-Seven

GEORGE SCOWLED. Something's not right here.

He stared at Alison and scratched his beard. Sure, he'd slept with someone else last night, someone much more willing, and given Alison the "I'm so exhausted" excuse. She seemed to buy it, the same way she bought his swearing that he'd never been in a threesome. He also got her into the show. He didn't have to do any of these things, and he wouldn't have done if she weren't so pretty and didn't remind him of his Auntie Bonnie. So why did she feel so ... far away.

He and Keith took their seats with the others while they waited to be served. That Lucy who came with Keith stayed at the serving area to help Alison, chatting away to her as she prepared drinks and brought them over to the table. Keith didn't seem to care, talked to Rob about the tunes they were working on, never gave Lucy a second look.

He himself was having trouble keeping his eyes off her, what with those tight blue trousers and skinny top she was wearing. She was quite the looker, but not as pretty as Alison. He should know, he'd had more women than all the others combined. He kept track in a little notebook and also collected nude snapshots with his Polaroid camera when the girl was willing. He tried to get Dunk to give him all the photos left for Jack, but Dunk gave them to the crew, said those poor buggers needed them more than he did. He wasn't sure what to make of Jack. The guy never seemed to get laid. Him and Randy both. That's why they were so wound up all the time. A man *needed* a good lay. At least he knew *he* did or he'd go crazy what with all that drumming. Made a man downright horny, it did.

Alison came over to serve meals, gave him, Rob, and Sam their burgers, Keith his steak, and Randy his lobster tail again. She seemed to be giving Randy a lot of special attention, asked him did he want this or that, put her hand on his shoulder and gave him a big smile. Randy didn't notice at all; a chick could hit him over the head and drag him away by his hair and he still wouldn't get that she wanted him to shag her. The guy was hopeless.

George went over to the serving table and flashed Alison his sexiest smile. She just looked at him and asked what she could get him, did he need some ketchup for his burgers and fries. What the hell. He nodded and went back to his food. He wolfed it down and sat there feeling pissed off.

Alison brought his ketchup and put it on the table near him. No word or nothing. He asked for another two burgers with all the works, feeling like he could eat a horse. Of course, she told him, went off to make it, no smile for *him*.

He sat there stewing until she brought the burgers. He wolfed those down too. Now he felt sick to his stomach and pissed off. Alison leaned over Randy to refill his glass and pressed her knockers against him. He couldn't remember exactly what happened. All he could remember was that he lunged across the table and punched Randy, and Rob punched him back, and one of the girls was screaming, and Keith and Sam were holding him and Rob apart, and everyone was yelling at him. Then the others came in and the red mist went away.

Twenty-Eight

JACK WAS WALKING with Dunk toward the Hospitality Room when they heard the screaming. Dunk was telling him about some problems with the staging. He hadn't even had a chance to mention Lucy and the lax security situation yet. For god's sake, now what? They ran down the corridor and into the room.

Keith had George up against the wall and Sam stood in front of Rob, his arm across Rob's body, telling him to calm down. Randy had blood flowing from his nose and was trying to stem it with his hand. The food server, Alison, and that Lucy stood near the food table watching. Alison had her hand over her mouth; she must have been the one screaming. Lucy quietly watched everything, keeping her cool when everyone else was melting down. Huh. Intriguing.

"What in the bleedin' blazes is going on here?" said Dunk.

Jack had to let Dunk handle this because he was in Victor mode and couldn't blow his cover as Jack's personal assistant. Besides, it would give him an opportunity to watch this Lucy interloper. Why was she even *in* here with the band, in the middle of everything? She wasn't the cause of this, was she?

Everyone looked at Dunk and started talking.

"One at a time," Dunk shouted. "Keith."

Keith stepped away from George and gave him an apologetic look. Keith *was* like a big brother to the boys, no matter what Dunk said. "So George here lunges for Randy," he said. "Wallops him a good one. Rob wallops him back. And that's about it, really."

Dunk walked over to George. "What the hell, George?"

George looked down at the floor, sullen, and mumbled something about "me bird."

"Something about me bird," said Keith, trying to be helpful.

"I heard him," said Dunk. "So this is about some *chick*?"

George stared at the floor and didn't say anything. This was so un-George. He never got into any trouble. Well, other than all the activity with underage girls Jack had just learned about from Dunk and Barry. Other than that.

Dunk walked over to Randy. "You awright, kid?"

Randy had picked up a napkin and was using it to pinch his nose shut and stem the blood. Sensitive, considerate, peacemaker Randy. What in the world could cause George to hit *him*?

Randy looked at Dunk, his face full of righteous indignation. "I didn't do anything! He punched me all of a sudden, for no reason at all. I was just minding my own business eating my lobster."

"Yeah," said Rob. "What the hell was he thinking? You don't go around punching a Rickman like that."

Dunk scowled at Rob. "That's exactly the point. He wasn't think-ing, and neither were you." He turned back to Randy. "So ya got no idea why George hit ya?"

"I think I can tell you," said Lucy.

Aha! Jack knew it. She was involved. That woman had trouble written all over her.

Dunk turned toward her and gave her his deadpan glare. Dunk had perfected that look back in public school—his "don't piss me off or you will live to regret it" look—and it made most people freeze and quake in their boots. Jack knew why he was using it. Groupies were not allowed to interfere in band business, and Dunk had to be thinking she was a groupie.

She ignored it and plowed ahead, didn't seem fazed by it at all.

"So George was interested in Alison here," she said, waving her hand toward Alison.

Alison looked back at Lucy and nodded. How does Lucy know this? She just got here, didn't she?

"And she was interested in him too. I mean, look at him, he's so sexy."

Everyone looked over at George. He looked back down at the floor with one of those half-smiles. Yeah, Jack could see it now. George was sexy. If he were a girl ... for god's sake, what was he thinking?

"But George told her he'd never been in a threesome," Lucy continued, "and she didn't believe him."

Alison shook her head. Smart girl.

"And then last night he gave her the 'I'm so exhausted' excuse and slept with someone else."

"You idiot," said Rob.

No, he wasn't an idiot. The guy was a sex maniac. Full stop. And Alison clearly wasn't that kind of girl.

George looked off to the side, sheepish. He didn't even look embarrassed, just caught out.

"So she decided she wasn't interested in George anymore," Lucy said. "She didn't want to be with a Sex God type of guy like George."

What type? Do women put us men into types?

George looked over at Alison, and Alison walked over to him. Jeez, this was like watching a play.

"I'm sorry, George, you are terribly cute, and I think you're really sweet too. And you're a great kisser. But I really want to be with a Charlie Watts kind of guy."

OK, that made sense. Everyone knew about Charlie Watts and his devotion to his wife Shirley.

George smiled at her. "S'okay."

Wow, he was OK with losing Alison to someone else. That was a first.

Alison walked over to Randy. "So I couldn't help noticing that Randy is really into fine food, like me. And he always asks me how I'm doing and really listens. And he even cleans up after himself. So I said, I bet he's a Charlie Watts. He's really cute too, and, well, I couldn't help but flirt with him a bit. In front of George. Sorry, George."

OK, now it all made sense. Jack couldn't blame her; she wants a Charlie Watts. She's so right, that's clearly Randy and not George. The problem was her flirting with another guy. That would set off any man. What was she thinking? She was lucky George was so easy-going and forgave her so easily. Jack wouldn't. He'd want an admission of guilt and a profuse apology. A man had to have his principles.

Rob gave Randy a man-to-man smack of approval on his arm—even though Randy had been totally clueless about Alison's interest. If he didn't do something now, with this opportunity landing right in his lap, the kid was hopeless.

Randy stood up and turned to Alison. "I, yes. Yes, I think I *am* a Charlie Watts. Well, I might be. Um, Jack ..."

He turned toward Jack. Oh no, what is he doing? Is he planning to consult me on his type? Are you kidding, Randy? And blow my cover in front of Alison and that Lucy? Jack glared at him and shook his head very slightly. Hopefully Alison and Lucy wouldn't see.

Randy looked startled and turned back to Alison. "Um, Jack ... isn't here." Phew! The kid got the message. "But he said I'm going to make someone a great husband someday. I mean, not that I'm looking to get married; I'm too young right now, and I have to focus on my career first, he said. But—"

"Get to it, you ninny. Be the man," said Rob.

Thank you, Rob. Otherwise we'll be here all night.

"Um, Alison, would you like to see my keyboards?"

"Yes, Randy, I'd love to," said Alison.

Why did Jack feel like cheering? Their boy Randy was getting together with Alison, who had not two seconds ago dumped George in front of everyone.

Except, hold the phone. What was going on in this band? First there was that crazy thing that happened with Ruth and Clint, and now this. Everything was starting to go out of whack. He and Dunk had to get things back under control. Pronto. They could not let there be any risk whatsoever to finishing the rest of the tour or to securing the bonus.

"But first, can I get some ice on that bloody nose for you?" Alison said. Randy nodded. She took his hand and led him out of the room.

Jack looked over at Lucy and she was swiping tears from her eyes. He felt the same way, but he'd never in a million years admit it. He wondered what she had to do with this. He was sure she had a hand in what happened. She seemed to know everything that was going on and be in the middle of things. Had she orchestrated it?

The tense air in the room dissipated with Alison and Randy's departure. The rest of the band gathered around the spurned George and commiserated with him.

"Tough luck, dude," said Keith.

"Hey, Randy's got the Rickman charm,' said Rob. 'What can you do?"

Sam smirked. "How come it skipped you?"

Dunk hit George in the arm. "Ooh, yer so sexy, Georgie. Yer so cute, Georgie. Yer so sweet, Georgie. Yer such a great kisser, Georgie. We'll nae hear the end of this, will we?"

Keith tousled George's hair.

George grinned. "Stop."

Lucy walked over and inserted herself under Keith's arm. She sneaked a glance at Jack. He narrowed his eyes and pursed his lips. What was she playing at?

Dunk turned to her. "I didn't catch yer name. I'm Dunk."

Keith answered for her. "Her name's Lucy and she's with me." He pulled her tight to him.

What the ... She's already got Keith wrapped around her little finger?

"So nice to meet you, Dunk," said Lucy. "Can I tell you how impressed I am with how you handled that?"

"Is that so?" Dunk smiled down at her. "Go ahead. Tell me more." He shouted across the room to Jack. "Ya hear that? *She* thinks I'm a great manager." And now she had Dunk wrapped around her little finger too.

"Oh yeah?" said Jack. He stared at Lucy. Exactly as he suspected, this woman was going to be trouble with a capital T. Well, little missy, let me tell you, you may not realize it, but you have met your match. Have I got your number, and am I going to dial it.

Twenty-Nine

DUNK STOOD, hands on hips, watching Jack go back and forth.

"She has to go," said Jack as he paced in his hotel suite. "Did you see what she did? Did you see it?"

"Yer bum's out the window, mate. She didn't do anything."

Jack stopped pacing and scowled at him. "When have we ever had a fight *in* the band? I mean a real fight, not the twins wrestling around on the floor. Never. And when have we ever had the boys fighting over a woman? Never."

Dunk looked confused. "Right. But Luce had naught to do with it. That was all Alison."

"See!" Jack pointed at him like a madman. "You're already calling her Luce, like she's your best friend or something."

"That's her name. Well, Lucy really. But she said Luce was fine."

Jack grimaced. "Don't you see? She arrives, all soft and smiley and girly and charming everyone, and all of a sudden we have a fight. And—"

"Hold on, hold on, hold on." Dunk held up his hands in a stop gesture and raised his eyebrows. "Did I hear ya right? Did ya say soft? Did ya actually *touch* her?"

Jack glanced at Dunk and away again. He went over to the table and fingered the *Wall Street Journal* lying there. "Well, yes, I had to. She fell and I had to catch her. I couldn't let her fall on the floor. That was earlier, when I met her. It doesn't really matter when it was. But she tripped on her shoe and I caught her. And yes, I have to admit, she was rather ... soft."

He could feel Dunk staring at him. Jack never touched anyone or let anyone touch him. If he could help it. Except for Ruth.

After a long moment, Dunk said, "And ya weren't wearing yer gloves?"

"Well, no. But I washed my hands ..." He mumbled "later" under his breath.

"What was that?" Dunk said.

Jack ignored the question. He wasn't going to admit that he didn't want to wash off the smell of her skin, that he kept sniffing it off and on afterwards, that he hadn't actually washed it off yet. That washing his hands "later" was still in the future. "You're missing the point here."

"Yeah, I *am* missing the point."

Jack started pacing again. "What if George had knocked Randy out and he couldn't play? That could've happened. George has biceps the size of the Incredible Hulk's."

Dunk smirked.

"OK, that was an exaggeration. But you know what I mean. And what if Barry found out Randy missed a concert and refused to pay our bonus? Then where would we be?" He stopped in front of Dunk. "You know where we'd be. Stuck in recording and touring hell again."

Dunk looked at him with a sad expression. "Would that be so bad?"

"How long can we keep this up? My father picked up the phone when I called home yesterday. What if he had the call traced? What if he finds us? What if that Lucy figures out who I am and tells the press before we finish the tour? You saw it, Randy almost outed me in front of Lucy and Alison today."

"So this Lucy. Ya think—"

"I think we can't take any risks. I mean, we know who Alison is, don't we? She works for the arena. But what do we know about this Lucy? Who is she? What's she doing here all of a sudden?"

"She's with Keith. He'll dump her in a day, maybe two, and then she'll be gone."

"We only have six more concerts to get through. Keith will get over it." Jack looked at Dunk with a pleading expression. "Do this for me. Please."

"Right." Dunk sighed. "Done."

"But do it after the concert," added Jack. "Give her a great seat for the show. We have some comps left, don't we? A flight and limo wherever she needs to go. And our best merchandise, something to remember us by. We can at least do that for her."

Dunk cocked his head as he stared at Jack.

Jack was well aware that he wasn't acting like his usual self. For some reason that eluded him, he needed her to know that he wasn't an arsehole, that he didn't *want* to kick her out. But he had to protect what they'd spent years building, and make sure they all got that bonus. Under other circumstances, he would really like ... well, he wasn't going to go there, because what was the point.

Dunk nodded and went to the door. "I'll talk to the both of 'em after."

As Jack got ready for the concert, he took special care with his costume and makeup. If this was the only Pirate concert Lucy was going to see, it was only fair that it be a good one. No, a great one. He didn't know why, but he felt he owed her at least that much.

Thirty

LUCY AND ALISON made their way to the VIP section. Dunk had told them they were getting the absolute best seats in the house, compliments of the band. Lucy was surprised by that. When did girl-friends and groupies get the best seats over journalists and VIPs? He wouldn't meet their eyes, guilt all over his face. That probably meant she was going to be banned from the tour, if past experience was any guide. Like the time she'd been kicked off the Netherlude tour and neither Tate nor Russell would look at her.

That Vic was behind this, she was sure. He had narrowed his eyes and pursed his lips at her in the hospitality room, like she had done something wrong, when she was simply trying to help things work out the best they could for everyone. Didn't Alison and Randy end up together? A much better match than Alison and George. Well, Vic had no idea who he was dealing with. Lucy L'amour, that's who. Someone who'd dealt with many miscreant rock stars in her day. He had met his match, that's what.

As they entered the VIP section, she caught sight of Howie. He looked over and startled when he saw her. Wow, that was a bit of a surprise. Barry hadn't said anything about Howie being here. He hadn't said anything about having a chat with Keith, either. It looked like Barry was hedging his bets at least three ways.

She already knew Howie from his visit to the ashram. Some other guest—she didn't know who—had raved about her music to Barry, and Barry had sent Howie as an advance scout. Howie had come to her chanting sessions and her evening concerts. He'd hung out with her, chatting about music. The kid was a musical sponge, clearly a wannabe musician with either no training or no talent, she wasn't sure which, who had settled for being a music aficionado. He seemed to know everything about the rock scene and could talk for hours about the different bands. He was, literally, a walking rock 'n' roll encyclopedia. She had been shocked to find out that he even knew about her time with Magnus and her sudden disappearance after the Buffalo concert.

He apparently recommended her to Barry, who hightailed it up to the ashram. But then Mandy the Snake caught word of his visit, and Barry was lured away for the so-called VIP treatment by the swami and Ramakar, while she was pushed into the background—despite the fact that it was *her* music. Barry had insisted that she be involved in discussions, much to the swami's displeasure and Ramakar's clumsy machinations to exclude her. She strongly suspected that they had persuaded Barry to send them the contract for review, again without including her. But now—ha!—he'd promised to give her the contract, rather than those sleazy slithering snakes, if she succeeded in babysitting this band. It meant she had a chance to keep control over the music that she had composed and slaved over to perfect during her three years at the ashram. She'd be damned—Hail Mary, full of grace—if she'd let anyone prevent her from getting that contract. No one, but no one, including Howie or that Vic, was going to stand in her way.

Lucy and Alison took their seats at the back of the VIP section, right behind Howie.

Lucy leaned forward and murmured in his ear. "Howie Bartholomew. Fancy finding you here." She almost gagged at the overpowering smell of pot and beer, and quickly leaned back again.

A young woman sitting next to him twisted around and looked at her. "Howie, do you know this lady?"

Howie turned his head toward the two of them. He had clearly been planning to ignore her. Maybe he didn't know she was there for his uncle and was afraid she'd expose him.

"Yes, I do," he said. "Lucy, meet Carly." He waved to his other side. "And this is Suze."

Lucy held out her hand to Suze and then Carly, shaking their hands in turn. They both looked taken aback by this turn of events. Lucy introduced them to Alison.

"Yes, we've already met." Alison nodded at them. "In the Hospitality Room. Hey there."

Lucy could tell they were groupies who were following the band everywhere, the signs being all over them. It looked like they'd latched onto Howie as their meal ticket, probably knew his uncle was a big record producer, could get them concert tickets and backstage passes. Nothing wrong with that, as long as Howie didn't get hurt. He was a sweet kid, really naive and impressionable, and afraid of his uncle. She'd have to make sure they were treating him right.

"I'm Lucy L'amour. Here with Keith. Alison is with Randy." It was best to get the groupie dominance hierarchy in place quickly. They were at the bottom of the totem pole and she wanted them to know it, wanted them to be cooperative and give her the gossip she needed. No time for niceties with only five more concerts to go after this one.

Carly turned in her seat. "Lucy L'amour? *The* Lucy L'amour?" She looked at Lucy with awe and leaned across Howie. "Omigod, Suze, this lady is a groupie legend. Used to be with Magnus." She turned to Lucy. "Then you disappeared from the scene for a few years. What happened?"

Lucy gripped Howie's shoulder to warn him not to answer. Howie tensed up and sat there looking straight ahead.

"I kind of went off to India to find myself," Lucy said. "Tired of the scene. But now I'm back and doing some scouting for the right opportunity, if you get my drift."

"Wow," said Carly.

"Got it," said Suze, winking at Lucy.

The lights went down. Lucy leaned forward and whispered into Howie's ear. "Your uncle sent me. Top secret. Talk to you later."

Thirty-One

LUCY SAT BACK. She grabbed Alison's hand and gave it a squeeze.

Alison leaned toward her and murmured, "Get ready for a wild ride."

"Oh, I'm ready," said Lucy. "I'm more than ready."

She didn't have high expectations of this band, having met all of them except Jack St James. Although, to be fair, she *had* been impressed by that MTV video her nana had shown her.

She jumped as the sound of a screaming guitar ripped through the darkened auditorium like a cannon being fired, accompanied by a flashing light and smoke coming from the broadside of the ship. The audience screamed with shock and delight, and goose bumps burst up and down Lucy's arms.

The cannon shots repeated over and over, getting louder and brighter and faster, until one last volley lit up the auditorium with flashing lights and rapid-fire guitar licks.

A spotlight lit up a man standing alone on the quarterdeck, immediately recognizable by his long black beard. "King of these seas, that's who I am," he belted out without accompaniment. "Blackbeard to you, death to the Man." The crowd went crazy again, so loud Lucy wanted to turn the volume down on their noise.

Jack St James in his pirate guise was dressed in knee-high black boots and a long sapphire blue coat over jet black clothing. His heavily bejeweled fingers pushed back his long blue-black hair to reveal dangling sapphire earrings. The pièce de résistance was a wide hat that lit up from within, making his ornately painted face look fearsome and otherworldly.

He stepped forward, the spotlight following him, and revealed Randy at the helm of the ship. He put his hand on Randy's shoulder and Randy joined in with his keyboards.

"My rule is law, my world this ship, obey me do, I'll make you rich." As Jack finished singing the phrase, he looked at the audience and indicated Randy. "Allow me to introduce the Gentleman Pirate Stede Bonnet, onboard this ship as my guest."

Dressed in a white nightshirt and breeches and sporting a wide blond mustache, Randy brought a big grin to Lucy's face. He broke into a brief solo, banging the ivories up and down on his Roland Jupiter-8 keyboard.

The audience went wild again, as they did when each band member was introduced. One spotlight stayed on Randy as he kept the melody going, while another followed Jack as he climbed around the ship, revealing each member of the band, singing a phrase with them, announcing them to the audience, and letting them do a brief solo.

He continued by climbing to the crow's nest, where he introduced Rob as "my most trusted officer, but with a troublesome eye for the ladies, Lieutenant Richards." Rob was dressed in breeches and a frilly white shirt completely open in front, with his hair held back in a ponytail with a ribbon. As soon as the spotlight hit him, girls let out shrill screams, shouted "I love you," and threw items of underwear at him. Unfazed, Rob improvised a solo, closing his eyes as he contorted his body in sync with the screaming sounds issuing from his Rickenbacker bass guitar.

Another spotlight stayed on Rob as Jack climbed down to the section in the middle of the ship and introduced Sam as "Black Caesar, the African chieftain brought over here in a slave ship, who heroically escaped during a storm and turned into a highly respected, but not entirely respectable, pirate, having, so I hear but have not seen, a thousand women in his own personal harem." Sam wore silk pants and a gold-embroidered, multi-colored cloth wrapped around him, with a collection of bead necklaces down his chest and long feathers sticking out of his Afro like a crown. He launched into a solo on his Fender Stratocaster, demonstrating some Hendrix moves and doing a moonwalk, which drove the audience to their feet.

Blackbeard turned to George on drums, sharing the middle of the ship with Sam, and introduced him as "Captain Jennings, treasure hunter extraordinaire and leader of the Republic of Pirates in Nassau, where we stop to take our rest and our pleasures between ... engagements." George was wearing nothing but breeches and a necklace that looked made of animal teeth, his hair pulled back with a leather thong, and he got the same hysterical reaction as Rob. He gave a mischievous grin and launched into a solo on his Tama Imperial Star drum kit, cycling through drum styles for different types of music and developing a heavy sheen of sweat on his bare chest within seconds.

Finally, Blackbeard climbed to the raised deck near the bow and introduced Keith as "Calico Jack, one of the most colorful and clever pirates in these dangerous waters, the first to have female pirates in his crew, Ann Bonny and Mary Read, the bonny Ann being his true love and mother of his soon-to-be child." Keith was dressed in a bright calico coat over orange togs and knee-high brown boots. Unlike the others, his hair hung loose and covered his face as he played his Gibson SG double-neck guitar like a man possessed.

Despite Keith's colorful appearance, not to mention the need to keep up her public persona as his "girlfriend," Lucy found she could not keep her eyes off Jack. She followed him as he moved about the stage, picking up instruments here and there—he seemed to be able to play everything—supporting others when they took the singing or playing lead. They all got plenty of opportunity to shine and flaunt their stuff.

Even if the playing hadn't been spectacular, the story would have mesmerized her. This was no rock concert; it was a rock opera on a par with The Who's *Tommy*, or Pink Floyd's *The Wall*, or David Bowie's *The Rise and Fall of Ziggy Stardust*. Each member of the band sang songs about their pirate exploits. Sam, as Black Caesar, sang "Buried Treasure," about raiding ships in the Florida Keys and amassing treasure beyond the wildest dreams of an African chieftain, treasure he had buried in places where no one would ever find it "in a million years, so don't try you poorly thief."

Randy, as Stede Bonnet, sang a humorous song called "Life is Not Faire," about being driven from his estate by a nagging wife, leaving behind his children and the life of a lazy gentleman to become a pirate on the stormy seas, only to be wounded in battle and confined in Blackbeard's ship with "such reekin' pirates you ne'er would believe."

Jack, as Blackbeard, countered with his own song, "Grog Blossoms," about ungrateful guests and a crew that took any opportunity to "open the Madeira and carouse with the ladies." He bemoaned "the need to keep my fearsome reputation intact, lest they discover my soft and yearning heart." As he looked into the audience, pleading for sympathy, she almost felt as if he were speaking directly to her, telling her that he was a good guy forced to act tough to keep his rowdy crew under control.

Rob, as Lieutenant Richards, swore his allegiance and innocence in "Walk that Plank," singing his regret about messing up his mission to get medicines for the ship by losing the other pirates to "demon drink and the sirens of the night, those ghosts of beautiful face that no pirate can resist." He followed with "Blue Lagoon," the song her nana had played for her from MTV, about being rescued from an island and having to leave behind the native woman he loved.

George, as Captain Jennings, growled out a song called "The Best of Times," about being rich "'cause I know how to reach the sunken treasure in these there depths" and "come take your rest in this Republic of Pirates, and let me show you the best of times." Lucy and Alison looked at one another and rolled their eyes. Lucy wondered if this was life imitating art, or art imitating life.

Her eyes teared up when Keith sang a ballad called "Your Face," about missing his love, bonny Ann, and not knowing if he would ever see her again "in this godforsaken world, caring naught about our hearts." She started sobbing when Jack joined in harmony and they sang "tell the child not my exploits, but of my true love for you."

She was overcome with how amazing the entire production was, but especially the music. Every single one of these guys was a brilliant musician and a compelling singer. But it was the songs that blew her away, especially the last one. Simple but elegant, a song that affected her to her very core, a song that as a musician she could only dream of writing.

She kept tearing up right through the other songs, "Bounty" and "Man-o-War," and through the final battle song when the ship engaged in "Firefight" like it had at the beginning, and through a fight on the deck involving flintlock pistols, cutlasses and swords, and through a death scene in which Blackbeard sang "Forget Me Not," about dying too young and wondering if he would ever be remembered by anyone.

When the concert was over, the audience gave the band a standing ovation that seemed to go on forever. Lucy stayed in her seat, wiping the tears from her cheeks as they kept flowing. Alison stood next to her cheering and punching the air, occasionally reaching down to pat her back.

Thirty-Two

JACK LOOKED DOWN at the dimly visible VIP section. There was Alison, clapping and jumping up and down. Howie was there too, with Carly and Suze. But no Lucy to be seen. Maybe she left early to beat the crowds. Maybe she had to go to the loo. Maybe she didn't enjoy the show and went back to the hotel.

He had put everything he had into this show, had pulled out all the stops. He was wrung completely dry. There was nothing more he could give. He just wanted her to enjoy it before she left, since he was kicking her out and it might hurt her feelings. That was all.

He swallowed the bitter taste of disappointment—his old companion disappointment. He wondered why he even tried. What was the point? All the effort never seemed to give him what he really wanted, never seemed to lead anywhere worthwhile. Except to more work, more problems to solve, more demands on his time, more worries about money.

The band took their final bows. Jack left the stage, followed by the others. He needed to get back to the hotel and strip off this costume and makeup. It made him look ridiculous, like a clown. He was a grown man, and yet he was still behaving like a schoolboy acting in amateur dramatics. Would he never grow up?

Everyone was smiling at him and congratulating him on a great show. Lucky that he had the makeup on; he could smile and they wouldn't know that he didn't mean it. That he was being overwhelmed by the darkness again. That he needed to find Dunk and get back to the hotel.

He hurried to his dressing room and stuffed everything into his carryall. He would sort it all out later. He rushed down the hall, looking into rooms as he passed. Dunk was probably in the Hospitality Room stuffing his face and congratulating the boys.

As he approached that room, he heard a female voice sobbing and other voices comforting her. This wasn't like Ruth's sobbing, that deep sob that took over and racked her entire body. This seemed more like an excited sob, if that was even possible.

He stood at the side of the door, out of sight, listening. Omigod, it was *her*. She hadn't left. She was in there raving to them about the show and the music. Going on and on about how amazing it was, how over-come she was with emotion. Relief and joy and terror cycled through him all at the same time.

"Who wrote that song 'Your Face'? Who wrote that song?" she asked in a teary voice. "I don't even have words."

"Well, uh, that would be Jack," said Randy. "Yeah, it's a brilliant song, isn't it? He writes all the songs, does Jack."

"Brilliant doesn't do that song justice. It was … it was a piece of heaven."

Dunk came up behind him and bellowed, "What are ya doing standing here? Ya must be famished." Dunk waited for him to enter the room. There was nothing for it; he would have to face her.

He walked into the room, Dunk behind him, and stopped inside the doorway. Dunk walked past him to the food table, oblivious to anything but throwing some food down his gullet.

Jack stared at Lucy and she turned toward him. When she caught sight of him, her expression changed from teary excitement to—there was no other word for it, was there?—joy.

Now she was running toward him and putting her arms around his neck and pulling him to her and squeezing him tight again and again and going on and on in his ear about "that song" and kissing his neck here and there in her excitement.

He stood there in shock, unable to move. But it wasn't repulsion or pain like it usually was when someone touched him. It was just the surprise of it. It actually didn't feel bad. No, to be honest, it felt good. He liked it. He maybe even really liked it.

She let him go and apologized for being so excited, but kept holding his hand in her own and crying and telling him how brilliant the show was and how much that song affected her. And how she would never forget it as long as she lived. A bar of music came into his head in that moment, a bar of music for her. The essence of her.

He kept staring at her as she talked. He didn't hear a word she said. He was in his head composing her song, Lucy's song.

Dunk's face came into view, concern across his features. "Luce, I need to have a word."

"No, you can't have a word." Was that his voice? "No, no words."

Jack and Dunk looked at one another. Dunk nodded. "OK, no words."

He had to get a hold of himself. He had to say something. "I ... I ... I'm writing another song. This is the beginning." He sang it to her.

She stared at him and teared up again. She liked it.

"I have to go." He turned and left the room.

He heard Dunk say "Scuse me, folks" and follow him out of the room.

"You OK?" Dunk said.

He looked at Dunk. "I have this song."

Dunk took him to the hotel suite, got the keyboard and acoustic guitar delivered, and by morning he had a new song. Her song.

Thirty-Three

"UM, LUCE, YOU TOUCHED HIM," said Randy after Jack rushed out of the room.

Lucy had stopped crying, but she knew her face was still red and tear-stained. She rubbed the moisture from her cheeks. "I know. I got a little carried away."

She wasn't sure what to make of Jack St James. He didn't seem to mind her throwing herself at him in her excitement, and he just stared at her while she was babbling on about the concert and that song. Then, all of a sudden, he shared a new song he was writing and sang some of it to her. Darned if it didn't sound as amazing as "Your Face." Jack was clearly a masterful songwriter, and as mesmerizing in person as on stage and in that MTV video. He reminded her of someone, but she couldn't think of who that was. But one thing she did notice: he and Vic both smelled like Wipe-It-Fresh. Could it be their laundry detergent?

Keith breezed into the room. "I could eat a giraffe."

He hadn't changed or showered yet, his clothes soaked with sweat and his makeup smeared. They all reeked of male sweat. It took her right back to her days with Magnus.

"Tell her, Keith," said Randy.

"Tell her what?" he said.

"About Jack and his ... you know."

Keith looked over at Alison standing next to Randy. "Now then, Ali, can I get some pizza and chips, you don't mind?' He grinned. 'Y'know, what you Yankee doodle dandies like to call frenchy fries."

Randy stood as tall as he could. "Um, Keith, well, um, she is ... her name is Alison, not Ali. And well, um, she's not working here anymore, so um, she can't get your pizza and chips."

Alison smiled at Randy and stroked his arm.

Keith looked as if he couldn't compute what he was hearing. "What?"

"She's with me now, and um, I said Alison, um, why don't you come with me. And she said—"

"Oh, for eff's sake," said Keith. "I don't care if she follows you around the bloody world. Me stomach thinks me throat's cut and me mouth superglued shut. I've been playing me nuts off and—"

"Cool your jets, loverboy, I'll get your pizza and fries," said Lucy. "It's the least I can do as your *girlfriend*."

Keith looked sheepish. He clearly had forgotten about their arrangement. He rushed to cover up. "Oh, yeah, that's right. *You* should be getting me me tea. Get a move on, woman."

"*Men*," she said as she smiled at him and went behind the food table. They watched as she prepared the plate and set it on the table, along with a mug of beer. Keith sat down facing them and shoved some fries in his mouth.

"She hugged and kissed Jack," Randy said to Keith.

"What?" said Keith, talking with his mouth full. "You're having me on."

"No, no. I wasn't *cheating* on you," Lucy said, giving Keith a meaningful look. "I was expressing my excitement about 'Your Face.'"

"Oh, yeah?" said Keith. "You liked it?"

"She hugged and kissed him," repeated Randy

"You wanna hear me tunes?" asked Keith. "I can play 'em for you tomorrow on the bus." He took a slurp of beer.

"Jack never lets anyone touch him," Randy said to Alison. "And he let Lucy touch and kiss him for ages."

"Yes, I'd *love* that," Lucy said to Keith, hoping that he would ignore Randy and Randy's obsession with her behavior toward Jack.

"I saw," said Alison to Randy. "He seemed to ... really enjoy it."

"Wait, what?" said Keith. He pointed his pizza slice at Lucy. "You stay away from that guy. He's a bona fidey freak."

"Well, of course I'm going to stay away from him. I'm with *you*." She gave Keith another meaningful look.

"And that Vic. You stay away from him too." Keith got up from the table. "OK, I'm done." He started walking toward the door.

"Didn't you forget something?" said Lucy.

Keith gave her a blank look.

She grabbed her things from a chair and rolled her eyes at Randy and Alison. "*Rock stars*. OK, loverboy. Let's go."

After Keith and Lucy left, and after he and Alison had eaten and done some really great snogging, and after he'd seen her off in a taxi, Randy returned to the hotel. He went to Keith's room and knocked on the door.

Keith opened it in his briefs. "What, man? Can't you see I'm busy?" A woman who wasn't Lucy smiled from under the bedcover.

Just as he thought. Randy made up some excuse and went back to his room. He mused it over in the shower and came to a decision. He couldn't keep this to himself. He was going to have to tell him.

Thirty-Four

THE NEXT MORNING, Cindy was summoned to the swami's office. Lucy often got summoned there, but this was her first time. She would have preferred to keep it that way, because she knew she was going to get a grilling about where Lucy was and she could not, under any circumstances, spill the beans. She saw only one way for the swami to apply the proverbial screws and make her crack—put her in the corpse pose for an extended period. That would be pretty quick, because she'd never been able to lie still and empty her mind. And damn it, why should she? Her active mind was her best feature.

She took a couple of deep breaths, said her favorite affirmation, "Calm and courage in the face of chaos and calamity" three times, and knocked on his office door.

The swami's imperious nasal voice penetrated through the solid wood. "Come!"

The door flew open before she could move. Ramakar held it and gestured for her to enter.

The swami was sitting behind his desk massaging some prayer beads, and didn't even look up to see who it was. The vibe in the room was definitely chilly. Like she'd been summoned to the principal's office and was about to be expelled from school. Jeez. Was this any way to treat the assistant director of the music program?

Ramakar indicated a low chair in front of the swami's desk. "Sit."

Cindy gave him a half-smile. "Oh, thanks anyway. I've got a back problem and have to stand. Health and safety." She put her hand on her back and grimaced, to make it official. Neither one of them ever came to yoga or kirtan, never talked to anyone in the ranks except to make speeches, so they'd never in a million years know it wasn't true. Unless Ramakar checked with that viper Mandy. Let him check, she didn't care. She could file an official health and safety complaint for lots of other things if they wanted to make an issue out of it. Bring it on, you sleazoids.

The swami pursed his lips as he played with the beads and made her stand and wait. Ramakar shifted on his feet, clasped his hands in front of his groin, and mindlessly twiddled his thumbs.

Cindy took the opportunity to scan the swami's desk for the Dolos contract. It wasn't easy reading things upside down. If only she could find a way to stand on the other side of his desk.

"We seem to have lost Jakananda," the swami finally said as he looked up at her.

"I'm not sure what you mean," Cindy said, even though she knew what he was *trying* to say.

"Jak-ka-nan-da," he said, insulting her like she was an idiot or hard of hearing.

"Oh, *Jakananda*. I didn't understand your accent there for a moment." Two can play this game, smarmy swami.

He glared at her. "This is not funny. Jakananda has disappeared. No one has seen her for a good while ... and we are very concerned about her."

"Oh, didn't she tell you?" She made her face a picture of complete innocence.

"Tell us what?" said the swami.

"Her grandmother suddenly got ill. They thought it was a heart attack or stroke, and she rushed back home. Nana is very old, and they're very close, and—"

Ramakar interrupted. "So why didn't she report it before she left?"

Cindy turned to Ramakar. "I'm sure she meant to. But I mean, you know Jakananda." If they knew Lucy and her haphazard organizational skills, they wouldn't even be asking this question. *She*, yours truly, was the one who really kept things humming.

"No, I don't *know* Jakananda," said the swami. "And I don't appreciate your tone. This is a very serious matter."

And I don't appreciate your sexism. "I'm a bit confused here. Her nana got ill and she ran home to see her. Shivarandiman did the same thing with his dad, so I'm not getting what the big deal is."

"Because her safety is our responsibility, that's why." The swami glared at her without blinking. "It's not for you to question, it's for you to tell us what we need to know. Do I make myself clear?"

Cindy stared back at him. "Yes, abundantly." You don't like to be called on your shit, do you, sleazy swami?

The swami threw down the prayer beads and stood up. "Get her on the phone. You know where she lives. Get her on the phone, right now."

"Oh, uh ... OK," said Cindy. This was unexpected. Think, Cindy, think. "Um, there's no phone."

The swami pulled it out from under some papers and slammed it on the desk in front of him.

She started to reach across the desk to pull it toward her.

"No, come here," said the swami.

Cindy hesitated for a moment. She didn't want to be that close to the swami. He creeped her out. But it looked like she'd have to take this on the chin for the team. Team Lucy. She walked around the desk. The swami didn't move an inch, just glared at her. She reached forward past him to pick up the receiver, keeping her eyes on the phone and holding her breath. Did he always have to wear so much of that stinky hair oil? She dialed Directory Assistance and kept her eyes on the desk. Hmmm, a lot of intriguing papers here.

"Yes, I need the number for Constance Sabatini in Endwell, New York ... Yes, that's the one. Could you connect me, please?"

Cindy gestured to the swami that it was ringing. Let it be Lucy's dad, she prayed. Her mom would launch into talking and for sure spill the beans before Cindy could even get a word in edgewise. But her dad was really into conspiracy theories, so if she could only find the right code word to signal him. Think, Cindy, think.

Cindy held up the phone so the swami and Ramakar could hear the ringing. She returned the receiver to her ear.

Someone answered the phone, shouted "No, we don't want," and hung up. Cindy knew immediately who it was—Nana. Oh no, that meant Nana was alone in the house. But Nana was supposed to be ill, so she couldn't let the swami talk to her. She had to convince him to give up.

She held up the phone so the dial tone was audible in the swami's office. "Someone answered and shouted and hung up. I think it must be the wrong—"

"Do it again," the swami ordered. "And write down the number." Cindy called Directory Assistance a second time, wrote down the phone number on a stray piece of paper, and had them make the connection.

The phone rang again and Cindy held it so the swami could hear. Nana answered again, shouted "No, I tell you we don't want," and hung up.

The swami looked affronted at the dial tone. "It sounds like an old woman. Maybe it's Lucy's grandmother and she's not so sick after all." He glared at Cindy. "Dial again and put it on speakerphone."

Cindy dialed. Que sera, sera. She did her best. It was out of her hands now. Besides, if the swami discovered that Lucy had absconded, what could he do about it? Fire her? He'd never do that. Lucy drew a lot of people to the ashram with her music and chanting, and the swami had a "thing" for her. Knowing the swami, she herself would be the one to get fired for being Lucy's accomplice, while Lucy would get off scot-free. Perhaps it was time for that big change she'd been dreaming about. A trip to the roof of the world, Tibet. Or an ayahuasca adventure in Peru. Or a yoga retreat on the beach in Bali.

The phone rang and rang. Cindy looked at the swami for guidance. He stared back at her unblinking, as if she was at fault for this fiasco. Like she or anyone else could control those crazy Sabatinis.

As soon as Nana answered, Cindy hit the speakerphone button and replaced the handset. She let out a deep breath she didn't know she'd been holding.

"Nana? Is this Nana?" the swami shouted. He thought her name was Nana. What a dummy.

"Hello?" said Nana on the other end.

"Nana?"

"Antonio? Nana not so good today. No food. The son's wife, she starve Nana."

Cindy stifled a smile. Vintage Nana.

"Listen! Listen to me. This is not Antonio. This is Swami Zukeeni."

"Zucchini? No zucchini. The son's wife no go shopping—"

"No, no! This is *Swami* Zukeeni. I'm calling to find Lucy, Lucy Sabatini. I need to speak to her. Urgently. Do you know where she is?"

"Lucy? You want Lucy?" said Nana.

"Yes, she's gone missing here at the ashram where she lives. We're very concerned. I need to be sure she's safe."

"Lucy very safe, you no worry."

"I want to speak to her ... to reassure myself she's OK."

"No, Lucy busy, no come to phone. But you no worry, Lucy safe." There was a click and the dial tone resonated in the swami's office.

Thirty-Five

IN THE SABATINI RESIDENCE, Nana hung up the harvest yellow wall phone. Lucy was gone now, but she had told that bad man *niente*. That man was no good. Bad voice. He would not find her Lucy. She would keep her Lucy safe.

She watched as her son and her son's wife banged through the front door and came into the kitchen with bags of groceries in both arms.

Nana waited until they had deposited the bags on the table. "Man called. Zucchini. I said, no, no zucchini, no food here—"

"Mama, whatsa problem? You knew we were going shopping," said Constance, her very handsome son.

"What's he think we are, a supermarket or something?" said Isabella, the wife. Always with the attitude.

"He call and call," said Nana. "Bad man, very bad man."

Her son stopped emptying the bag and raised his arms in dismay. "What? That's it. We're changing our number. First it was those kids calling all the time and making bad jokes about letting the king out of the can. Now it's a bad man calling my mama. Enough is enough."

"It was Prince Albert, not the king," said the wife. Always with the criticism.

Her handsome son shrugged. "Prince Albert, the king, what's my business? No one threatens my mama."

"Fine, fine," said the wife. "Just get a good number. They always give us the leftovers." Look who's talking. Always with the orders.

"Don't worry. Only the best for my family."

Nana grinned and shuffled out of the kitchen. Mission accomplished. She always kept her Lucy safe. And she always got out of putting things away. Like she tells her Lucy—smart like a fox. The only way to be.

Thirty-Six

AFTER NANA HUNG UP, the swami paced in front of his desk and rubbed his chin.

Cindy stayed glued to the same spot. She kept her eyes downward and her body in a humble pose. She was scanning the papers on the swami's desk. She didn't see the recording contract, but there were some other papers that intrigued her. The swami seemed to be involved in some sort of real estate deal involving the ashram. But how could that be? He didn't have the power to sell the ashram's land and buildings, did he?

The swami stopped pacing and turned to Cindy. "Say nothing to anyone about this. We don't want word getting around that Jakananda went absent without permission. Do you hear me?"

Cindy looked up at the swami with a solemn face and nodded.

He waved his hand. "You may leave."

She walked around the desk and to the door. Turning to face them, she bowed. "Namaste."

Well, of all the ... neither one gave her the required greeting. Besides being remarkably disrespectful, it meant their plans were so far along they couldn't even be bothered keeping up appearances. This was much more serious than she thought.

She slipped out the door and shut it loosely behind her. It was not closed all the way and she could still hear their conversation.

"Pack our bags," said the swami. "We're going to Endwell, New York."

Oh no. They don't believe Nana and they're going to travel all the way to the Sabatinis to see if Lucy's there.

"I'll get Mandy to book a limo. When do you want to leave?"

"Right away. Don't tell her where we're going. At this point, we can't afford any slip-ups. And I want you to take back her key to this office. Hide it someplace no one can find it except us. Now go."

Cindy rushed around the corner and pretended she was doing a stretching exercise against the wall. She heard Ramakar come out of the office and slam the door behind him, then walk quickly down the corridor in the other direction.

He would be going to Mandy's office to arrange the limo and get the key. Cindy knew a shortcut to the admin office most people didn't know. She ran down a short corridor, took two flights of stairs down to the basement, ran past the laundry room, the bike rack, and the men's sauna, and up one flight of stairs. She peered around the door to the first floor and there was Ramakar entering the admin office.

Several men came down the corridor toward the staircase holding towels and personal care products. She had nowhere to hide. She sat on the stairs, closed her eyes, put her hands in prayer mode, and pretended to be meditating. Through slits in her eyelids, she saw them pass by on their way to the men's sauna. They checked her out but didn't say anything.

As soon as they were down the stairs, she jumped up and peered around the corner. Ramakar was coming out of the admin office and had something in his hand. Mandy came out after him and shut the admin office door. They both looked up and down the corridor and then did a quick kiss.

"Check in with me, sugarpuss," said Mandy.

"I'll try, sweet pea," said Ramakar.

Cindy couldn't believe it. Everyone swore a vow of chastity when they came to the ashram, and here was the second-in-command getting it on with one of the admin staff. Even worse, he was her supervisor. Liars and cheats, both of them. And throw-up mushy too.

Mandy went back in the admin office and shut the door. Ramakar proceeded back the way he came and Cindy followed him. She stayed a healthy distance behind and pretended she was doing a silent walking meditation so no one would stop her or speak to her.

A little ways past the Sun Room, Ramakar was accosted and detained by a pair of guests. He turned halfway in her direction as he stopped to deal with them. She darted into the Sun Room and peeked out through the window in the door. Two ladies were already in the room, sitting in easy chairs by an open window.

"Excuse me," said one of the women with Dolly Parton-ish hair, "but aren't you the lady who took over for Jakananda in kirtan?" She got up and walked toward Cindy. A tiny little lady with red hair rose from the other chair and followed her. "Norma here and myself—"

Cindy cut her off by grabbing her hands and speaking very rapidly in a hushed voice. "I know exactly who you are. And I know what you said to Jakananda. You have no idea what it meant to her. Listen, we don't have time." Cindy pulled her to the window in the door and pointed. "You see that man?"

"Yes, we know Ramakar."

"He and the swami are trying to steal Lucy's—I mean Jakananda's—music, and they're planning to sell the ashram to some corporation."

The Dolly Parton look-alike and Norma both gasped, exactly the reaction Cindy was hoping for.

She barreled on, keeping an eye on Ramakar. "Can you help us stop them? Would you be willing to follow Ramakar—without him knowing—and find out where he hides the key he's got in his hand?"

The two women looked at one another and back at Cindy. "We love this ashram, honey," said the Dolly Parton look-alike, "so you bet your sweet bippy we would."

Cindy noticed Ramakar finish his conversation and resume striding down the corridor. "He's on the move. Go, go, go! I'll meet you back here as soon as their limo comes and they leave."

The one with red hair grabbed her friend. "C'mon, Delta. We can pretend we're on another power walk."

The two of them slipped out of the room and began power walking down the corridor after Ramakar.

Cindy hightailed it to her room, got some change, and sprinted down the stairs to the pay phone in the basement. She had memorized the latest phone number for the Sabatinis when she was standing at the swami's desk. She deposited the money, dialed the number, and prayed someone would answer.

"Hello," shouted Lucy's father.

Cindy talked as fast and loud as she could. "Mr. Sabatini, this is Cindy. I'm calling to warn you that two bad men are on their way to your house."

"What?"

"Swami Zukeeni and Ramakarshivenenda are on their way to your house, right now. They're out to hurt Lucy and you can't tell them where she is."

Cindy gulped breaths as she explained the situation. Mr. Sabatini reassured her they would handle it.

After she got off the phone, she sprinted up five flights of stairs to the top floor of the ashram. Gasping and holding her side, she ran to the window overlooking the back of the ashram, the area where the guests unloaded their luggage. The limo wasn't there. She ran to a room across the hall that overlooked the front drive. No limo there, either. She ran back to the first window just as a limo pulled up. No surprise, they were using the more secretive loading zone. The driver got out and Ramakar rushed up to him and handed him two overnight cases. The swami followed, and in moments the limo was lurching away and speeding down the drive.

Cindy made her way to the Sun Room. The two women were waiting for her. As soon as she entered the room, Norma held up the key and grinned.

"Excellent work," said Cindy. "They left with overnight bags, so I'm going in tonight to do some sleuthing. Are you with me?"

They looked at one another and back at her.

"Does the pope wear dresses?" said the one called Delta.

Thirty-Seven

JACK PULLED Mick aside and offered him five hundred dollars cash, payable when they arrived in Phoenix, if he kept his walkie-talkie in transmit mode for the entire trip and hid it somewhere in the lounge of the band bus. Mick also had to keep his bus traveling right behind Jack's so Jack would always be in receiving distance and could hear everything that was said. Jack waved the brand new cash—he always carried fresh new bills with him "just in case"—and Mick instantly agreed.

Jack didn't trust Mick to put the walkie-talkie in the right place. So he came on the band bus to "consult" with Mick on where it should go. Jack didn't tell him why he was doing it; he was the damn boss and that's all Mick needed to know. Besides, he could see that Mick was desperate to get on his good side after what happened on the interstate the other night.

Jack hadn't been on the band bus in a while and he couldn't believe the overwhelming smell of beer and pot. Mick had tried to cover it up with air freshener, but that made it reek even worse. It was especially bad in the combination lounge and galley area where the boys hung out, not so bad in the area with the bunks at the rear of the bus. Jack was not well pleased. He was planning to sell the buses on to another rock band at the end of the tour, and getting the smell out was going to cut into the profit. These boys seemed determined to foil his plans at every turn. Why couldn't they grow the hell up and act like adults?

He also didn't think Lucy or Alison should travel on a bus smelling like this, but there wasn't much he could do about it. Keith wasn't allowed to bring a groupie on the bus, but he could bring a girlfriend, and he had made a point of calling Lucy his girlfriend a ridiculous number of times. Like he didn't want anyone to forget. And yet most of the time he ignored her. There was something very fishy going on there. And, of course, Alison was coming on the band bus with Randy. She had quit her job to accompany him for the rest of the tour. Jack would never have believed that Randy succeeded in getting a girlfriend if he hadn't been there to see it for himself.

After some consultation, Jack and Mick agreed on where to put the walkie-talkie. Jack made sure the batteries were new, that the placement was ideal for catching conversations, and that Mick was sworn to silence. Attention to detail was one of the keys to his success—and under no circumstances did he want anyone to know what he was doing. That was the main reason he'd paid Mick so damn much.

The tricky part now would be getting Dunk to ride on the band bus. He almost always rode with Jack so they could review how things were going and tweak their game plan—except when they were having a big row. Jack told Dunk he was exhausted from writing music all night and needed to sleep. He also suggested that Dunk go on the band bus so he could try to weasel more out of Howie. It was far easier to convince Dunk than he had expected.

Shortly before they took off, Jack told Gus he was taking the walkie-talkie to his bedroom so he could chat to someone on the other bus. Gus waved his hand and grunted. Jack went in his bedroom at the back and made himself comfortable. He sprawled across the bed with his hands behind his head, food and drink within reach, and the walkie-talkie next to him.

He hoped this paid off, because if anyone found out he'd done this, they would think he was out of his mind ... or worse. He knew why he was doing it. That Lucy, he had to know more. Who was she? What was she doing here? Dunk never would have agreed to "bug" the bus, which was essentially what he was doing. Dunk would have told him to get his arse on the band bus if he wanted to know more about her. But he could never do that. He was the leader of the band and needed to maintain his distance, and that bus was a veritable cesspool of germs, as he'd now confirmed. Riding on there was not something he would ever do willingly.

He listened to everyone board the band bus—Rob and Sam, Keith and George, Howie with Carly and Suze, Dunk and Randy, and, finally, Alison and Lucy. He heard Lucy near the walkie-talkie. "You guys, what about Jack? I saw Vic get on the other bus, but I didn't see Jack." How adorable is that, making sure he's not left behind.

"Oh no, he's there. I just checked." Dunk's voice boomed in the walkie-talkie.

"But don't *they* want to ride with us?" said Lucy.

"No," said Dunk, "*they* have work to do."

"Yeah," said Keith in a smartass tone. "*They* have to buff each other's toenails, don't they?"

He better watch it.

"Yeah, and they have to trim each other's overgrown nose and ear hairs," said Rob, a bit harder to hear.

You watch out too, Rob.

"Yeah," said Sam, about as distinct as Rob, "and they have to give each other haircuts like Nigel Tufnel."

Oh, here we go again with Spinal Tap. The boys were obsessed with it.

"Yeah," said Randy, a bit closer, "and ... and ... and they have to play a song in D minor and weep in each other's arms."

"Yeah, and these go to eleven," Rob and Sam shouted at the same time. There was the sound of laughter and hand slaps.

"Oh, you guys are too silly," said Lucy, her voice getting less distinct as she moved away from the walkie-talkie. "Why don't I pop over and ask them?"

"No!" Dunk's voice was so loud it hurt his ears. "Jack's sleeping and we can't disturb him."

"Won't Vic be lonely by himself?" said Lucy.

"Get over here, woman," said Keith. "Forget about Vic. You're with me."

Lucy's voice got louder. "You're right, loverboy. You were going to play your tunes for me."

Loverboy? Has she ... ? No, she can't have.

Jack heard the sound of the band's bus door closing. His own bus started up and pulled out. He could hear indistinct chitchat on the other bus, then lost them altogether as they went out of range. He ran up to the front of the bus and told Gus to keep the band bus closer. Gus grunted and slowed down. Jack was a bit peeved. He hoped he hadn't missed anything.

He rushed back to his bedroom. Keith was now playing acoustic guitar and singing a song Jack had never heard before. He figured Keith must be singing one of his new tunes. Jack was pleasantly surprised. It was quite good, not the schmaltzy schlock Keith had been turning out before, but still a might too pop for his own tastes. Keith played two more tunes and Lucy kept exclaiming how good they were. She didn't say great, thank goodness. That would encourage Keith to be even more demanding about including his songs in the show, and honestly, how could Jack respect someone who thought Keith's songs were "great"?

"Now me," she said.

What did that mean? There was a pause and some low talking, and then the guitar playing started again. Lucy must have taken the guitar because the playing was far more gentle and folksy than the aggressive way the boys played. A female voice started singing his song "Your Face." How could she already know the words and melody? She'd heard it for the first time last night.

She had a pitch perfect soprano voice, but it was the passion with which she sang that got him. Keith joined in on the second verse and Jack felt a surge of jealousy. It should be him singing his song with her, not "loverboy." Then everyone else joined in on the last two verses. They were having a sing-along and he was the only one not there. That old sense of injustice reared its head and he squashed it back down. He didn't want to miss a note of her singing.

He lay there listening as the group sang song after song. They sang old rock and folk standards from the sixties and seventies, a few disco hits, nothing recent from the eighties. Lucy seemed to prefer the old tunes. She seemed to be able to sing anything within her range, even the difficult ones.

"Can I do one of my own songs for you?" she asked.

Everyone encouraged her. He almost shouted "Yes" himself, forgetting that he wasn't actually there.

She strummed as she introduced the song, like she was used to playing in front of audiences, or at least in front of other people. "This is a tune called 'Saying Yes.' I recently had this Southern lady with big Dolly Parton hair come up to me. She said that this tune had made her feel like living again, because you see, she had lost her son and she wasn't caring about anything at all anymore. And her friend Norma—she's this tiny little lady with bright red hair—well, Norma made her come there, um, where I was, and she heard this song, and she wanted to live again. And now she and Norma are going to open a business." Lucy's voice cracked. Someone murmured something he couldn't hear. "No, I'm OK ... So here it is. 'Saying Yes.'"

She played her song. He wasn't expecting much, some simple little tune. He sat up and turned up the walkie-talkie to hear more clearly. He was completely and totally stunned. This girl knew music at some fundamental, primal level. The melody was simple enough for the average person to pick up and sing, but the music had a depth and complexity only a professional musician would truly appreciate. It reminded him of some of his favorite Zep tunes—haunting and beautiful. He could imagine this song with all kinds of arrangements, including a full orchestra.

But it was the lyrics that got to him. She sang about the regret of not living the full life, of doing what everyone else wanted while denying one's own true calling, of letting life slip away until it was suddenly gone. "The robin comes, the robin goes, quicker every year, until our red breast breathes its last and death is at our door." Emotions chased through him—nostalgia, regret, resolve—the hallmark of a great song.

The bus slowed and turned off the highway. The bus drivers would need a break, the buses would need refueling, and the boys would need to stretch their legs before the confinement of the bus drove them nuts. Not to mention using the public toilets so they didn't stink up the bus, especially with ladies onboard.

His bus stopped and he heard the voices disappearing from the other bus. He stayed on his bed, not sure if he was up to leaving the bus and facing all of them. He closed his eyes. Maybe he'd take a quick nap. He *was* tired from not getting enough sleep the night before.

A voice unexpectedly came through the walkie-talkie. "What is it, Luce?"

Lucy spoke in a low voice, like she was afraid of someone overhearing. "Alison, I know this might sound crazy, but I don't think there's a Vic."

Jack's eyes popped open in shock.

"What are you talking about? We saw him get on the other bus."

You tell her, Alison.

"But did we see *Jack* get on the bus?" said Lucy. "No, we didn't. And here's the thing. When have we *ever* seen Jack and Vic at the same time?"

That girl is too smart for her own good.

"Huh," said Alison, "you're right. We haven't."

"And why did they almost jump down my throat when I suggested we invite Vic to join us?"

Because they know I'm not going on that germy bus, that's why.

"Yeah, what was that all about?"

Lucy's voice was nonchalant. "I wonder if Randy would tell you, your relationship being so new and everything."

Jack groaned.

Alison sounded indignant. "Well, he better tell me." He *will* tell her. Randy didn't have the experience to resist a persuasive female.

"It'll be hard to ask him with the guys around," said Lucy.

"Don't you worry," said Alison. "I know exactly how to get him away from them. Leave it to me."

No, I won't leave it to you!

"I bet you do," said Lucy. They laughed and their voices faded away.

"That little minx," Jack said aloud. He jumped up from the bed and went into the wardrobe area. Time to get in full Victor mode. He was going to have some fun with her. She doesn't know that I know that she knows. This is going to be *delicious* fun.

Thirty-Eight

JACK DESCENDED from the bus and strode over to Randy. He was standing with the guys but Alison was whispering something in his ear. Randy was starting to follow her when Jack zoomed in and grabbed Randy's arm and said in Vic's voice, "Beggin' your pardon, Alison me darlin', but I need to consult wif me boy Randy 'ere."

Alison looked surprised and displeased.

Jack gave her a killer smile. "Don't fret, me love, I won't be takin' 'im far." As he led Randy across the pavement, away from Alison, he spoke softly in his normal Jack voice. "Randy, I need to ask you for a very small favor."

"Yeah, sure, Jack," said Randy, also lowering his voice. "Anything."

Jack stopped and faced him. "Well, you know I don't normally go for groupies, but I'm quite taken with this Lucy. She's kind of cute, isn't she?" He looked across the parking lot where she was talking with Alison and sneaking looks in their direction.

"Um ..." Randy was at a loss for words.

"Not my usual type," continued Jack, "but I'm not talking about a relationship or anything. Just, you know, having some fun with her. Maybe a wild night or two. I bet she's a wildcat in bed, a wildcat I'd love to tame. Might even be into the kinky stuff, you know what I mean."

Randy looked shocked. "But um, well ..." His face suddenly lit up with relief. "She's kind of with Keith."

"C'mon, Randy, we both know Keith couldn't care less. So here's my tiny little favor. I want you to ask her to come to my room tonight. And to wear something very sexy, like what she was wearing yesterday. Something that's a total turn-on." Jack rubbed his hands together. This was so good.

Randy looked mortified. "Well, I don't know, Jack. I mean—"

"This one time, Randy. I won't ask you to do something like this again." Randy looked unconvinced, so Jack put on his most earnest look. "You know it's hard for me to approach women given my situation. And she seems like she'd be quite open to it. You saw her, she kissed and hugged me last night and I thought she'd never stop. She's clearly very attracted to me. So you'd be doing both of us a big favor, wouldn't you?"

Randy grimaced and looked at the ground. "I guess so."

"Excellent. Let's go chat to them, so I can say great things about Jack and get her excited about him again. Then you can ask her when you're back on the bus."

Jack left Randy and sauntered toward Lucy and Alison. Showtime!

Randy straggled after him.

"Allo allo, ladies," Jack greeted them. "Jus' stoppin' by to relay Jack's regrets for not bein' a better 'ost. 'E was up all the night composin' a new tune, all inspired by the reaction to the concert last night, and by your enfusiasm specially, Mistress Lucy." Jack gave Lucy a wide-eyed, innocent smile.

Lucy smiled back. "Oh, yes, I *was* impressed. I would really love the opportunity to tell him again. And I thought both of you might like to come on our bus for a while. We're singing songs and having a blast. Would he happen to be awake?" Point well played, Mistress Lucy. But not well enough.

"Oh no, 'e's quite the sleeper, is ol' Jack. No tellin' when 'e'll wake up. An' 'e needs 'is sleep after workin' all night, know what I mean?"

Lucy moved close to him, into his personal space. "Then why don't *you* join us, Vic? No reason you should stay on that bus all by your little old self with nothing to do."

Jack looked down at her and smiled with regret. "Oh, I wish I could, darlin', but I got me work to do. I'm Jack's assistant and 'e gave me some fings to ..."

He stopped speaking because she started fingering the front of his shirt and he lost his train of thought. She was touching him and he didn't mind it. In fact, it was kind of turning him on.

"Oh, that Jack, he's not very nice to you, is he? Making you work while he gets to sleep and everyone else gets to have fun. He sounds like a real slave driver. How can you stand working for him?"

Jack was momentarily speechless and then came to his senses. He couldn't let her get away with talking about him like this, especially when she didn't know that he knew that she knew. "Oh, no! Jack ain't no slave driver. 'E's the best." Jack turned to Randy for support. "Right, Ran?"

Randy had been looking at the ground and trying to avoid everyone's eyes. He looked up and Jack raised his eyebrows at him.

"Um, yes. Jack is great. I swear it."

Lucy moved up close to Jack, put her hands on his chest, and looked up into his face. "I just don't think he's that good to you, Vic. He keeps you all to himself and we never get to spend any time with you. I mean, I would love to get to know *you* better."

This was not going the way Jack had intended. She was supposed to be convinced that "Jack" was a good guy and be enticed to come to his room tonight. Did it matter? He was so distracted by her hands he couldn't think straight. "No, you need to give 'im a chance, me love. Listen to Randy. 'E knows. Jack's the best."

"Um, yeah," said Randy.

Lucy pulled away from Jack. "Oh, OK. If you say so. But don't forget you called me princess and told me to come to you if I ever needed anything. So don't you be surprised if I might need something from you, *Vic*." She gave him a coy smile.

Jack narrowed his eyes at her. He was being played. The question was, how far was she willing to go? He guessed he might find out tonight.

"Gotta get back to me work, ladies," he said. "Don't forget what we talked about, Randy." He doffed an imaginary hat and bowed to the two women. "Alison. *Princess*. Me pleasure."

He turned and strode back to the bus. He ignored Dunk calling his name, and as he climbed onto the bus he told Gus he was not to be disturbed. He went into his bedroom and locked the door, took off his shirt and smelled it. He put on the Jane Fonda tape, not for inspiration but to mask the sounds as he jerked off in seconds flat. He'd never been so turned on in his entire life.

Thirty-Nine

LUCY AND ALISON turned to Randy as soon as Jack left.

"What did he talk to you about?" said Lucy. She needed to know. She'd been very turned on sparring with Jack pretending to be Vic and not knowing that she knew who he really was.

"Oh, OK, well ..." Randy shuffled his feet.

"Vic is Jack, isn't he?" said Alison.

Randy looked at Alison with shock. "How did you know?" His expression changed immediately to chagrin. "Forget I said that. I can't tell you anything. I signed a contract, didn't I? And I don't want to lose my job."

Lucy gave him a reassuring smile. "We already knew, so *you* didn't tell us. But what did he talk to you about? He was looking at us the whole time he talked to you."

"I don't really want to," said Randy. "You're not going to like it."

"Get it off your chest, hon," said Alison as she rubbed his back. "You'll feel better."

Randy looked at Lucy with regret. "He wants you to come to his room tonight."

"Really?" said Lucy, her face breaking into a big smile. She couldn't stop it.

"You can't go. He's really crafty, is Jack."

"I'm really crafty too, Randy." Didn't he just see her in action?

"No, you don't understand. He wants you to come there in something really sexy so he can seduce you and have wild sex with you." Randy lowered his voice. "Even maybe, you know, kinky sex."

Lucy looked disbelieving. "Kinky sex? Like playing pirate and wench, and I get to walk the plank?" She and Alison looked at one another and laughed.

"No, he said you're a wildcat he wants to tame."

Lucy felt bad for Randy; he was so earnest and concerned about her wellbeing. "C'mon, he must be joking ..." She looked off into the distance for a moment, and suddenly it came to her. "Unless ... unless somehow *he* knows that *I* know. How would he know that I know?" He couldn't have. Could he?

She dashed over to the bus and climbed aboard, Alison and Randy rushing to keep up with her. She turned and put her finger to her lips. Tiptoeing into the lounge, she searched the cushions and then the overhead area. The walkie-talkie was hidden beneath a blanket. She picked it up and showed it to them, and pointed to the "on" transmission switch.

Randy beetled his eyebrows as if he couldn't compute what he was seeing, while Alison raised hers and mouthed "oh-mi-god."

Putting the walkie-talkie back where she'd found it, Lucy stood on the seat so her mouth would be as close to it as possible. This was going to be so much fun. "Alison, can I be honest with you?"

Lucy waved at Alison to respond.

"Yes, Lucy, you can." Alison was a bit wooden in her delivery, but it would have to do.

"I'm so surprised that Jack is interested in me. I thought he was gay."

Alison gave her a grinning nod. "Why did you think that, Lucy?"

"Well, because I hugged and kissed him last night, and he didn't react at all. He was stiff as a board."

"That sounds gay to me," said Alison.

"Um, I've never seen him with a woman," said Randy.

Lucy gave him a gleeful smile and a thumbs up.

Randy looked confused. "Well, I haven't."

"That's just it, Randy. I would love to have wild and kinky sex with him. But he doesn't seem to like women. Now Sam, on the other hand, Sam seems to have a real appreciation for women."

"Well, yes, but Sam likes *a lot* of women," said Randy.

"I guess I won't know for sure unless I go tonight in my sexiest outfit and see what happens. I would certainly enjoy some wild and kinky sex right now."

Forty

JACK LISTENED as he sprayed Wipe-It-Fresh and cleaned up the mess he'd just created. Omigod, could they be worse actors if they tried? It was clear they had found the walkie-talkie and were performing for his benefit.

"So that means she knows that I know that she knows that I'm Jack and Vic," he said aloud. "Game on, my fine wench, game on."

He fetched himself a glass of wine and got settled against the headboard of his bed as he waited for everyone to troop back onto the other bus. He half-listened to the chatter until Lucy's voice came through loud and clear.

"Sam, come sit next to me. I've been wanting to get to know you better."

"And Sam wants to get to know you better too," said Sam in his sexy voice.

"Rob also wants to get to know you better," said Rob in his alpha male voice.

After a pause, during which Jack was quite certain they were both putting physical moves on her, Lucy said, "Are you two looking for a threesome? I hear there's a lot of kinky sex going on in this band."

"No," Rob and Sam barked at the same time.

Jack laughed. Clever girl. She knew how to handle randy young men.

"Tell me, is Jack gay?" said Lucy.

Here we go again. Back to the gay repartee.

"I don't know about Jack," Sam said, again in his low, sexy voice, "but Sam is most definitely he-ter-o-sex-u-al and interested in a *twosome* with a very fine lady such as yourself."

"You want a real man?" said Rob. "Check this out ... Go ahead, feel it." No doubt he was showing her his bicep.

Lucy laughed. "Very nice."

Jack rolled his eyes. Like she would be impressed by that. Or, at least, he hoped not.

He only half-listened after that, plotting out his seduction if she showed up that evening. He changed his mind a half dozen times. Finally, giving up, he took a power nap and did what he often did—let his unconscious figure out what to do. When he woke up ten minutes later, a plan was taking shape in his mind.

Forty-One

RANDY NOTICED Dunk watching all the activity around Lucy and looking over at Keith, expecting him to react in some way. Keith was hunched over a guitar magazine, oblivious to everything else going on in the bus.

"Um, Dunk, could I have a word with you?" Randy said, indicating the sleeping area with his thumb. "Excuse me for a minute please, Alison."

Dunk followed Randy to the sleeping area. He looked down at him and raised his eyebrows. "What is it, kid?"

"Well, um, I know it looks like Lucy is cheating on Keith, but she's not. He was with someone else last night."

Dunk glowered and Randy took a step back.

"No, I'm not mad at you, kid. I'm just surprised that it didn't last even one single night."

Randy knit his eyebrows. "Oh, yeah."

"Good laddie," Dunk said, patting him on the shoulder. "Ya did the right thing telling me."

After Dunk went back into the lounge, Randy stood there trying to make sense of things and wondered whether he'd actually done the right thing telling Dunk. One thing he knew for sure, he was so happy he now had Alison to talk to.

Alison came in and shut the connecting door behind her. "You OK, babe?"

Randy grabbed her and gave her a long, passionate kiss. They climbed into one of the bunk beds and continued snogging.

"Whoa!" Sam said as he walked in and out again. Randy heard the door latch shut and Sam shout, "Off limits. Our kid is getting his groove on."

"Our kid" carried on through the laughing and hooting that came through the door. The guys might have to wait a while. He had a lot of catching up to do. It was his turn to monopolize the sleeping area. And he was planning to do a lot more than snogging.

Forty-Two

SWAMI ZUKEENI LOOKED out the window of the limo at the hometown of the absconded Jakananda. He was not impressed. Endwell, New York was a strikingly boring suburb where, obviously, nothing of any significance ever happened. Indeed, it was an offshoot of Endicott, the birthplace of IBM, a has-been company rapidly being superseded by the likes of Microsoft and Apple, dynamic companies in which he avidly invested.

He accepted the driver's hand as he alighted from the limo, ordering Rod to get out on the street side. His second-in-command was annoying him to no end these days with his nail-biting and second-guessing. He, Mac, knew exactly what he was doing and had the goods to prove it, with his thriving ashram and skyrocketing stock portfolio.

He was also not impressed with the Sabatini family home. How could an entire family live in a ranch house of such diminutive girth? His house was twice as big and he lived alone. The lawn and flowerbeds looked as if they had been mown, weeded, trimmed and pruned within an inch of their lives. Those petunias dare not bother their pansy neighbors or there would be hell to pay. He suppressed a smile at his internal wittiness; this was a serious endeavor and he must maintain decorum at all costs.

"Are we going in?" said Rod at his elbow.

The lace curtain twitched at the Sabatini's front window.

"Yes, Rod. I am surveilling the Sabatini premises for clues as to the whereabouts of our disappeared songstress, but my acute senses tell me that she is not here." He sniffed as he looked at grinning gnomes cavorting on the lawn around a statue of the Virgin Mary. "Bad taste. That is all we'll find, I assure you."

Waving at Rod to go ahead of him, he adjusted his robes and turban as he sauntered up the slate walkway to the tiny front stoop. The door opened before they reached it.

"Can I help you?" said a young man with a New York Mets cap. Even the sports choices of this family were losers.

"We're sorry to disturb you," said Rod, overly obsequious, "but is this Lucy Sabatini's house?"

"Who's asking?" The young man had the same impertinent tone as Jakananda and her friend Cindy. That Morgan girl could ask for a Sanskrit name until she was blue in the face, but she'd never get one until she cleaned up her smartass attitude.

"We're from Spirits Rising Center for Yoga and Meditation." Rod gestured toward Mac. "This is the head of the center, Swami Zukeeni, and I'm the director of operations, Ramakarshivenenda."

Mac bowed, his hands in prayer mode. "Namaste." Rod followed suit.

"So what can I do you for?" said the young man, grinning at them as he mangled the English language.

"Miss Sabatini has gone missing and we're very concerned about her safety," Rod said, using the tack they'd agreed. "We understand she might've come here, but obviously we had to check that out for ourselves. She's a very important person at the center, you see, being our musical director and a much-admired singer."

"Oh, yeah? C'mon in." The young man gestured for them to enter.

Rod turned and waited for Mac to precede him.

Mac was not surprised by the room they found themselves in. Italian American, ultra-formal, and kitschy. Crocheted doilies on the arms and backs of a floral sofa and matching armchairs. Wall-to-wall green carpeting crying out to be replaced. The odor of Pledge furniture polish hanging in the air. Mac was certain plastic coverings had been whipped off the furniture the minute they arrived. These were, no doubt, old-school Catholics who attended Mass every Saturday evening and said Hail Marys on their rosaries. He had to swallow the bile rising in the back of his throat. He and Rod would not be staying long.

A middle-aged man with a dramatic comb over and a woman clutching his arm smiled as he walked up to them. He bowed and intoned, "Namaste."

The man thrust out his hand. "I'm Lucy's dad, Constance Sabatini." The swami extended his own and allowed Lucy's "dad" to grab it and shake it. A male bonding ritual the swami had never enjoyed.

Gesturing to the woman, the man said, "And this is my wife, Isabella."

Lucy's mother kept one arm around her waist and waved with the other hand. A woman who obviously had a female relative dye her amateurish red hair and a hair "parlor" cut it. He knew her type.

"And that's my son, Tony," Lucy's father added, waving toward the door.

The young man gave a curt nod, crossed his arms, and widened his stance. He reminded the swami of a bouncer at a backstreet nightclub, a person with a taste for petty power and gratuitous violence.

Lucy's father indicated the other chairs in the room. "Please, sit."

The swami took the seat furthest from the Sabatinis and assumed an erect and commanding posture, staring at the couple as Rod galumphed into the armchair next to him.

"So, Swami Zukeeni," said Lucy's father. The smile had disappeared from his face. "How are—"

"Where is Lucy?" the swami said without ceremony.

The Sabatinis raised their eyebrows at one another.

"Can I get you some coffee or tea?" said Lucy's mother. "Coke? Fanta?"

Ramakar grinned. "A Coke would be—"

"No drinks," said the swami. "Time is of the essence. Where is your daughter, Mr. Sabatini?"

Lucy's father startled. "Well, uh, I've sent my daughter to Palermo.

My mother is not well, and Lucy's getting her birth certificate, in case, you know."

All three Sabatinis made the sign of the cross. The swami stifled a smile. So the innocent-looking Sabatinis had prepared for this little Nativity play too.

"When is she expected back, pray tell?"

Lucy's father made an exaggerated shrug. "That depends. Those Italians—"

"It took Rose Zucco three weeks," interrupted the wife. Her husband gave her a look and she added, "Well, it did."

"Three weeks," said the swami, staring at Lucy's mother.

"Maybe four, I can't remember exactly." She perked up, as if an idea had occurred in that small, red-helmeted head of hers. "You want I should call Rose? She might just be home. Oh no, wait, I think she's helping out to bingo today."

"Bingo," said the swami. He couldn't keep the sneer from his voice.

As he weighed his options, the moment's heavy silence was shattered by shouting from another room. "Nana, no!"

Everyone turned in the direction of the shout. An old woman came into view through the doorway into the family area, moving at a fast clip with her walker. A black cocker spaniel accompanied her, spinning and barking into the air.

A young woman followed behind, holding a bucking toddler. "Nana, come back to your room."

Jumping up, Lucy's father spoke in rapid Italian to his mother as she approached, remonstrating with her to go back to her room and leave things to him. Lucky for the swami, and unlucky for the trickster Sabatinis, he was fluent in Latin and most of the Romance languages, including Italian.

He stifled a smile as Nana gave her performance: shrieking at the top of her lungs and spewing insults—from her native Palermo no doubt, as these were new to him—followed by a string of incantations and curses as she waved her walker around and pulled on her clothing like a woman possessed, the dog barking as it circled around her. He wanted to shout "Bravo!" for the impressive performance. After a final shriek, she turned and toddled back toward the rear of the house.

"Sorry about that," the young woman directed at the Sabatinis. "Betsy, come," she ordered the dog as she made her exit. The dog gave a look around, made a satisfied yip, and padded after her.

"Bad," shouted the toddler, pointing at the swami over his mother's shoulder.

"You wanna see Cookie Monster?" she responded. The little brat nodded his head and clapped his hands. Why did anyone have children? Such irritating and useless creatures.

Mac rose and looked from one Sabatini to another. "That was quite ... dramatic. I see where your daughter gets it from." He sauntered to the door, Rod anxiously hovering on his heels.

The Sabatini bouncer opened the door for them.

Time for Mac to deliver some drama of his own. He turned and gave Lucy's parents a fierce stare. "Tell Lucy we are looking for her and we will find her if we have to call in the FBI. Tell her that her departure has caused me big problems and I am not amused. She will return to the ashram immediately or there will be serious repercussions."

Just as he turned to make a dramatic exit, he felt something rub against his leg. He looked down. A cat! There was one thing he was deathly afraid of, and that was cats. He turned in a circle as he shrieked and tried to throw the beast off his leg. The cat streaked into the other room.

"You don't treat our Mittens like that," the son said, glaring at him.

After the indignity of being assaulted by a mangy feline, how dare this upstart talk to him in such tone? Mac turned and flounced from the house. To make matters worse, he heard Rod apologizing for disturbing them. How dast he apologize to those inconsequential and appalling people?

Mac marched onto the grass and kicked over the gnomes. Gnomes should not, under any circumstances, cavort around the Virgin Mary. His father would file a lawsuit against the Sabatinis if he saw such sacrilege.

Mac could hear the son shouting at him so he hightailed it to the limo. The driver opened the door and he leapt in. Rod jumped in the other side not two seconds later.

The limo driver screeched away from the curb as Lucy's brother shook his fist and screamed at them through the closed window. Thank goodness it was an air-conditioned vehicle and the window was closed, or that Neanderthal might have grabbed him by the throat.

The swami reveled in the adrenaline high and beamed with satisfaction. He would laugh with unbridled glee if they were alone.

"Driver, raise the soundproof divider," he ordered.

As soon as the driver did so, Mac pulled off his turban and threw it on the floor. "That was quite the performance by Nana. Worthy of a Razzie."

"But we didn't find Jakananda."

"Who cares? They told us everything we need to know. Our little songstress has, indeed, absconded against ashram regulations. So we are going ahead with our plans, Lucy Sabatini or no Lucy Sabatini. The contract is going to Barry tomorrow and it's full steam ahead."

"But ... but ... we don't have her signature."

"You will practice it and sign for her. What do the kids say? Easy-peasy."

Rod began picking at his fingernails and the swami pulled the offending hand away.

"Relax, Rod. Everything's going to work out perfectly. You will have your music contract *molto presto*." Mac relaxed back in the plush seat. "Did I ever tell you about my sojourn in the gastronomically and oenologically stellar town of Montepulciano?" He expounded on his sojourn all the way back to the ashram as Rod surreptitiously picked at his fingers beside him.

Forty-Three

NORMA WAS KEEPING watch out the window, just in case the swami and Ramakar changed their plans and arrived back earlier than expected, while Cindy searched the swami's office and Delta made photocopies of anything interesting they found.

Lucky for them it was summer, still light out, and they could see without turning on a lamp. Lucky also that there was a Xerox machine in the office, an obvious manifestation of the swami's need for secrecy. If it had been efficiency he was after, the machine would have been in the admin office with Mandy.

Cindy had already searched the top of the swami's messy desk and the jumble of papers underneath it, had flipped through the files in the drawers, and was now making her way through the tall filing cabinet in the corner. She had found an unsigned copy of the recording contract and a draft proposal for the transfer of the ashram to a company called Naturisme Inc.

She wrinkled her brow in concentration. "This all seems to be old stuff belonging to a guy named Elmo MacFie." She pulled out a thick paper. "Hey, he got an A at Princeton University on this paper: 'Sensual Longings and Sexual Peccadilloes as Revealed in the Writings of the Sanskrit Scholars of Yore.'"

Norma watched as a limo pulled up on the drive below. "The eagle is landing! The eagle is landing!"

Cindy looked up from the file. "What?"

Ramakar and the swami got out of the limo and stretched. The swami looked up toward his office and Norma jerked out of sight.

"The swami is back and I think he saw me."

The women jumped into action, stuffing the Xerox copies down their yoga tops and bottoms, turning off the Xerox machine, and rushing out of the room. They locked the door and walked quickly down the hall.

"Split up and meet me in my room at o-nine-hundred," whispered Cindy.

Norma furrowed her brow. "O-nine-hundred or o-twenty-one-hundred?"

"Nine o'clock," hissed Cindy over her shoulder as she ran down the corridor. She ducked into a meditation session and took a spot at the back.

When they gathered in Cindy's room later, they figured out a place to hide the copies where the swami and Ramakar could never find them. They also agreed: as soon as possible, Norma would go to the nearest town and get her bright red hair dyed dark brown.

Forty-Four

THE PIRATE ENTOURAGE checked into their new hotel in Phoenix and got everyone settled in for the four-night stay. Tonight was a rare night off, followed by three nights of concerts. Dunk preferred a longer stay in one place to give the crew a break from putting up and taking down the stage. Jack didn't mind, as long as they could play a good-sized arena and sell out. It cut down on the amount of cleaning he had to do. Selling records and concert tickets had never been a problem in the southwest; pirates turned out to be especially popular in cowboy country. Although, at the moment, they weren't really having a problem selling out anywhere. Knock on wood.

Jack sprayed Wipe-It-Fresh and cleaned the coffee table, along with the remote control and telephone.

"I hate to say it," Dunk said, "but that Lucy? She's gotta go."

"What?" said Jack. "Why?" Only yesterday Dunk had been arguing to let her stay. It had to be something serious if he now wanted to banish her.

"Keith was with someone else last night. Not Lucy."

Jack straightened and looked for something else to clean. "So?"

Of course he was with someone else. She wouldn't be with *Keith*. He wasn't good enough for her. With that voice and that composing talent, none of the band members were anywhere near her equal, except maybe himself. She was … extraordinary.

"*So?*" Dunk said in a piqued voice. "Who said yesterday that we had to get rid of her because we don't know why she's here and we can't take any risks?" Putting a hand on his chin, Dunk looked upwards as if he were trying to remember. "Oh, yeah, that would be you."

Jack checked his teeth as he wiped down the full-length mirror. "Of course she's not with Keith. Odds are that Barry sent her. But so what? We use it against him. Use her to send back whatever we want him to hear." Which meant he would need to spend time with her to make sure she sent back the right things. A lot of time.

"Look, I hate to say this, because you'll never bloody well let me forget it, but you were right. She's turning everything upside down. Randy was having sex on the bus. Randy!"

Jack turned toward Dunk. "Randy? Really?" He broke into a huge grin. "Our little boy is growing up." If Randy could get hooked up like that, and that quickly, there was hope … for anyone.

Dunk threw up his hands in disgust.

Jack walked past him to the window and sprayed it. "Relax, I'm on top of it." He averted his face. "I'm going to … I've scheduled a meeting with her tonight. I intend to find out what she knows, and give her some tripe to feed Barry."

He had no choice, did he? She'd already figured out who he really was—in record time, actually. Alison hadn't even had a clue until Lucy pointed it out to her. Lucy was not just a pretty face, or, to be more accurate, a gorgeous face and a perfect body. But she could expose him, so he had to give his time and attention right now to managing the situation. He needed to know exactly why she was here, and make sure she didn't do anything to hurt the band or put the bonus at risk. That was his job as the head of the band.

"A meeting. Is that what ya call it?"

Jack turned and glared at Dunk. "Give me some credit. I know what I'm doing." Yes, Lucy was very smart; that was obvious. But everyone kept calling him a genius. So he figured he could bloody well handle it. Dunk seemed to be implying that he had other motives. That was ridiculous … and insulting. He was simply protecting the band.

Dunk went to the door and opened it. "I hope that's true, 'cause this time *yer* going to be the one picking up the pieces." He slammed the door on his way out.

Jack shrugged and started singing "Your Eyes" as he resumed cleaning. He wanted the room to be absolutely flawless if she showed up that evening. He prayed that she would come. He felt this weird fascination when he was with her, something he'd never experienced before, as if he could watch her and listen to her all day and feel perfectly content. And he also had this strange hunger to know more about her. He never wanted to know more about other people; he preferred to read books and write songs. But he wanted to know *everything* about her. Everything. And he wanted to be the only one who did. Just him. No one else.

Forty-Five

LUCY YANKED down her red miniskirt and adjusted the off-the-shoulder black top Alison had lent her. She couldn't believe she used to wear this kind of stuff all the time. The younger Lucy had been willing to suffer all kinds of discomforts to look sexy. From living in the ashram, she knew it didn't matter at all: men were men were men were men, as she liked to say. Wearing the lace-up stiletto heels from her younger days made her feel like a groupie again. But that was the point tonight, wasn't it? Or was it? She wasn't sure anymore. She wasn't even sure why she was here, or what she was expecting to happen. All she knew was that, for some reason, she was eager to know more about this Jack, or Vic, or whatever his name was.

She raised her hand, took a deep breath, and knocked on the door. She heard footsteps, and after a moment the door swung open. Jack stood there looking at her in that intense way that made her breath catch in her chest.

"Hello, Lucy. I'm Jack ... and Vic ... as I think you figured out." He motioned for her to enter.

She walked past him into the room. Darn, she had completely miscalculated. He was dressed in stonewashed jeans and a Pirate t-shirt, like when she first met him as Vic. He smelled good—that was Aramis cologne, if she wasn't mistaken—but with that intriguing undertone of Wipe-It-Fresh again.

Select lamps were on here and there, giving the room a relaxed but not intimate ambiance. He had a selection of cheeses and crackers on the table, and a bottle of wine chilling in an ice bucket.

"You look lovely," he said.

"No, I don't," she blurted. She knew she looked ridiculous.

He raised his eyebrows in surprise and laughed. "OK, should I say fetching instead?"

"Yes. Fetching some of that wild and kinky sex you promised. But that's not on the menu tonight, is it?"

"Not tonight, I'm afraid."

"Any night?" She had to know. Was he gay? She'd fallen for gay men before and made a blooming fool of herself. She promised herself she wouldn't do that again, but darn if the gay nation wasn't full of obscenely attractive men. A lot of gay men were hiding in plain sight in rock bands, as she well knew.

"Ah, the question of the day. Is Jack gay?" He smiled at her. "No, I'm not gay."

She felt a burst of happiness. "Do you mind if I take off these awful shoes? They're killing me."

"Please, be my guest." He picked up the bottle of wine. "Do you like chardonnay?"

She smiled and nodded as she took a seat on the couch, unlaced the stilettos, and nudged them off.

He poured them glasses and handed her one. Sitting on the couch next to her, he lifted his glass in a toast. "To what I hope will be a personal and artistic friendship."

Friendship? Is that all he wanted? Or was he playing it cool and being coy? After their sparring that afternoon, she wouldn't put it past him. She had clearly won that round. Or maybe she had wounded his ego and made him uninterested? Oh no, did she ruin things already?

They clinked glasses and sipped.

"I apologize profusely," Jack said, "but I need to get some business out of the way first."

Lucy sighed. Another bad sign, putting business ahead of her, and even worse, right after she got here. Maybe he *was* just another self-centered rock star and she'd let her attraction to him prevent her from picking up on the red flags. Well, to be fair, she hadn't spent that much time with him, and she was normally a pretty good judge of character, so maybe there hadn't been any red flags ... yet.

"Go ahead," she said without enthusiasm.

He grinned. "No, I mean with you. I promised Dunk I would find out what you're doing here. I bet him that Barry sent you to spy on us."

She choked on her wine, and he handed her a tissue as she coughed to clear her throat.

The jig was already up. He knew she'd been sent by Barry. A huge weight lifted from her shoulders that she hadn't even known was there. But how funny that he thought she came to be a spy. Why would Barry need to spy on one of his own bands?

"You're not the first, you know. Howie is Barry's nephew. And we suspect there are others." He smirked. "We tortured it out of Howie, with Suze and Carly's help."

Lucy's smart mouth started saying something before she could stop it. "Are you going to torture it out of me?"

He looked into her eyes. "Do you *want* me to torture it out of you?"

She couldn't breathe. He was flirting with her, and her traitor body wanted to fling itself at him, right now, this second. She was sure she was emitting enough sex pheromones to attract an entire beehive. But her mind was pulling on the reins and reminding her that she was here to get the recording contract, not to get it on with the lead singer of a rock band, no matter how good-looking, charismatic, and talented he happened to be. Not to mention she'd made a promise to Nana, although at the moment she couldn't for the life of her remember exactly what that was.

He moved a touch closer as he spoke in a soft, sexy voice. "Are you here to spy on us, Lucy?"

She wanted to say yes and see his response. Would he try to seduce her? She wouldn't be able to resist him. But she also didn't want him to have any misconceptions about her that came back to bite her in the you-know-what later. She didn't want to ruin this, whatever this was, or whatever it could be. He wasn't going to like it, and it might put him off her, but it had to be said. "No, um, actually, I'm here to babysit you."

"Babysit us?" He furrowed his brow like it didn't compute. "You're here to babysit us."

"Barry said he was worried about you guys making it to the end of the tour. He wanted me to come and keep an eye on you, try to keep you out of trouble and let him know if anything goes wrong. You know, like a babysitter."

She held her breath waiting for his reaction.

He stared at her for a few more moments and then burst out laughing. "That is priceless. I can't wait to tell Dunk. He's going to love it. Barry sending someone like you to babysit us."

What did that mean? He didn't think she was capable of babysitting them? "Someone like me?" She couldn't keep the irritation out of her voice.

His eyes went wide and he rushed to respond. "Yes, someone who's beautiful and an amazing musician. You're much more likely to cause trouble than keep the band out of it. I mean, Keith, Sam, and Rob are already vying with one another over you. So I'm guessing that's the real reason Barry sent you."

"You think I'm an amazing musician?" And beautiful?

"Yes, I heard you on the bus." He grinned. "When I was spying on you." He put down his wine and got up. "Hold on." He disappeared into the bedroom and came back with an acoustic guitar. Retaking his seat next to her, he strummed the guitar and tuned it up. He glanced at her shyly and launched into her song "Saying Yes." He sang the entire first verse to her in his beautiful tenor voice. It sent goosebumps up and down her spine.

He stopped and regarded her. "Has anyone told you that you have a real gift for composing, both music and lyrics? Not to mention a pitch perfect voice. If you had more songs, you could put out your own album."

"But I do have more songs." Why did she always tear up when she talked about this? "That's why I'm here."

She told him everything. About the swami trying to steal the music she spent three years of her life perfecting, then Barry offering her the deal if she flew out right away and babysat Pirate. How she had to sneak out of the ashram and go home and find her old groupie clothes. Keith thinking she was an A&R rep from Dolos and offering to pretend she was his girlfriend, then forgetting to pay attention to her, but it didn't matter because she'd already become friends with everyone else. Being completely blown away by the concert, and feeling so confused about her deal with Barry that she hadn't called him yet. What a great band she thought Jack had; she should know after traveling with Magnus and meeting tons of bands on the road.

She barely drew a breath because he asked a lot of questions—how she learned to sing and play, how she ended up in the ashram and what it was like living there, what her family was like and where they lived and what they did. She found herself opening up and telling him things she hadn't thought or talked about in years.

She was surprised when she caught sight of Jack's watch and realized they'd been talking for hours. He was so different from other rock stars she'd known, whose biggest interest was "are we going to shag, love?" or who was going to supply them with their next snort or guzzle. She didn't blame the guys in rock bands at all. Who could fault them for milking their fame and fortune for all it was worth? Most rock bands were like shooting stars—here today, gone tomorrow, soon forgotten except by die-hard fans. It wasn't the sanest career choice. More a brief window of time in which young men were allowed to pluck strings and bang sticks and make mind-blowing music together before being ushered back into a more normal life. No wonder they seized the day.

But this guy next to her sure wasn't your typical rock star. He wasn't drunk or high, for one thing. She was the one gulping down the chardonnay while he took random sips. He didn't seem to be interested in getting in her pants, and hadn't even made what could be considered a move. The strangest thing was his insatiable curiosity and his desire to know everything about her. Even her family and friends could care less about all this stuff, whereas he seemed to be hanging on her every word.

Suddenly it struck her. Could it be that, for the very first time in her adult life, a guy was truly—for real—interested in her?

She cocked her head as she regarded him. Huh, this was different.

He was saying something to her and looking at her expectantly.

She shook her head to clear her thoughts. "Sorry, but what did you say?"

"Forgive me. I was asking why you left Magnus. It's probably none of my business. You don't have to tell me. Although you can, if you want to."

The tears welled up; she couldn't help it. She was overwhelmed thinking that he might truly be interested in her—this very handsome, talented and fully conscious rock star—in her, little Lucy Sabatini from Endwell, New York. She realized that she was also a bit drunk; she hadn't even touched the cheese and crackers. Plus, talking about why she left Magnus was always very emotional for her.

He put down his wine and looked at her with a distraught and help-less expression. Poor Jack. Randy was so right; Jack didn't really know how to deal with women. First there was his utterly endearing ability to listen intently to what she was saying without interrupting. Like, what guy on the planet does that? Even the women in her family were chronic interrupters. Then there was his obvious struggle in dealing with his attraction to her, leaning toward her, and then when she moved toward him, unconsciously leaning away or jumping up to pour some more wine. The guy was clearly ambivalent about this, whatever this was.

She didn't know why she did it. Curiosity maybe, or her constant companion impatience. But she placed her wineglass on the coffee table, climbed into his lap, and put her head on his shoulder. After his initial surprise, Jack put his arms around her and held her. It felt so comfort-able and comforting.

She replayed that terrible night in her head as she recounted why she left Magnus. "I was standing in the wings, like usual, watching him sing. He was on fire that night, which might be why it happened. When he did call-and-respond, the sound coming back from the audience was like a massive roar. It was thrilling and scary at the same time. You know what I mean?"

"Yes, I do."

"He was cracking me up, doing all kinds of funny poses while he sang. Like singing backwards through his legs, or reclining and stretching his top leg toward the ceiling, like he was doing aerobics or something. He's always tons of fun, but he was off the chart that night. Snorting lines of coke behind the horn section."

Jack tensed and frowned.

"He looked over at me and winked, and that's when it happened. The barrier separating the audience from the stage gave way, and the audience surged forward, overpowering the security guys and climbing onto the stage. The band got up and ran, and the roadies grabbed Magnus and carried him off the other side of the stage."

"But what about you? What happened to you?"

She took in a deep breath and exhaled slowly. "I couldn't move. I just stood there watching what was happening in total shock. A roadie —Butch was his name, I found out later—scooped me up and carried me away. He saved me from ... from ... from what happened to those other people." Tears were streaming down her cheeks now, and she swiped at them with her free hand.

Jack squeezed her. "You don't have to say any more. I know what happened."

"Nine of them trampled to death, and I saw it."

"You couldn't have done anything."

"Yeah, but I lived, and they didn't. It wasn't ... it wasn't fair. Some of them were younger than me ... just kids."

"No, it wasn't fair. That shouldn't have happened. The arena and the band should have had security measures in place. What did Magnus say about it?"

Lucy gave a shaky sigh. "They bundled him into a limo and got him out of there ... before the police arrived. Because he was off his head, y'know."

Jack clutched her arm. "So, hold on. What about you? You weren't with him?"

"No, they left me with the others in the band room. But that was OK, because we were kept safe until the police got there. They interviewed us, and took us back to the hotel, which managed to find rooms so we could stay there another night. My parents drove to Buffalo as soon as I called them. It's an eight-hour drive, so they got there the next morning. I lay on the back seat and cried all the way home."

"And Magnus didn't go to the hotel to take care of you?" Jack asked in an outraged voice.

"I know it looks bad. I can't tell you where he went because he made me swear on a Bible. But you can't blame him. He did what he needed to do, and I forgave him for leaving me there."

"Well, I can't forgive him," Jack said in a fierce voice. "That was absolutely inexcusable, from start to finish. I would have protected you and taken care of you. That would have been my top priority. Full stop. No question whatsoever."

"It would?" She looked up at him with genuine surprise.

He nodded, then leaned down and gave her a gentle kiss. When he pulled back and looked at her, she lifted her head toward him and kissed him back. It was a grateful rather than a passionate kiss. She didn't want to scare him away by seeming too needy or demanding, something Russell Hammond of Netherlude had accused her of several times. Although she'd found out later from one of the Flying Garter Girls that the guy was a major-league commitment-phobe. So she liked to make out? Was that a crime, Russell?

Jack kissed her again, this time shifting his body to bring her closer and angling his head to kiss her more deeply. She opened her mouth to give him access, and he suddenly pulled away, scrunching up his face in confusion. "Uh ... I'm not sure ... I think I should get you home."

"Home?"

"Back to your room, I mean."

She did a heroic job of hiding her disappointment as she extracted herself from his lap. After straightening her errant clothing and putting the stilettos back on, she allowed him to walk her to her room several floors down. He turned to her at her door and she looked up at him. She felt nervous again and started babbling. "Thank you for such a wonderful evening, Jack. Or should I say Vic? It was so much better than I expected. Not that that wild and kinky sex you promised wouldn't have been wonderful too, but—"

Her words were cut off by his mouth suddenly on hers, no longer kissing her like the polite gentleman he'd been upstairs. This was Jack the entitled and voracious rock star, putting his tongue in her mouth and exploring it like he had to know every single bit of her, like he could never get enough.

She put her arms around his neck and her hands in his hair, and used her tongue to duel with his own. She was so incredibly turned on. If he had wanted to invite himself into her room and ravish her, she couldn't have stopped him.

But, of course, he didn't know that, and she wasn't going to tell him or show him. Men needed to feel that they had won the treasure, not had it given to them. At least that's what her mother, her aunties, and even her nana told her over and over again, like they didn't trust her to get a man and keep him. Yes, it was the eighties, they said, and yes, women had been liberated. But men—forget about it!—they would never change. Men would always be men.

So she had to pretend she didn't want to drag Jack into her room and ravish *him*. The thing was, she'd never wanted someone this much before, and she didn't want to jinx it. So in case they were right, she would let him take the lead. And as they had reassured her, everything changed when you got married. You just had to be patient and wait your turn.

She had no clue how long they were standing there kissing. He had backed her up against the door and was holding her face in his hands. She would have been happy if it went on for hours, but he finally broke the kiss. He looked down at her, his eyes dark and intense.

"Um ... I should let you get some sleep," he said. "Do you have your key card?"

He pulled away from her to give her room. She rummaged around in her bag and pulled out her key card.

He took it from her and opened her door, then handed it back as he wedged the door open with his foot. "Are you coming to the concert tomorrow ... I mean, tonight? It's already tomorrow, so the concert would be tonight, actually." He appeared to be holding his breath, afraid she might say no.

"I wouldn't dream of missing it." Oh no, how could she say something so drippy, like she was a character in a sickly sweet romance novel. Yuck.

"Good night, Jack." She made herself go inside her room and shut the door. She stood there listening and wondering if he was still on the other side. She didn't dare look through the peephole. She heard the door to the staircase down the hall close. He was gone.

Lucy bounded over to the bed and threw herself on it. It was covered with all the clothes she'd tried and rejected earlier that evening. She couldn't even be bothered to remove them; she was floating on cloud nine and couldn't care less.

She relived the entire evening in her mind, spending extra time on the kissing part. As she was reviewing it a second time, all of a sudden it hit her. She'd done *all* of the talking and had learned nothing whatsoever about him. Like literally nothing, not one single thing. What a major league idiot she was. She had even freely admitted that she was there to babysit them for Barry. Jack had found that funny, but what if he found it insulting and unforgivable in the light of day?

Randy was right. Jack was *very* crafty. Out of her league, that was for sure. Let's hope he was a good guy, or she might find herself kicked out of the tour and kissing her music contract goodbye. She wasn't sure which of those two outcomes would disappoint her more.

She tossed and turned all night, excited and worried in turn, surprised at how much the lead singer of Pirate was unsettling her.

Forty-Six

WHEN JACK LEFT LUCY, he went straight to Dunk's room. He was flying and this was the only way he knew to bring himself back to earth. Plus, he had to tell Dunk about why Lucy was here. Dunk would die laughing. He had to share it with him, right away.

He knocked on Dunk's door. There was no response at first, but he kept on knocking. He should let Dunk sleep; he worked so hard. But how often did he wake him up like this? He could do it this one time. That wasn't unreasonable.

After what seemed ages, he heard Dunk growling and swearing as he came to the door. Dunk yanked the door open and glared at him.

"This better be good or I'm going to throw ya to the fans and let them tear ya limb from limb."

"It's good, it's good," said Jack, crowding Dunk back into the room. "It's really, really good."

Dunk padded to his bed and Jack followed. Dunk got into the bed and pulled the covers up to his chin. Jack dragged a chair next to the bed and dropped into it.

"So?" said Dunk.

"Lucy's here to babysit us. Can you believe it?"

"Babysit us?" Dunk rolled his eyes. "That's pure barry."

"Isn't it?" Jack said, ignoring Dunk's clever play on words. He launched into an account about why Barry sent her, and segued into a detailed accounting of the entire evening, relating to Dunk everything Lucy had said—about her time at the ashram, and about the swami and Ramakar trying to steal her music, and about her big family somewhere in New York State in a town called Endwell, such a charming name for a town, and literally everything else. He left out the kissing parts. That was between him and Lucy and none of Dunk's business.

Dunk began snoring around the time Jack started talking about Nana. It was too bad. Nana was a real character and Dunk would enjoy Lucy's funny stories about her. Jack kept right on talking even though Dunk was sleeping. He needed to get it out of his system or he wouldn't be able to get any sleep himself. He probably wouldn't anyway; he never slept well and he was really wired. But he didn't want to forget anything she had said, either. He wanted to remember every little thing. She had opened up and trusted him with the story of her life, and he wanted to be worthy of that trust.

Now that Dunk was asleep, he could talk about the kissing. "She's even more beautiful and sexy than Jane Fonda. She feels and tastes like heaven. She's so soft. And her touch is so light and gentle, it doesn't even hurt ..." As Dunk snored like a trucker after a cross-country gig, Jack talked on and on, repeating everything a second time and then a third. He could talk about her all night.

Forty-Seven

BARRY BARTHOLOMEW KNOCKED the ashes from his cigar and brought it near his lips.

"Swami, to what do I owe the pleasure of this call?" he said before indulging in a series of puffs.

The swami's nasal tones came through the line. "We've got Lucy Sabatini's signature and she's on board for future projects."

Barry choked and went into a coughing fit. After a few sips of water, he said, "Sorry, swami, new brand of cigar. Not used to it yet."

"We're sending the contract by courier," said the swami. "You should have it later today. We've done our end, now things can move quickly on yours."

"Yeah, sure. Soon's I receive it, I'll get right on it."

Once he got rid of the swami, Barry shouted for Rhonda to get Keith on the phone, pronto. He needed to know if the swami was pulling a fast one, and Keith might know the whereabouts of the broad. She might even be in his bed, an image that excited and annoyed Barry in equal measure.

Keith sounded half asleep. "Hiya, Bar. I was gonna ring you."

Barry couldn't hide his pique. "What the hell is going on out there?"

"Yeah, OK. So Lucy's with me. I said why don't you be me missus and she said that was cool."

A woman's voice mumbled something in the background.

"Babe, come back to bed. I know your name is Becky. It's this other chick I'm talking 'bout. Babe, be reasonable. Babe!"

Barry heard the phone drop and Keith remonstrating with the broad for a minute, followed by the door slamming.

"Chicks!" said Keith, coming back on the line. "If she'd stayed for a morning shag, I woulda got her breakie. She was a good one."

"Tough luck, kid," Barry said as he rolled his eyes. "So back to business. Are ya tellin' me you gave Lucy a cover story?"

"Yeah," said Keith. "Kissed her in front of the guys, let 'em know she's with me. Only Rob knows what's really going down. It's all cool."

Barry wasn't happy about this turn of events. Keith and Lucy weren't supposed to know about the other being in cahoots with him. And that Howie hadn't called either him or his sister yet, despite Jack promising to have him do so. Not one of them was reporting back to him every day as agreed and letting him know what was going wrong. Now that damn swami had clearly forged Lucy's name on the contract and expected him to get it finalized. Every goddam thing was going tits up. He sure hoped Keith had some good news—or bad news, to be more precise.

"Is everything all right out there? Any problems I should know about?"

"That Lucy," said Keith. "Man, can that chick sing."

Barry was pleased Keith thought so, at least one thing he was doing right, giving that hippie broad the recording contract.

"But I had to get her to cool her jets. A bit too keen, if ya know what I mean. Tried to get Jack on our bus, and when that didn't work, she tried to go on his bus. Had to tell her, 'Woman, get your arse over here, you're with me.' Saw her chatting to Jack when we stopped, said yeah, OK, no harm in that. But I'm keepin' an eye on her, make sure she don't overplay her hand."

"So where is she now?"

"At this hour, in her room I s'pose."

"Ya think that's not suspicious, she not sleeping with you?"

Keith got louder. "Listen, man, that's what I said, we gotta authenticize it. But she said no hanky panky 'cause her nan would get wound up. She's some sort of Catholic chick. Nothing personal, she said, I'm a handsome dude and all that. Just have to put on a good show. So I touch her every chance I get, y'know, keep it real. But what's a man to do? *Women.*"

Barry put his head in his hands. Oy vey. He had to get out of this business. These rock stars were going to drive him insane. They had already driven him to drink and drugs.

"Great work, Keith," he said. "Check back in with me tomorrow. And get Howie to call me, will ya? Wanna make sure the youngster is keeping his nose clean."

After he hung up the phone, Barry leaned back in his chair, puffed his cigar, and prayed to the god of music for a miracle.

Forty-Eight

THE TABLE TOP shuddered as the private investigator laid a map of the United States in front of Jack's father and stabbed an area in the southwest.

"The call from your son came from a hotel here. We were lucky. He stayed on the line just long enough for us to trace it. I'm waiting on a list of guests at the hotel on and around that date. But I checked the newspapers and broadcasts. Seems the big news was a visit from the rock band Pirate. A band out of Manchester."

"A rock band." Winnie would not be surprised at his son being involved in something so childish and entirely at odds with his station in life.

The P.I. laid out photos of the band on top of the map. "Here are the latest publicity shots. All of their official photos are in their pirate costumes. Anyone look familiar?"

Winnie picked up the photos one by one and examined them. "I can't be sure."

The P.I. splayed a series of photocopied pages from celebrity magazines on top of the photos. "These are pap snaps of band members and staff."

"Well, well, well." There was the unmistakable hulk standing with some others. "If it isn't Duncan MacGregor."

"You know him?"

"Wherever goeth Duncan MacGregor goeth my son, and vice versa."

Winnie picked up another photocopied snap. "And alas, here he is. My wayward son." He read the caption. "Victor Slonimsky. Personal assistant to Jack St James, alias Blackbeard."

"Duncan MacGregor is the band manager," said the P.I.

Winnie threw the snap on the table. "I have to give my son credit. He's always been a master of defiance, even if he is terribly unimaginative. Nicolas Slonimsky is a famous composer, something my son will never be."

"You want us to pin down where they are?"

"I want him back here for our thirtieth anniversary. It's the only thing that will make my wife happy. So yes, find him. Whatever it takes."

"We're on it."

"And look into Pirate. I want to know whatever you can dig up on them, including anything on their ... financial status."

The private investigator left and Winnie tapped his finger against his chin. Perhaps there were more opportunities here than he had originally thought.

You've evaded and defied me for four years, my boy. And now it's time for me to even the score.

Forty-Nine

DUNK PULLED up at the hotel entrance in a taxi. He'd been troubleshooting all morning at the new arena and had a list of worrisome issues he and Jack needed to iron out. Not to mention the fact that he was exhausted from too little sleep—not just the night before when Jack had droned on and on for what seemed like hours, talking about Lucy and her family and Nana and the bloody price of tea in China, but throughout the entire blasted tour. He couldn't wait for the scuttering shitestorm to be over.

As he got out of the taxi, a crowd of excited fans took snap after snap. It seemed a much bigger than usual crowd, and a bit weird that they were taking photos of him. He strode into the lobby and the hotel manager rushed over.

"Excuse me, Mister MacGregor." The manager put up his hands in a defensive gesture. "I know you paid extra for a quiet stay, but there was no way I could stop him."

"Him who?"

"Magnus. He demanded to see Lucy Sabatini. Said he'd been sent by her family to deliver some bad news. She insisted we send him up. So what could I do?"

That explained all the extra hubbub. "He's with her now?"

"Just went up."

"Right." Dunk had to take charge of the situation. The manager looked like he was going to have a stroke at any moment. "Send your security guys to cordon off the hotel. I'll get a bunch of my guys as well. Less ya want a major incident on yer hands."

The manager looked horror-stricken. "N-n-no! I mean yes. I'll do it immediately." The manager pulled out a handkerchief and wiped his brow as he hurried away.

Dunk turned on his heel and hastened toward the elevator bank. One of the elevators pinged and its doors opened. "Coming through! Emergency!" he shouted at a couple about to get on. They turned, blanched, and scrambled out of the way as Dunk barreled past them into the elevator. There were distinct advantages to being a huge man with Scottish warrior blood running through your veins.

On the trip up, he checked himself out in the mirror and sighed. His hair looked wilder than usual—he'd been pawing at it as one problem surmounted another—and the black bags under his eyes made him resemble a hungry Count Dracula. No wonder that couple had leapt out of the way.

He frowned as it suddenly hit him: there was no security guy in the lift, like he'd ordered. He was relieved to see a security guy when the doors opened on the top floor. At least one bloody thing was going right.

After shouting at the guy to get someone in the lift, he legged it to Jack's suite and knocked on the door.

"Come in," Jack called.

Dunk always had a duplicate key or keycard to Jack's room for security purposes. He let himself in and found Jack at the table eating his lunch. It looked like spaghetti bolognese with a side salad. No french fries he could nab. He hadn't eaten since early that morning and realized he was utterly famished.

"How goes it at the arena on this glorious day, my good man?"

Jack was uncharacteristically perky and chipper. Dunk wanted to punch him, his own day having gone from bad to worse, while his partner here lolled about his suite, no doubt dreaming about Lucy and letting him deal with all the shite. He was so tired. But he had to keep his cool and prevent Jack from doing something stupid. Not bloody likely, but he had to at least try.

He spoke in a nonchalant tone, leading with the important news and hoping Jack ignored the rest. "I got some urgent concerns about the arena we need to discuss. I'm worried about the staging and security. And oh, a little side note: Magnus is here visiting Luce."

"What?" Jack jumped up from his chair. "When was this?"

Dunk sighed. He just didn't have the energy to deal with Jack in manic mode. "'Bout ten minutes." He watched with resignation as Jack grabbed his key card and slammed out of the room without even saying goodbye. That was gratitude for you. Dunk goes to the arena and takes care of one huge problem after another, and Jack abandons him to go chasing after some girl. Why did he even bother?

He picked up the plate of spaghetti and poured it down his throat, fed himself the salad with his fingers, couldn't be bothered using a fork, and gulped down the sparkling water from the bottle. Still hungry, he ate three Kit-Kats and two Milky Ways from the mini-bar in rapid succession.

He suddenly felt so tired he could barely stay upright. A quick nap would restore his energy and put him in a better mood. He was too tired to go to his own room on the next floor. Besides, if any of the band members saw him, they would collar him and moan about this and that and he wouldn't get a wink of sleep. Making his way into Jack's bedroom, he eyed the made-up bed. Jack would be upset at Dunk sleeping on top of his bed, absolutely irate if he slept in it. He smirked as he pulled back the covers and got into the bed, shoes and all. The minute his head hit the pillow he was dead to the world.

Fifty

JACK RAN DOWN three flights of stairs to Lucy's floor. He knew exactly where she was staying from the night before when he walked her "home" from their date, as he liked to think of it.

He wasn't exactly sure why he was there and what he intended to do. Granted, Magnus had done the unforgivable by abandoning Lucy in an extremely traumatic and dangerous situation, a situation she had spent three years trying to get over. He didn't think she was even over it yet. But he also recognized that it was her inalienable right to decide whether to see Magnus or not. Still, the guy was an undeniable cad and Jack felt obliged to make sure she didn't get hurt even more.

He tiptoed to her door, looked up and down the corridor to make sure no one was looking, and pressed his ear against it. He could hear some voices but he couldn't make out what they were saying. He cupped his hand and strained to hear.

The door of the room to the left opened. He stood up straight and put his hands on his hips as a maid backed out, pulling a trolley of cleaning items. She looked in his direction and startled when she saw him. A red mark ran the length of her face, as if she'd been taking a nap. How lucky was that? She'd feel guilty and be putty in his hands ... he hoped.

He plastered an aggrieved look on his face, put a finger to his lips to indicate silence, and waved her over. He whispered, "Can you hear anything they're saying in there?"

She stared at him for a long moment, as if deciding whether to comply. She sidled close to the door, cupped her hand against it, and listened. "No, señor," she whispered. "I don't hear."

"I'm trying to find out if my wife is in there cheating on me with another man."

The maid opened her eyes wide and put her hand to her mouth in shock. "No!"

"Yes." He looked at her name tag. "Maria, I think we can hear better in that room." He indicated the room she'd just vacated.

"Oh, no, señor," she said as she straightened and moved away from the door. "I get such big trouble."

He gave her a pleading look. "I need to save my marriage, Maria. I love my wife ... so much. You want to help me save my marriage, don't you, Maria?"

Maria worried her fingers as she stared at him, indecision on her face. He pulled out a wad of cash from his pocket and pushed it into her hands as he gently removed her master key card. She looked down at the cash and splayed it like a hand of cards. It was the five hundred he liked to carry around for emergencies. She gasped and her eyes lit up, like she'd come up with the winning hand in a major poker tournament.

"Don't move, Maria," he said as he opened the room next door and engaged the lock to prevent it from closing. He turned back to her and held out the key card. "Here, take this back. If anything happens, your story is that you didn't see me come in. I came in while you were cleaning the bathroom and hid in the closet. Yes?"

She beamed at him. "Si, señor. I am so happy lady. Uno momento." She turned away from him, and he could see she was secreting the cash in her brassiere. She turned back, took the key card from him, and put it in the pocket of her uniform. She raised her arms as if to give him a hug, and he put up his hands and backed away.

"No, not now. He might be doing things to my wife as we speak. You go clean another room and pretend you haven't seen me." He waved her in the other direction. "Hurry. Go, Maria, go!"

She winked at him. "Si, I pretend." She grinned as she grabbed the cart and pushed it down the corridor, not stopping at the next room. She appeared to be going on break. OK, whatever.

He slipped into the room, shut the door, and engaged the lock and the security latch. He didn't want anyone disturbing him until he was ready to be disturbed. He rushed to the wall adjoining Lucy's room, cupped his hand against it, and listened. Damn, it was still impossible to hear anything. He tried with a glass, but that didn't work either. He searched along the wall for a radiator that might have a connecting vent, but no such luck.

Opening the balcony door, he looked in the direction of her room. The two rooms had balconies that were only three or four feet apart, and her balcony door was open. Jackpot!

He sidled to the edge of his balcony and cupped his ear. He could hear Magnus talking in an insistent voice and Lucy responding in what seemed to be a tearful one. What the hell? How dare he talk to her like that? As if he hadn't hurt her enough already.

Jack leaned as far over the balcony as he could without falling off, straining to hear what the two of them were saying.

Suddenly she cried out, "No! Oh no! Don't tell me that!"

Magnus murmured something, followed by a smack.

"No, no, no," Lucy screamed and started sobbing.

Jack didn't think. He rushed back into the room, grabbed the chair from the desk, dragged it outside next to the balcony railing, got up on it, balanced himself and leaned forward ready to leap. Taking a short step on the chair and another step on the balcony railing, he pushed off with all the strength he could muster and catapulted across the gap between his balcony and hers. He landed on her balcony railing and took a few moments waving his arms as he tried to regain his balance. Good thing he was used to leaping about the ship on stage, which took a lot of stamina—plus doing aerobics every day with Jane. Some sort of commotion drifted up to him from below, but he was too focused on saving Lucy to pay it any mind.

He dropped from the railing onto her balcony. As he landed, Magnus turned in his direction. Seething with adrenaline, Jack ran over and punched him as hard as he could. Magnus went down and lay unmoving on the floor.

"Oh no," Lucy screamed. "Jack, no."

Why was she screaming at *him*? He was here to save her from that abusive mingebag. Didn't she see that?

She knelt next to Magnus, took his face in her hands, and called his name. He half-opened his eyes and mumbled something.

She looked up at Jack, anguish in her eyes. "He's sick. He's got HIV and he might die." She started sobbing again as she leaned over Magnus.

The air sucked out of Jack's lungs. He hadn't rescued her. Instead, he'd punched a sick man, a man she clearly still cared deeply about. What a major fool he'd been. Would she ever be able to forgive him? He had no choice whether she did or not, but one thing was sure: he had to make things right.

He rushed over to the desk, picked up the phone, and dialed his room on the off chance Dunk was still there. There was no answer, so he called the front desk and they told him Dunk had not yet come back down. He asked them to connect him to Dunk's room, but no response there either. Maybe he was visiting the boys, but Jack rather doubted it. He had a strong suspicion where he was. He called his own room again and let it ring and ring and ring, until a very groggy Dunk finally picked up.

"We have an emergency here," Jack said. He summarized the situation as succinctly as he could. Dunk swore at him for only ten seconds, to his relief, and then said he would take care of it. When had he ever not been able to rely on Dunk?

Jack walked over and knelt on the other side of Magnus, feeling helpless and like the biggest fool in the world. Magnus was conscious and blinking at Lucy. She was crying and imploring him to stay with her. She gripped his hand and told him over and over again that she loved him very much, and that he was not allowed to leave her, never ever.

One emotion after another chased through Jack: embarrassment, chagrin, shame, severe disappointment, the bitter taste of rejection and defeat, and finally a growing sense of resolve. He had to marshal all of his strength to help Lucy through this. He owed her that. He *wanted* to give her that. What he wanted for himself wasn't important now. What was important was what *she* needed.

Magnus turned his eyes toward him. "Great right hook."

Jack half-smiled. "I apologize unreservedly. I thought you were hitting her, and I simply lost it."

Magnus turned his eyes back to Lucy. "I need some water."

Lucy looked at Jack. "Could you?"

He nodded and started to get up.

"No, you," Magnus said to her. "Not him." Odd. Why not him?

After she got up and went into the bathroom, Magnus turned his head toward Jack. "Take care of her, will you? Save her from that swami."

Jack stared at him, not clear on exactly what he meant and unsure how to react.

"Promise me?" Magnus said as Lucy returned with a glass of water.

Jack nodded. He lifted Magnus's head as Lucy held the glass to his lips. Magnus took a few sips. He turned his head away from the glass and toward the balcony as a helicopter arrived and hovered near the hotel.

"That could be the medical helicopter," Jack said as he lowered Magnus's head. He stood up and rushed out onto the balcony. He waved to the helicopter to let the medical crew know their location. That's when he realized it was a news chopper with a cameraman pointing a long-lens camera at him. Below, the road and parking lot were filled with satellite news trucks and a line of cameras with their telephoto lenses focused on Lucy's room.

He rushed back inside, slammed the balcony door shut, and closed the curtains. "I'm terribly sorry to tell you this, but it seems the cat is already out of the bag. That's a news helicopter."

Lucy got up, went over to the balcony door, and peeked out through the curtain. "Oh, no! How are we going to get him out of here?"

"Dunk will think of something. He's a jujitsu master in the face of any kind of crisis."

Jack picked up the remote and turned on the TV news. He flipped between the three major network affiliates in Phoenix, and the whole sorry saga was playing on one station after another, including footage of Magnus arriving and of Jack leaping across the balcony and waving his arms to get his balance. Lucy gasped when they showed the leap, and he himself watched with his breath caught in his chest. What was he thinking leaping across a chasm that large eight stories above the ground? If he'd missed, it would have been certain death; that is, unless a balcony or awning broke his fall, in which case he would probably be in some sanatorium with a dented head, playing chess with imaginary people and calling everyone Sybil or Archie.

Not surprisingly, the news was making it out to be a love triangle between super-groupie Lucy L'amour, her old lover, the disappeared rock star Magnus, and her new lover, Victor Slonimsky, personal assistant to Jack St James, aka Blackbeard, lead singer of the rock band Pirate. Jack was relieved his cover was still intact. That was something at least.

A forceful knock sounded on the door.

"That should be him." Jack clicked off the news and went to answer it. He looked through the peephole and there was Dunk, looking rumpled and out of sorts. Jack knew he was going to get a bollocking, but a huge dam of tension released inside his body just the same. He opened the door and moved inside so Dunk could enter.

Dunk strode in, slamming the door behind him. He put his hands on his hips and glared at Jack. "Ya doaty dobber. What the hell were ya thinking? Ya coulda been killed. And ya coulda killed him."

"We can yell at him later," said Lucy. "What about an ambulance or medi-vac?"

"Waiting nearby." Dunk hung onto the bed as he eased himself down to the floor and kneeled next to Magnus. "How ya doin', mate?"

Magnus managed a weak smile. "That was quite an entrance. Feel a little dizzy ... looking at you." Dunk and Magnus stared at one another for a moment.

Dunk sat back on his heels and addressed Jack. "So here's the plan. We're taking him out in a laundry truck waiting in the loading dock. Gurney is on its way up." He looked back down at Magnus. "Have to cover ya with a lot of sheets, but I swear we won't suffocate ya."

Magnus grinned. "Whatever you want."

Jack glanced sideways at Lucy. She had her arms folded across her chest and an obstinate look on her face, like she wasn't happy with the turn of events.

Dunk regarded Jack and Lucy standing near one another and scowled. "I don't want any lip from either of you. Once he's away, you're going out front to give an interview in front of the cameras. It was a mistake. Ya thought she was cheating on ya and were off yer head, but she wasn't; he was just an old friend visiting, kiss for the cameras, come back in. She sits front and center in the VIP section tonight. Tomorrow it's old news and we all go back to being the same old eejits we've always been. Got it?"

"Yes," said Jack.

"No," said Lucy. "I'm going with him."

"Do as he says, squirt," said Magnus. "Don't be a royal pain in the ass."

Jack narrowed his eyes. What a terrible and unfair thing to say to Lucy. Look at her. She was a goddess. And squirt? What was that? An insulting nickname?

Lucy teared up. "How can you talk like that?" Yes, exactly.

Magnus waved at Jack. "Hug her, would you?" Hug her? What?

She stepped away from Jack. "No, I don't want him to hug me. I'm mad at him." Wait, what? She was mad at him after he almost killed himself to defend her?

Magnus managed a weak grin. "That's my girl." He turned his eyes to Jack. "She's your problem now. Sucker."

Jack stifled an intense spurt of happiness. Did Magnus say she was his problem? Does he think Lucy is his? Really?

"I hate you," said Lucy, tears rolling down her face as she hugged Magnus goodbye.

Fifty-One

LUCY AND "VIC" gave the interview and did a kiss in front of the cameras. The media scrutiny was intense. They were used to attention from the rock 'n' roll news and broadcast media, and from their fans and fan clubs, but not from the celebrity news media. Magnus's visit, Jack's leap, and their assumed "fight" over Lucy had put Pirate in an unaccustomed spotlight. Everyone loved a story of passion, jealousy, and betrayal among the rich and famous.

Bleary-eyed and short-tempered, Dunk issued orders and no one dared disobey. Everyone was assigned rooms on the top floor of the hotel. Lucy got the room connecting to Jack's "so the maid doesn't squeal to the media about something fishy." Jack was not about to complain, even though Lucy still seemed to be mad at him. Howie and his ladies got connecting rooms, Randy and Alison got a room together "because I said so," and Dunk gave himself and the boys the remaining rooms spread around the floor. He banned any guests "until this hoopla dies down, and you'll all shut yer mouths about it." The boys whinged to one another and to Jack, but didn't dare utter a word to Dunk.

The security guys, along with crew members co-opted onto the security detail, had the next floor down. They took shifts guarding the staircases and elevator doors and picking up and delivering food and drink orders. Dunk even convinced the day and night managers that he needed a security guy in the elevators at all times. The night manager appeared terrified of the enormous Scotsman, quivered and repeated over and over "whatever you say, Mister MacGregor."

Getting everyone to and from the concert proved to be a logistical nightmare. The police directed traffic because the roads were clogged with media trucks and gawkers, and despite the band leaving an hour early, the concert still ended up starting late. As Dunk had ordered, Lucy sat in the VIP section, surrounded by Alison, Howie, Carly, Suze, some local bigwigs, and a cordon of security men, most of them drawn from the crew. Jack sang his heart out again, knowing that Lucy was watching and feeling that she deserved an amazing show after all the trouble he'd caused her.

After the concert, once everyone was safely back in the hotel, Dunk came into Jack's suite and dropped down on the sofa. He clicked on the TV and flipped to *Entertainment Tonight*. "They're running this bloody nonsense nonstop."

The two of them watched as correspondent Mary Hart reported on the love triangle between "the charismatic and reclusive rock idol Magnus, super-groupie Lucy L'amour, and the handsome Victor Slonimsky in rock band Pirate."

Dunk threw a box of tissues at the TV. "Since when is Victor Slonimsky a member of Pirate? Get your facts straight, you mingers." He glared at Jack. "Rona Barrett and Robin Leach are both asking for exclusive interviews, along with every pond scum, sleazeball gossip journo in this gormless excuse for a country."

Jack laughed. "Go to bed and get some sleep before you murder someone. I can handle anything that comes up. You know I won't be able to sleep."

"Ya won't be laughing, mate, if this crosses the pond and your da finds out where you are. Or if Barry the Bastard decides to make an issue of this and claims you're violating the bonus agreement."

"OK, first, this news is too small to play in England. And second, Barry can't do that. It's a legal agreement with fixed terms."

"Oh, yeah? You trust those bassas to play by the rules? Ya believe that, maybe you'll believe I'm going to Sweden next week to accept the

Nobel Peace Prize. They like the way I extract information and money from people. Think I should be an example for kiddies around the bloody world."

"I'm not worried about Barry as long as we have Howie. But my father … do you really think he might see this?"

Dunk forced himself off the couch and stood up, swaying on his feet. "Yer da may not even be yer biggest worry, mate." He dragged himself to the door and turned. "If this hoopla keeps up, a Nobel Peace Prize-winning band manager is going to go starkers and murder yer sorry arse. Count on it."

Jack frowned as Dunk slammed the door on his way out of the room. Jack didn't think the news would cross the Atlantic. The American news media were insatiable when it came to celebrity news, so naturally they had jumped on the story. But he doubted the British news media would find someone leaping across a balcony all that exciting. However, in future he would have to be more careful about appearing in public without costume and makeup. Not a good idea to tempt fate.

A minute later there was a tentative knock on the connecting door. He went over, undid the latch and bolt, and opened it. Lucy stood there in bare feet and her pajamas and robe.

She looked off to the side. "I wonder if I could talk to you."

He held the door open. She walked past him to his bed, climbed on top of it, and got into a cross-legged position, as if she were about to have a heart-to-heart with her best friend. He hid his surprise and followed her to the bed. He plumped a pillow and put it behind him as he sat against the headboard facing her.

She picked at some imaginary scab on her ankle and he stared at his hands. They started speaking at the same time, apologized and insisted the other go first. He stayed silent. He had learned that that was usually the best strategy when you were the guilty party.

Lucy looked up at him. "Magnus called me, said you had him flown to San Francisco Medical Center, the best place for HIV treatment in the country, and told them you would foot the bill. He's very grateful … and me too."

Jack waved his hand. "Dunk arranged it." Dunk was the big hero here, and she should know that.

She cocked her head, as if assessing him. "My family saw us on TV. My mom and nana both think you're hot."

He grinned. "They do?"

She picked at her leg again. "They asked me to apologize for them. They think none of this would have happened if they hadn't done what they did. You see, my best friend Cindy told the swami I left the ashram because my nana was on her deathbed. That was my excuse for leaving. But I forgot to tell my boss, Ramakar, before I left. So the swami and Ramakar made Cindy call my parents in front of them, and who should answer but Nana." She shrugged her shoulders. "They jumped in a limo and went to my house looking for me."

"Wait, what? Where your parents and Nana live?"

"Yes, can you believe it? They showed up and demanded to see me. The swami wouldn't even let Mom get Ramakar a Coke, and when they told him I was in Palermo getting Nana's birth certificate in case she kicked the bucket, he gave Mom the heebie-jeebies with his creepy stare. Then Nana escaped from her room—Em couldn't stop her—and pretended to be a madwoman. I think she wanted to make up for when they called and she sounded normal. Dominick—that's my nephew—called the swami a bad man. So the swami threatened to contact the FBI to find me, and then he kicked my cat, Mittens, and my gnomes on the lawn." She looked triumphant. "But my brother Tony chased him to the limo and threatened him with a fist sandwich."

Jack grinned. "They take good care of you, don't they? I like the sound of your family. But why should they feel responsible for what happened?"

"Oh, yeah. Because they had this crazy idea to send Magnus out to warn me. I mean, they could have picked up the phone. But my family is all about the drama."

One thing puzzled him. "Your parents met Magnus?"

Lucy smirked. "Met him? I grew up with him. I'm not supposed to tell anyone this—he even made me sign an NDA before I could go on the road with him—but his real name is Carmine Matarazzo and he's my cousin."

"You're related to him?"

She looked at him like he was crazy. "You think Italian or Greek parents would let their teenage daughter go on the road with a rock band without a chaperone? They would shoot her first."

He felt his heart leap. Magnus hadn't been her boyfriend.

"He also gave me the name 'Lucy Lamour,' after the actress Dorothy Lamour. She was in all those on-the-road comedy movies with Bob Hope and Bing Crosby? Mister Funnypants said *I* was a traveling comedy. But then everyone thought it meant L'amour. Y'know, 'love' in French? So the last laugh was on my wisenheimer cousin."

His heart leapt again. Magnus hadn't been her boyfriend. She wasn't mad at him for interfering with their love affair, as he'd assumed, but instead because he'd hit her sick cousin. She wasn't *with* Magnus. Which meant that she could be with *him*. Emotion surged inside of him, along with an overwhelming desire to kiss her. But he was also a bit aggrieved at what she'd put him through. He'd leapt across that balcony and almost killed himself to save her, and she'd acted mad at him the entire day. At *him*, the little minx.

"Get over here."

She looked up at him through her lashes. "What?"

"Come here, right now. I'm going to kiss you."

She gave him a mischievous look. "No."

"No?"

He lunged and grabbed her, flipped her onto the bed, and lay on top of her. "No, huh?"

Lucy laughed as he tried to kiss her and pretended to evade his kisses.

He stopped. "OK, if you don't want to."

She smirked at him, grabbed his face, and pulled his lips to hers. It was as good as the kiss the other night. No, it was even better. She still had the softest lips, but now he was laying on top of her soft body, and he couldn't believe how comfortable and welcoming it was, and how perfectly it fit with his own. Plus, she smelled divine, what he thought of as "essence of Lucy." Thank god she didn't wear perfume or cologne and mask her natural scent. Her smell made him mad with desire.

She put her arms around his shoulders and her hands in his hair, which turned him on even more. She angled her head and explored his mouth with her insistent tongue, and he allowed her access as his erection grew even more intense. It was getting uncomfortable in his jeans, and she was starting to grind her hips against him.

A feeling of confusion and panic surged inside him, competing with the desire. Things were moving too quickly and getting out of his control. He didn't feel ready for this. They were not going to be taking it all the way tonight. He needed to feel ready, didn't he? It had to happen in the proper way, didn't it? Because he wanted a relationship with this woman and not a quickie roll in the hay. Besides, he didn't have a condom and he didn't know if she was on birth control. No, he was going to have to be the man and take the lead here.

He rolled his body to the side while still kissing her, so he wasn't laying on her anymore. She groaned into his mouth in protest. Even though it took all of his willpower, he pulled away and looked at her. "I think I need you to go back to your room."

She looked back at him with dismay, her hands reaching for him and her face full of desire. God, she was beautiful. She furrowed her brow and pouted. "No. I won't."

His resolve was wavering. He had to say something to convince her to go. Something that would set her off, and he could say sorry in the morning. But in the meantime, he needed to get some distance between them. "Your cousin warned me that you're a royal pain in the ass, and I'm not sure I don't agree. And he also made me promise I would take care of you."

She came right back. "Well, you're not doing a very good job, are you?"

He stifled a smile. No, not the way she wanted. But he was doing it for the greater good. *Their* greater good. He was not going to have sex with her tonight. He would *make love* to her when the time was right. When they were both ready and not a moment sooner. But if she wasn't willing to go back to her room, he wasn't going to make her. He didn't want her to go back, anyway. He still wanted to be close to her.

He got up from the bed and pulled back the covers on one side. "Get in."

She shimmied onto that side of the bed and looked up at him, expectant. He would use that to his advantage.

"Don't move," he said, pretending to be gruff. He loved ordering her around. It made him hard again.

He went around the rest of the suite turning off the lamps. He came back to the bed and stripped off his shirt and socks, pursing his lips as he stared down at her. He kept his jeans on. No point in tempting fate. She stared back at him with wide eyes.

He put his knee on the bed. "Turn around and move over."

She made a great pretense of doing it unwillingly. He almost laughed. She was utterly and totally adorable. There was no other word for it. He switched off the bedside lamp, slipped in next to her, pulled the covers over them, and spooned her.

Putting his arm around her and pulling her close, he put his mouth near her ear and talked in Vic's voice. "Now get some shut-eye, me love. We's goin' to do fings the proper way, ain't we. And don't be givin' me no sass, girl, or I'll be tannin' your hide, I will."

"Promises, promises," she said.

Always with the best come-backs. Could she be more brilliant? He squeezed her and kissed her shoulder.

He thought he would lie with her until she fell asleep, then get up and do some work once he got bored lying there. He'd told Dunk he would handle any problems that came up, but damn if it wasn't so warm and comfy in that bed. He yawned and snuggled closer to her. He could get very used to this. He stuck his nose in her hair and closed his eyes just for a moment. And that was the last he remembered.

Fifty-Two

DUNK SPRAWLED on the couch in Jack's suite, watching him pace back and forth as he tried to convince Clint to work with them. Clint was sitting at the table cradling a mug of coffee. The cowboy was looking polite but unconvinced.

Clint and Ruth had disappeared off the map for a few days, no one in the band hearing a single word from them. Dunk had felt a wee bit annoyed by that, what with the tour almost over and the crew needing adjustments. But it turned out Ruth didn't abandon them; it was Clint's fault. He'd taken her back to his hotel and insisted on taking care of her. He claimed that she was "tuckered out and needed some tender lovin' care," some "spoilin'" by a man who adores her."

Dunk rolled his eyes when Clint said this. She was a grown woman, f'crissakes. She could make up her own mind. Ruth being Ruth, the minute she saw all the hoopla with the band on television, she'd put her foot down and said they had to help Pirate. So now, at this very minute, she was over at the arena giving the crew adjustments. And she had insisted that Clint come over to the hotel and meet with Jack and Dunk and help out however *he* could.

Jack was now ranting about Dolos and Barry the Bastard cheating the band. "The good news is that sales are going through the roof with all this publicity. The bad news is that we already know Dolos is ripping us off on expenses." Jack stopped pacing and turned toward Clint. "It's a simple proposition, Clint. Hold their feet to the fire and make sure they abide by all contract regulations, meet the sales demand, and pay us everything we're entitled to. In return, we give you a goodly percentage of everything you recoup for us."

Clint stared into his coffee mug, avoiding Jack's expectant look. "Don't get me wrong, Jack, I'm really flattered that you've asked me. But ... don't you have a lawyer?"

Dunk scowled. The guy was a liar and a cheat. "That scunner deserves to be hung up by the bawsack and—"

"He's not someone we trust, let's put it that way," said Jack. "Turns out he and Barry went to the same law school, go to the same temple, eat at the same deli, play in the same poker game every Thursday."

"Screw the same 'broads' and snort from the same bag," Dunk added, rolling his eyes.

"You get the picture," said Jack.

Clint looked apologetic. "I would really like to help you fellas. But keep in mind, even if I chase the accounts, you'd still have to hire an attorney for legal matters."

"Agree with you one hundred percent," said Jack. "We were thinking Allen Grubman. He's representing a lot of people, like Spring-steen and Joel. But we wonder how many rock stars he can handle at the same time. Or there's Leonard Marks, who handles the former Beatles and Bowie. But now we're thinking maybe John Branca, Michael Jack-son's guy."

"Yeah, I hear good things. But he's in L.A. and Dolos is in New York."

"Our contract with Dolos is ending. And that's the other big prob-lem, Clint. Barry's making noises that we still owe them—"

Dunk had to interrupt, he felt so aggrieved. "After we gave those bassa bloodsuckers one album that did good, followed by two hit albums and a bunch of top hits. But, oh no, yer still our organ-grindin' slave monkeys forever, because we're chargin' ya for all the meals we had in fancy restaurants where we said yer name one time in passing, and we said yer name again when we were doing promo for another artist so we're chargin' ya for that, and oh yeah, we mentioned yer name to impress that hooker, so we're chargin' ya for her too."

"Oh, don't think I don't know their tricks," said Clint. "You're right to want some barracudas on your team. But, well, the other problem is that I'm kind of busy ... I could really use your advice on this actually. I'm ... well, the fact of the matter is, I'm making plans to marry Ruth."

Dunk grinned from ear to ear. "Aaaaaw." He was surprised at how soppy that made him feel. Their Ruth getting married to this kind-hearted cowboy who adored her and wanted to take care of her.

Jack gaped at Clint. "Are you serious? Oh. My. God. We love Ruth. Have you popped the question? Has she said yes? Can we come to the wedding?"

Dunk had never seen Jack as animated as he was this morning, except when he was doing a theatre production. It was like he was on some sort of upper. Dunk hoped he wasn't taking something. Jack and drugs had never been a good combination; he always had some sort of off-the-wall reaction.

Clint pulled a ring box out of his pocket. "I went out yesterday when she was sleeping and got this." He snapped it open. "Do you think ... will she like it?"

Before they could respond, the connecting door banged open. Lucy scuffled in wearing those pink fluffy slippers girls seemed to like and Minnie Mouse pajamas. Her hair was sticking up like a fountain orna-ment or a gargoyle or something, and she didn't look like she'd slept well, with big dark bags under her eyes.

She went straight over to Jack. "Good morning, handsome." She put her hands on his chest, stood on her tiptoes, and gave him a kiss. "You woke me up with your yelling. What's all the excitement?"

Jack was grinning like a right ol' muppet. He inclined his head toward Dunk and Clint. "Um, Luce ..."

She looked around and saw them. "Oh, goodness. I didn't see you guys. Hey Dunk, hey Clint." Dunk raised his eyebrows in response. Not sure how he felt about this.

Her gaze went to the ring box. "Omigod. Is that what I think it is?"

"For Ruth," Jack said. "It's for Ruth. A ring for Ruth."

Dunk stared at him. Boy, was he acting strange today.

Lucy ambled over to the table. "Can I see?" When Clint showed it to her, her eyes teared up and she put her hand on her heart. "It's beautiful."

Clint beamed. "Do you think she'll like it?"

Lucy sat down at the table across from Clint. "She'd be crazy not to. When are you going to ask her?"

Dunk watched as Jack went to the phone and placed a room service order for everything on the breakfast menu—"Yes, that's what I said, one of everything please"—while Lucy and Clint chatted away. He couldn't believe it when Jack sat down next to Lucy and put his hand on her leg, and she brought her hand under the table to hold hands with him. This was a guy who hated to touch and be touched, except by Ruth. Would miracles never cease?

Not to mention the fact that Jack was now engrossed in a conversation about Clint's secret wedding plans. Jack talking about a wedding with any real interest? That was a new one.

Dunk got up from the couch, none of them paying him any mind whatsoever. He went to the door and stood there observing them for what seemed a dog's age. Jack *finally* looked over at him.

"I'll get the guys to bring up the food."

Jack mouthed "Thanks" and went back to staring at Lucy.

Dunk stood there for another moment, realizing that he was now the third wheel. He'd put her in the connecting room and the inevitable had happened. His best friend was falling in love. And like new lovers everywhere, Jack couldn't seem to focus on anything for more than a minute before his lover stole back his undivided attention.

Trouble was, the timing totally sucked. For the first time since they formed the band, Dunk was truly worried about security onstage. The arena was old and poorly maintained, and the stage was much too low for his liking. But every time he tried to talk to Jack about the problems, something else got in the way.

To add fuel to the fire, the media coverage was drawing large crowds looking to bag a Pirate ticket any way they could, and unscrupulous scalpers were out in force selling forged tickets at exorbitant rates. It was never a recipe for a peaceful, manageable crowd when you had to turn away people who had paid hard-earned money in good faith. He was doing everything he could to rout the scalpers and tighten security, but he worried it wasn't enough.

Not to mention that the band seemed to be hemorrhaging money, and Clint had yet to commit to helping them hold Dolos' feet to the fire. He hated to be suspicious, but hadn't Barry the Bastard succeeded in getting two of his spies—Howie and Lucy—in the middle of the band, where they could see and report back on everything? Jack had insisted they both stay, and Dunk had agreed, maybe against his better judgment.

The biggest problem of all—Dunk was just physically and mentally exhausted. Normally, he and Jack could handle anything that got thrown their way. But with Jack missing in action, Dunk was struggling to bear the full weight of the tour on his shoulders. Maybe his shoulders were massive compared to everyone else's, but there was a limit to what they could bear. No one seemed to recognize that. They took his shoulders for granted. They took *him* for granted—as they chased after tiny women with bags under their eyes and hair that looked like fountain ornaments.

As he left the room, Jack was talking about flowers. Wedding flowers. Dunk rolled his eyes in disgust.

Fifty-Three

HALF A WORLD away in southeast England, in the very house where Jack had spent his life until the age of six, Jack's father walked into a darkened bedroom and clicked on the TV. He turned and glared at Jack's mother lying in the king-sized bed.

"I want you to see what that son of yours has become."

Jack's mother pushed herself up against the headboard as he flipped to the cable entertainment news channel. The same footage playing in the US had made its way to the United Kingdom. She watched in utter disbelief as her son launched himself across a balcony eight stories above the ground. The news anchor identified her son as Victor Slonimsky.

"Personal assistant to the lead singer of a rock band." Jack's father threw the remote control on the bed. "Absolutely disgraceful. If he's going to piss his life away, the least he can do is piss it away here and not hanging about with that jock and a bunch of talentless plebs."

"So he's with Duncan."

"I knew I should have separated those two years ago and sent him to Tufferson's. They would have made a real man out of him. Instead I listened to you, and now look at that poor excuse for a son."

Her mouth dropped open when she saw him kissing the young woman. They looked ... in love. She had always worried her son would never be able to let go, never be able to fall in love. Lucy. She liked the sound of her. She liked the look of her.

"Lucy L'amour. A common little guttersnipe slag," said his father. "I ask you, Pippa, is there any length to which that ungrateful brat won't go to spite us?"

"So they think he's Victor ..."

"Victor Slonimsky," said his father. "Let's just hope they don't discover his real identity before I get him home. It would be an unmitigated disaster."

She feigned her usual illness. "I can't handle this. I've got a migraine. Leave me be, Winnie. I need to be alone. And close the door."

He swore at her and slammed the door as he stalked out of the room. After he left, she flipped around the channels and watched the news about her son again and again. It made her so terribly happy and gave her energy she didn't know she had. She was not going to take this lying down. She was not going to let her husband impose his will and get away with murder yet again. She didn't know what, but she was going to do something to help her son. To help him have the life he deserved.

Fifty-Four

LUCY CAME RUNNING into Jack's suite from her adjoining room. "Turn on the TV! My parents are on."

Jack loved to see her so excited. Dunk and Clint had left for the arena, *finally* leaving them alone. Clint had solicited advice from Lucy on how to propose to Ruth, and, in the throes of his excitement, had agreed to help them with Dolos. Jack gave her the credit; she just had a way of making everyone happy. And Dunk looked in a much better mood after scarfing down all of the room service breakfast Lucy didn't want. He and Dunk probably should have talked, Dunk mentioning some concerns about the arena. But Jack simply couldn't seem to focus with Lucy nearby. Was it a crime that he wanted to spend some time getting to know her better?

Jack clicked on the remote and switched to the entertainment news channel. He held out his arm to Lucy and she inserted herself underneath it and snuggled against him. He kissed the top of her head and caressed her upper arm as they stood together watching the TV.

A middle-aged man with a dramatic comb over was on the screen. He stood stiffly by himself in front of a small ranch house and a well-kept lawn, where several grinning gnomes appeared to be cavorting around a statue of the Virgin Mary. The subtitle read: *Constance Sabatini, Father of Lucy L'amour.*

Lucy grinned up at Jack. "That's my dad, and our house, and my gnomes."

"We haven't met Vic yet," her father said, looking off-camera, "but we hear from Carm he's a very nice boy."

Lucy's mother sidled into view next to him. "From Magnus. You mean from Magnus."

"What'd I say?" Lucy's father put his arm around his wife. "This is my wife, Isabella. Lucy's mama."

Izzy smiled and waved at the camera.

"That's my mom," said Lucy.

Nana sidled in front of them, only coming up to Connie and Izzy's shoulders. The camera panned down to get her in shot. "And this is my mother, Lucy's nana. Luisa Victoria Sabatini."

"She good girl, my Lucy," said Nana, shaking her finger at the camera. "This boy very lucky be with my Lucy."

A young man holding a toddler, with his other arm around a young woman, moved into the space behind Connie and Izzy. "And this is my son Anthony, Lucy's brother, with his wife Emily and my grandson Dominick."

Tony and Em smiled and Dom buried his face in his dad's shoulder. "Wave to the people, Dom," Tony said, lifting his son's hand and waving it.

"No!" said Dom.

Tony beamed and Em stroked his hair.

The news correspondent came into view. "And there you have it, folks. Lucy L'amour's family."

"It's Lucy *Sabatini*," said Izzy looking offended.

"What? What'd he say?" said Connie.

"He said Lamour. What's with this Lamour? Like she's a movie star or something."

The news correspondent shrugged and smiled. "Back to you, Kate."

Jack clicked off the remote and looked down at Lucy. "So, I understand from Nana that I'm very lucky to be with you."

Lucy gave him a coy smile. "And don't you ever forget it, mister."

"Maybe I should show you why you're lucky to be with *me*."

"I dare you." She darted out from under his arm and ran around to the other side of the table.

He pretended to twirl an imaginary mustache. "Get ready, my pretty, because I'm going to catch you and have my way with you."

She screamed with delight as he chased her around the suite and finally cornered her in the bathroom. He scooped her up, carried her over to the bed, and threw her on it.

He kneeled on either side of her and pinned down her arms.

"OK, now I'm going to show you how lucky *you* are."

"Like I said last night ... promises, promises."

He leaned down and kissed her, then let go of her arms and lowered himself onto her and gave her a long, passionate kiss. She caressed his hair and his back, and then ran one of her hands down his buttocks. Jerking at her touch there, he grabbed it and moved it upwards.

"We can't disappoint Constance and Isabella," he said against her lips. "They think I'm a very nice boy."

"What they don't know won't hurt them," said Lucy, moving her hand back down again.

He rolled away and sat up. He wanted this, but it didn't feel right. Now was definitely not the time. Their first time had to be romantic and memorable, something they would never forget. Call him an incurable romantic, but *this* was not it. And he had to feel ready, if that was indeed possible.

"OK, Lucy L'amour, time for you to get dressed and act like a groupie, and time for me, Victor Slonimsky, to do some personal assistant stuff."

"I *am* acting like a groupie. You're the one who's not cooperating. What kind of rock star *are* you?"

He smiled at her. "Hopefully the fairly effective kind."

She sat up and smiled back. "Well, me too. I'm going to go chat with Suze and Carly about how to up my groupie game. I hear they've been having threesomes and orgies down the hall with the boys."

"What?" said Jack.

Those idiots! They could be jeopardizing the bonus, although he wasn't quite sure how. Could you be arrested for a threesome or an orgy in Arizona?

Fifty-Five

JACK ROUNDED up the band members for a meeting. Dunk was over at the arena, so Jack took the unusual step of meeting with them on his own.

He was disappointed with their lack of judgment at a time like this, with all the heightened media scrutiny. They should know better. It was one thing to entertain a woman in one's room, quite another having threesomes and orgies that could be reported to the media. With only one leak by a hotel employee, they could lose a large part of their American fan base. Americans were a religious people and more conservative when it came to sex; not to mention the fact that many of the band's fans were teenagers, whose parents could ban them from buying Pirate records or attending Pirate concerts. As Dunk would say, what were these numpties thinking?

He had them gather in Keith's room. Sam and Rob sat on one bed and George and Randy on the other. Keith slouched in the desk chair, his legs crossed at the ankles.

Jack put his hands on his hips as he looked around at them. "OK, first of all, I want to talk to you about sex."

"Shouldn't Georgie be giving this lecture?" said Keith.

George grinned.

"George?" said Rob with a mock outraged face. "Yeah, if you want it short and sweet. But if you want it long—"

"Then come to me, pretty mama," said Sam. "Sam will take care of all your needs."

"Who you callin' pretty mama?" Keith pointed to himself. "Me? I didn't know ya felt that way 'bout me, Sammy Wammy."

"Yeah, you so cute," said Sam.

"Alison says I'm very good," said Randy.

Rob made a duh face. "Of course. You're a Rickman."

Jack sighed. He needed to get them to focus. "I'm not talking about ... OK, what I'm talking about ... OK, we can't be having threesomes and orgies and such ... with Howie here ... and letting that kind of thing get out with all this media scrutiny right now."

Keith sat up. "You're having us on, man. Howie's the one been having the threesome, and he's right in there with the or—" He stopped abruptly, as if he'd said too much.

"Hold on," said Rob. "You've been having an orgy and I wasn't invited?" He turned to Sam. "Were you invited?"

"No, man, I wasn't invited either. I been making do with little Sam here." He smiled coyly at Keith. "But hey, now I know about pretty mama over there."

Rob was not to be deflected. "That's not fair." He looked at Keith and George. "Maybe Sam and I will have an orgy and not invite you. How about that?"

"Will you invite me?" said Randy.

"No, you're with Alison."

"But I want to be invited."

"Alison won't let you, so what's the point."

"I can do an orgy if I want to."

"You can join our orgy," said Keith.

Jack put up his hands in a stop gesture. "OK, there aren't going to be any more orgies."

Keith glared at him. "Ya can't tell us not to have orgies. We got nothing else to do, cooped up here. And you'll hurt Suze and Carly's feelings. Did ya think about that?"

"Yeah," said Rob and Sam at the same time, now seeing their shot at getting some real sex.

Keith pointed at Jack. "Besides, you're getting it on with Lucy Lovergirl, so who're you to tell us to keep our bleedin' willies on ice?"

Jack realized he'd lost control and blurted out the first thing that came to mind. "Because you're going to be too busy preparing to sing one of your own songs ... in the encore."

Keith looked at him with shock. "For real?"

"Lucy said they're really good." It wasn't really a lie saying that. He *had* heard her say it over the walkie-talkie, just not in person. "But only the one for now. We'll see how it goes. OK?"

Keith was beaming. He stood up and looked at the others. "C'mon, boys, we got ourselves a song to rehearse. Let's get cracking."

Jack stood there watching as they talked with great excitement about the arrangement. He wondered why he'd never done this before. He congratulated himself on his fast thinking and good management. The encore was not an official part of the setlist, so they could play whatever they wanted without violating the bonus agreement.

Bill would be damn proud of him. He was damn pleased with himself. He couldn't wait to tell Lucy.

Fifty-Six

IT WAS AN EXQUISITELY sunny day outside in the heart of the beautiful Berkshires, but the weather was doing nothing to brighten Ramakar's mood. He stood in front of the swami's desk, tense to the max and picking at his already raw fingernails. Mac was not going to be pleased.

"The key you told me to get from Mandy and hide somewhere is gone."

"What?" said the swami, his dark brows beetling together. He got up and walked around the desk, stopping directly in front of Ramakar. "Where did you hide it?"

Ramakar wished he could move back a step. Mac's intensity was making him terribly nervous. "Um, in the drainpipe. That's supposed to be a good place."

The swami stared at him for a long moment. "Hmm. That *is* a good place. That's where I always put it."

Ramakar let out the breath he didn't know he was holding.

"You know what this means, don't you, Rod?"

Ramakar knew the question was rhetorical. The swami was talking his thoughts out loud more and more, and they were often paranoid and crazy thoughts.

"It wasn't my imagination," said the swami. "There *was* a redhead in this office when we got here last night. We have to find her. *You* have to find her, because this is *your* fault." He waved his hand like a king dismissing a subject. "Report back to me in an hour."

Ramakar backed out of the office and shut the door. He hurried around the corner, leaned against the wall, and tried to get his breathing under control. He really believed Mac was losing it. But he wasn't sure how to get himself out and take Mandy with him.

He pawed at his shirt trying to loosen it. He really couldn't breathe. He felt like he was going to die. Right here in the hallway of the ashram, right now on this ludicrously sunny day. Would Mac give a damn? Would anyone mourn him?

Fifty-Seven

DELTA STROLLED DOWN THE HALLWAY, trying to decide whether to go to yoga or hang out in the hot tub. She had just about made up her mind to do neither, and instead browse the bookshop for something new to read, when she saw Ramakar leaning against the wall. The poor man was gulping in air and sweating profusely. He looked to be having a panic attack.

She rushed over and put her hand on his arm. "I'm here, sweetheart. I'm here. Close your eyes and breathe real slow." She rubbed her hand up and down his arm to calm him. "That's it, darlin'."

His breathing slowed and he opened his eyes.

"I want you to come with me, sweetheart. You need to lay down."

Ramakar looked panicked again. "I can't. I have to find a redhead. In one hour."

Delta was having none of it and pushed Ramakar into a standing position. "You come with me, and I'll get you that redhead. Promise."

She escorted him down the hallway to the double room she shared with Norma. Good thing their room was on that floor and a short walk. Ramakar looked to be in a real state.

She opened the door a crack and said, "Hey, you decent?"

Norma's voice came into the hallway. "Is the Dalai a llama?"

Delta snickered. "Is Siddhartha Buddhist?"

She pushed open the door and guided him in ahead of her. Norma was standing there in her bra and panties.

"Hey," said Delta. "You said you were decent."

"Decent as the day I was born," said Norma. "What in all that's holy are you doing bringing Ramakar to our room?"

Delta guided him to her bed and helped him lay down. "There you go, darlin'." She looked over the bed at Norma. "The poor man's having a full-on panic attack."

"Well, I don't doubt it, hanging around with that crazy swami. What're you going to do with him?"

Delta looked down at Ramakar. "I'm going to take care of him. And you're going to get some clothes on and go get Cindy."

Ramakar tried to sit up. "No, no, not *Cindy*."

Delta shushed him. "Lift your head, hon." She removed the pillow and inserted herself into the area where it had been. "Now lower your head into my lap. I'm going to massage your temples and do some Ayurveda on you. All you have to do is breathe in and breathe out."

She mouthed at Norma to go as she massaged Ramakar's temples. He groaned in relief.

Norma threw on her yoga clothes and flip flops and hurried out of the room.

Twenty minutes later the door cracked open and Norma put her head around the door. "You decent?"

"Hardy-har-har," said Delta. She was still massaging Ramakar's temples as he snored softly. "He's young enough to be my son. Where you been all this time?"

Norma came into the room, followed by Cindy. "I couldn't find her. Little missy here was raiding the pantry and sweet talking that cute little French busboy."

"I was hungry," said Cindy.

"Hungry for *something*," said Norma.

Delta gave them both a reproving look. "We got a situation here, ladies. Ramakar needs to report back to the swami with a redhead in half an hour and the poor dear is petrified."

"So let me see if I have this straight," said Cindy. "He needs to produce the redhead the swami thinks he saw in his office last night."

"Well, he did see me," said Norma. "He might be loony tunes, but he sure ain't blind."

Cindy looked up at the ceiling as she thought out loud. "If he saw a redhead, that means he knows someone got into his office while he was gone, and that means he knows someone found the key. So the key is the key. A redhead with a key. Why would a redhead with a key want to go into the swami's office? What excuse would the swami believe? Think, Cindy, think!"

"I can tell you," said Ramakar in a groggy voice.

"You awake, hon?" said Delta, caressing his face.

Ramakar opened his eyes. "He thinks he's god's gift, and every woman wants him, and every man wants to be him. Or else they're out to get him and bring him down, because he's the good guy and they're the bad guys."

"Your classic narcissistic psychopath is what you're telling us," said Cindy.

"Is he a psychopath or a sociopath?" said Norma. "I always get the two mixed up."

"Po-ta-to, po-tah-to," said Cindy.

"Focus, ladies," said Delta. "We can't send Ramakar back into that lion's den. We've got to do something."

Norma put her shoulders back and her chin up. "It was my fault. I was the redhead standing in the window like a big fat dummy. So it has to be me who goes back in."

Cindy put her arm around her. "You're not a big fat dummy. You're memorable."

Ramakar sat up and swung his legs over the edge of the bed. "You don't have to go in. I'll tell him I couldn't find a redhead. You've got brown hair now, anyway."

Norma walked around and faced him. "Yeah, except I think the swami took a good look at me when you two were rushing to the office and we were power walking away. And I'm pretty sure he recognized me."

"Hey, I've been in the lion's den," said Cindy. "It's not so bad ... as long as he doesn't like you."

Ramakar looked at Norma. "OK. We'll go together. It shouldn't be too bad. And if he tries to ban you from the ashram, you'll just have to sneak around. I'll have Mandy keep you on the books."

Delta put her hand on his shoulder. "You sure you're up for this, hon?"

He stood up and faced her as he yanked his clothes back into place and patted down his hair. "You remind me of my mom," he said as he leaned down and kissed her cheek. "God rest her soul."

Delta wiped away a tear as they left the room. "Good luck," she called after them.

Fifty-Eight

"MY DEEPEST APOLOGIES, SWAMI ZUKEENI," said Norma. She was standing in front of his desk next to Ramakar.

The swami was massaging some prayer beads and pursing his lips as he watched her. He reminded her of a cobra contemplating its prey right before it strikes.

She bowed her head and looked at the floor to seem as contrite as possible, and also so he couldn't stare into her eyes. He had the most piercing gaze she had ever encountered, and she was afraid he would suck the truth right out of her through the pupils of her eyes if she didn't avert them.

Ramakar stood to the side, clasping his hands in front of his groin and picking at his fingers. Norma wanted to slap his hand away from there; he was making her nervous, not to mention calling attention to that particular part of his anatomy like a ninny.

"I see you've dyed your hair," observed the swami. "Out of guilt for desecrating my office, no doubt."

Norma peeked up at him and put on her best innocent face. "No. Well, actually yes. Out of guilt. But no, I wasn't here to desecrate your office. I was here to touch your things and be close to your ... essence. I revere you, Swami Zukeeni."

268

"My essence, you say?" The swami got up, walked around the desk, and came to a standstill in front of Norma. "Look at me."

Norma looked up and the swami stared into her eyes. Oh, OK, they were going to do eye staring, which was different from just looking someone in the eye. Norma was good at eye staring. They did it as a regular exercise in her Ayurveda classes, and she and Delta practiced it in their room. It was a good way to connect with the client and assess the state of their health at the same time. She held the swami's gaze without blinking for what seemed like forever, but was probably less than a minute. She fantasized about that gorgeous Bobby Ewing on *Dallas*. Piece of cake.

The swami cocked his head to the side, considering her. If she wasn't mistaken, his holiness was smirking at her. "You wanted to be close to me? To my essence?"

"Yes, my esteemed swami," said Norma.

The swami returned to the chair behind his desk. "Your wish is granted."

Norma looked over at Ramakar and back to the swami in confusion. "Pardon?"

Ramakar looked at the swami with alarm. "But—"

"When you're not in class or sleeping, you are with me. Ramakar, get her a key to my house so she can attend to my affairs as needed."

Ramakar and Norma looked at one another, both speechless.

"What's your name, my dear? Your Sanskrit name," said the swami.

"I don't have one yet."

The swami played with his beads for a long moment. "I award you the name Sashwatimundi, which means handmaiden to the divine."

Why did she feel he was playing with her? Like a cobra dancing with its prey?

Norma bowed. "Thank you, Swami Zukeeni. I am ... honored."

The swami looked over at Ramakar. "Take her and show her around my house, so she knows where everything is."

Ramakar stood there, rooted in place, staring at the swami.

"Now," the swami barked.

Ramakar and Norma backed out of the room in the Namaste

posture. Ramakar shut the door and the two of them rushed down the hallway toward her room.

"What the heck, Ramakar?"

"I ... I ... I don't know what just happened," he said.

Norma didn't even check if Delta was decent or not. She slammed the door open and marched into their room, full of righteous indignation. Ramakar was so hard on her heels that he crashed into her.

Delta startled and dropped the book she was reading. "Heavens to Betsy! What happened?"

"Disaster, that's what happened. Take a good look at your dearly departing friend, *Norma*, because you won't be seeing her anymore. Big fat dummy here," she said as she pointed at herself, "just talked our crazy swami into making me his worshipful and devoted slave. Sasquat-timuddy."

Fifty-Nine

IN THE HOTEL where the Pirate entourage was holed up, Suze stood next to the bed in Howie's room holding the phone to her ear and smirking at Howie. "Relax. It'll be fine."

Yeah, like she had a clue.

"Hello? Is this the Bartholomew residence? ... Please hold for Howard Bartholomew."

Suze handed the phone to him. "I think it's your mom."

"Mom?" said Howie, putting the phone to his ear.

He had to immediately pull it away as his mother shrieked at him. "Howard Bartholomew, where have you been? I've been waiting for days for you to call me. Your uncle and I have been beside ourselves with worry. Haven't we?"

A man's voice shouted something in the background. Oh no, oh no, oh no. His uncle was there. He had only called home because Dunk ordered him to, and he was terrified of that guy. He thought he would just call and reassure his mother he was fine, and then he could go back to hanging out with his ladies and the guys in the band. He was having the time of his life, and he didn't want his mother or his uncle ordering him back to New York City like he expected they would. He had to think of a quick excuse, one that would buy him time and let him stay until the end of the tour.

"I've been b-b-busy for Uncle B-B-Barry." His stutter always got worse around his mother.

"He said he's been busy for you," his mother said to her brother.

Howie could now hear his uncle and his mother battling over the phone.

"Gimme the phone, Mave," his uncle shouted. "I got business to do with my nephew."

"He's my son," she yelled back. "Let go of this phone."

A squeaking sound came over the receiver as they grappled with the phone, and then clattering as it fell on some hard surface.

"You can talk to him after. I promise," said his uncle. Oh no, his uncle had the phone. "Leave the room, Mave. And shut the door. We gotta talk business."

A door slammed in the background. Double oh no, his mother was going to be furious with him. Which was totally unfair because it was Uncle Barry's fault, not his. How come he always got blamed for everything?

"Howie," his uncle shouted into the phone. "Didn't I tell you to call me every single motherfucking day? You better have some *el primo* dirt for me or I'm going to make mincemeat out of those tiny little nuts of yours and feed it to some pigs in Mongolia. That's a promise."

"I do," said Howie. Quick, think of something, anything, to appease Uncle Barry. Anything at all.

"OK, let's hear it."

"Jack's sleeping with Lucy." That should make his uncle happy and get him off his back.

He could hear his uncle puffing on a cigar. "I know that, numnuts. The whole world knows that. Course they don't know Jack's Vic and vice-a versa, like I do. But there ain't no percentage in that. Those cock-sucking limey journos be figuring it out soon enough. So what else ya got for me?"

Howie was silent, wracking his brain for something else to feed his uncle.

"So," Uncle Barry said, "ya hear anything and ya says to yourself, 'huh, that's inneresting,' or 'huh, that's kinda oddball,' or 'something seems a little smelly here'? Something like that?"

"Oh, yeah," said Howie. "There's this guy, Clint Pomeroy. He's b-been hanging around Jack and Dunk."

"Clint Pomeroy? Guy wears a fancy cowboy outfit?"

"Yeah," said Howie.

Howie had to pull the phone away from his ear as his uncle swore up a storm, using every swear word in the Barry Bartholomew book, which he suspected was close to every swear word that existed in the English language.

Suze strode over, a look of determination on her face, grabbed the phone from his hand and hung it up. "That's enough, love monkey. You got better things to do than listen to your asshole uncle, don't you?"

Howie was no fool. He'd watched his uncle and learned from him how to play the percentages. "Yes, I do," he said, pulling her onto the bed. He was a man now and couldn't seem to get enough of his two sexy ladies. That trumped his fear of his Uncle Barry any day of the week—as long as his uncle was 2,500 miles away on the other side of the country.

Barry heard the dial tone and completely lost it. How dare his nephew hang up on him! He threw the phone across the room, hitting his sister's prized ceramic vase from Jerusalem and knocking it from its pedestal to the floor, where it shattered into pieces.

She rushed through the door and stood gaping at the carnage, a look of disbelief on her face. Her wail could wake the dearly departed as she raised her hands to her face, let out a primal howl, and staggered back and forth in front of him.

Mave was Barry's one and only relative left in the world besides Howie. Panting as he stood there watching his sister's distress, Barry promised himself that, even if it cost him his career, that little cocksucking limey control freak Jack was going to pay dearly for this. No question about it, everything bad that was happening lately was that little cocksucker's motherfucking fault.

Sixty

WHEN JACK TOLD Dunk there would be two extra songs that evening as an encore—his song for Lucy, as a surprise for her, and Keith's song because he'd had to keep the boys out of trouble—he didn't expect it to be a big deal. But Dunk had the biggest meltdown that Jack had seen in years.

"I been trying to tell ya we got big problems," Dunk shouted, "but all ya can think 'bout is being with yer lady, and sleeping with yer lady, and serenading yer lady."

How dare he make this about Lucy. Jack couldn't help but shout back. "It's only another fifteen minutes. It's not going to affect the setlist or the bonus. So what is the big deal?"

Dunk stomped around the suite, picking things up like he wanted to throw them and then tossing them back down. "Nah, mate, it's goin' to add a *half hour* to the concert, and that's goin' to give me an even bigger headache with this bleedin' excuse for an arena. Do ya have any idea what me and Manny are dealing with over there? Do ya? Or have ya been too busy with yer lady to give me the bloody time of day?"

Phew, this wasn't really about Lucy. Dunk had some problems at the arena and needed to unload and blow off steam. OK, that he could deal with.

"What's happening at the arena? Is it worse than Syracuse? Tell me. I want to hear."

Dunk stopped in front of him and put his hands on his hips "Syracuse? Syracuse, did ya say? That was bloody nirvana compared to this. These bawbags are from the dark ages. Signed the bloody contract without even readin' it, so naught—and I mean naught—is the way it should be. The electrical systems are so ancient they can't handle modern-day requirements, let alone sophisticated kit like ours. Bonesy got a big shock, thought he was a goner, but only went out for a few minutes."

"What?" Now Jack was truly concerned.

Dunk continued on his roll. "Rider? Rider, did ya say? These wallopers wouldn't know a rider if it walloped them upside the head. The lavvies are rank and the food shite. They gave us their standard codswallop, had the nerve to call it their deluxe menu, naught what we specified, and even Dogger is complainin' 'bout it. But you wouldn't notice, would ya, 'cause yer floatin' on cloud nine and couldn't be bothered with the likes of us."

Jack grimaced at Dunk. That was certifiably bad, if Dunk thought the food was shite and Dogger didn't want to eat it. It had to be not only unsavory but unsanitary. He didn't usually eat the arena food himself, dined beforehand at the hotel. But knowing this, he would warn Lucy not to go near it either. She didn't seem to be particularly discriminatory about what she put in her mouth. That would definitely have to change now that he was kissing that part of her anatomy. That glorious part of her anatomy. He started fantasizing about it when Dunk yanked him back to reality.

"But that's not the worst of it. If ya didn't have yer head in the clouds, ya woulda noticed last night that yer body was on a stage so low any Tom, Dick or Harry—or any Maddie, Hattie or Nelly, for that matter—could climb right onto it. So we had to ring our men round it, 'cause those wankers didn't bother to hire enough security. Ya don't even know what it's costing us, do ya?"

Now this was concerning. "What do you mean 'our men'? Our security men?"

"I knew *that* would get yer attention." Dunk rolled his eyes. "Naw, mate, I'm talkin' 'bout payin' the crew even more overtime to be secu-rity guards during the concert—when they're already burnin' the candle at both ends. It's a recipe for disaster. But you been too busy with Lovergirl to help me and Manny deal with it."

Jack sighed. "Will you stop calling her that? She's not the problem. The problem is the arena. So what are you telling me? That we shouldn't do the encore?"

Dunk dropped onto the couch and it made a cracking noise. He rolled his eyes again and let out a huge sigh. "Naw. I jus' wanted ya to know what we're dealin' with and that it's goin' to cost us. Manny and I will deal with the arena and—"

"Not what you did in Syracuse."

"Listen, mate, don't tell me how to do my bloody job. You have yer ways and I have mine."

"Why are you even dealing with it? Isn't that the promoter's respon-sibility?"

"Well, it would be, but we didn't use a promoter here. Arranged it ourselves, didn't we?" Dunk held up his hands in a stop gesture. "Big mistake. Even if it does give us a much bigger profit."

"I'm not blaming you. But maybe we need to hire someone to do the promotion side of things, so you and Manny and the crew aren't burning the candle at both ends. Especially with all this other hoopla. And never mind arranging an end-of-tour party in L.A. to thank every-one, like we were thinking. We'll do gifts instead. How about that?"

Dunk rubbed his temples and looked up at Jack with bleary eyes. He did look utterly exhausted and defeated. Maybe it was time for a motiva-tional talk to inspire him to soldier on, the kind Bill would give.

"Look, I know you and your team are doing a cracking job, and have done for the entire tour. We're almost there, at the finish line. Only two concerts here and two in L.A., then we're finished for good. Then we can get the money that's coming to us and retire to the countryside and live the life of Riley. Like we planned. But let's not fall at the last hurdle or crawl across the finish line. Let's make a mad dash and finish in style. I promise I'll hold up my end of the bargain and keep the band together for four more concerts. Which is why they need to sing their song tonight. Just another ten minutes. Mine can wait. OK?"

Dunk sighed. "Nah, I'm jus' knackered from dealin' with those heidbangers. You sing yer song too. I wanna hear it, and see what that Lucy Lovergirl's got that I ain't got."

Jack went over to the window and looked out. Why did finding a new love have to mean sacrificing something else? Why did this feel like the end of an era, rather than the start of something new and exciting? How could he feel so happy and so sad at the same time? Bittersweet, that's what this feeling was.

"I guess I should get ready to lead tonight's charge," he said without turning around.

He heard Dunk grunt as he got off the couch, and could feel his eyes on the back of his head.

"Be back soon," Dunk said as he lumbered over to the door and opened it.

Jack flinched at the slam behind him. Navigating the situation with Dunk was not going to be as straightforward as he'd hoped. At least things were going brilliantly with Lucy. Knock on wood.

Sixty-One

JACK SNUGGLED UP against Lucy on the band bus, his arm around her. The guys needed to know that she was his. Hands off. She was so beautiful, outgoing, and charming, he couldn't blame them if they wanted her. But they were not going to get her. Case closed.

He could not believe what a major operation it had been getting everyone over to the arena for that evening's concert. Dunk and Manny had had Mick pull the band bus up at the hotel's service entrance, which appeared to fool no one. A massive crowd of fans and paparazzi had followed the bus and gathered between the bus and the entrance. Mick whinged about fans trying to sneak onto the bus and paps offering him bribes. The guy was angling for a raise, and they'd have to give him one. He hadn't signed up for this circus.

The band members and their guests had been brought downstairs in several trips. A security cordon two men thick was placed around the entire group and escorted them from the service entrance to the bus. The security team joined them on the bus so they could go through the same maneuver on the other end, at the arena.

A small contingent of security guys had been left behind to guard the two floors in the hotel. They'd had to promise them hefty bonuses.

Each had already signed an NDA prohibiting them from talking or giving information to, or in any way abetting, the media or any outside party. But you could never be too careful given how much money the entertainment channels were willing to pay for an exclusive, or how wily the paparazzi had become.

On the way to the arena, Jack told Lucy he had a surprise for her. Her eyes lit up. He loved seeing that. He loved making her happy. She kept pleading with him to tell her what it was, but he had always been very good at keeping secrets. It would be much more special if the song for her was a surprise. He couldn't wait for the end of the concert to see her reaction.

Once they reached the arena and got everyone inside, Dunk ordered them all into the hospitality room for an announcement. Jack had already told Dunk to do whatever he thought best to keep everyone safe.

"No one's sitting in the VIP section tonight," said Dunk, facing the group with hands on hips and a don't-cross-me expression on his face. "Things are getting out of control and we can't protect you there. So ya got two options: watching from the wing, or staying here. Yer choice." When someone groaned, Dunk looked about to lose it. "Shut it or I'll throw ya out and ya can watch from the car park and find yer own way back to the hotel. Do I make myself clear?"

Dunk strode out of the room and Jack looked at Lucy. She was the one who'd groaned. He took her hands in his. "I understand you're afraid to go near the stage, but you'll be with everyone else." He looked around the room. "Alison. Howie. Suze. Carly. You won't be there alone."

Lucy grimaced at him. "I don't know."

"And I'll be there." He gave her a reassuring smile. "With your special present."

She jiggled with excitement. "Please don't make me wait. Can't you give it to me now? I hate to wait for presents. I can't stand it. I really can't."

"I'm going to give it to you later." He grinned at her excitement and squeezed her hand. "At the end of the concert."

Her smile faltered. "I don't know if I'm going to go. Maybe if you gave it to me now, I'd have it to keep me company ... during the concert."

"I'm not going to give it to you now, *here*. That would spoil it."

"So why did you even tell me about it?" she muttered. "That's not fair."

The words escaped Jack's mouth before he realized it. "Don't be childish. You'll get it when I'm ready to give it to you."

Did he just say that? Oh god, he sounded exactly like his father.

Lucy snatched her hands away and frowned at him. "Childish? Did you just call me childish?"

Jack sighed. "OK, hold on. I didn't mean to say that. What I meant to say was that we all have to learn to have something called impulse control. We can't have everything in life exactly when we want it. We have to learn to delay gratification. It's something I've spent a lot of time learning myself. Impulse control." He felt quite pleased with the rational argument and the calm tone with which he'd said that. She obviously needed to learn some impulse control, something she couldn't possibly dispute wasn't true.

Lucy folded her arms like a defiant child. "Well, OK, *Dad*. Thanks for the lecture. I'm sorry I'm such a fucking disappointment to you."

He recoiled in disapproval. *He* was being perfectly logical and reasonable here, and only trying to help, whereas she was, indeed, behaving like a child. "There's no call for using language like that, is there? I'm trying to reason with you, is all. Do you really consider it necessary to use the f-word?"

"Um, yes, I think I do." She walked around him in a circle, saying "fuck" over and over again at him.

The others looked over, shocked by what they were witnessing.

Jack folded his arms. "Lucy, you're behaving—"

"Like a child. You already told me that. I'm just living up to your *high* expectations of me."

"Now stop it. Right now."

"Or what?"

"Or ... or ..."

"Or ... or ..." she mimicked him.

God, he hated to be mimicked, had always hated it. It really set him off.

"Or I'm going to have to spank you," he blurted.

She looked at him in shock. He looked back at her, dismayed at what had just come out of his own mouth. Did he just threaten her?

Lucy's lip started to quiver and Alison rushed over to comfort her.

"I didn't mean it," he said. "Luce?"

But it was too late. Everyone was looking at him like he was a complete and total arsehole. All he'd wanted to do was give her a present he'd slaved over to make for her. How had it all gone so wrong, and so damn quickly?

He fled from the room and rushed blindly down the corridor, only stopping when he found himself on the left wing of the stage where he couldn't go any further. He could hear the audience finding their seats and talking to one another in voices filled with anticipation and excitement, while members of the crew climbed up and down the set making last-minute tests and adjustments. Unlike Lucy, he found it calming being close to the stage like this. He stood to the side, out of the crew's way, playing "'Round Midnight" in his head and with his fingers, so he wouldn't have to think about what he'd just done. How he'd ruined the greatest thing that had happened to him since he met Dunk. Maybe the best thing ever. If he thought about it, he might cry.

Dunk found him like that a few minutes later. "I can't leave ya alone for two damn seconds, can I?" He crossed his arms and stared at Jack like he was an idiot of the highest order. "I'd yell at ya, but 'twouldn't do any good. After seventeen years of trying to reform yer sorry arse, I know it's a lost cause."

"Tell me she's OK. That's all I need to know."

"Here's the thing, *Einstein*. I can't tell ya she didn't cry, and I can't tell ya she's not mad. But I can tell ya that she wouldn't act like that if she didn't care."

"Really?" Jack was desperate to believe that—that he hadn't ruined things for good.

"Yeah. Really. I'm not an emotional eejit like you, so you can believe me. But ya gotta make it up to her, ya royal rocket. So get ready to sing yer heart out to her and win her back."

"But she doesn't want to come near the stage. It's a long story—not my story to tell—but it scares her."

"Then ya sing to her later, in yer suite. F'crissakes. Do I have to tell ya *everything*?"

Sixty-Two

ONCE LUCY CALMED DOWN, she realized what an idiot she'd been. Magnus was right. She *was* a royal pain in the ass. And she hated to admit it, but Jack was right too.

She had no impulse control. At least not when it came to presents. Whereas Tony would open his presents very slowly and carefully on Christmas morning, savoring and admiring each one before moving on to the next, she would tear all of hers open inside of a minute. She'd made him cry at the age of three when, having finished hers, she tore open all of his as well. Her parents made her go to her room, no new presents to play with. She'd never done that again, but then she started searching the house for presents in the weeks leading up to Christmas. Her parents switched to hiding them at relatives' houses, but she searched those too. She wasn't sure where her parents finally ended up hiding them, but she wouldn't be surprised if her dad hadn't rented a storage unit for the Christmas season and stashed them there. Or even begged some complete stranger to store them.

Now everyone was leaving to go listen to the concert from the side of the stage. No one wanted to stay in the hospitality room where you couldn't hear as well, and she didn't feel it would be fair to keep them there just because she didn't want to be alone. Alison offered to stay with her, but Lucy insisted that she was fine and Alison should go along with the others and watch Randy play.

When Dunk heard she was alone in the hospitality room, he sent a security guy to stay with her. The guy took the opportunity to wolf down some food, said he'd never worked so hard in his life and was absolutely famished. He told her that they'd had to work through a lot of problems they weren't expecting, and how he didn't mind because Dunk and Manny were paying them extra. He said people didn't know the huge amount of work that went into an operation like this. It was like a traveling carnival, only bigger. For sure, she had no clue, had enjoyed the spectacle of the concert and had never given the enormous amount of work behind it a second thought.

What he said made her think about how much Jack was dealing with. Besides these problems with the production, which she hadn't known about, there were all the financial concerns she'd heard him discussing with Clint, and the huge security issues resulting from the incident with Magnus, and complaints from members of the band about not being able to come to the arena and rehearse the new song they were doing in the encore. The guy was drowning in problems.

If she thought about it—and she didn't want to think about it, but she was going to make herself—a lot of the problems had been caused by her. Well, at least half of them. To add insult to injury, in the middle of everything she decided to have a major hissy fit over having to wait for her present—a present he had somehow found the time to get for her—and, even worse, made herself look like the victim and him look like the bad guy in front of his own band. My god, could she have been a bigger brat if she tried?

Yes, he had blurted out something about spanking her, and no question that was wrong, but he took it back as soon as he said it. It was almost like he was parroting something that had been said to him. And he looked so devastated when she started crying. She should have gone after him when he left the room, but she was so outraged at being called a child that she couldn't think about anything else. She'd spent three years talking about this in group therapy, and it was her emotional trigger, but for crying out loud, when was she going to be able to control it?

And wasn't he right? He might have acted like a sanctimonious dad, but she acted like a big fat baby.

Lucy needed—she wanted—to make it right to him. Here he was performing and she wasn't even there in the wings like everyone else. She wanted him to see her when he came off the stage, to know that she was sorry, that she cared, that she was there for him too. Only that meant going to the side of the stage, which terrified her. She'd talked about that fear in therapy for three years too. And learned about how you have to face your fears or you'll never get over them, and how you had to acknowledge the trauma you'd experienced but not let it rule your life and prevent you from living it.

She asked the security guy to get Alison for her. Alison came right away, and Lucy told her what had happened in Buffalo. She asked if Alison would hold her hand as she went to the stage, she didn't think she could do it on her own, and Alison said she would be honored to help her. She felt like someone learning to walk again as she gripped Alison's hand and painstakingly made her way toward the stage. The others saw her coming and made a space for her. She took a spot in their midst and kept a grip on Alison's hand.

The terror started to surge up and she took huge gulps of air. Alison pulled her close and held her. She'd been taught to move toward the center of the terror and touch it and let it speak to her. She closed her eyes and moved toward it, asking it what it wanted from her. Shockingly, it had wanted *this*, had wanted to come back to this situation and see that it wasn't the place itself that was terrifying her. It was the death that she had witnessed and hadn't been prepared for, the death that had haunted her, and had haunted Magnus. The death that seemed so senseless and unfair and tragic, a major violation of the laws of the universe.

Lucy kept touching the terror until it changed into something more like normal fear. She was still afraid of being here on the side of the stage, afraid of the possibility of fans getting out of control and charging onto the stage, trampling people underfoot and killing them. But that was a normal, rational fear. It could happen here, as it had happened in Buffalo and Altamont and Cincinnati and other places. She opened her eyes and realized that her breathing had slowed to normal. As she glanced around, everything no longer seemed so magnified. It looked downright ordinary. They were in the staging area, with equipment, ropes, crew, people and other concert stuff. That was it, and that was OK.

She had Barry to thank for this opportunity to face her fear. If he hadn't sent her to babysit Pirate, this never would have happened. When she saw that man, she was going to give him a huge hug and find a way to repay him. But in the meantime, she would relish the opportunity to enjoy the concert and support her wonderful man. And wait for him to come offstage so she could apologize and make it up to him in a heartfelt way.

Sixty-Three

"THANK YOU, THANK YOU SO MUCH," said Jack as the applause finally died down. "As an encore, we thought we might play two new songs for you. We've never played these before, and we hope you like them. The first one is 'Jungle Fever.'"

He signaled to Keith, and the boys broke into the opening chords of their song. Keith had asked him to sing quiet backup and play the maracas. He was touched and grateful to have been included, given they had done all the rehearsing and could have asked him to sit the song out.

It was a fast song with a Latin beat, about a saucy senorita with a come hither look who led the guy on a wild chase, only to disappear into the jungle and leave him wondering if it had all been in his imagination. Each of the guys had a solo and played it for all it was worth. Keith led the audience in learning and singing the very catchy refrain. The audience loved it and Jack could tell the song would be a hit. He also realized that Keith might be ready to start his own band; he'd really come into himself as a songwriter and creative leader. It gave Jack an unexpected pang in his heart to think about Pirate breaking up.

Finally the boys' song was over and it was his turn. A crewmember ran onstage and handed him an acoustic guitar. He adjusted the mike and looked at the audience. He felt nervous the way he had back in the beginning when they first started touring, not because of the audience, but because the song was so intensely personal. He was going to be wearing his vulnerable heart right there on his proverbial sleeve for everyone to see. About as taboo as an Englishman—or any modern-day man, for that matter—could get, but he didn't feel he had any choice. He had to let her know how he felt. He couldn't lose her before they'd even begun and had a chance to see if it would work. That is, if she heard it, if she was willing to give them a chance, if he hadn't already fucked it up. There, he could say the f-word too. Not that he liked to— it was such a lazy, unimaginative word—but he could.

He spoke very quietly. "This is a song called 'When Lightning Strikes,' and it's for Lucy." The audience was silent, as if they knew something very special was coming and they didn't want to miss a single note. He played the chord progression through once before launching into the first verse.

> Tis fine, all fine
>> An easy lie
>> It's all I need
>> This music high.
>> Life's best alone
>> Without the pain.
>> This something life
>> This gentle rain.
>
> Then lightning strikes
>> Flashing hazel
>> Red and white tube top
>> Astrape chortles
>> My head splitting
>> My soul searing
>> She's got my number
>> This lightning lover
>
> It hurts, my girl
>> I can't deny

Your Zeus-like aim
Your thunderous lie.
Pain is pleasure
Pleasure pain
A bolt from the quiver
Of love insane.

When lightning strikes
Flashing hazel
Blue flare trousers
Astrape chortles
My head splitting
My soul searing
She's got my number
This lightning lover

A mouse in a cat's jaw
A Rottweiler's bone
A stag fearing rivals
An Odyssey home
How did this happen
In one fell swoon
Now yours to torture
Your monogrammed loon.

When lightning strikes
Flashing hazel
Bright red lipstick
Astrape chortles
My head splitting
My soul searing
She's got my number
This lightning lover

A man mighty flawed
Full of bravado

Make me, I beg,
Your inamorato.
Say you'll stay
My lightning lover
Say you'll strike
Again and forever.
Say you're mine
My lightning love.
Make your home
In my aching blue boughs.

He played the last chord and looked down, exhausted and afraid of leaving the stage. What if she hadn't heard it? What if she didn't feel the same way he did? What if she didn't want him after those stupid remarks he'd made earlier?

After a collective gasp from the audience, he looked up to see Lucy running across the stage toward him—across the quarter deck, down the stairs, across the amidship, up the stairs to the forecastle—her face streaked with tears. He turned toward her and she ran into his arms, sobbing and hugging him and saying "I love you" over and over again. The mike was still on and the audience went wild.

Jack was still holding the guitar and embraced her with it. A crewmember ran out and removed it from his hand.

She found his lips and they kissed, the audience cheering them on. She stroked his face. "Let's go home."

He picked her up in his arms and carried her off the stage to wild cheering.

When they got offstage, he put her down but kept his arm around her. The guys came by and congratulated him on a great song, and all he could manage was a wooden thanks and a half-smile. The fog had already descended and he was enveloped in it. The darkness. The terror and the panic: those unwelcome and persistent guests who never failed to show up at a time like this.

"Keith, could you please get me Dunk," Lucy said in an urgent voice.

Jack looked down at her and she was regarding him with concern.

He wanted to comfort her, but he felt lightheaded and she seemed so far away. It felt like déjà vu, as if he'd been through this exact moment before. He wanted to cry, but he remembered he shan't or something bad would happen.

He heard Keith shouting and Dunk's booming voice. "What the bloody hell is it … ?" Dunk's face loomed in and out of his vision.

"Dunk, can you get us back right away?" said Lucy.

"Manny, get the band loaded into the bus, pronto," Dunk shouted.

"I'll round up the lads," said Keith.

Jack knew this urgent activity was about him, but he couldn't seem to function, like he was experiencing everything from a distance, almost as if he was hovering outside his body watching someone else be him. Someone terrified of moving and doing the wrong thing. Someone trying his best not to moan or cry.

Lucy was peering up at him through a tunnel. "I'm with you, sweetie. I've got your hand and I won't let go. I'm taking you to the bus now. You're with me, OK?"

Yes, it was déjà vu, wasn't it? Or maybe he was living the real thing again. A lady came and took him away. She kept telling him it was going to be OK, but it wasn't OK. It wasn't OK for a very long time.

Sixty-Four

LUCY HAD him by the hand and led him into the suite.

"Do you want me to take care of him?" said Dunk. "He'll be fine in the morning, but it could be one of his rougher nights."

"No, I'll take care of him," said Lucy. "I'll call you if I need you, OK?"

The door slammed and Lucy led him over to the bed.

Jack stood there as she pulled back the covers.

"Sit down, sweetie, and let me get your boots off."

He obeyed and she pulled off his boots. That meant she was going to leave him. He felt tears streak down his cheeks.

"Don't leave me. Please don't leave me." He grabbed her arm. "You can't leave me." As he continued to plead, he expected her to pry his hands off and tell him to *buck up, everything will be fine*, and then depart the room and leave him alone. But she didn't. This time was different.

"Oh, sweetie, there's no way in the world I'm going to leave you. Just give me some room to get in bed with you." She put a pillow against the headboard and sat against it, then held out her arms to him.

He looked at her with confusion. He couldn't make a decision about what to do without getting some sense of what she was feeling. He didn't know what would please her.

292

She had a concerned look now. "What if you put your head in my lap?"

That was clear enough. He could do that. He lay alongside her with his head in her lap and she began to stroke his hair. He still wasn't sure what to do, and lay there stiff as a board as he waited to see what she wanted.

"How about if I sing to you, sweetie?"

"OK," he managed to whisper.

She sang some sixties songs from the Beatles and Peter, Paul, and Mary, and even that silly "Incense and Peppermints" song by Strawberry Alarm Clock. He and Dunk had made up their own version with lewd lyrics during an especially boring Chaucer lesson.

But now she was singing nursery rhymes. When she started on "Sing a Song of Sixpence," he clutched her legs like a lifeline. He heard himself start sobbing as he slipped down into the familiar darkness. He had to hang on or he would be lost, for good. He had been so close so many times. If not for Dunk.

Her voice crooned at him from a distance as she continued to stroke his hair. "I have you, sweetie. I'm here. Let it out, my love. Let it all out. Nothing else to do, nowhere else to go. I'm here. I'm not going anywhere. Just let it all out."

Not that he could stop or anything. It was a torrent that kept on coming, and coming, and coming. First was the sobbing. Then his brain seemed to wake up and demand to be involved—to explain what was going on. She had to be made to understand, or it could all go pear-shaped again. He could be left, again.

He moved his head to look at her. "Let me tell you. I have to tell you. Can I tell you?" When she nodded, he continued. "Mummy and Daddy left me at boarding school when I was six years old. Mummy was crying and Daddy told her to stay in the car. When I started crying, he hit me in the face and told me to buck up and stop making a scene. He told me I was a lucky boy, because he had wanted to bring me at the age of four, right after my brother died. But he'd let my 'poor excuse for a mother' talk him into keeping me in the local day school for another two years. He told me I could come home for visits if the headmaster said I was good and if I got top marks. Otherwise, I was no longer welcome at home."

She wiped tears from her eyes. "But how could he do that, to his own son?"

He plowed on. He needed to get it all out. "The headmaster didn't like me at first because I was artistic, not an athlete like the top boys. He was big on team sports. He punished me whenever he felt like it because he knew my father had no problem with it. He liked to pull down my pants and hit me with a hairbrush, or a cane, or a switch, or sometimes his hand."

The tears were streaming down her face now.

Jack hurried on, the words falling over one another now in his rush to get them out. "Then things got worse. He said my father had told him to make me into a man, and that was his excuse to abuse me. I wasn't the only one, but I was one of his favorites. He used to call me into his office, make me pull down my trousers and pants, spank me for being bad, tell me to fondle myself, and then jerk off in front of me. I think he did other things. I don't remember. He told me my thing belonged to him and I wasn't to share it with the other boys. I guess the other boys didn't mess with me because they knew he would punish them for it, so I didn't get the bullying and ... attention some of them got. But I got a lot of attention from him ... for the first two years. I never knew when I was going to be called to his office. That was the worst part, never knowing when it was going to happen."

"But what about your parents? Couldn't you tell them?"

"He told my father I was uncooperative to prevent me from going home for visits, and to make sure I didn't have the opportunity to tell them what was going on. I doubt my father would have cared and my mother would have been powerless to do anything about it. By then she was ... well, that's another story. So I was at the headmaster's mercy for two years. That was when I learned to separate from my body and not feel anything. And that's when I started to hate to be touched ... by anyone."

"Oh, sweetie! I hate that man! I hate him!"

"Then Dunk came and the headmaster tried the same thing on him. Dunk was a lot smaller then, but he's always been a fighter and bit him straight through the finger. When the headmaster said he was going to turn him in to the police, Dunk threatened to tell his parents and to expose him as a pervert. I don't know how I found out about this, but I did. And the next time the headmaster called me into his office, I paid Dunk to go with me and tell him never to bother me again or else. It worked and his reign of terror over me ended. But I hate to say that he simply moved on to other little boys and forgot about me. He liked them really young."

"Is he still alive? Because I'm going to kill him."

"Dunk and I became friends and discovered that we both loved music and acting and things like that. We set up an amateur dramatic club and put on plays with the other boys, until a new headmaster came and put a stop to it. So we started sneaking out to act in the local pantomime, got caught several times, and finally got kicked out of the school. This happened at a few different schools, and whenever my father enrolled me in a new one, Dunk would have his parents enroll him in the same school so we could be together."

Lucy gave him a wan smile.

"By that time, I was spending all my holidays with Dunk's family. We had faked a letter from my father authorizing it, and the headmasters were only too happy to get rid of me during break. Cheaper and less bother for them. Dunk's family became like my own family. His parents hadn't wanted to enroll him in boarding school in the first place, but his father got this prestigious fellowship for a year in a part of Africa with a lot of malignant malaria, and they didn't want to take any risks by bringing Dunk with them. When they returned from Africa, they planned to bring him back home, but he and I had become best mates by then and he begged them to leave him in boarding school with me. The MacGregors thought that maybe, instead, I could come live with them and go to the local school with Dunk. So his father went to talk to my father, and my father told him to keep his dirty son away from me."

"That asshole," said Lucy with a fierce look. "Your dad, I mean."

"Well, he really said a lot worse than that, but I don't want you to hear those words. I think Dunk's parents felt really sorry for me, so they allowed him to stay in boarding school. They weren't that well off like my parents, but Dunk was so smart that he was always able to get one scholarship or another to stay there."

"Wow."

"Yeah. People call me the genius, but he's really the one. When it came time for university, we both applied to Cambridge because we wanted to join Footlights. That's the dramatic club there. My father was determined that I do the PPE course at Oxford and get into economics or politics, and I was equally determined that I wouldn't. By some miracle, I got a scholarship to Cambridge and he threatened to have it withdrawn."

"Hold on. He doesn't want to raise you, but then he wants to control your life as an adult?"

"So I threatened him back with exposure. I knew things. Plenty of things. He gave in and let me go there, to Cambridge. And while we were in Footlights, Dunk and I did a drag show and my father got word of it and threatened me with prison under the Sexual Offences Act."

Lucy shook her head in disgust.

"I didn't believe he'd actually do it, but he threatened Dunk too. So I agreed to behave, quote unquote, appropriately. That was when we plotted my liberation from my father, a completely new identity for me. I had written a pirate parody, including all the music. We put it on at a local pub and it had gone down a storm. That was when Pirate was born. When we graduated, we went underground and decided on Manchester as our new home. I won't go into all the boring details, but we recruited the members of the band and began performing, and things took off from there. I always appear in costume so my father has never been able to track me down."

"Or you go out as Vic."

"Exactly. But, to be honest, I think my father was happy to have me disappear and never really looked for me, until now. It's my twenty-fifth birthday in three days and I come into control of the trust fund my maternal grandfather set up for me. You see, my father has been the trustee my whole life, and I'm quite sure he has engaged in some serious breaches of the trust, which I will discover when I get control."

Lucy grunted. "Why is that not a surprise?"

"Now he wants to get *me* under his control in whatever way he can to prevent those breaches from coming out. Let me make this clear, my father will stop at nothing. You see, Lucy, my father is a hereditary member of the House of Lords."

"Wait. What?"

"Yes. And believe you me, he loves being a lord like life itself. It's absolutely everything to him, and he will destroy anyone, including me, who he perceives as any sort of threat to that. I'm afraid he might be coming for me, and that's why you should run as far away from me as you can. I love you, and it would kill me if he did *anything* to you. But ... I can't let you go. I can't. So you have to decide. You have to decide, Lucy. You have to, because I can't."

"Oh, sweetie. There's—"

"Don't tell me now. You have to think about it. Tell me tomorrow."

He had to pull his gaze away. Her eyes were puffy from crying and she looked so sad. What was he doing to her? How could he deserve her after everything he'd just told her, and what he might put her through if she stayed with him? The problem was, he didn't have the willpower to give her up, to be the better man and do what was best for her. He now realized, not only was she what he wanted, but she was in fact exactly what he needed, what had been missing in his life all these years. The Princess Leia to his Han Solo. The Corrie to his Paul. The Peg to his Bill. What fool in his right mind would willingly give that up, except an idiot saint?

Sixty-Five

JACK HAD FALLEN asleep with his head on Lucy's legs, his arms tight around her at first, but easing as his breathing deepened. He finally turned away from her, and that's when she felt able to get out of bed and use the bathroom.

No wonder the poor guy didn't sleep. He was dealing with post-traumatic stress disorder. She'd had training in how to recognize it at the ashram. It was startling how many guests came there suffering from it; the ashram, with its promise of spiritual sustenance and solace, was a magnet for troubled people. It was obvious that she'd been suffering from the disorder herself after Buffalo, and it made all the difference in the world to be able to put a name to it and learn strategies for dealing with it. As tonight showed, after three years, she was still not completely over it—if she ever would be. And here was poor Jack dealing with post-traumatic stress disorder from the age of six on his own. Well, except for Dunk.

As she returned to the bed and stood looking down at Jack, she realized that there was something else she had to know, and only one person who could tell her. She grabbed the key card, opened the door to the suite, and closed it as silently as she could.

She padded down the hallway in her bare feet. She hadn't even changed into her pajamas yet; there hadn't been time. Stopping in front of Dunk's room, she put her ear against the door. She couldn't hear any sound, but that didn't mean he wasn't awake. She *had* to talk to him because it would decide everything. She had to know.

After a few calming breaths, she rapped on his door. She heard the bedsprings as he got up and his heavy tread as he trudged to the door. A moment later, he pulled the door open and looked down at her. He pulled it all the way open and she walked past him into the room.

"He's finally asleep," she said as she took a seat in the guest chair, perching on the edge.

Dunk grabbed a clean glass from the dresser and poured her a shot from a half-empty bottle of whiskey. As soon as he handed it to her, he topped up his own and laid back on the bed against the headboard. She took a sip as he downed his entire glass and poured himself another.

She let out a shaky sigh. "He told me everything."

"Everything?"

Lucy teared up. "If not for you ..."

He stared into his glass and swirled the whiskey around.

She looked at him with a pained expression. "I have to ask you, Dunk. I came here to ask you. Are you ... in love with him?"

He kept his eyes down. "No."

"I have to know ... that I won't be sharing him with you ... in that way. I have to know ... that he will be mine heart, mind, body ... and soul."

Dunk finally looked at her, a world of pain in his eyes. "He already is."

He put the glass down and pulled himself to the edge of the bed, sitting there for the longest time staring into space, as if he didn't know what to do with himself. He looked so lost and forlorn.

She watched him as conflicting emotions warred within herself. She hadn't known until now, and now that she did, what could she do? Her eyes started welling over.

He finally roused himself and got up from the bed. He lumbered over to the door and opened it. "If ya don't mind, Luce, I got a big day tomorrow."

Lucy put down her drink. She walked over to the door and looked up at him, tears streaming down her cheeks. "Don't leave him, Dunk. Please don't do that to him. I don't want that either."

He stared into her eyes and then looked away.

She turned and left the room. The door clicked shut behind her as she walked back to the suite. She hated how she felt right now. She just felt so damn sad.

Sixty-Six

THE NEXT MORNING Jack woke up feeling as if he'd been hit by a truck. He had a headache and a crick in his neck. Lucy was holding him from behind and her saliva was on his shoulder. Somehow that didn't bother him as much as it should have. It was *her* saliva. But he did have the urge to remove it with a wet wipe.

He moved around to face her and lay there watching her. Her hair went into strange and funny shapes when she slept, something he found amusing and charming. She still had dark bags under her eyes, no doubt because of what he'd been putting her through.

She hadn't run away when he told her everything. She had stayed and listened, her face full of concern and sometimes horror. He knew it was bad, but it was what it was. He couldn't change what had happened to him. God knows he wished he could. The question was whether she could live with someone who'd been sexually abused and didn't really know how to have a normal relationship with a woman, sexually or otherwise. He wanted to try, but would she? And then there was the issue of his father, an unpredictable but very real threat. He wanted her to know what she was getting into, to make an informed decision and not be conned into something she later regretted.

He pushed her hair back from her face and she stirred. She opened her eyes halfway and he couldn't help it, he couldn't wait for her to wake up and tell him where things stood. He whispered, "Good morning."

She opened her eyes all the way and smiled. "Hi." She shimmied closer to him, put her head on his arm, and fell back asleep.

He felt a spurt of joy leap inside him.

He couldn't sleep any more but didn't move for another hour, didn't want to disturb her, and just lay there watching her. He finally had to get up because he was dying to pee. He was in the bathroom brushing his teeth when she strolled in, pulled her panties down, sat on the loo, and peed in front of him. He looked at her in surprise, then realized the significance of what she was doing and beamed at himself in the mirror.

He stopped brushing for a second. "Do you want me to order you some breakfast?"

"Yes, please." She wiped herself, pulled up her panties, flushed the loo, and inserted her fingers under the running water, then strolled back out of the room.

OK, they were going to have to have a talk about that. That was unhygienic and quite alarming. She didn't even use any soap.

But she wasn't going to leave him. He heard the "Hallelujah Chorus" strike up in his head and he hummed along out loud.

Sixty-Seven

JACK GOT BACK in bed with Lucy. He tried to act nonchalant, even though he was dying for verbal confirmation. "Um, so ..."

"Sweetie, can I tell you a story about my family?"

He hadn't been expecting that. "OK."

"I want to prepare you, so you know what *you're* getting into. It goes both ways, you know."

Huh. That was true. He was so focused on himself, he hadn't thought about what problems her family might bring.

"If it's about hygiene." He stopped as he clocked her expression.

"It's not, but can I say that you and my mother are perfect for each other? No germs or wrinkles in my mother's world. Same for my friend Cindy. She's single, in case you decide to go back on the market and find someone more hygienic."

He moved close and kissed her. "Or maybe someone who remembers to wash their hands?"

She exhaled. "OK, I usually do that. But I got no sleep last night and you were over the sink brushing your teeth."

He grinned. "Well, in that case, I think I'm still off the market. Your mother, who thinks I'm hot, and your best friend Cindy will both have to look elsewhere."

She grinned back. "So about my story. Would you believe that my entire family got kicked out of Yellowstone National Park?"

"But ... out of the whole park?"

"Yeah, because my parents never stop arguing, and they don't know how to talk softly. And they love to be the center of attention. And they're also very loud when they ... you know."

Jack frowned at her. "Really?"

"Yeah. They were scaring the animals and annoying the people, or vice versa. I forget which. The park rangers told us we had to leave. Tony and I were so mortified that we pretended we were with another family, the Zehners, who were staying next door. We almost got away with it too, but then they found us and dragged us out."

"Where were you?"

"Against the wall in the upper bunk, hiding behind blankets."

Jack cocked his head. "Where was Nana? Who, by the way, is also single and thinks I'm hot."

"That was when we were kids. So Nana was with Pappap then. But Nana ... there are things you don't know about Nana. She can be naughty too."

Jack put his finger to his upper lip and looked at the ceiling. "A family that gets kicked out of Yellowstone National Park. A naughty nana. I don't know. That's quite extreme."

Lucy moved his finger and gave him a passionate kiss. He pulled back.

"Oh no," said Lucy. "I'm sorry, sweetie. We can take things very slowly. No rush."

He furrowed his brow. "Um, it's not that. It's that ... well ..."

"Oh!" said Lucy. She jumped out of bed and ran to the bathroom. He heard the water running, and then she was back with a big smile on her face. She exhaled toward him. "How's that?"

He pulled her to him and gave her a deep kiss. He wanted her so much, but not until things were right. Not until he knew she was his, for sure.

It was as if she read his mind. "Sweetie, the reason I told you about my parents is because they have fights all the time. I mean constantly. Tony and I are always fighting. My aunts and uncles are screamers. I was so surprised when you ran out of the room last night. I was expecting you to yell back, like you do with Dunk."

"But you had tears in your eyes."

"You better get used to that. Sabatinis are criers too. Even the men. We cry at the drop of a hat."

"But I don't want to be the one who makes you cry."

"Oh, sweetie, it wasn't just what you said. I was scared." She heaved a big sigh. "I did a lot of thinking while I was in the hospitality room by myself. You know what? I think we both have post-traumatic stress disorder."

Jack frowned at her. What was she saying? That they were mental cases?

"It's something we learned about at the ashram. Lots of people come there with it. It means you went through something traumatic and it's still having an effect on you. Like you with boarding school and me with the stampede."

Huh. That was interesting. Something he could learn about and work on in his quest for excellence. "Is there an expert on it? I'll call them ... Um, I mean, we could call them."

She beamed at him. "Omigod, I am so hot for you right now ... But no pressure. You don't have to—"

He smothered her words. Of course he wanted to kiss her. It was the other stuff that needed to wait. For the right time. When he was ready.

Sixty-Eight

JACK FINALLY PULLED AWAY from their kissing and said he had to do some work. Lucy could have carried on all day. He went off to take what he called a power shower. Apparently he could shower in four minutes, one of the most ridiculous things she'd ever heard. As if getting clean was the only purpose of a shower. The man didn't know pleasure. She'd have to break him in, slowly but surely. Her shower had taken so long that he'd ordered room service, and it had arrived, before she'd even finished toweling herself off.

Now she was munching on some toast in a leisurely manner as he had his so-called power breakfast. The man was all about power this and power that. He was talking a blue streak, and jumping up from the table to get this and that, while she sat there staring into space as she chewed. He'd already downed three cups of coffee; maybe that's why he seemed to be moving at one hundred miles per hour while she was chugging along at ten.

"I'm going to have a word with Dunk," he said as he leaned down to give her a kiss.

"OK, sweetie." She smiled as he hurried out of the room and took another bite of her toast.

The phone rang. Murphy's law that it happened as soon as he left. Or Sod's law, as her gorgeous new man would call it.

She groaned as she pulled herself up from the table and slogged over to the phone. She swallowed and cleared her throat as she picked up the receiver. "Hello?"

There was a moment of silence.

"Hello?" she repeated.

A woman's voice with an English accent came through the line. "Is this Lucy?"

Hmm, this was suspicious. Lucy knew how ruthless the celebrity news media could be in going after a story. The caller could be a reporter from one of those horrible tabloids.

"This is her assistant. May I tell her who's calling?"

The woman hesitated. "This is Victor Slonimsky's mother. Penelope."

Omigod, it was Jack's mother. She'd probably seen him on the news as Victor Slonimsky and assumed that was what everyone called him. So his mother now knew where he was. If this was indeed his mother.

"I have to check that you're who you say you are. Tell me something about Victor only his mother would know."

"Oh, goodness." She sounded flustered. "Well, for one thing, his real name is not Victor. And he's played the piano since the age of three. And his favorite toy was a stuffed Tigger, which I still have. In my cupboard."

Lucy could tell this was Jack's mother. There was something similar to Jack in the way she talked. And she sounded like she was pulling things from her memory, not making them up.

"Um, this is actually Lucy. I was pretending to be my assistant in case you were a journalist or something."

"Oh, of course."

"Penelope, did you say? That's a beautiful name."

"Everyone calls me Pippa."

"I like Penelope," said Lucy. "Would you mind if I called you that?"

"I would like that." There was another silence. "I'm calling because ... well, first because I wanted to tell you, he looks so happy. I've never seen James look this happy ... since he was four. And second—"

"Did you call him James?"

"Oh, dear. He didn't tell you."

Lucy knit her brows. "OK, I'm confused. His real name isn't Jack St James?"

There was a gasp from the other end of the line. "Jack St James?"

"Yes. Is that not his name?" Lucy could hear Penelope blowing her nose. "Are you OK?"

Penelope sounded tearful. "Jack is his brother's name. His name is James. James Stevens. Actually, James Augustus Percival Stevens."

Lucy dropped onto the couch. "But ... but even Dunk calls him Jack."

"Now I know why my husband was never able to find him. Never in a million years would he expect James to use the name Jack. It's ... it's going to enrage him."

"I'm sorry about your son Jack. My Jack—I mean James—said he died young. So maybe he wanted to keep his brother's memory alive, or pay him homage? He's that kind of man, isn't he? Very generous and romantic."

"I like you," said Pippa. "I liked you the moment I saw you. I thought you would be very good for my son."

"I'm glad you think so, because if we got married and had kids, we would be hitting you up for babysitting." After a silence she added, "I'm kidding. Well, no, not really. We would love having you around and doing some free grandma labor, if you wanted to."

"My dear, I do hope it gets to that, but I'm calling to warn you. My husband, he's planning to force James to come home. He saw him on the news and he knows where you are. I don't know what he's planning, but please believe me when I say that you cannot underestimate him. He's quite ... good at getting his own way."

"If that man lays a finger on him, I'll kill him. I mean it. I will kill him."

"I'm so glad James has you on his side." Pippa sounded wistful.

"Did you want to speak to him?" said Lucy. "I could have him call you."

"No, dear, that would not be advisable right now."

An idea popped into Lucy's head and she blurted it out. "You have to come to his birthday party. As a surprise. It would make him so happy. It's his twenty-fifth—silly me, you know that!—and I'm going to throw him a surprise party. Tell me you'll come." She hadn't thought of the party until that very moment, but she immediately knew it was what she had to do.

There was a long silence on the other end. "I don't know if I can manage it. My husband—"

"I'll leave a ticket for you at the airport. London to L.A. Easy peasy. Just tell me which airport and which airline."

Pippa was quiet for a moment and Lucy waited with baited breath.

"You know what?" Pippa said. "Get me on that brand new airline the lovely Richard Branson has started. Virgin Atlantic out of Gatwick. My husband and his people will never in a million years look for me there. Tomorrow evening."

"I'll arrange it right away. We'll have someone at the airport to pick you up. I can't wait to meet you."

"And I you. Au revoir, Lucy L'amour."

309

Sixty-Nine

JACK RETURNED to the suite as Lucy was hanging up the phone.

She was beaming. Who made her beam like that? He didn't like it. Making her happy was *his* job.

"Who was that?" he said.

Lucy skipped over and leaned against him. "Um, sweetie, can I please use your credit card?"

"What?" The request threw him for a loop. Why would she get a phone call and need his credit card?

Lucy had an expectant look. "For something really important I need to buy."

He narrowed his eyes. This was totally fishy. "I'll give you some cash." He went to reach for his billfold in his back pocket.

"No," said Lucy. "I already have cash. From Barry. But I don't have my own credit card, living at an ashram and everything. And right now I really, really need one. It's ... urgent."

Jack wracked his brain for a way not to give it to her. It had his real name on it, and he hadn't managed to tell her that yet. And truth be told, he wasn't ready to let her have it. Their relationship was too new. They hadn't talked about money yet. A huge topic. Couples broke up all the time over money. And he was still worried about having enough to retire at the end of the tour. No, absolutely not. He couldn't hand it over to her. That would set a very bad precedent. Damn it, how did other guys handle a situation like this? Not having a lot of girlfriend experience was a real drawback.

A brilliant idea suddenly occurred to him. He smoothed out his furrowed brow and gave her his most earnest look. "It's better if you use the band's corporate card. Tell Dunk I said you could. He's not here right now, but I'm sure he'll be back soon."

She fingered his shirt. "I can't use the corporate card, sweetie. That would be fraud, wouldn't it? Because I'm buying something personal, for you."

"Oh, that's so considerate." He smiled down at her. "But I don't need anything. Really. Now that I have you, I have everything in the world I need."

Hey, he was going to be good at this boyfriend stuff. Clear and firm in his communication, like a good manager, with a compliment thrown in to make her feel good.

She smirked up at him. "It's for your birthday, *James*."

His mouth fell open. "Um ..."

"I had a chat with your mom, *Penelope*. That's who I was on the phone with. She saw us on the news and called to say that she's so happy about us. And she gave me an excellent idea for your birthday present, and we agreed I would get it for you. But if you want me to tell her that's not possible ..."

He looked at her and sighed. Damn it, damn it, damn it. Lucy had spoken to his mother. That in itself was alarming, as if everything was spinning out of his control. But then his mother reveals his real name to Lucy with no by your leave whatsoever. Before he has a chance to do it himself, making him look as if he's hiding things from her. Important things, like his real name. Now she'll be wondering if he's truly the son of a ruthless lord, as he said he was, or something far more nefarious, like a Tory taxidermist or an astrologer from Arundel.

There was no comeback for this, was there? He pulled out his bill-fold and handed over his American Express Gold card. "There's a low limit, just so you know. And I'll need it right back ... for something I have to pay for ... uh, today."

She took it and read out his name. "James A.P. Stevens." She looked up at him and grinned. "James Augustus Percival Stevens. It suits you. You're not really a Jack or a Vic, are you?" She got on her toes and gave him another kiss. "Thanks, sweetie."

"I'm going to see the guys." They might know what he could do to make sure he got his card back with minimum damage. Or at the very least, they would commiserate with him. How had this happened, and so quickly? He slammed out of the room without looking back.

Seventy

JACK KNOCKED on Keith's door. He could hear Keith and the guys practicing their song.

Randy opened the door. "Oh, hey, Jack."

Jack strode past him, running his hand over his head in frustration. He stopped and looked at the guys.

"She got my American Express Gold card."

There was a chorus of sympathy.

"You should have given her your Sears card, man," said Rob, looking at him like he was an idiot. "Not your AmEx."

Keith raised his eyebrows. "That's a true catastrophe, that is."

"Yeah," said Sam. "I hide my cards where the ladies can't find them."

"That ain't all the ladies have trouble finding," said Keith, grinning.

"At least they find *something*," Sam retorted. "Pretty *mama*."

Rob scowled at Jack. "Why don't you call AmEx and tell them to lower the limit to like ... five thousand or something?"

"Nah man, can't. She's his missus now," said Keith. "It were only a matter of time, weren't it?"

"Alison took mine the first day," said Randy.

"You bonehead," said Rob. "Cancel it."

Randy turned red. "But she's going to take care of the bills. And she's talking about a down payment on a house."

"What?" said Rob. "You just met her."

Keith and George looked at one another and smirked.

"Ya dodged that bullet, dint ya, Georgie?"

Randy glowered at Keith. "Take that back. You can't talk about Alison like that. She's not a bullet. She's my ... missus."

"Sorry," Keith and George mumbled at the same time.

"And my future wife," Randy added.

Rob exploded. "What?"

"I asked her and she said yes."

They gathered around Randy, slapping him on the back and congratulating him. Except for Rob, who stood off to the side, a look of outrage on his face. He opened the door, looked back at his beaming brother, and stalked off down the corridor.

"Not to spoil your excellent news, Randy, but you're not the only one," said Jack.

"Oh, Jack, congratu—" said Randy.

"No, not me," said Jack. "We haven't even slept together yet."

"Ya haven't done her yet?" said Keith. "Were me, I'd be right in there."

"Yeah, like me." said Randy. "I was right in there. She really loved it."

"No, no, Jack's got it right," said Sam. "You make 'em wait till they're begging you 'do me, do me now.' You do 'em and they're so grateful they make you coffee and iron your shirts. And you let 'em because it makes 'em happy to spend more time with you. Right, George?"

"I make 'em come first," said George. "That's it really."

"Alison came twice last night," said Randy. "She told me."

"Try and top this, me lads," said Keith. "I once shagged a bird seven times in one day. No joke."

Sam smirked. "Yeah, and the score was Keith seven, lady in heat zero. She came to my room after, got herself some satisfaction."

Jack was really enjoying this, being one of the guys. "Does anyone have some condoms ... please?"

314

He didn't want to ask Dunk, and it would be embarassing to call the front desk.

Keith grimaced. "I only shag chicks on birth control."

Sam laughed. "Yeah, bunch of little Aldcroft monsters running around out there, causing murder and mayhem."

"Child support," said George.

"What's that, Georgie?" said Keith.

George fixed Keith with a stern look. "I pay child support. Use a condom is my advice, Keith."

Keith stared back at him with a look of horror.

"I don't have to because ... well, we're trying for a baby, Alison and me. We want one," Randy said hesitantly.

Keith threw his head back and emitted a deep groan that turned into a howl. "Jesus effin' Christ mother of Mary, pass me the fuckin' Buddha bowl and call me Harry. I can't believe it, man. What is happening to this band? We used to screw our way round the world, but we've become nowt but a fuckin' band of pussies controlled by a demonic warrior class called the ladies."

"I got plenty of condoms, Jack," said Sam. "You can have your own box."

Keith shook his head, as if to clear it. "So who's the other poor sod, Jack? Ya said Randy weren't the only one. Who else is getting hisself chained to one of them demon warrior ladies?"

"Clint," said Jack, grinning. "He said he's going to marry our favorite demon warrior lady. Ruth."

Seventy-One

MAC LOUNGED IN HIS CHAIR, fondling his prayer beads. Rod and Norma stood in front of his desk, listening as he conversed with Barry Bartholomew by speakerphone.

"Swami," said the Dolos A&R man, "both you know and I know that ain't Lucy Sabatini's signature on the contract, don't we?"

Mac glared at Rod. He had specifically told him to practice until the signature was perfect. "Whatever do you mean?"

"This here ain't her genuine signature," said Barry. "I think she did a runner on you, and your man Ram-a-ding-dong there, trying to be a good boy scout, went ahead and forged her signature."

Rod opened his mouth to protest and Mac held up his hand to silence him. It was too late for Rod to argue his case now. Mac valued him as his second-in-command, but the guy seemed to be coming apart at the seams the past few days and was making a veritable mash of things. First the key, now this.

"I know where our little singer is," said Barry, "and I suggest you go fetch her and bring her back to the ashram so we can have a pow-wow with her and convince her to sign. Capiche?"

"Oh, yes, I do capiche," said Mac. "Where is our little songstress, pray tell?"

"With Pirate," said Barry.

Mac furrowed his brow. "With a pirate, you say?"

"Yes, you could say that, swami." Barry gave an extended sniff.

Mac smirked at the phone. It was always advantageous to know one's allies' weaknesses, especially in the pharmacological department.

"With Jack, the lead singer of Pirate," Barry continued. "Also known as Victor Slonimsky. They're on tour and ... cohabiting."

Mac lurched up in his seat. "What?" He had been cultivating Lucy to be his consort. This was an unforgivable outrage. "Tell me where they are and we will go fetch her immediately."

The sound of a lighter snapping shut came over the line, followed by a puffing sound. Barry hacked and cleared his throat as he kept them waiting.

Mac rolled his eyes at Rod and Norma. These corporate types, he knew them entirely too well. Always swinging their little dicks around, making fools of themselves, until they came up against a real dick. A big dick like his. Then they didn't play all their tiresome little power games anymore. It was only a matter of time. He could afford to be patient.

"Listen, swami, this is a delicate operation. They got security up the kazoo at their current locale, but they're going to be moving to the final locale tomorrow—L.A.—the last stop on their tour. I gotta man on the inside, gives me intelligence on everything going down. He can advise on the best way to make the snatch. In the meantime, sit tight and be ready to move at a moment's notice."

"Excellent," said Mac, grinning with delight at this invigorating turn of events. "Count us in, As soon as you have the plan, let me know and I'll have my assistant, Sashanimoody here, make all the arrangements."

Seventy-Two

"WE'VE GOT to contact the FBI," said Norma, back in her room with the others. She had told the swami she needed a "ladies break" to get some time away. Ramakar had said he needed to do some "admin."

Cindy knit her brows. "Think about it. We've got a recording contract, some papers about a possible sale of the ashram to a corporation, and some guys talking about making a snatch. Basically, we got squat."

"But we can warn them a kidnapping is going to take place," said Norma, "so they can foil it."

"The FBI's not going to believe us," said Cindy. "We're airy-fairy people in an ashram."

"Hey!" said Ramakar. "I work here. Have some respect."

"She does, hon," said Delta. "She's just saying the feebs have their own way of looking at things. And they've never gone for hippie types, have they?"

"I'm not a hippie," said Ramakar.

"No one's saying you are, sweetheart," said Delta.

"I think the best thing is if I get ahold of Lucy and warn her," said Cindy. "That way she can foil it on her end. We need to call the record company and find out where the band is staying."

"I can have Mandy do it," said Ramakar.

"No!" Cindy, Norma and Delta all said at once.

Ramakar recoiled. "Why not?"

Cindy didn't sugar coat it. "We don't trust her."

"You can trust Mandy," said Ramakar with conviction.

Cindy gave him a test for her. He had to tell Mandy something and see if it got back to the swami. It did—almost immediately.

Norma felt bad for Ramakar when they reconvened.

"That traitor!" he said. "I thought I had a future with her."

"Don't you worry, sweetheart," said Delta. "You're a prime catch, and there's much better fish in the sea than that Mandy. You'd have all the ladies down in Pensacola in a right tizzy, I can tell you."

Norma wasn't sure she'd go that far. But Ramakar would be a good fixer-upper for some take-charge lady who liked the codependent type. A lady like Delta, only younger.

They discussed "strategy" again, as Cindy called it, and agreed that Norma would call Barry's assistant on the pretext of making "advance arrangements" and get the hotel name and number.

"Then you pass me the key," said Cindy, "and I'll call Lucy from the swami's office this evening. We'll meet back here at Checkpoint Delta at oh-nine-hundred."

"Aye aye, commander," said Norma, saluting her. Anything to get out of being Sascatchiwoody.

Seventy-Three

DUNK STOOD next to the hospital bed in the San Francisco Medical Center, looking down at the occupant. "Awright, Carmine? Or should I call ya Magnus?"

Carm looked back at Dunk with suppressed joy. "Call me Carm. My Magnus days are over and done with, thank you to all that's holy and blessed. Not that I didn't enjoy being a rock star while it lasted. But never mind that. To what do I owe this unexpected and wonderful visit?"

"I thought I'd come check on ya. Make sure yer getting everything ya need."

"All the way from Phoenix? To see little ol' me? I'm thrilled and flattered beyond belief. But don't you have something called a tour to manage?"

"Yeah," said Dunk.

Carm waited for him to say more, in vain. "A man of few words. Refreshing, given that I have way too many, as my cuz Luce the Goose will tell you if you take the trouble to ask her."

Dunk stared out the window for a minute, giving Carm the opportunity to study his arresting face. He was one of the most masculine men Carm had ever met. If he had to use a single word to describe him, it would be "glorious."

Dunk finally looked down at him. "I've been with him almost seventeen years."

"You're lucky. I've never been with anyone longer than two weeks."

"Will she take good care of him?"

Carm laughed. "She'll drive him mad. But I think she'll make him happy ... if my experience is anything to go by."

"We're gonna take good care of you."

"Will you?" Carm said, searching Dunk's eyes. "Promise?"

"I best be getting back."

"Stay a while ... please. Tell me a story. Tell me your story. I want to hear everything." Without thinking, he reached out and grabbed Dunk's hand.

The Scotsman stood unmoving, glowering in a way that would scare a lesser man.

"Listen," said Carm, seizing what he knew from experience might be his only chance. "If I have to be in a hospital getting god-awful tests for a pathetic disease, the least I deserve is to stare at a gorgeous man like you."

Dunk pulled his hand out of Carm's, turned, and walked to the door. He stood there, in front of it, for what felt like an eternity. Carm watched without moving or breathing, until Dunk quietly shut the door. He exhaled a long, shaky breath and tamped down his eagerness lest he scare the man away—the story of his sordid love life, if you could call it that.

Grabbing the visitor's chair, Dunk brought it next to the bed and lowered himself into it.

"Ya know Rob Roy of the clan MacGregor?" he said. "That's my clan."

"I adore a man in a skirt," said Carm, beaming with happiness.

Dunk put on a thick brogue. "It's nae a skirt. It's a kilt, me laddie. And a kilt that's seen many a ferocious battle." He launched into a story about the Highland Rogue and proceeded to tell Carm one story after another—until a stern nurse told him visiting hours were long over and kicked him out.

Carm managed to hold Dunk's hand the entire time he was there. His eyes never left his beautiful face. He felt an overwhelming sense of loneliness and desolation when Dunk left. But also the first hope he'd felt in three years, since that terrible stampede that killed nine people and ended his life as Magnus.

Seventy-Four

MANNY SHOWED up without Dunk to transport the band to the arena for that night's concert. Jack couldn't hide his surprise. Dunk normally took control of the transport and security situation, especially with the kind of extreme publicity they were facing.

"Manny, where's Dunk?"

Manny wouldn't look him in the eye. "Can't say."

Jack put his hands on his hips and stared at Manny. "Manny. Tell me."

Manny sighed. "He woke me up 'bout five this morning, tells me he got to go somewhere, be back whenever, don't tell Jack."

"Do you know where he went?"

"Wouldn't say." Manny grimaced. "Picked a bloody good time to be leaving us high and dry, I tell ya. Me and the boys been working our arses off, one thing after another in this fuckin' arena. Manager a wanker of the highest order, always getting on our tits 'bout this and that while givin' us fuck all help. Dunk properly exploded yesterday, said I'll smash yer head in with a cricket bat you don't get this mess straightened out. Guy got proper nasty, said I'll call the coppers. Dunk said the fuck you will, got him up against the wall and told him shut yer geggie or I'll stuff your bawbag in it and make ya swallow it. Never seen him so mad, said go easy, man, fuckin' chancer needs his head smashed in but not till it's over and we can do a runner. So I'm all on me own here, Jack."

Lucy strolled up. "Hey, Manny. How are you?"

"Proper buzzin', ain't I, Jack?"

"Oh, that's great," said Lucy, smiling at him. She strolled away to talk to the others.

Jack couldn't hide his concern. "Is everything under control? Is it safe?"

Manny waved his hand. "Yeah, there's nowt to worry 'bout. Jus' me frustration is all."

Jack frowned. He'd never known Dunk to do anything like this. That he up and left the tour was unimaginable; it was his tour as much as it was Jack's. Where in the world could he have gone? If something had happened to Dunk's parents, he would have told Jack because they were like parents to him too. It was certainly worrying, but what could Jack do?

Dunk was going to get a big piece of his mind when he saw him again, that was for sure. He was putting the tour at risk, not to mention the bonus. In the meantime, there was nothing for it but to do the concert and hope everything went to plan. And that Manny was up to the job.

Seventy-Five

LUCY SNUGGLED under Jack's arm on the ride over to the arena.

He had become so much more relaxed when she handed back his AmEx card. As if he'd been afraid she was going to keep it and run up a huge bill. First off, they weren't even an official couple yet, let alone committed. That would be entirely different, and then they'd have to have the money talk. Second, she was probably a lot more frugal than he was, coming from an immigrant family that had had to scrimp and save to keep their heads above water. All he had to do was look at her clothes, for crying out loud. But it was good to know he was careful with money too, because she couldn't commit to someone who wasn't, like that spendthrift Russell of Netherlude.

The bus passed the main entrance to the arena and headed for the artists' entrance.

"Is it just me, or does the crowd look a lot bigger tonight?" said Alison.

Randy peered out the window. "Maybe they came to hear our new song."

"I love your new song," said Lucy.

Rob sneered at Randy. "It's sold out, you moron. They're not going to come if they can't get a ticket, are they?"

Alison turned and glared at him.

"A big problem with scalpers," said Jack, "according to Dunk."

"Oh, right," said Rob in a stroppy tone.

Lucy glanced over at him. Poor Rob looked like a sulky little boy. She whispered in Jack's ear. "I think he's still upset about Randy's engagement."

Jack looked over at Rob. "You think so?"

After they pulled up, Manny made them wait while he set up a security cordon from the bus to the entrance. As they came out of the bus, Manny urged them to hurry into the arena. "Get your arses in gear. Go! Go! Go!"

Lucy and Jack ran past Rob as he ignored Manny and strolled through the cordon, waving and grinning at the girls who yelled his name.

"Ow!" Rob screamed.

Lucy looked back to see Rob grabbing the back of his head. Two security guys had wrestled a man to the ground and were taking turns punching him. The man protected himself from the blows as one of the security guys yanked Rob's hair tie from his hand.

"Hey! What the fuck," yelled Manny as he rushed over.

"Did you see that?" said Alison, stumbling inside as she looked back at the guy on the ground.

"Yeah," said Randy as he put out his arm to steady her. "I don't think they're supposed to do that."

"So you think it's OK for the guy to assault me?" said Rob, ambling up to them as he massaged the back of his head. "Wanker!"

"Rob," Jack said in warning. "Mind the fans."

"I'll mind the fans when he minds me," said Rob, scowling.

The door clanged shut behind them as they got inside and a security guard secured the door.

"I'm not a wanker," Randy muttered as they made their way further into the arena.

Jack leaned down and kissed Lucy. "Be right back." He continued down the corridor as everyone else went into the hospitality room.

Lucy followed the others into the room and leaned against the wall, crossing her arms and staying out of the way. She needed to have a little think before her sweetie returned. She'd arranged the ticket for his mother, but now she had a mere two days to plan and execute his birthday party. It was a milestone birthday—a quarter century!—and as his mom said, he hadn't had a real birthday party since he was a little kid. So it needed to be super special. She was going to get everyone involved, because many heads and hands were better than just her own, and of course he was a special person to everyone, not just to her. And his mom might be coming. But it had to be hush-hush, so Jack didn't suspect a thing. Maybe she should have a word with Alison now and get the ball rolling.

Just as she uncrossed her arms and pushed away from the wall, Alison made a beeline over to Randy. He'd been standing at the food table since they'd entered the room scarfing down slice after slice of pizza.

"Hon, you're going to make yourself sick," said Alison. "You don't want to throw up on stage, do you?"

"Why don't you nurse him as well?" Rob taunted, watching them with his arms crossed.

Alison turned to face him. "I beg your pardon!"

"You heard me," said Rob.

"What is your problem?"

Rob glared back. "My problem is you. You meet my brother and within minutes you're acting like his mother and telling him what to do."

"No, I'm not," said Alison. "I'm showing concern for him. Something I've noticed you never do."

"Don't you tell me how to treat my brother," Rob yelled, moving close and standing over her in a threatening manner.

Randy grabbed Rob's arm. "Get away from her."

Keith and Sam rushed over, pulling the brothers away from each other and standing between them.

Leaning around Sam, Rob pointed his finger at Alison. "You're not going to marry my brother, you gold digger."

Alison teared up as she glared at him, and shrugged off Randy's arm when he tried to put it around her.

OK, Lucy thought, time to defuse things and inject some TLC.

"I've got this," she said to Randy as she eased her arm around Alison's waist.

At that moment Jack strode back in the room.

"Sweetie," she said as she signaled him with her eyes to deal with the brothers. She led Alison over to the sofa in the corner.

Jack sighed and put his hands on his hips. "So what did I miss? What's going on here?"

"Nothing," both brothers mumbled.

"Well, it's got to be something," said Jack.

Randy looked at Jack. "He keeps disrespecting my lady."

Rob made a scoffing face. "That's rich. She keeps disrespecting *me*."

Jack pursed his lips and nodded his head. "Got it. I think it's very simple, actually." He looked at Rob. "Randy has someone new in his life, and, understandably, you're jealous because he's not available to you anymore in the same way he was before. So, unconsciously, you're acting out your frustration and taking it out on Alison, because she's the one who took him away from you. Do you see?"

"No, that's not it at all," said Rob. "I don't like her. She's a gold-digging tart and she doesn't deserve him."

Jack gave Rob a disapproving look. "Now you know that's not true."

"Yeah," said Randy. "You don't even know her and you haven't even tried."

"Oh, I get it," said Rob, putting his finger in the air like he was having an aha moment. "That must mean Dunk is acting out right now, yeah? I don't see him here, and we haven't seen him all day. And we have a big show to put on and he's not here to do his *job*. I guess that means he's acting out and taking it out on *Lucy*."

Jack narrowed his eyes at Rob. "OK, hold on, that's not the same thing at all."

"Oh, yeah?" said Rob, glaring back at him.

Lucy couldn't believe it. Her sweetie was making things even worse. She excused herself from Alison and rushed over to Randy. "Hon, I think Alison needs you."

Looking over with concern, Randy pulled out of Keith's grip and loped over to Alison.

Lucy maneuvered her way past Jack and Sam and grabbed Rob's arm. "Excuse me, guys, but now that he's lost his hair thingamajig, I think I need to help Rob with his hair. Quick, before the concert starts. C'mon, handsome," she said to Rob as she pulled him away. "Let me find something to hold that back."

She gave Jack a mock chiding look as she led Rob past him. He rolled his eyes at her and she grinned back. Could he be more cute?

Taking Rob over to a wall mirror, she pulled a chair in front of it and made him sit facing his reflection. She stood behind him as she plumped and played with his hair.

"You know what I think?" she said. "I think you should keep it down. You'll have the ladies salivating and chomping at the bit. They love long hair."

"If you say so," said Rob, grinning at her.

"I do say so." She looked at him in the mirror. "Randy, he's different from you, isn't he? He needs one woman to adore him and take care of him, like Alison, whereas you're waiting for that one woman you can adore and take care of in that manly way of yours. When you're ready. No rush."

Rob stared back at Lucy. Good. He seemed to be truly listening and taking in what she said.

One of Manny's guys popped in and shouted. "Ten minutes to showtime, everyone. Ten minutes."

The room exploded into action. Rob got up, turned around, grabbed her face, and kissed her hard on the lips. He gave her a triumphant smile and strode away.

Lucy looked after him with astonishment. OK, that's not good. She glanced over at Jack to make sure he hadn't seen Rob kiss her. Phew. He was busy talking to Manny. She didn't want him to know that she might have made things worse herself, after giving him that chiding look. Maybe much worse from his guy perspective.

She'd forgotten how unpredictable and unruly rock stars could be. She'd have to stay on her toes with these guys, even if she was the lead singer's girlfriend. Especially as the lead singer's girlfriend—a veritable minefield of emotional cross-currents and rivalries.

Seventy-Six

SAM AND GEORGE peered from the wings. The audience was on its feet, chanting "Pirate! Pirate!" over and over again.

"Wow, man," said George.

"Yeah," said Sam. "Intense."

Keith came up behind them and put his hands on their shoulders. "Heard they had to turn away hundreds of people. Problem with them arsemongering scalpers. Coppers had to bash some heads."

George grimaced at him. "You're having us on ... Right?"

"No faffing about tonight, ladies. Or these punters will be calling for your heads on one of them spikes." He leaned between them. "Holy Horatio, look at the Belisha Beacons on that one. John Thomas here is already standin' to attention."

"Sam called dibs," said George with disgust.

Keith smirked. "Soz, boys, but I don't get a leg over tonight, I'll be knockin' on your doors." He goosed Sam.

Sam jumped. "Hey!"

"Ya called me pretty mama, Sammy Wammy. I been waitin'."

Manny strode over. "Get your lazy arses in gear, girls. You're on."

Seventy-Seven

STANDING in the wings with Alison, Lucy couldn't believe the response the band was getting. The audience never sat down, sang along and waved their arms or punched the air to every single song. It was like a stadium full of people on ecstasy.

Deafening screams issued from the girls in the audience whenever the boys performed solo, especially Rob with his new hairstyle and the way he was thrusting his hips forward even more than usual. The guy was working it. Girls at the front threw their bras and panties at him, many of them falling on poor George.

Not to be outdone, George removed his rubber band and let his own hair hang down, and flashed his mischievous grin whenever something got screamed or thrown at him. The guy was a very sexy devil, no doubt about it.

Sam competed with his bandmates and elicited cheers from the audience when he went into full Jimi Hendrix mode, playing between his legs, getting on his knees and leaning all the way back until his head hit the floor, and making love with the wall. Gosh, he was flexible. Lucy should get him into yoga.

Sweet little Randy more than kept up with them, playing like his life depended on it. Keith—what could she say? His guitar riffs and licks were "electrifying"—no other word for it—and often took her breath away.

The entire band seemed to be singing at some heightened level of passion and synchronicity. She kept wiping away tears; it was sublime. And to think, her man had composed all of this. Was she a lucky girl or what?

The encore was no less exciting. On the first song, the entire stadium sang the refrain with Keith, throwing a deafening sound back at the band. The applause went on for what seemed like forever.

As the boys were taking their bows, Jack got ready for his solo. A roadie ran out and handed him an acoustic guitar. Once he was settled and the applause had died down, he looked out at the audience. "This is a song for my love. It's called 'When Lightning Strikes.'" Lucy put her hand on her heart. Alison gave her shoulder a squeeze.

Jack strummed a few chords and stopped. "Should I get her out here?"

Lucy's eyes went wide with shock. The audience screamed and waved their approval.

He looked in her direction and smiled, although she knew he couldn't actually see her. "Can someone get Lucy out here?"

She stood rooted to the spot. Didn't he remember what she'd told him about Buffalo and how traumatized she was by that? But then hadn't she also stood up to her fear the night before and everything had been fine? Hadn't she even run across the stage to him? She could do this. She knew she could. She could face her fear again and show her man how much he meant to her. Show him that if he could face his fear in telling her about his abuse, and even reliving it in his mind, she could face her own fear of a stampede.

She made her way to the edge of the stage, where a crew member helped her onto the ship.

"Is she coming?" said Jack.

Lucy stepped onto the deck and looked out at the audience. They screamed and it was deafening. She looked over at Jack. He turned in her direction and extended his left arm toward her. There was her gorgeous man, waiting for her. She took one tentative step, and another, and then she scurried the rest of the way across the decks and ran into his open arm.

"Sing with me," he said in her ear.

Letting her go, he adjusted the mike to accommodate her and tuned the guitar. After a few strums, he launched into the chord progression, playing it all the way through as he had the night before. The audience linked hands over their heads and swayed from side to side.

As he sang the first verse, he encouraged her with his eyes to join him. She made a small shake of her head. She wanted to hear his beautiful tenor voice, and besides, she didn't remember the words and there was no band or backup singers to hide behind. He smiled and kept singing, staring into her eyes as he sang about "this something life" and "gentle rain".

In the following three verses, he sang about "love insane" and her being his "lightning lover," describing what she was wearing when they met—something that would always make the song special for her. For both of them. She teared up, wiping the tears away with her hand. She could hear a wave of sound from the audience, but was too overcome with her own emotions to pay attention. He looked almost beseeching as he sang the final verse, begging her to be his inamorato and make her home in his "aching blue boughs." No one would know how utterly accurate that phrase was, except for Dunk. She had to hold herself back from grabbing him and plastering him with reassuring hugs and kisses. The sound of sniffling and sobs floated up from the audience.

She finally joined him as he repeated the final verse, stepping up to the microphone as they sang to one another. He wove his tenor voice around her soprano, and encouraged her to take the lead as he sang softly and brought the guitar sound forward to accentuate the words. When she began to crescendo, he opened his voice full-throttle to join with hers. A combination of joy and elation surged up through her body—the same feeling she had when she was whirling in kirtan meditation and entering that state of ecstatic bliss.

Just as they were reaching the end of the verse, a bright red garment arced toward them and landed in front of the line of security guys facing the audience. As one of them bent to pick it up, a member of the audience seized the opportunity to step on his back and leap onto the stage.

The fan ran directly toward Lucy, a manic smile on his face. She froze in shock as Jack stepped in front of her and delivered a punch that sounded like a loud pop and sent the fan spinning to the ground.

In a matter of seconds, the stage was being overrun with crazed fans. Jack threw down the guitar and covered her with his body.

She could see and feel people grabbing at her and Jack punching their hands away. She heard a whimpering sound and realized it was coming from her own mouth.

"Don't move, my love. I have you," Jack said in her ear.

Jack twisted and shifted over her as people grabbed at them. It felt like forever that he was fighting them off. There was a ripping sound and he jerked and sucked in his breath.

"Get off 'im, motherfucker!" Manny screamed.

One guy hit the floor in front of them with a thud. He scuttled to the edge of the stage clutching his side and dropped over the edge.

Whack! Another guy landed on their left, drops of blood spraying across the floor.

"Go! Go! Go!" Manny shouted. Jack lifted her into his arms and carried her offstage, Manny and two crew members forming a human shield around them. "We got everyone in the hospitality room."

Jack ran in that direction with Lucy in his arms. She peered ahead from under his chin and marveled at the carnage. Fans were running amok everywhere: not only in the backstage area, but also in the off-limit areas where only the band, crew, and arena personnel were allowed. Shouts, screams, and thumps reverberated through the concrete structure. It was like a riot.

They reached the hospitality room and Jack entered sideways, maneuvering her through the doorway with great care.

"Nowt to worry 'bout, Jack," said Manny. "Be back in two ticks when we get rid of that bastard lot. Two guys right out here, yeah?" He slammed the door.

Jack carried her over to the sofa and sat down with her in his lap. He inspected her face with concern. "Are you OK, my love? Are you hurt?"

She snuggled against him and sobbed her heart out. He held her close and crooned into her ear. "I've got you. You're safe, my love. No one's going to hurt you when I'm around. I'm here, my love."

When her sobs finally subsided, she turned in his lap to look up at him and gasped in shock. "Omigod! You're hurt. We need to get you a doctor. There's blood all over you!"

"Calm down. It's nothing, my love."

"I wouldn't be calling that nothing," said Keith. "Would you, lads?"

Lucy turned her head. Alison and the band members were gathered around them. Howie, Suze, and Carly were sitting on the other sofa, watching them and looking shellshocked.

"Got everything but your boots and trousers," said Sam.

"Stripped the shirt right off your back," said Rob, grinning.

George smacked his arm.

"What?" protested Rob. "It's true."

"I bet if you clean the blood, it won't look so bad," said Randy. "Does anyone know first aid?"

"Yep, I do," said Suze. "I trained in that. But I don't have any supplies with me."

Alison waved toward the rest of the room. "Hospitality rooms like this are supposed to have first aid kits."

Alison, Suze, and George spread out and looked around the room.

"Here you go," said George. He brought over a metal container with the Red Cross on it.

Suze took charge and ordered people around, telling them to bring over a table and go get her this and that. Despite his protests, she ordered Jack into a chair and swabbed his wounds.

Lucy insisted on holding his hand through the whole thing. There was no question: if he hadn't protected her, this never would have happened to him. He would have fled with the other members of the band and would still be in tiptop shape. She couldn't believe how brave and self-sacrificing he had been—for her. Especially when he found it so painful to be touched, and those fans had touched him everywhere.

She started crying when she saw the patches where fans had torn his hair out and the rips in his earlobes. How could they do this to him? She wanted to kill them.

Suze gave her a direct look and said, "I'm going to stitch him, so ..."

Lucy blanched and nodded. She grasped Jack's hand with both of her own.

Suze turned to Jack. "It's up to you. You can wait for a doctor or I can do it for you."

"Do you have any experience?"

Suze leaned close so only Jack and Lucy could hear. "Look, in my real life I'm a nurse and I work for Medics on the Frontlines. I do this all the time. But can you keep that under your hat? I'm incognito at the mo."

Jack looked at her in surprise. "OK. Well, I hate doctors. So I'd be grateful if you did it, Suze."

Lucy stared into Jack's eyes so she wouldn't have to look at what Suze was doing. Jack talked through all the stitching, keeping his eyes on hers. Other than tensing up and sucking in his breath here and there, he got through it. Her incredibly brave man.

After Suze finished, Jack inspected himself in the mirror. "What do you say, boys? Shall we change our show? A new version of Frankenstein maybe?"

Not only was he brave, he was funny in the midst of tragedy.

"Dibs on Igor," said Randy quickly.

"Nah, I vote for Dracula," said Keith, leering and lunging at Randy's neck. "I love the taste of blood."

"Ow!" Randy glared at Keith and rubbed his neck.

"Dracula is too close to KISS," said Sam. "Or Ozzy Osbourne."

"Wolf Man," said Rob. "Top dog, that guy."

Rob didn't even notice he'd made a joke. None of the guys seemed to.

"You're already the Wolf Man," said Sam. "No need to play him, dude."

Rob nodded and grinned. "Yeah."

"I vote Godzilla," said George.

"No," said Sam, "because Blue Öyster Cult already did it, with a big monster onstage and everything."

George scowled. "So? We can still do it."

"No, we can't, bro, because we're not losers, are we?" Sam playfully pushed George off-balance. "King Kong beat Godzilla's arse. He the man, man. And he get the ladies too, like that sexy Fay Wray. So it has to be the King."

"We should've stayed and fought the punters," said Rob. "My blood's up."

Sam pushed Rob into Keith. "Wolf Man, meet Dracula."

"Saw that film," said George. "Godzilla was much better."

"Hey, do one, will ya?" Keith said to Sam, pushing him back. "Dracula be suckin' the blood right out of your mingin' monkey."

The door crashed open and Manny strutted in.

"OK, listen up. Me and me crew got it all under control. Bus pulling up in five, gotta get you all outa here. Arena wankers ain't too happy. So, ladies, get your arses in gear." He reddened and pointed at the guys. "I mean these ladies, not you real ladies. Um, what I mean ..."

"Manny," said Jack, waving him over. "What's the damage?"

"Yeah, so," said Manny, turning serious. "We got two guys in hospital, the security guy caused the whole shebang by bending over like a wazzock, and the tosser nicked Rob's hair doodah. Might be some equipment walked out the door. When we load it up, that's when we know."

"Have you heard from Dunk?" said Lucy.

"Nah," said Manny. "But me boys was brilliant, I tell ya. Made me proud tonight. Best crew in a bust-up I ever seen."

Jack held out his hand. "Thank you for saving me and Lucy. We will be eternally grateful."

Manny shook his hand, looking down at the ground and clearing his throat. He clearly realized how unusual it was for Jack to shake anyone's hand. "Yeah, well, um. Bus in five." He turned and strode back out of the room

Lucy grabbed Jack's hands. "I think you shocked him there."

"We owe him. That Dunk, on the other hand. I don't even have words, but we will be having words. A mountain of words. Bad words. For what he did to you."

Suze ambled up to them with a plastic bag. "Jack, you're gonna need this. All the drugs I could find. Got the others to chip in." She opened the bag and peered in. "Some painkillers, a bottle of sedatives, bag of pot. Enough to keep you comfortable tonight. I'll get you some better stuff tomorrow. Gotta check for infection every day, take the stitches out in three to five days. Cool?"

"I don't know how to thank you, Suze. Can you let me know if you need anything? Will you do that?"

She winked at him. "Sure thing." She ambled back to Howie and Carly.

Lucy turned to Jack. "James Augustus Percival Stevens?"

"Yes?" he said.

"I want you to know that I love you."

He grinned. "Finally. I wondered how many times I was going to have to sing that damn song in front of fifteen thousand people, and protect you from deranged fans, and do all those other foolish things men do when they're in love."

She grinned back. "You're not going to do all those other things? I feel so cheated."

His smile faltered. "Sorry, my love, but I think I need one of those painkillers."

"Finally. My turn to take care of you." She fetched him a painkiller and a glass of water.

"Thanks, Nurse Lucy."

She lifted his arm and inserted herself underneath. "You poor baby. Let me help you to the bus."

"What? You're not going to carry me? I feel so cheated."

Seventy-Eight

THEY GOT BACK to their suite without incident.

Jack was touched and amused by all the care Lucy was giving him, as if he was an invalid. He'd got hurt much worse on the cricket pitch and in rugby games.

"You've got to get into bed, mister. You're injured and it's my job to take care of you."

Actually, on the painkiller he felt rather good. Putting on his sexy voice, he said, "Is that an order, Nurse Lucy?"

She looked at him with regret. "Sweetie, you're in no condition tonight for anything, I'm afraid. When you're better, OK?"

He knew what he needed to do. "I don't think I can undress myself. You're going to have to do it for me."

She narrowed her eyes at him. "And that's all I'm going to do."

He was already getting excited. He tried to calm himself down. He didn't want to give himself away.

She had him sit down and pulled off his boots, followed by his socks. She helped him take off his rings. He sat there shirtless in his breeches and smiled at her, so happy.

"Stand up, mister," she ordered him.

He stood up. He wouldn't be able to hide it now, he was properly turned on.

She knelt down to unbutton his breeches. Little did she know he had nothing under them. When she got to the lowest button, she stopped and stood up. "Um ..."

"You didn't finish," he said. He reached down, unbuttoned the bottom button, and dropped his breeches. His erection sprang free, standing at full attention. He kicked the breeches away.

She looked with wide eyes at his body. He didn't mind; he expected, he hoped, that she would be seeing a lot of it. She didn't seem put off by it.

"Come here," he said.

She went up to him and he took her face in his hands and kissed her. A deep kiss that went on and on. He could have kept on going if not for her roving hands. She moved them all over his chest and his back, then down his abdomen, and finally touched his knob.

He jerked and pulled her hand away.

"Oh, I'm sorry," she said, looking at him with concern. "If you're not ready—"

"No, it's not that. You'll make me come. I want it to last. Besides, it's your turn."

"What?" she said.

"Take off your clothes. Nice and slow. Just for me."

"Oh."

He sat back on the bed.

Lucy raised one eyebrow at him in a provocative manner. She unzipped her trousers and wiggled her backside as she peeled them off, turning to give him a full view as she did so, and tossed them away with a flourish. Grabbing her blouse on both sides, she tried to pull it over her head, but it got caught on her face and she struggled with it for a moment, until he got up and freed it for her. As she pulled it off and tossed it away, she gave him a saucy look, then pulled down one bra strap followed by the other, slowly pulling her bra down inch by inch, until it was just covering her nipples.

Jack couldn't take it anymore. He jumped up, grabbed her, and threw her on the bed, yanking down her bra and sucking on one nipple as he played with the other. She gasped and clawed at his back. He switched his mouth to the other and she cried out and grabbed for his penis.

He moved up to face her. "I'm sorry, my love, I can't wait."

"Me too." She rushed to pull off her panties with his help. As she opened her legs, he guided his knob into her and pushed in. She opened wider and clamped onto him as he kept pushing and pushing until he was as far as he could go.

"Omigod, you're so tight," he said. He stayed still for a moment, hoping he could hold off his ejaculation long enough to give her some pleasure.

"Is it OK?" she said.

"It's perfect, my love. Perfect." He went back to kissing her. She started moaning and moving against him and tightening her grip without realizing it. Damn it, he couldn't hold off much longer. He started pumping as hard as he could. He stuck his finger next to his penis and massaged her clitoris, feeling her contractions as she started screaming into his ear. He pumped faster and faster and came in one long, glorious ejaculation.

As he lay there inside her, he turned his face toward her and kissed her ear. "Are you OK?"

She sniffled and burst into sobs.

He was speechless as he pulled out of her and gathered her into his arms. Had he hurt her? Had it been that bad? Hadn't she had an orgasm? Or had she faked it, like he heard some women did to get the thing over with? Maybe he was not good at this sex business. What if he'd met the woman of his dreams and she didn't enjoy sex with him? His mind went around in a circle of self-doubt as he held her.

Lucy stopped sobbing and nuzzled against him.

That was a good sign, wasn't it? He raised his head to peer down at her. Her face was tear-stained, but she looked relaxed. "Are you OK, my love?"

"Mmmmmmm. I feel fabulous."

"What? I mean ... brilliant." Maybe he wasn't a crap lover after all. She said fabulous, so maybe he was a good lover, maybe even a very good lover. He could relax now. Everything was cool. Lucy was not repulsed by him, and she probably didn't fake the orgasm, but the jury was still out on that.

God, he felt sleepy all of a sudden. Just as he began to drift off he heard a voice in his ear.

"Sweetie, I think we need to talk about this."

He pulled himself back from the brink of sleep and mumbled, "What?"

"What just happened and why I'm crying. I think we should talk about it ... while it's fresh."

That might make sense, but his body didn't agree. It wanted to go to sleep. He started to drift off again when he felt Lucy lay on top of him and grab his face. Now you're talking, his knob said. He opened his eyes a crack and Lucy had her face inches from his own, grimacing at him. Oh no, this didn't look good. His knob retracted, disappointed.

"OK," he managed to say as he felt himself drift away.

She squeezed his nostrils shut and his eyes popped open. The little minx was grinning at him. "I always do that to my brother to wake him up. It works every time."

He blinked his eyes to focus. "Could we sit up? Otherwise, I might fall asleep."

They rearranged themselves so she was sitting in his lap with her head on his shoulder, the same as on their first date when she talked about the stampede. Now he got it. This was going to be one of those conversations.

"I wasn't crying because of what we did. That was ... everything I imagined it would be, and more."

He couldn't help but dig for some reassurance and validation. After all, he wasn't that experienced with real women. Jane didn't really count; she was on a screen. "So it was as good as ... up to ... those other rock stars?"

She lifted her chin to look at him. "You thought I slept with other rock stars?"

"You didn't? I just assumed."

"Sweetie, I'm Catholic. I didn't let them get to home base."

He swelled with pleasure at that news. He was the first to get to home base. But what did that mean? He knew it had something to do with baseball. Was it some sort of metaphor, like a "clean bowl" or a "hat trick" in cricket? Wait a second. Did it mean rock stars had gotten to other bases? All of a sudden it dawned on him. "Oh, is that what 'Paradise by the Dashboard Light' was about? That Meat Loaf song?"

She smirked. "You're dying to know what the other bases are, aren't you?" She turned serious. "We do need to be honest with each other, don't we? Get the sex conversation out of the way. So ... first base is kissing, second base is doing stuff above the waist, third base is, you know, fingers down there, and home base is intercourse. That's about it." She played with his chest hair. "So ... what about you?"

Oh no. How did she manage to bring it to his sexual history so quickly? He was planning to bypass this entire topic. Idiot! He should have left well enough alone.

"You don't have to talk about it," she said quickly. "I know it's a difficult topic for you."

He took a deep breath. If he had a real relationship with her, shouldn't he tell her everything? He might spend the rest of his life with this woman, and this might be the one time they opened up enough to talk about this. It was now or never. "I did stuff with boys at school. Most of us did. Well, that's not really true. I let them do stuff to me. You know, get me off. But not the other way around. I could never ... the germs ... you know."

"I have to ask, was Dunk one of those boys?"

He looked at her. Would this be the deal-breaker? Would this send her packing? Maybe she already knew, or suspected. "Yes. But that ended, a long time ago. It just felt   wrong."

She got very solemn. "OK, we need to agree, if we're together, there can't be anyone else. My boyfriend in middle school, Billy Dwornik, went out with Irene Defazio behind my back, and I don't ever want to feel that way again. It almost killed me. Besides, in my family cheating and divorce are cardinal sins. You can drive each other crazy and fight like dogs, but you stay together through thick and thin. I mean, that's if you want—"

He took her mouth with a fervor he didn't know he had. She wasn't put off by his sexual history. And now she knew about Dunk, his biggest secret. He didn't have to hide that from her. In fact, she appeared to already know. But who cared? She seemed to be willing to have a relationship with him, an exclusive relationship. "Paradise by the Dashboard Light" flooded his head as he took first, second and third bases in rapid succession and then scored another home run. Hard to top Meat Loaf for an exciting soundtrack.

Lucy didn't let him get much sleep that night. The girl was insatiable, but then so was he. Lucky for her, the injuries didn't seem to slow him down at all. They had sex every way they could think of, and then some.

It was after one especially vigorous session that she wormed his other big secrets out of him.

"Sweetie, how do you know so much about women's bodies? You seem to know a lot of different positions ... and where to touch me so I come ... and stuff like that."

He tried to act nonchalant. "Well, I read *The Joy of Sex* and *The Kama Sutra* first. Then *The Hite Report*." Was she impressed? "I wanted to be ready ... for you. Most women need clitoral stimulation to reach orgasm, you know." He kept babbling, not sure what she wanted to hear. "I passed them on to Randy, but now I think I'll get them back and read them again."

Lucy fingered the hair on his chest, avoiding his eyes. "What about getting it on with girls? Have you done that?"

Phew. That's all she wanted. "Oh, yeah. I forgot to tell you about all the women stuff."

She looked up, startled. That was interesting. Maybe his little goddess worried about being compared against past lovers too.

He grabbed her hand and played with her fingers. "There was a night with a girl at Cambridge. Priscilla Wiggins. Everyone called her Priss. I don't even remember what happened, but she claimed I got her pregnant."

"How did you not remember?"

"Magic brownies, and Dunk thinks she put something in my drink. I woke up the next morning in my bed, déshabillé, with her next to me. Dunk was beside himself, as you can imagine. Said everyone knew she was hunting for a husband and gave me a good bollocking. But he took care of it when her father insisted that I marry her.

Demanded evidence of her pregnancy and threatened to ruin her reputation."

Lucy grinned. "Remind me never to cross Dunk."

"Next thing you know, she was engaged to Ramsy Bigglesworth, poor devil."

"Um ... anyone else?"

He steeled himself for a reaction. "Jane Fonda."

"Jane Fonda? You've had sex with Jane Fonda?"

He nodded. "Many times over the past three years."

She stared at him, and then burst out laughing. "Oh, not you too! Everyone watches Jane when they want to, you know ... I mean, every guy."

He grimaced at her. How dare she laugh at his fantasy paramour? Jane had been very special to him. "Well, if that's so pedestrian, then tell me, what's yours?" When she looked away, he felt entirely justified in pushing. She was hiding something. "C'mon, tell me. No more sex until you tell me who my fantasy competition is."

"Fine. Well, the order varies, depending on my mood, but there are five who are always on the list."

"You have a list? At least I'm faithful to Jane."

She counted off on her fingers. "Davy Jones of the Monkees. I've never gotten over my girl crush on him. Erik Estrada in his police uniform. He's on a TV show called *CHiPs*. Cary Grant in *North by Northwest* or *The Philadelphia Story*. Billy Dee Williams as Lando Calrissian in *The Empire Strikes Back*. Whenever he comes onscreen, I swoon. Paul Newman and Robert Redford in *Butch Cassidy and the Sundance Kid*, together. So that counts as one. Then the other five keep changing."

"Wait. Paul Newman and Robert Redford together? Like a ménage à trois?"

"No, more like I couldn't decide between them. I think I'd die if I had them both at once."

He suddenly pulled her to him. "What a boring list. How about adding an exciting rock star to spice it up?" He didn't want to mention that he might not be a rock star for long, if they got the bonus. That was a conversation for another time.

"Well, actually, I was thinking of adding either Bruce Springsteen or George Harrison. They're both gorgeous."

She shrieked as he flipped her onto the bed and made her forget those pretty boy musicians in short order. Jack better be at the top of that damn list, or else.

As he drifted off in the early morning, it hit him. He hadn't used a condom the entire night. But it didn't matter. He was going to marry and have babies with this woman. Whether anyone else liked it, come hell or high water. She was his and he was hers, and that was all there was to it. *Punto*. Full stop.

Seventy-Nine

LATER THAT MORNING, after only a few hours' sleep, someone pounded on the door of their suite and woke them up. Jack shuffled to the door and looked through the peephole.

"Speak o' the devil," he said in an exaggerated Scottish accent as he yanked the door open. "Here for a skelping, are ya, ya gormless, manky, reekin', knobhead skiver?"

He waved Dunk in and shut the door after him. "Lucy, look who it is. That heidbanger who used to manage a band called Pirate." Jack put his hand on his chin and looked at the ceiling. "What was his name?"

Dunk went into his Hell's Angel stance in the middle of the suite, while Jack glared at him, hands on hips. Lucy scrambled onto the loveseat, drawing her legs under her and watching the two of them from the sidelines. Smart girl, because this was likely to get ugly after what that humongous tube did the night before. Or did not do, as the case may be.

"Where the hell have you been?" said Jack. "Do you *know* what happened?"

"Yeah, Manny and the boys told me."

Jack put his hand up to his ear. "Eh? I'm not hearing it. That enormous apology I'm expecting from you. And I'm not seeing it. You. On the floor. Groveling and begging for mercy."

Dunk gave him his unblinking police stare. What incredible wankery.

"Do you know how irresponsible you've been? Cat got your tongue? OK, let me enumerate the ways." Jack began pacing, something that always helped him think better, and counted on his fingers. "One, there are people injured and in hospital, thanks to you. Two, some of our equipment has been stolen, equipment that costs a great deal of money and that we won't have for the remaining concerts. So your bad behaviour is also going to cheat our fans. Not to mention put our financial targets in jeopardy. Have you thought of that? Three, the entire band was set on by mad fans and had to flee the stage. They were like rabid dogs—"

"The band?" said Dunk.

Jack stopped pacing and directed an outraged look at Dunk. "You think this is funny? Lucy could have been killed. As it was, she was terrified and cried in my arms for a long time afterwards. And look at me. I had to have stitches, and you know how much I hate doctors. Thank god Suze was there and could do it on the spot. But look at me, for god's sake. I look like Frankenstein."

Dunk shifted from one foot to the other and looked down. Jack couldn't see his face—was that a grin or a frown?—but the guy should be ashamed of himself, putting Lucy through that. "My pirate costume is ruined and look at my earlobes. I can't wear earrings anymore. It hurts and I have to take painkillers all the time. By the way, I need you to get me some more painkillers. I'm almost out."

Dunk raised his eyebrows at him. "Anything else?"

Jack started pacing again so Dunk couldn't see his face. He was scraping the bottom of the barrel here, but he wasn't done venting his spleen yet. "Rob had a ribbon stolen from his hair—right off his head! He had to wear his hair down and that drove the female fans especially crazy. So, naturally, George put his hair down too, and that drove them even crazier. Then Sam went 'full Hendrix' to keep up and drove everyone off the deep end. You tell me: how are we going to deal with that going forward? And now everyone knows that Vic is me and I'm

Vic, and I can't go anywhere incognito anymore. Do you even realize how outrageously inconsiderate and self-centered you've been? I should fire you, that's what I should do. I don't know that you're fit to run this band. You've gone all Malcolm McLaren on us. Maybe you should contact the Sex Pistols and see if you can convince them to get back together. Maybe that's where you belong. With a punk group that cares more about creating chaos and inciting riots than it does about keeping people like Lucy safe so they can attend a concert and listen to some decent rock music."

Jack stopped pacing and faced Dunk, daring him to disagree.

"Is it my turn now?" said Dunk.

Jack waved his hand to indicate permission.

Dunk smirked at him. "Ya can't fire me, can ya, mate? 'Cause it's my band too. Yer the one outed yerself to the world the night before last when ya sang to Lucy, so that's on you, ya numpty. The boys always drive the girls crazy and Sam always does his Hendrix moves, as ya well know. Ya do look like Frankenstein and I think it kind of suits yer personality. Ya got a lot of pirate costumes, so stop yer havering about losing the one. The people in hospital are fine and the equipment's covered by insurance. Me and Manny paid a visit to the arena manager and he gave us a princely sum for all our trouble, so we came out well ahead. But I am sorry about one thing." He turned to Lucy. "I'm sorry ya went through that, Luce. I know that must of scared ya to death. If it's any consolation, I saw Carm and he sends his love, said there's no need for ya to worry 'bout him."

"Oh, Dunk." Lucy jumped up and ran over to hug him. "You don't know what that means to me. I have been terribly worried."

Dunk enfolded her in his arms and the two of them had a long hug.

Jack stared at them in disbelief. He was the injured party here, and the thoughtless culprit responsible for everything that had gone wrong was getting a hug. That wasn't fair! But what could he say when Dunk had checked up on Carmine and made Lucy happy? He would put up with anything—well, almost anything—if it made his love happy like that.

Dunk and Lucy pulled apart. Dunk ambled to the door and turned. "Bus leaves in an hour." He looked over at Lucy. "I don't have a clue what ya see in this eejit. But whatever yer doing, keep it up. 'Cause he never let me off this easy before. I owe ya one." He smirked at her as he yanked the door open and strode out of the room, letting the door clang shut behind him.

Lucy turned to Jack and inclined her head. "You poor thing."

He stuck out his lower lip in a pout. "I know."

She sauntered over, a seductive smile on her face, and put her arms around his shoulders. "I don't think I told you how grateful I am that you saved me last night."

He suddenly felt a great deal perkier. "No, I'm quite sure—actually, *very* sure—you didn't." He leaned down and kissed her. "I'm also sure I won't be convinced unless you *show* me."

"Oh, you do, do—" Her words disappeared into his mouth.

Eighty

AFTER TWO BOUTS of what she now thought of as reaching nirvana—it reminded her so much of her chanting, not at all of those clinical descriptions of the Big 'O' in biology class with Mr. Sipowicz—Lucy reached over to grab a tissue and caught sight of the alarm clock on the end table.

"Oh no! We're supposed to be downstairs in twenty minutes." She tried to pull away but Jack held onto her. "Sweetie, we have to shower and pack, and I've got to check in with Barry or I'll lose my recording contract."

"Let's stay in bed and let them go without us. We can fly over later, or hire a limo. Have some more 'us' time."

She disentangled herself and got out of bed. "Silly man."

"I'm not silly. I'm in love. That's different."

"I love you too," said Lucy as she walked naked into the connecting room. "But I have to make this call, or else."

"Four minutes, tops." He hurried into the bathroom and shut the door.

Lucy sat on the edge of the bed and dialed the ashram. She should be calling Barry, but she was dying to tell Cindy about falling in love—

without Jack there to hear her swoon over him like a smitten teenybopper.

A man answered on the other end. It sounded like that intense young guy with dreadlocks who called her to the swami's office. She put on the voice of her high school principal. "Yes, I need to speak to Cindy Morgan immediately. There's been an accident."

"Hold on." The guy put down the phone with a thump.

Lucy hummed "When Lightning Strikes" while she waited.

A minute later Cindy came on the line, breathless and anxious. "Hello?"

Lucy spoke quickly. "It's me, so act natural and pretend I'm telling you about an accident. Well, actually, the reason I couldn't call you back last night was because there *was* an accident, and Jack looks like Frankenstein now, with stitches all over his head and on his earlobes, but he saved me and we had sex all night and now he's fine."

"Wait, what?" said Cindy.

"Oh, you're a very good actress," said Lucy.

Cindy kept her voice low. "Tell me what happened. Tell me *everything*."

"Hold on a second." Lucy got up and closed the door. Jack was still in the shower, but she didn't want to take any chance of him overhearing. She got back on the phone. "Omigod, Cin! Why didn't anyone tell me it could be like this?"

"How bad is it? And don't spare me any detail."

Lucy sat cross-legged and got comfortable. "First of all, he holds my face and looks into my eyes and then leans in to kiss me really slowly. I feel like I'm with a leading man in a Hollywood movie."

"Oh, my!"

"And then he spends forever on my breasts, can you believe it? Not like they're a quick pit stop on the highway to petticoat junction like every other guy on the planet."

"I'm shocked to hear that."

"I know," said Lucy. "He puts his finger down there and I explode. That's just my first orgasm."

"What?"

"Yes, he says he wants to go slow and really savor it. So then he goes down on me and that lasts forever too."

"I can't believe it, I really can't."

"And finally he comes inside me and—"

Jack opened the door. "Hey, why's the door closed? Are you hiding from me?" He was fresh from the shower, wearing only a towel wrapped around his waist.

"Is that him?" said Cindy.

Lucy spoke over the receiver. "I'm on the phone with Cindy. Could you—"

"Not for long, you're not." Jack dropped his towel, revealing a growing erection. He climbed onto the bottom of the bed and began crawling toward her.

"What's he doing?" said Cindy.

Lucy tried to twist away from him. "He's being ..."

He moved up behind her, pulled her against him, and put his hands on her breasts. He began fondling her nipples and nuzzling her ear.

"Stop ... um ... oh ... ah ...." said Lucy.

"What's happening? Tell me what's happening."

Jack grabbed the phone and spoke into it. "I'm sorry to have to interrupt your tête-à-tête, Cindy, but Lucy cannot speak to you henceforth." He grinned and pressed the off button.

Cindy stood there in shock. She stared at the young man with dreadlocks. "What's your name?"

"Jeremy."

"I need your ... help, Jeremy. Can you come with me?"

She took him to her room and gave him an unexpectedly good time. Afterwards, he admitted that he wasn't sure they should have done what they did, but far be it from him to argue with a more senior member of the ashram. She gave him a gold star for attitude, among other things.

Only later did it occur to Cindy that she never told Lucy about Barry's and the swami's plans to kidnap her. When she finally got the opportunity to call Lucy back, the band had checked out of the hotel and no one at the front desk knew where they were headed.

Eighty-One

EARLY THAT EVENING IN LONDON, on what was an unconscionably sunny day, Lord Winston Stevens stood on a carefully selected spot with the Houses of Parliament in the background. His media man had contacted the BBC with an exclusive.

He was furious at the news coverage on Pirate. First there was his son parading around as a personal assistant with a Cockney accent and kissing that little tart in front of the cameras. Then there was his unmasking as the lead singer in disguise. Winnie had already got comments at the club on how "that Pirate fellow is a doppelganger for James, isn't he?" and "I always knew you were pirate stock, Winnie."

But the absolutely unforgivable thing James had done was take his brother's name. How dare he. He was desecrating the memory of a truly brilliant boy, a boy who would have put James to shame with his intelligence and talent. The real Jack would have followed his father into politics and distinguished himself. Not become something utterly disgusting and tacky like a rock 'n' roll singer.

Enough was enough. Time to get the truth out there—that Jack St James was, in fact, his second son, James. Time to get ahead of the media coverage rather than being on the back foot, and get this *thing* behind them as fast as possible. There were much bigger issues to deal with—

namely, getting James back home and in his proper place. James had never seen the trust agreement and didn't have a clue about the assets he'd inherited. He could not be allowed to question how his father had managed them. That would not do. Winnie would not stand for it.

The BBC correspondent thrust the microphone in his face.

Winnie looked at the camera with a serious expression. "Thank you for coming. I would like to read a statement on behalf of myself and my wife Penelope." He pretended to be reading from the piece of paper he held in front of him. "Our son, James Stevens, has been the lead singer for the rock band Pirate under the stage name Jack St James. To protect his privacy and safety, he has also posed as Victor Slonimsky, the personal assistant to the lead singer. We are very pleased that his theatrical training at Cambridge has stood him in good stead."

He looked at the camera and smiled, and the correspondent laughed as expected. "And we are glad he enjoyed his time in the music business. We look forward to having him back home in England, at the completion of their American tour this week, and returning to the family business and the family fold."

He stopped speaking and put the piece of paper in the inner pocket of his suit jacket. The correspondent realized the interview was over and pulled the microphone away. "And that's a wrap. Thank you very much, Lord Stevens. We'll get it on air as soon as possible."

Winnie had not been pleased with the BBC coverage to date. "You tell Alistair to stop showing all that Pirate nonsense. No one cares about a pathetic little rock band. There are far more important things for the BBC to cover."

"Yes, of course, I'll tell him. But unfortunately for poor Alistair, he may not have any choice. It's one of the highest-rated stories we've had all year."

Winnie leaned close to the correspondent. "You tell Alistair to keep the Pirate footage off the air, or the BBC will face an audit the likes of which it has never seen and will never wish to see again in a million years."

The correspondent's eyes went wide. "Yes, Lord Stevens."

Winnie started to turn away, stopped for a moment as if recalling something, and turned back. "And give him this little message from me as well: Justine and Marguerite."

"Justine and Marguerite?"

"He'll know," said Winnie, grinning as he turned to his media man. "Get me to the club, Trev. I need a stiff drink. And call my wife. Tell her I will not be home tonight."

He went to the club and had drinks with some of his cronies, and then found an eager prostitute. He upended her on his lap, clamping her in place with his left arm and right leg, both toned to peak strength by playing squash and riding to hounds. He whipped her with his belt until he was dripping with sweat and her buttocks were dripping with blood. Now fully turned on, he had his way with her every which way he desired, beating her in between to bring back his erection. That was why he kept an isolated and soundproofed flat, and why he guarded his status with his life. No one would ever believe a harlot over a lord. Never. He didn't even pay her, just turned her out and told her to keep her mouth shut. If the past thirty years were anything to go by, he had nothing to fear.

Now that he'd cleared his head and restored the feeling of power and control to which he was legally and rightfully entitled, he could make plans to bring his wayward son home, willingly or otherwise, and bring him to heel—once and for all.

THE END

What Next?

Hey again. It's me, Dunk, as promised. Your favorite band manager.

Enjoyed that, did you? Course you did. The boys are great entertainment. Our lead singer, on the other hand—jury's still out, isn't it?

If you're wanting more, you can read the first chapter of our next book, *Pirate Booty,* starting on the next page.

You can sign up for our newsletter at piratetherockband.ck.page, if you want the delight of hearing from me and the boys on a regular basis. You'll also get free access to an interview *R Squared Magazine* did with me and Jack, back before all this kicked off. Kind of makes me nostalgic.

And be sure to check out our website, where you'll find band news, profiles, interviews, links to our merch, and more:
PiratetheRockBand.com

If you're wanting to contact us to advocate for equal representation of downtrodden voices in the band, or to give us feedback or point out mistakes, send an email to dunk@piratetherockband.com.

Right, time for me to get back to work. And time for you to stop havering and get on with things. You think I'm gonna hold your hand or something? I'm not the Beatles, mate.

Pirate Booty

Want to know what happens next? Read on for an excerpt from the next exciting book about Pirate, available now to hard-rocking readers everywhere.

CHAPTER 1

Jack and Lucy stood behind the security guy as they descended in the hotel elevator. Jack held her tight against him. He couldn't stop leaning down and kissing the top of her head or inhaling what he thought of as Essence of Lucy. If he could, he would bottle it and carry it with him everywhere, snorting it like a coke addict whenever his energy or spirits flagged. He was sure he could even sell it and make a fortune—it was that entrancing and irresistible.

Things were going wrong with the tour that would have sent him into orbit even yesterday. But he'd just spent all night making love to Lucy—well, to be perfectly honest, except for a few hours' sleep and a couple of rests here and there—and then another two times this morning. It was something he'd always considered outrageous exaggeration when other men made similar claims, but now he'd done it himself and become a bona fide member of the all-night-long club. He might look like Frankenstein from all the stitches on his head, but he'd made love *all night long* to the most beautiful woman in the world. He was on a dopamine high—or was it oxytocin?—not to mention some powerful painkillers, compliments of Suze.

The elevator heralded their arrival in the underground garage by throwing its doors open and making a dramatic ping. The welcoming committee when they stepped out was not nearly as exuberant. Dunk stood glaring at them, hands on hips, while Manny slumped next to him, hands in his pockets and eyes on the ground.

"Where in bleedin' blazes have you two been?" said Dunk. "Did I not tell ya to be down in one hour?"

Jack dropped his arm from Lucy as he started to explain. "We were busy getting—"

"Oh, I know why ya were busy. Only one reason why ya couldn't be bothered to answer the phone."

"I'm really—" said Lucy.

"Or open the door when Manny knocked and knocked. Ya kept the poor guy standing in the hall listening to all yer racket."

"Yeah, I was shocked by it," said Manny in an emotionless voice.

Jack smirked. "Did he tell you to say that?"

"Yeah," said Manny, peering up at Jack. "I wasn't really shocked. I was like, finally, Jack's getting rid of some of his baby batter. Good stuff."

Dunk and Jack both gave Manny a chiding look.

"What?" Manny said. It took a moment, but then it dawned on him and he reddened. "Oh, sorry, Lucy. I, um ..."

Lucy gave him an indulgent smile. "It's OK, Manny. I love Jack's baby batter." She moved around Manny and Dunk and walked toward the buses.

Dunk grinned at Jack, his outrage instantly vanished.

"I know," said Jack, grinning back like an idiot.

The three men turned and followed Lucy. Jack rushed to catch up with her. A handful of fans had managed to get into the underground garage, and even though the security guys seemed to have them

360

corralled, he wanted to be there to protect her should one of them manage to break away. Fans could be very willful and wily.

Lucy headed for the band bus.

"Uh, Luce, we're on the other one. My bus."

She acted as if she hadn't heard him. As she reached the band bus, the door opened for her.

"Hi, Mick," she said to the driver as she started to board. Jack grabbed her hand, making her swing around on the first step and face him.

"We're not going on this bus, my love." It was clear she thought they were going to hang out with the band and have a sing-a-long, like she'd done on the way to Phoenix. But he had other plans.

She grabbed his face with her free hand and gave him a quick kiss. "I need to chat with the ladies. OK, sweetie?"

He put on his sexiest voice and spoke low, so Mick couldn't hear. "I've got some champagne chilling on the other bus. We're going to have some more 'us' time."

"You are such a sweetie pie." Instead of following him, she pulled her hand out of his, turned and disappeared into the bus.

He avoided looking at Mick as he rushed after her. The guy would undoubtedly be smirking after the walkie-talkie incident, even though he'd been handsomely paid for his discretion. Not that Jack entirely trusted Mick to remain discreet no matter how much he paid him.

Jack came up behind Lucy in the lounge area, where the band members and their so-called girlfriends were gathered. Well, Alison was now Randy's fiancée, actually. He didn't know what to call Suze and Carly. Howie's entourage, maybe? Funny how Howie was the only one who wasn't in the band and yet he had an entourage. Funny that.

"Hello, everyone." Lucy pointed at the three women in turn. "You, you, and you need to come with me on the other bus. It's the ladies' bus today, and this is the guys' bus."

"What?" said Jack. "No!"

She turned to him. "Sorry, sweetie, but we have to plan something and you guys can't know about it." She leaned against his chest and smiled up at him. "But don't worry, I guarantee you'll love it."

"Is it a fashion show?" said Sam, strumming a guitar.

"A striptease?" said George, grinning at Lucy. The guy who had one or more groupies strip for him every single night.

"An orgy?" said Howie in a hopeful tone. The guy who was sleeping with both Suze and Carly.

"Hey, my lady wouldn't do that," said Randy, glaring at them as he pulled Alison closer to him.

"Yeah," said Rob, scowling at George and Howie. "Don't you even think those things."

Keith put his hand on his chin and pretended to be thinking those things. "Wow. Well fit, ladies. Well fit."

Rob stood up and glared down at Keith. "I'm warning you."

"Get a grip, mate," said Keith, giving him a scornful look. "It's called comedy. You should try it sometime."

Lucy stood on her tiptoes and gave Jack a kiss. "You don't mind, do you, sweetie? You'll have a great time with the guys."

Jack looked down at her in despair. "OK, but don't you think—"

"Come on, ladies." Lucy squeezed past Jack and moved toward the front of the bus. "Oh, and Dunk is riding with us, sweetie," she threw over her shoulder.

What? Hold on. That wasn't fair. What was going on here? What could she be planning that he and the guys couldn't know about but Dunk could? Not his birthday, thank goodness, because the guys would be in on that.

Jack watched her go, racking his brain for an excuse to follow her and talk his way onto the other bus. He was just too addled by making love all night to think straight. And thinking was usually his strong suit. This sex stuff was like kryptonite.

As the ladies said their goodbyes and trooped after Lucy, he looked around with a rising sense of dismay. He might have designed the band bus, like he had the management bus, but he'd only ridden on it back and forth to an arena, not on any lengthy trips. It was a thing of beauty when he and Dunk turned it over to the band, all gleaming surfaces and smelling of new wood and carpeting. He'd been so proud of it. Now look at it. Stains everywhere, like a posse of schoolchildren had been living on it. Except for the overpowering stench of stale beer and pot, so replace that with a posse of teenagers. After all the money he'd spent making it nice for the boys and they'd treated it like ... what did the Americans call it? Oh yeah. A frat house.

He could still escape, couldn't he? Insist on riding on his own bus and maybe stay in his own room while they took the lounge. That could work, couldn't it? He was willing to compromise to make his little woman happy. He turned toward the front of the bus just as the door slammed shut and Mick started to pull away.

He lurched to the side and righted himself. Damn it, now he was consigned to this bus until they made the first pit stop. Yes, he could demand that the buses stop so he could switch to the other one, but then he'd look like an arse in everyone's eyes, including Lucy's. No, he'd just have to grin and bear it for an hour or two.

He looked around for a place to perch. He couldn't stand like an idiot the whole damn trip. He didn't really want to sit on the vinyl couch without cleaning it, but if he asked for Wipe-It-Fresh and paper towels they'd think he was a nutter. Only Dunk knew the full extent of his cleaning fetish. The area where Suze was sitting was probably the most hygienic, Suze being a nurse and educated in the hazards posed by germs. She'd stitched his wounds last night, hadn't she? And there wasn't any noticeable infection on his scalp yet. He'd have to suck it up and sit there. He lowered himself onto that area of the couch—good thing he did squat thrusts every day and could do it without touching anything—and perched on the edge with his hands on his knees.

"Here," Keith held out a bottle of beer. They were all holding beers. When did that happen? He took it, being careful not to touch Keith's hand and wiping off the top of the bottle on his shirt before taking a swig. Of course he'd had beer before, having gone to university and all. But he was a committed wine drinker himself, occasionally indulging in cognac or celebrating with champagne, as he had expected to be doing at this very moment. Still, ice cold like this the Corona Extra wasn't half bad, lemony actually, and quite refreshing on such a hot day. Especially since that hapless Mick had not got the bus cooled down before they boarded.

"Can't say as I don't feel for ya, mate," Keith said, sprawled on the opposite couch staring at him. "She might be a major looker, but she's already got ya spinning round her axis, don't she?"

Keith's words and the beer, not to mention Mick's ineptitude, seemed to unleash the frustration he was feeling. "She is ... I can't ... I don't know how she does it, but by the time I figure out what she's up to, it's too late to do anything about it."

"I know," said Randy. "Alison always seems to know what I'm going to say before I say it, and then she tells me why it's wrong. I never even get to say it!"

Rob looked at him with contempt. "Just tell her you're the man and what you say goes. That's it."

"Yeah, just act like a caveman and she'll fall right into line," said Sam, rolling his eyes at Randy.

"It works for me," said Rob.

Sam smirked. "Yeah, for the whole three hours you spend with a lady."

"We don't need more than three hours, do we, Robby me boy?" said Keith. "Jus' enough time to taste the honey without being sucked into the honeypot and getting swallowed hook, line, and sinker."

Jack grimaced. "But that honey ... it's irresistible. I can't seem to get enough of it. And she keeps walking around ... flaunting it in my face."

"Me too," said Randy. "She keeps saying we just did it, and I keep saying but that was a while ago. And she says it wasn't even an hour. So I keep watching the clock, wondering how long I have to wait. It's not fair."

Keith ruffled Randy's hair. "No, it's not, our kid. That's why I have me a different lady every night, maybe two at once. Ya see, it's all about this thing called lib-i-do. The ladies got small ones and we got big ones. Mine's huge. Yours too, Georgie."

George shrugged his shoulders. "Yeah. Gotta have it."

"Me too," said Howie. "Gotta have it. And boy do Suze and Carly give it to me."

Randy was on a roll with his outrage. "But it's not fair. They've got these lovely bits and can play with them whenever they want, while we have to beg to play with them. How fair is that? It's not."

"You have bits you play with all the time too," said Sam, laughing. "I hear you."

"Yeah, he's playing with his jubblies," said Keith, pretending to grab for Randy's boob as Randy fended him off.

Keith got up and passed around more bottles of beer. "Time to get this party started, gentlemen. The ladies don't want us, then screw 'em. We're gonna show 'em how it's done."

Jack noticed that the guys just dropped their empty bottles wherever. Sam had even knocked his over and left a beer puddle on the floor. Somehow it didn't seem to bother him as much as it usually would. He'd never been one of the boys, but now he was ... what did they call it? Kicking back with the guys and really enjoying it. You can go ahead and suck socks with the ladies, Duncan Iain MacGregor.

Rob took out a bag of pot, rolled a joint, lit it up, and took a puff. Jack watched with fascination. So that's how you did it. Rob passed it on to Sam.

"Roll one for Jack," Keith said to Rob.

Jack put up his free hand. "No, that's OK. Really."

Keith gave Rob a look and Rob stared back at him until realization dawned. Of course Jack wouldn't smoke if he had to share it. Even half drunk that was an absolute given. It was one thing to share Lucy's saliva, abhorrent to share anyone else's.

Rob rolled a joint and passed it over to Jack with the lighter. OK, fine, he didn't normally use pot, hadn't had any since that one crazy night at university; other than the magic brownies incident, that is. Of course, Dunk had been there that time to rescue him and pick up the pieces. But he was feeling good and enjoying being one of the boys. Jack lit up and took a puff. Besides, honestly, he was on a bus. What was the worst that could happen?

Six beers and two doobies later, Jack realized that he really, really loved these guys and wanted to bare his soul to them. They were his band, and the very best guys in the whole world. He stood up and waved his bottle of beer. "Hey, everyone, I have to tell you something. Guess what? You're not going to believe this."

They were sprawled out and looked up at him with bleary eyes.

"My name's not Jack," he said. "It's James. And my daddy is a lord.

And he's going to do something really bad. To me, and probably to this band too, when he finds out where I am. What d'ya think 'bout that?"

"Cool," said Keith.

"Ace," said Sam, giving a lazy thumbs up.

George grunted something, Jack couldn't say what.

"Beat his royal arse," mumbled Rob.

"Yeah, arsehole lord," said Randy. "Gets too many bits. S'not fair."

Acknowledgments

The band wishes to thank its fans for their love and support, including all the photos, apparel, gummy bears/cookies/treats, and other items bestowed upon it, which have become a cherished part of the Pirate "entourage" and lore. Gratitude also to everyone at Dolos Discs who provided valuable and timely support on our albums and tours over the past three years.

Our biographer E.Z. wants to thank a slew of folks who gave feedback on early ideas, initial drafts, and the cover, including Doc Pruyne, Gail Clarkson, Mike Kelly, Sue Motulsky, Ellie Rudolph, Anton Snowsill, Anne and Mike Hagan, Oliver Mawdsley, Cheri Robartes, Shawn Jarrett, Katharyn Lanaro, John Eyes, Jurga Sakalauskaitė, Sally and Richard Lincoln-Vogel, and Auden Lincoln-Vogel. A special thanks to Clive Pullan for sharing his personal experiences and unique knowledge relevant to the Stevens' world, and for his cover ideas.

A heartfelt thanks to editor extraordinaire Carmen Erickson, who made a world of difference in so many ways. Any errors are solely the band's or author's and not hers.

Thanks to the many experts who shared their knowledge and wisdom about writing and publishing, with special gratitude to: Mrs. Carr in 9th and 12th grades; Chris Jones, Karol Griffiths, and everyone involved with the virgin Talent Campus at the London Screenwriting Festival; Adam Croft, Joanna Penn, and David Gaughran on publishing; ALLI; Jericho Writers; Masterclass, especially the classes with James Patterson, David Baldacci, Margaret Atwood, Dan Brown, and Walter Mosley;

Steve Kaplan on comedy; Scott Myers on screenwriting; Kim Hudson on structure; and Frazer Flintham (in whose screenwriting class Ruth and Clint showed up).

Thanks also to Dan Mazer, whose advice that "you're about as likely to sell a screenplay as you are to become a professional footballer," steered E.Z. towards writing novels rather than screenplays. Voila.

About the Author

E.Z. ("Easy") Prine writes about the escapades of Pirate, an eighties hard rock band out of Manchester, England. The Beatles' appearance on the Ed Sullivan Show in 1964 sparked what has become E.Z.'s lifelong devotion to "classic rock" and fascination with those luminaries we call rock stars.

The Pirate series is E.Z.'s love letter to rock 'n' roll and personal thank you to all the artists and supporting others who brought this amazing contribution to our world. May we always rock on.

Wanna read more about Pirate?

Pirate Booty (Book Two)

Pirate Penance (Book Three)

piratetherockband.ck.page - our newsletter

PiratetheRockBand.com - our website

Made in the USA
Middletown, DE
16 August 2022

70662106R00227